UPON A STARLIT TIDE

By Kell Woods

After the Forest
Upon a Starlit Tide

UPON A STARLIT TIDE

Kell Woods

TOR PUBLISHING GROUP • NEW YORK

This is a work of fiction. All of the characters, organizations, and events portrayed in this novel are either products of the author's imagination or are used fictitiously.

UPON A STARLIT TIDE

Endpaper art by Lindsey Carr

A Tor Book
Published by Tom Doherty Associates / Tor Publishing Group
120 Broadway
New York, NY 10271

www.torpublishinggroup.com

The Library of Congress Cataloging-in-Publication Data is available upon request.

ISBN 978-1-250-85251-9 (hardcover)
ISBN 978-1-250-85253-3 (ebook)

Our books may be purchased in bulk for promotional, educational, or business use. Please contact your local bookseller or the Macmillan Corporate and Premium Sales Department at 1-800-221-7945, extension 5442, or by email at MacmillanSpecialMarkets@macmillan.com.

First Edition: 2025

Printed in the United States of America

0 9 8 7 6 5 4 3 2 1

For my husband, Luke.

A light in the darkness.

Far out in the sea the water is as blue as the petals of the most beautiful cornflower, and as clear as the purest glass.

Hans Christian Andersen, “The Little Mermaid”

UPON A STARLIT TIDE

PART 1

Their world seemed so much wider than her own, for they could skim over the sea in ships, and mount up into the lofty peaks high over the clouds, and their lands stretched out in woods and fields farther than the eye could see. There was so much she wanted to know.

—Hans Christian Andersen,
"The Little Mermaid"

1

Wrecked

Clos-Poulet, Bretagne
May 1758

She thought him dead at first.

A man, draped lifeless upon a wedge of broken hull, cheek pressed against the timber as tenderly as a lover's as he rose gently up, gently down with the exhausted breath of the sea. The storm had raged all night, howling and hurling itself against the shore, rattling the windows so hard that it had taken all of Luce's will not to fling them open and feel its cold breath on her face. Only the chintz drapes, her mother's great pride, had stopped her. Papa had brought the fabric all the way from India, and there was no telling how Gratienne would have reacted had Luce allowed the weather to spoil them. And so, she had kept the window closed, watching the storm as it battered the gardens and orchard and pried at the roof of the dovecote as though it would rip it free and toss it, rolling and bouncing, down the sweep of rain-soaked fields and into the furious waves.

It was the kind of weather that stilled the world and sent folk hurrying indoors, that closed shutters and covered mirrors for fear of lightning strikes, that caused ships to fly before it into the harbor at Saint-Malo. One ship, at least, had not been fast enough.

Its remains dotted the gray water. Shards of decking, slabs of hull, tangles of rigging. Luce narrowed her eyes against the glare of the early morning sun, skirts held out of the weed and foam. She had seen the sea's victims before, of course. Many times. Could not avoid it, with the storms that blew in from the northwest, tearing down the Manche, leaving ruined ships and their dead strewn across the beaches of Clos-Poulet like flowers after a wedding feast. Faded petals across the sand. This man's face, however, lacked the telltale pallor of death. And did he cling to the timber? She had seen men who had lashed themselves to ships as they broke apart, only to wash ashore, drowned, their fingers open and empty. But no rope bound this man to his floating sanctuary.

Not dead, then.

A quick glance down the cove's curved, rocky shore. There were folk from Saint-Coulomb about; she had seen them as she'd climbed down the steep path from the cliffs. Men in their low boats and shawled women, heads bowed as, like Luce, they combed the beach for treasure in the storm's wake. Brandy and waxed packets of silk; coins and tea and candles. The men, however, had pushed out into deeper water, sails cutting the gray horizon, while the women had rounded the rocky point separating the cove from the next beach, where, farther along the shore, the path to the village lay.

But for a scattering of foam and weed, the beach was empty.

Decided, Luce tossed her boots, stockings, and garters to the gold-gray sand and shrugged out of her heavy men's overcoat. She wore it like a shell, that coat; a briny leather casing that hid the soft, female truth of her. Her long, dark hair had been tucked safely within its collar; it unraveled around her shoulders as she bent to unlace her woolen caraco, then unbuttoned her breeches, sliding them down her bare legs. A final glance along the beach and her battered black tricorn joined the motley mound of clothing upon the sand. Clad in her chemise and stays, Luce picked her way to the water's edge.

One, two, three steps and she was shin deep. Four, five, six and the fine cotton of her petticoat was dragging at her thighs. Luce's skin prickled. It was May, and the Manche had not lost its wintery bite. Seven, eight, nine and she was pushing off the sandy bottom with her toes, diving clean and strong into the first rush of sea and salt. She opened her arms and scooped them back, gliding toward the man.

A feeling of dread as she neared him. What if she was wrong? What if he was tangled, not clinging? Dead instead of living? Would he roll languidly to greet her, already bloating, eyes glazed and sightless?

Too late now. She had to know. A few strokes more and she was at his side: a man from the waist up, clinging to the surface while his legs fell into shadow. His eyes—to her relief—were closed, his skin pale against his dark hair, but when Luce touched his wrist she felt the fluttering of his heart. A tattered sail and rigging trailed about him. She grasped the rope and turned for shore, swimming hard, towing the cumbersome load behind her.

The tide was coming in. Papa always said that Saint-Malo's tides were the most powerful in Europe and that, together with the city's position, surrounded by the Manche on three sides with a happy proximity to the trade routes between Spain, Portugal, England, and the Netherlands; its treacherous necklace of reefs and islands that caused even the staunchest of navigators to falter; and the legendary, protective storm-stone forming its mighty walls and ballasting the hulls of its ships, was what gave it its enviable strength.

Luce let the water help her, let it push broken man and ship both toward land.

When the hull scraped against sand, she drew away the rigging holding him to the timber. He sank beneath the surface as though he were made of marble and not flesh. Panicked, Luce dived after him, wrapping her arms about him as the Manche dragged him hungrily down. How heavy he was! She opened her eyes—the familiar salty sting—and checked to see if the ropes that had saved him were now conspiring to drag him to his death. They were not. Yet still he sank, arms trailing slowly upward, dark hair wafting like weed. She kicked harder. Felt, through the water around her, a nameless prickling against her skin. Surprised, Luce stilled and heard, clearly, the rumble of distant thunder.

Storm-stone.

Sailors on stricken ships sometimes helped themselves to its storm-stone ballast, hoping the stones' magic might save their hides. Luce plunged her hands into the pockets of the man's breeches, scooping the fist-sized ballast stones free. They grumbled as they sank, tiny granite storm clouds heavy with magic. Lightened of his burden, the sailor lifted easily in Luce's arms. She pulled him to the surface and on toward the shore, his head lolling against her shoulder, his fingertips trailing in her wake.

He was taller than she, and well-knit, but she managed to drag him clumsily onto the beach, her chemise twisting around her thighs, her feet sinking in the wet sand. His own feet—bare, perfect—were hardly clear of the water's grip when she lowered him onto the beach and sank down beside him, gasping. The Manche hissed regretfully, stroking at the young man's bare toes, the cuffs of his breeches.

Be still, Luce told it silently. *You have had your fill of sailors today. You shall not have this one, too.*

The sun slid above the storm clouds tattering the horizon, washing the water in weak spring sunshine. It drifted over the near-drowned man, catching at his face. He groaned a little and frowned, closed eyes scrunching tight as though he feared the day.

Luce could not blame him for that. His ship, his crew were gone, the former heaving and rocking itself into death in the deeps of the night, dragging the latter down with it. It seemed that only he had survived.

The strike of a ship's bell drifted faintly from the clifftop above. Eight strikes; eight of the morning. Luce pushed herself to her knees.

He lay on his back, eyes closed, dark hair—as dark as Luce's own—fanning across his brow. Long black lashes were startling against his skin, his eyelids the faint mauve of the palest mussel shell. Beads of water glimmered silver on his skin.

Luce shifted closer, heedless of the cold, her exposed skin, the open beach. Took in his generous lips, the stubble on his jaw, the column of his neck. His forearms, tanned to smoothness. The lean and clinging shape of him beneath his shirt. Luce swallowed, exhaustion forgotten. He was waterlogged, near death—and yet he was as beautiful as the dusk.

Her heart panged hard against her ribs as the young man's eyes flickered open.

Dark eyes, like a moonless night. He blinked twice, rapidly. Frowned. His gaze settled on Luce's face. The frown deepened, then smoothed away, replaced by something else. Fear? Wonder? And then, before Luce knew what he was about, he raised himself up on one elbow, reached out with his other hand, and cupped her cheek with his palm.

Strong he was, deceptively so, and Luce knew a flutter of anxiety as he drew her face toward his. Then he was kissing her, the rush and the shock of it, the taste of his mouth, saltwater and the stale, almost-death of him. There was life, too—warmth and wanting, and Luce found herself kissing him back, pushing her body against his, wrapping her cold, bare arms about his neck. She was soaking wet, shivering, water breaking jealously over her hips, yet nothing, *nothing* mattered but the two of them, his arms locked about her, her legs and hair twined about him.

No, she thought to the sea. *No. You shall not have him.*

Voices drifted from the path along the cliffs above. More of the villagers from Saint-Coulomb coming down to search for survivors or goods that had washed ashore, whichever they happened upon first.

Upon hearing the voices, Luce lurched away from the sea-man, her breath coming fast, his fingers snarling in her hair. Without her to hold him upright he flopped back onto the sand. His eyes drooped closed.

As the voices continued to carry to her from around the headland, Luce crabbed away, seizing up her clothes and concealing herself in the tangle of weedy granite beneath the cliffs.

"There's someone lying on the sand, there!"

Luce hunched further against the rocks. It would not do to be seen; whoever approached—a hasty glance revealed a handful of folk from Saint-Coulomb—would recognize her. As though to prove it, the little band of jetins who were wont to patrol the cove marched from between the rocks, brandishing sticks and swords, stones and mutinous expressions.

"What's afoot?" the first of the fae demanded.

"Something's afoot . . ." His comrade took in Luce, his wrinkled face suspicious. "'Tis the Lion's youngest daughter."

"The Lion's youngest daughter?"

"Been swimming again, has she?"

They gathered around Luce, a tiny, disreputable crew dressed in pebble-grays and moss-greens, their wild beards woven through with feathers, shells, and bones.

"Save your stones, lads."

"Off we go."

It was as polite as the creatures were ever likely to get. Through a narrow sliver in the rocks, Luce watched as they strode across the sand to where the fisherfolk had reached the still-motionless man. She winced as the jetins, ever protective of their territory, began to pelt the rescuers—fishermen, mostly—with pebbles, then took advantage of the ensuing commotion by scraping herself into her breeches, shrugging her coat straight on over her soaking chemise and stays, and tucking her caraco and boots under one arm. One last peek revealed two familiar forms among the fishermen—there was no mistaking Samuel with that height of his, and Bones, his cousin, almost as tall but lanky as a coatful of shins—as, dodging the korrigans' stones and insults, they hefted the young man between them, carrying him toward the path cutting into the cliffs.

". . . take him to the Lion's house," one of the men huffed.

"Be well tended, there . . ."

"Better than he's used to, most like."

Luce's heart sank: they were taking the sailor to her father's house.

It made sense, she supposed, pulling her tricorn low and tucking the ends of her wet hair deep into her collar. Nowhere was closer or more comfortable than Le Bleu Sauvage, while Jean-Baptiste Léon himself—shipowner, erstwhile corsair captain, and gentleman—would know precisely what to do with the rescued man.

What he would do if he discovered Luce's part in said rescue was another matter entirely.

She hurried through the rocks, away from the fishermen and their catch. She knew this cove better than anyone; knew its paths and its secrets. What appeared to be a thick bank of pink sea thrift, for example, might in fact be a perfectly serviceable path, while a thick carpet of reddish maritime pine needles might hide a forest-trail that ended at the broad stone wall surrounding the Léon estate. It was damp and shady there, thick with waist-high billows of cow parsley, and Luce paused to catch her breath and put on her boots, wincing at the pain that was steadily worsening in her feet. She pressed on, ignoring the pain, determined not to imagine what would happen if her family discovered her absence.

Do not think of it, she told herself firmly. *Just keep going.*

Just keep going.

The forest soon gave way to bocage. Luce avoided the road—it was used regularly by the workers employed by her father to tend the estate's crops and orchards, its vegetable plots and livestock, all of which would sustain the household when it returned to the walled city in the autumn—in favor of the tall hedgerows, where oak and chestnut trees lent their generous shadows. A robin tittered as Luce limped by—*I see you, I see you.*

Luce squared her shoulders and lengthened her strides—enhancing the illusion formed by the tricorn and overcoat—as she emerged from the hedgerow and onto the road. There was no one about. The malouinière's main gate—a grand arch in the stone wall revealing a wide graveled court and a tantalizing glimpse of the house beyond—was deserted, the road before it meandering peacefully through the bocage to join the highroad that would eventually lead to Cancale in the east, and Saint-Malo in the west.

At any moment the fishermen—and the pair of smugglers in their midst—would appear behind her, dangling their catch between them as they approached the gate. Luce *must* be safe inside the walls when they did.

Keep going, keep going. Every step a fervent wish that she would make it home in time, that her feet, wailing in protest now, would not fail her.

At last, *at last*, the old chapel came into view., lay the old chapel.

Luce's salvation, and her sin.

Laying half within and half without the somber expanse of wall, the tiny stone church—indeed, it was not as large as Maman's sumptuous dressing room—had two entrances, one on either side. The first, an unassuming door that opened straight onto the road, had been used by long-ago villagers in the days before the newer, larger church had been erected in Saint-Coulomb. The second, which was broad and intricately carved, opened into the private domain of the Léon family, the gardens and pathways and fountains that seemed to be from another world, so different were they to the rolling countryside with its rough stone dwellings and wide Bretagne sky.

The second door was never locked, for indeed any member of the Léon household was free to pray in the chapel whenever they liked. But the first? It opened so rarely that everyone—from Luce's father to the lowliest kitchen boy—had all but forgotten its existence.

Everyone, that is, but Luce.

By the time the fishermen reached the road, Luce was in the chapel, locking the outer door and brushing the sand and guilt from her overcoat. She undressed once more and bundled the men's clothes together before hurrying to one of the chapel's deep, high windows. A beautiful sculpture nestled before it: Saint Sophia and her three daughters, their faces vibrant in the glow of the colored glass. Balancing on the edge of the nearest pew, Luce reached behind the ladies' carved skirts—*pardon me, mademoiselles*—and retrieved a second, smaller bundle of clothing stashed there. Dropping it to the floor, she shoved the coat and breeches in its place, then tucked her tricorn in as well, the key to the outer chapel door—a copy made from one she had filched from the femmes de charge, Claudine, two Christmases ago—hidden in one of its triangular folds.

The second set of clothes was entirely different to the first: a soft cotton petticoat and a fine woolen skirt that matched the dark blue of Luce's damp caraco. She dressed quickly before cracking the chapel's second, opulently carved door, and then, when she was certain it was safe, slipped back into the confines of her life.

Lions of the sea. That's what they called the Léons, one of the oldest and most distinguished of Saint-Malo's ship-owning families. The family coat of arms, a golden lion against a background of Bretagne white and blue, testified to this. For generations they had ruled the seas, as merchants and sea captains, navigators and explorers. Luce's father, his father, and *his* father before him had been shipowners and corsairs, amassing an impressive fortune. None of which, unfortunately, had been left to Jean-Baptiste. As the youngest son, he had received anything but the lion's share. Even so, through cleverness, chance, and no small amount of bravery he had made his own wealth, including a splendid town house in Saint-Malo. It was the malouinière, Le Bleu Sauvage, however, that was his true pride.

Built by some long-ago member of the Fontaine-Roux family,

the large and luxurious manor house sat upon a broad estate twelve miles from Saint-Malo—a distance great enough to offer respite from the crowded city in the summertime, yet close enough to be within riding distance should a pressing business matter require attention. Other shipping families had constructed their own malouinières over the decades, so that the countryside was dotted with stately granite homes, their fountains and formal gardens hidden behind high walls.

The scent of roses replaced the tang of salt in Luce's nose as she hurried along the gravel pathway, past reflecting pools, garden beds bristling with lavender, and boxwood hedges trimmed with maritime precision. The ordered gardens soon gave way to a wide lawn surrounded by stone benches and chestnut trees. Twin lions carved in creamy stone guarded the steps leading to the house, which reared, as stately as one of her father's ships, over the green lawn. Two stories of white-plastered granite from the Storm Islands, its stern façade lined with rows of tall windows with frames painted a fresh white, their edges lined with gray stonework. The roof was steeply pitched, the perfect shape of an upturned ship's hull in austere, storm-gray symmetry. Narrow chimneys rose above it like sails, defying the laws of balance. The house, like the walls surrounding the estate and Saint-Malo itself, was made from storm-stone. Luce felt its low, not-unpleasant rumble, the nameless prickling against her skin, as she tucked herself behind a pine tree and surveyed the house.

All was still. Within, the domestiques would be quietly beginning another day. Papa would be sipping coffee while his valet helped him dress, his thoughts already on the letters, account books, and fresh pastries waiting in his study. Luce's mother and sisters would be abed, or lazily drinking their morning cups of chocolate; joining the morning slowly, reluctantly, as they always did. All of them blissfully unaware that the peace of the morning, as ordered as the watches her father insisted be rung on the old ship's bell in the vestibule, was about to be shattered.

The house was framed on either end by smaller wings, built, like the main house, of storm-stone: the servants' kitchen and quarters, and the enormous main kitchen where the family's meals were prepared. Beyond it, built into the walls on each side of the gate through which the fishermen would at any moment arrive, lay the stables, the carriage house, and—closest to Luce—the laundry. It was there that she limped, skin prickling at the nearness of the storm-stone, the rose bushes growing beneath the laundry window catching accusingly at her skirts as she slipped inside.

Was that voices she could hear, on the path beyond the walls? The scrape of rough boots, the low grunt of men heaving and hoing a weight between them?

Hurry. Hurry.

The stone room was dim and cool, clinging still to the stormy dark of the night before. Luce crossed the uneven floor and hastily perused the wooden rack fixed to the ceiling, thick with the Léon family's freshly washed linens. Chemises and shirts, laces and ribbons, stockings and petticoats. And there—*thank you*—several cotton caps. She chose the plainest—one of Charlotte's—and rolled her damp hair quickly at the back of her head, tucking the cap over it and tying the white silk ribbons. All the while it was not her hands but the young sailor's she felt in her hair. His hands, his arms, his lips . . .

The ship's bell tolled once—one bell, eight thirty. A shout rose from the yard. Through the laundry's grimy little windows Luce glimpsed the fishermen crossing the smooth gravel of the yard, the sailor dangling between.

Luce slipped out of the laundry, listening as the house was shaken rudely from its rest. The rapid tread of domestiques in the vestibule, the crunch of shoes on the gravel of the yard, the creak as the enormous front doors were thrown open. A confusion of voices: fishermen and laquais, maidservants and stablehands, questions and answers moving between like goods at a busy market. Luce wandered toward them, doing her best to appear calm and slightly curious. Not a moment too soon: Jean-Baptiste Léon strode from the main doors, splendid in his favorite morning coat. Luce's mother and two sisters poured out of the house behind him, gloriously en dishabille in morning robes frothing with ruffles and ribbons. They clustered around the fishermen, peppering them with questions and exclaiming over the ailing man, until Jean-Baptiste ordered the men to bring their cargo inside. He met Luce's eyes briefly before he led them in, sparing her one of his smiles; distracted, kindly. Gratienne, Veronique, and Charlotte were on his heels, as well as the laquais and the maids. The stablehands returned reluctantly to their duties.

The courtyard was quiet once more.

Only then did Luce limp to the well, tucked away beside the laundry, and draw a bucket of fresh water. When she was sure the rose garden would block her from the sight of anyone looking out of the house, she pressed her back to the stone wall and sank gratefully down, stretching her long legs out before her.

Finally, *finally,* she could finally turn her attention to her feet.

To the pain that, even now, felt as if a hundred newly sharpened knives had been slicing into her skin, her flesh, her very bones.

2

Rough Water, Dark Moon

Luce's unfortunate affliction, Gratienne called it. Or *Luce's curse,* when she thought her youngest daughter was not close by. Charlotte called it far worse—hurtful things that made Luce want to curl her legs beneath her skirts, or run away, if running had not pained her so.

She removed her boots and stockings, wincing. Unlike her legs, which were long and smooth, her feet were as gnarled and brittle as driftwood. Oddly curved, they turned inward and under, so that her toes were a mess of misshapen, flattened bones, thick with calluses and pain. And pain. And pain.

The surgeons had no name for it. Jean-Baptiste had summoned several over the years, along with barbers and apothecaries. He had even taken Luce to Paris to see the kingdom's finest healers. On one thing they all agreed: Luce had been born with a rare and terrible affliction, and there was no means of curing it.

"Look here, then," came a tiny voice from the rose bush. "What's happened to *you*?"

Luce sighed. "Nothing you need concern yourself with."

"I disagree!" A woman no taller than a cat hopped from between the roses. She was dressed all in green, with red stockings and a jaunty red hat. Before Luce could say otherwise, the lutine—for that is what she was—was examining Luce's feet with an air of scientific curiosity, her hands clasped behind her back.

"What have you been doing?" she asked, *tsk*ing as Luce

scooped water over her feet. *Oh, sweet relief.* It was as nothing to the succor that seawater would have brought her, but it would do. "Not being careful, eh?"

Ordinarily Luce was mindful of her feet. She walked slowly, considering the placement of each step, the surface and angle least likely to cause her pain. The rapid climb up the rocky path and back to the house had been just the thing to set them on fire.

"You could say that." She dipped into the bucket again. The water was blissfully cold, and it was taking all her willpower not to plunge both feet in at once and dabble them like a duck.

In the house, the sound of voices receded and then sharpened as their owners flowed into the grand salon. The doors overlooking the lawn were open, and Luce clearly heard her mother telling the servants, Nanette and Marie-Jeanne, to bring hot water, towels, and blankets.

The little creature *tsk*ed again, waggling her fingers, and a piece of clean washing that looked suspiciously like one of the embroidered handkerchiefs Luce had seen drying in the laundry room appeared in her tiny hand. "Voilà!"

"Is that—"

"Be grateful, not nosy, tall one."

Luce bit back a smile as she thought of Veronique's face, should her sister discover what her beautiful handkerchief had been used for. "Thank you."

"Welcome."

The lutine watched as Luce dabbed at her foot with the kerchief, smoothing away the sand and heat. The little rose-woman was not the only Fae creature living on the malouinière grounds. There were korrigans in the kitchens and water sprites in the well. The scullery maid was always careful to leave a flat stone or three before the oven each night for the little folk to warm themselves upon, as well as bread and other treats. It would not do to lose them, after all. Everyone in Saint-Malo—from the wealthiest shipowner to the lowliest kitchen boy—understood that. The steady hum of the storm-stone rising from the house and the estate walls, the protection and peace it offered, was entirely due to the presence of Fae Folk and the magic they imparted. Stone, sea, earth—they blessed it all.

"Rude not to answer questions," the rose-lady said. "What has the tall one been doing?"

"I dragged a drowning man out of the sea."

The lutine blinked. "The tall one lies!"

"Not at all." Luce told the tale while she washed her other foot. Well, *most* of the tale. She left out how cold the sailor's hands had felt through the sodden cotton of her chemise, and the startling warmth of his tongue as it brushed against hers.

Her cheeks flooded with heat. *This* was not what she had expected of her morning. She had risen early to comb the shore for storm treasure, nothing more. Unusual shells, she had thought, as she slipped through the chapel and out into the freedom of the early morning. Or, if a ship *had* wrecked out in the Manche, something more substantial. A spy-glass, perhaps, or a sounding line, its cordage knotted, but salvageable. Once, after a storm, she had found a wooden box floating in the cove. It had contained a sextant of gleaming brass, perfectly safe, perfectly dry. It was her greatest treasure, taking pride of place on the rough stone shelves of Luce's sea-cave—her greatest secret. It was there that she kept all her salvaged treasures, and there that she retreated when the strictures and bustle of her family, her entire life, became too much to bear.

But then this morning, there *he* was. As strange and unexpected as the rarest shell. Just waiting for her to find him.

The lutine was watching her, eyes bright as jewels in her crinkled face.

"Dangerous path you're treading," she said quietly.

"What do you mean?" Luce's blush deepened. She wondered if the little lady could somehow see the mark of a kiss on her lips, the imprint of hands upon her skin.

"Only a fool steals a soul from the sea once the sea has claimed it."

"That's just sailors' superstition." She had heard it often enough from Bones, and even Samuel. Most sailors, smugglers, and fishermen hesitated to rescue their stricken brethren from the sea, for fear that their own lives would be forfeit.

"'Tis true enough. Now *you* owe the sea a soul."

A prickling of foreboding whispered across Luce's skin. Beyond the lawn, the house, the sea pines whispered, as though a new wind had woken. "You don't really believe that, do you?"

"Foolish," the lutine said, with a solemn shake of her head. "Foolish to risk your soul like that. I will ask the wind to watch over you."

"And I you."

Another snap of those tiny fingers, and a set of clean silk stockings and two pink garters appeared in her hands. These, Luce saw with relief, were her own, and she felt no guilt as she slid her clean toes inside the stockings and drew them up to her thighs, securing them with the ribbons. When she looked up, the lutine was gone.

Luce waited until she was sure the fishermen had left the grounds—until the low whickering from the stables and the contented clucking of the chickens wandering near the gates were the only sounds—before she returned to the house. The vestibule, with its imposing ceilings, marble floors, and enormous stone staircase, was empty.

"Those fools didn't know a thing," Luce heard her sister Charlotte say from the grand salon. The enormous, ornate double doors were slightly ajar, hiding the activity within. "Who is he, do you think?"

Who, indeed? Luce considered that as she crossed the vestibule. She knew all the great ship-owning families of Saint-Malo: the Gaultiers and the Desailles. The Fontaine-Roux and the de Châtelaines. The Le Fers, the Landais, and the Rivières. Perhaps this man was a foreigner? From Amsterdam or Spain? Perhaps—she hesitated, steps slowing—he was English?

The war with England was in its fourth year now. "Tussocking over the Americas," Samuel called it, though Luce's father would have disagreed. "It is a matter of French pride," Jean-Baptiste had told her. "We cannot let the English take the Ohio." The fighting was not limited to the New World. There had been fighting in Saxony, Bohemia, and Moravia, as well as the Mediterranean. It affected everyone in Saint-Malo—merchants, traders, and shipowners alike. With trade interrupted, and the Manche and Atlantique bristling with enemy ships, men like Luce's father turned, as they had always done, to privateering. Armed with a Letter of Marque from the king, he would swiftly pull together investors, a crew, and a captain. "It is not only our right, but our duty," Jean-Baptiste would oft proclaim. By disrupting English shipping and destroying or taking its ships, the corsairs of Saint-Malo were assisting the king by distracting the English Navy, as well as adding to the French war coffers by sharing their spoils with the Crown. They were also—Luce glanced at the Italian marble floor, elaborate golden candelabra and matching mirror, still covered by layers of linen after last night's storm—making a great deal of money. Of course, it was not only France who took to privateering. England, too, had its own raiders. Just like the gentlemen of Saint-Malo, they scoured the Manche, the Atlantique, and beyond, attacking, sinking, and stealing enemy ships, fighting for country and glory. If this man was an English privateer, he was her father's, Saint-Malo's, and all of Bretagne's enemy.

Guilt of an entirely different kind rose within Luce. She hurried toward the grand salon, then whirled as someone hissed her name.

Samuel and Bones were standing in the shadows beneath the stairs, tricorns in hand, grinning.

"Found your clothes, then," Samuel whispered, with an amiable wink. "Good for you."

"I'll thank you to keep a civil tongue in your head, Samuel," Bones muttered, turning to his cousin in mock disapproval. "Anyone would think you *enjoy* glimpsing well-bred young women swimming in their underthings."

Framed by the intricately carved pair of fish bearing the bronze ship's bell, their overcoats of oiled leather stark against the pastel paneling on the walls—dove-gray, cream trim, the height of fashion—the two smugglers looked large, rough, and completely incorrigible.

"What are you still doing here?" Luce hissed, hurrying toward them.

"The same as you." Samuel looked wounded. "Saving that poor soul from certain death."

Bones was no longer smiling. "Tell me you didn't pull him from the water, Luce," he said, his usually good-natured face grave. "That he was already on the beach when you found him."

Luce sighed. Bones wholeheartedly believed, as all seamen did, in the superstitions that soaked their craft. Customs that could save your life or doom it. Habits that could change the whim of the weather, the will of the waves. "You're as bad as the lutine, Bones, with your superstitions."

"You know better than to do something like that, Luce," he scolded. "The sea must have its number."

"I—" Luce froze as the voices in the salon drifted closer, as though someone—Nanette, perhaps—was about to step into the vestibule. Bones, swearing softly, bolted through the front doors and across the courtyard, out of sight. Samuel merely stood his ground, grinning in a way he knew Luce found to be most disagreeable.

"Curse you, Samuel." She placed both hands on his chest and pushed him further into the shadows. Though he could have stopped her easily—he was a full head taller than she, and strong from years of sea-work—he retreated obediently, ducking his tawny head to avoid bashing it on the stairs. A moment later Veronique's chambermaid, Anna-Marie, hurried intently by, her neat, capped head bent low.

"You took an age to come inside," Samuel said, when Anna-Marie had gone. "Bones was worried your mother would catch us loitering and toss us arse-first into her rose bushes."

"Keep your voice down, or she will toss us *both*!" Luce's hands were still on his chest. Carefully, she removed them.

"You're in a foul mood," he observed. "Feet hurting?"

"I'm fine. I just . . . I don't want my family knowing what happened this morning, that's all."

Samuel frowned. "That man owes his life to you, Luce. Why should you hide it?"

"Because—as you well know, Samuel—my entire family believes I was at prayer in the chapel this morning, not . . . not running about the shore in my chemise."

Or kissing strangers, for that matter. She glanced up at him, at the curve of his lips, lifting in a half smile.

"Well, no need to worry about that. No one saw you but Bones and me."

Those words from any other man might have made Luce shudder and draw away. They implied an intimacy, after all: an unseemly, uninvited, knowledge. In Samuel's rough French, however—he, like Bones, was English, though decidedly more interested in profits than patriotism—they were a reassurance, nothing more. In all the time they had spent together, on the shore and in his boat, he had never once made her feel uneasy.

She watched him a moment, wondering if he had seen *more* than just her underthings on the beach: Luce, wrapped in the near-drowned man's arms, kissing him as though she alone could push the life back into him. *No.* No, the young man had flopped back onto the sand well before the fishermen, Samuel among them, rounded the headland. And Samuel, for his part, was calm as always. There was no question in his gray eyes, no. . . . what was she looking for? Jealousy? Consternation?

She ought to know better.

Samuel and Bones were part of a small operation that smuggled contraband from Bretagne to their village in Dorset. Tea, wine, and brandy. Silks and lace and fine Breton linens. When Luce and Samuel first met, he had been searching for a place to store contraband between Manche crossings—space in the crowded warehouses in Saint-Malo and Saint-Servan was far too expensive for smugglers of his ilk, he later explained. Somewhere close to his lodgings at a Saint-Coulomb farmhouse, where an elderly widow gave both him and Bones a meal a day and rough beds in the loft above her barn. There were several caves that had caught his eye, but all were occupied—tide-women, though rare, were still about, as well as fions and the same crotchety band of jetins Luce had met that morning at the cove. Samuel was stumbling up the beach, suffering the indignation of having curses as well as stones hurled at him by the latter, when he came upon Luce swimming. Later, he had admitted that he had thought her one of the sea-folk, at first, with her long dark hair. It was only when she swam into the shallows and banished the furious jetins with a word that he realized she was *not* one of the Fae as he had supposed, but the daughter of Jean-Baptiste Léon.

Turning his back while she emerged from the water and dressed, Samuel had expected nothing more from his future than swift punishment for encroaching upon not only Monsieur Léon's property but the privacy of his youngest daughter. He had not anticipated being the subject of Luce's keen appraisal. She had known within a moment of hearing his spluttered apologies and curses that he was English—thanks to the many tutors her father had procured for her over the years, she not only spoke fluent English, but Latin and Spanish, too—and wasted no time in asking him what his business was. Stunned into honesty, he explained his predicament: he was in need of a cave. Somewhere large and dry. Somewhere secret.

Luce had known the perfect place. A sea-cave hidden amid the tumbling rocks beneath the cliffs and protected by the presence of the powerful groac'h, or tide-crone, who lived in her own cave nearby. Despite the many stories of the fae woman's wickedness and savagery, Luce had always found her to leave well enough alone, if the same courtesy was bestowed upon her. Even better, her presence caused the local fishermen to give the cove a wide berth. Luce showed Samuel the cave—he agreed that it was perfect—and offered it to him on two conditions: one, that he avoid the parts that Luce had already claimed for her own use, and two, that he teach her to sail.

Samuel was unable to pass up such an opportunity—a cave protected by the presence of a malignant sea hag? It was more than he had hoped for. "By all means," he had said in his still-clumsy French. "I will gladly teach you to sail, mademoiselle."

"Then we have an agreement," Luce replied in perfect English, shaking his hand.

Samuel had honored it, too, arriving at the cove at least once a week whenever Luce and her family were residing at Le Bleu Sauvage, in the quiet of the mornings when the rest of her family slept or sipped coffee in their chambers, completely unaware that Luce had slipped through the chapel and gone out on the water with an unscrupulous smuggler from Dorset. Samuel's presence was an island in an otherwise dreary ocean of tutors and music lessons, embroidery and tiresome social engagements; suppers and lunches, piqniques and dances. Luce did her best to avoid them. She had little in common with the other young ladies of Saint-Malo, with their talk of marriage and trousseaus and shopping trips to Paris. She had her father, of course, and the many books he brought for her—geography, natural history, and mathematics.

But it was only Samuel who gave her what she most wanted: the open water, and its freedom.

Footsteps. Nanette, bearing a pitcher, scurried by, followed by Claudine, her arms loaded with blankets. Neither servant so much as glanced under the stairs before hurrying into the salon.

"Very good," came Gratienne's voice from within. "Now, take that blanket and spread it out under him. No, *this* way. Here, lift him, lift him. That's right. No point ruining that chintz."

"I wonder who he is," Samuel said, tilting his head in an effort to catch a glimpse of the goings-on between the crack in the salon doors. The ends of his brown hair, crisped gold by long days of sun and salt, glimmered gold as her mother's candelabra. "Did he say anything to you?"

"No." Luce's cheeks flamed. She was glad of the cool shadows beneath the stairs.

"I suppose we'll find out when he wakes."

"I suppose we will." A moment of dread. Would the sailor reveal her part in his rescue? He was, at this very moment, surrounded by her family. It would take only a word or two for him to reveal all.

Samuel was watching her. "I doubt he'll recall much," he said, as if perceiving her thoughts. "God alone knows how long he was drifting, cold and exhausted. It will be a miracle if he remembers anything at all."

"I hope that's true." *Please, be true.* Relief, and something else. Disappointment? She feared that the sailor might remember her, it was true; yet, at the same time, she loathed the notion of him forgetting. The memory of his kiss was warm on her lips; she touched her fingertips to them guiltily.

"One can only hope," Samuel said with a shrug.

Luce narrowed her eyes. "You're thinking of the ship."

He grinned. "I'm thinking of the ship."

Smuggling was not the only unlawful pastime with which

Samuel filled his days. He was also a storm diver, a hunter of the precious storm-stone ballast used by Malouin shipowners and captains to protect their vessels from foul weather, attack, and mutiny alike ("Not all storms are related to the weather, after all," Papa was fond of saying). Harvesting the stone from wrecks and reefs was illegal—Samuel knew this as well as anyone. But storm-stone was no longer as plentiful or powerful as it had been a century ago, when Bretagne's population of Fae creatures had been larger, and there were strict laws in place to protect the city's supply. There had to be. As more and more of the Fae left Bretagne, it became harder and harder to find good quality stone. A thriving black market had developed, which Samuel had no qualms about levering to his advantage. The rarer something was, after all, the higher the price.

"I gave him a discreet little slap or two on the way up," Samuel admitted. "Hoped he might wake and say what kind of cloud the ship was carrying, and where it went down. He wouldn't rouse, more's the pity."

"You didn't!" Luce tried, and failed, to keep from laughing. "That man almost died, Samuel—his crew are unaccounted for—and all you care about is whether he might help you line your pockets!"

"We're not all of us lucky enough to be Léons," he said, with a meaningful glance at the opulent vestibule. It was the first time, Luce realized, she had ever seen Samuel in her father's house. Beside the spindly side table with its ridiculously ostentatious decorations—flowers and birds, swirls of leaves and sea shells—he looked supremely out of place.

. . . *And no less attractive for it*, said a small, rather irritating part of Luce.

"If we're going to talk about who owes what," Samuel was saying, "let's talk about what *he* owes *you*. You put yourself at risk when you swam out to save him."

"Nonsense. I'm a strong swimmer."

"You are," he agreed. "But that's not what I'm talking about.

You stole a soul from the Manche when you saved him. It will not forget."

"Heavens above, Samuel. Not you, too?"

She should have known. Samuel was not as effusive as his cousin when it came to sea lore, but he saw omens in the clouds and portents in the color of the water just the same.

"The Manche has never been anything but kind to me," she said. "I am not afraid."

"I wish I could say the same," he said soberly. "Lend me some of that confidence, would you? I'll need it tonight."

"You're making a run?"

"Looks like it. The moon's new and the weather's lurking. Perfect night for a little 'fishing.'"

Luce frowned. "The crossing will be rough."

"It will. The Manche is in a foul mood."

"Why tempt it, then?"

"You know why. Rough water, dark moon—good smuggling."

Luce nodded. Dark moons hid sails, and bad weather kept customs men—and their speedy clippers—at bay. Even so, the thought of Samuel and Bones sailing their little two-masted lugger, the *Dove*, across the dark expanse of the Manche filled her with misgiving.

"I thought you said you weren't afraid?" Samuel teased. "There's no need to look so worried; we're only going to Guernsey."

The salon doors creaked open, and Marie-Jeanne bustled through. She spared not a glance as she passed by, hurrying toward the kitchen.

"How many servants *are* there?" Samuel asked in wonder.

"I should see if they need help," Luce said. The urge to see the sailor again, to know how he fared, was suddenly strong.

"Of course." Samuel watched the salon warily. "Much as I've enjoyed lingering with you beneath these fancy stairs, I have things of my own to see to. Is it safe to leave?"

Luce peered out from beneath the stairs. "I think so."

He ducked out from the cover of the shadows, overcoat swirling as he strode for the door. At the last moment he stopped, came back. "I'm going to search for that wreck when we get back from Guernsey. The tide will be just right in the morning. Come with me. Six bells?"

Despite herself, Luce nodded.

"If for some reason you can't meet me"—he inclined his head toward the grand salon, and her family—"leave a note at the chapel."

"I will. Take care tonight, Samuel. The Manche is in a greedy mood."

"Then I'll be in good company." He threw her another wink and settled his battered tricorn on his head. "But I'll take care, just for you."

3

Wolf Cub

Le Bleu Sauvage was a confection of luxury and light, fantasy and fashion. Furniture embellished with carved flowers and shells, palm leaves, and foliage adorned every room. The high walls were a tasteful shade of pearl-gray, bedecked with sumptuous mirrors and art. No room, however, was more breathtaking than the grand salon.

With two sets of high double doors opening at either end, one could walk from the vestibule to the center of the room, where silk-covered chairs and chaise longues were artfully arranged, passing beneath an enormous crystal chandelier before pushing aside the gauzy curtains and stepping down to the sweeping expanse of lawn.

The dark-haired man was oblivious to his elegant surroundings. He lay, eyes closed, upon the largest of the chaise longues. Luce drank in every part of him: the black hair flopping over his high brow, the triangle of pale flesh peeking through the laces of his shirt.

"Fetch Jean-François, Nanette," Jean-Baptiste was saying. "I must send word to the harbormaster at Saint-Malo."

Nanette obeyed at once, hurrying out into the gardens where the dovecote lay. At the same moment, Marie-Jeanne came back through the doors behind Luce, bearing a tray loaded with bread and broth.

"Ah, well done, Marie-Jeanne," Gratienne said, pointing. "Put it there. He will be famished when he wakes. Poor wretch." Her gaze fell upon Luce. "There you are, Lucinde. I wondered where you had got to."

"Why do you bother, Maman? You know exactly where Luce was," Veronique said patiently. "She always begins her day in the chapel."

"Whatever do you pray about, day after day?" Charlotte inquired. "You missed all the excitement this morning." She gestured to the unconscious sailor, lowering her voice as though he might hear. "The fishermen found him on the beach!"

"Goodness," Luce said, feigning surprise. "Is there anything I can do?"

"Your mother has everything in hand," Jean-Baptiste said, tilting his cheek for Luce to kiss. He smelled of ink and coffee; warm, and comforting. "I knew the weather would be foul last night."

"Oh?" Luce, noticing that his lace jabot was crooked, reached up to adjust it.

"Indeed. I was at the dockyards in Trichet yesterday," he explained. "Monsieur Gaultier's new ship is near complete. And what do you think, one of the carpenter's apprentices stuck his knife in the *mainmast* in his haste to get to his dinner!"

Luce's hands stilled. "Papa. You're not truly blaming that boy for the storm?"

"I most certainly am, mon trésor. A knife in a mast will always raise the weather. If he'd been less eager to drop tools and fill his belly, he'd have remembered it."

Luce hid a smile. Her father was dressed impeccably in a lace-cuffed shirt, silk faille waistcoat, and breeches. Still, it was impossible to separate the gentleman before her from the young sailor he had once been—along with his superstitions. The ship's bell and hourglass in the vestibule—manned by the four laquais and rung on every watch except the deeps of the night and early morning—were proof enough of this, as was Jean-Baptiste's unabiding dislike of reversed maps, upturned shoes, and whistling, which he swore would turn a stiff breeze into a gale. It was an unconditional rule that the women in his household—domestiques included—refrain from brushing or dressing their hair after dark, lest they rouse the weather and endanger his ships.

"Maman, he is still so cold." In her lace-edged peignoir, her golden hair loose around her shoulders, Veronique looked like she was sitting for a portrait, not nursing an unfortunate sailor. She was also, Luce noted, clasping one of the young man's hands. "His skin is like ice."

Gratienne rustled to the chaise, held a hand to the sailor's brow. "You are right, ma chère fille." She frowned about the room, then gave a determined nod. "Very well. Out, my daughters. You must leave the room at once."

"But, Maman!" Charlotte exclaimed.

Veronique pouted. "Might we not stay and help?"

"We must remove his wet clothes and warm him," Gratienne said crisply. "Decorum must be maintained. Besides, neither of you are dressed to receive visitors."

"He's hardly a visitor," Veronique said.

"He's not even awake!"

"But he *is* about to be undressed," Jean-Baptiste said, a laugh tickling the corners of his mouth. "Off with you, ma filles."

Luce's sisters dragged themselves to the door, Veronique clinging to the sailor's hand until the last possible moment.

"How disappointing," Charlotte muttered. "This was the most exciting thing to happen since we left Saint-Malo."

She gave Luce a pointed look. Le Bleu Sauvage was the family's summer home, a retreat when the walled city became an odious, simmering cauldron. Ordinarily the move occurred when the weather warmed—usually in June. But this year, like the year before, and the year before that, Luce had begged her father to take the family to the malouinière much earlier. Saint-Malo, home to twelve thousand souls, was crowded, noisy, and unbearably close. Yes, it was surrounded on all sides by the sea; but its high walls and ramparts, its locked gates and strict curfew, made reaching it difficult. By the end of March, Luce was climbing the walls. Her father, taking pity on her, had moved the entire household to Le Bleu Sauvage at the end of April.

Luce had almost cried with relief. Her sisters, too, had shed a tear, though for entirely different reasons. With the rest of the wealthy families still in the city, the usual summer pastimes—balls and receptions, piqniques and long, lazy walks followed by cards, music, and even longer suppers—had not yet begun. To Veronique and Charlotte, the Léons were alone in the vast emptiness of the countryside, with neither excitement nor diversion. Since neither could tolerate missing any social engagement, no matter the occasion, they had in no way forgiven their youngest sister.

"He is most handsome, is he not?" Veronique whispered. She glanced back at the chaise. "I wonder what color his eyes are."

"Black," Luce murmured without thinking.

"What did you say?" Charlotte's sharp gaze caught Luce, pinned her.

"I *imagine*," Luce said quickly. "I *imagine* they're black."

"*Girls!*"

"Yes, Maman," Charlotte and Veronique said in unison, dipping their heads. Luce followed them slowly out, watching as her mother and Alis, the eldest of the domestiques, bent to strip away the sailor's shirt. A glimpse of his bare torso, his shoulder, the skin smooth and pale, before Gratienne turned.

"*Lucinde!*"

Luce bowed her head and hurried for the door. She could not help but turn back, at the very last. Warmth flowed through her, head to toe. The young man's eyes were open. For one sweet moment, before they closed again, they met Luce's own.

"Ah, there she is; lingering at Papa's door again like a lost hound."

Luce, waiting outside her father's study, turned to see Charlotte on the stairs. It was evening, and the servants had lit the candles, but the golden light did nothing to warm Charlotte's countenance. "Waiting for scraps, are we?"

Luce was tempted to remind her sister that she was not the only one who had been waiting at doors that day. Both Charlotte and Veronique had discovered countless reasons to linger on the second-floor landing—which offered a clear view to the guest room where the young sailor was resting—despite Gratienne's informing them that *under no circumstances* would they be permitted to enter.

"Don't be unkind, Cee," Veronique said, gliding down the stairs. Like Charlotte, she had changed for supper and glowed in a gown of ivory silk faille, her blonde hair pinned elegantly at the back of her head.

Charlotte ignored her older sister. "What will Papa give you this time, Luce?" she mused. "Are we to pack our belongings and move again? Or will it be more rubbish from one of his ships?"

Luce said nothing; there was nothing *to* say. Papa had always delighted in bringing her things. Rare sea shells, carved hair pins; a precious copy of *Systema Naturae.* Feathers from the French Antilles, tiny bottles of pink sand. Cakes of indigo, which he knew to be her favorite, its beautiful blues shallow or deep depending on the dyer's whim. She was always careful to take these gifts straight to the cabinet adjoining her bedchamber, tucking them away before her sisters noticed them. Charlotte, however—always watching, measuring, judging—noted each and every one, down to the tiniest shell.

"What do you and I care for trinkets and feathers, Cee?" Veronique, who owned half a hundred feathers in various shapes, colors, and sizes, examined her flawless face in the enormous gold-framed mirror—now free of its storm-coverings—and brushed at one delicately powdered cheek. "After all, we may buy whatever we wish."

But it was not the same, and they all knew it. A gift from Papa—one of the busiest men in Saint-Malo, which was, in its turn, one of the busiest seaports in Bretagne—was not only a sign of his esteem and affection, but a sign that you, the receiver of the gift, were important enough to have been in his thoughts. Feathers and trinkets they might be, but the fact that Luce received so many tokens from her father merely proved what Charlotte had accused Luce of since they were but tiny girls: of his three daughters, Luce was Jean-Baptiste's favorite.

It was a dire crime at the best of times, but today it was even worse. For when Jean-Baptiste had heard from the servants that his guest had awoken, he had gone directly to the chamber on the second floor, knocked politely, and closed the door behind him. Clustering on the landing, ears pressed to the door, his three daughters—Luce, too, was incapable of withstanding the chamber's siren-song—had heard the low rumble of their father's voice. And, even more exciting, an answering one. There followed a muffled scrap of a conversation—Luce caught the words "dauphin," "Cádiz," "English," and "storm"—before Jean-Baptiste had come out again—his daughters had straightened guiltily—and, after giving them a brief, knowing glance, walked down the stairs and into his study, closing the door firmly behind him.

He had remained there throughout the afternoon, protected by one of the household's most enduring laws: when Jean-Baptiste was about his work, no one, not even Gratienne, was permitted to disturb him.

No one, that is, but Luce.

Charlotte, who was clearly aware of this fact (and, of course, that Luce was the only one among them who might prevail upon their father to share their guest's identity) opened her mouth to say more, then closed it again at the sound of her father's muted voice.

"Is that you, mon trésor?"

Luce winced.

"Run along, *treasure*," Charlotte mimicked. "You know he only treats you so because he pities you. Your wretched feet, your awkward ways. It's no wonder—after all, you're not *really* a Léon like the rest of us, are you? You're just another piece of flotsam he brought home when he went to sea."

"Cee!" Veronique was shocked enough to look away from her reflection. "You *didn't*!" She turned to Luce, her face soft with pity. "Take no heed of her, Luce. She's just jealous. . . ."

Luce barely heard her sister over the storm of shame that had woken in her heart. Shoulders hunched, she stepped into her father's study, closing the door softly behind her.

"There you are," Jean-Baptiste said, from behind his enormous desk. "I have been hoping you would come in and rescue me from these wretched accounts."

"Do you need help, Papa?"

"Not tonight, mon petit oiseau. I intend to do nothing but enjoy my supper and partake heartily of that new wine from Bourgogne. Such an aroma!"

Walking into her father's study was like entering another world. Unlike the rest of the house, the room clung stubbornly to a masculine soberness. Letters, accounts, and ledgers covered the desk, which was overlooked by dramatic paintings of his favorite ships—the *Lionne*, the *Thétis*, and his pride and joy, the *Fleur de Mer*.

Shelves and cabinets lined the heavy oak-paneled walls, bursting with books and maps, models, rare stones, and strange coins. He loved treasure, had acquired it in every port he had ventured to: dried starfish and carved whale bones. Feathers, fishhooks, and coral. Turtle shells. The twisted horn of a narwhal and the startling, spiny jaw of a swordfish. Spears and swords, powder horns and pistols. Shells of every color and description. Luce loved to explore those shelves, to imagine the places he had been, the shades of those distant seas and the scent of different winds. Spices and salt, flowers and tropical rains.

"And what of my youngest daughter?" Jean-Baptiste asked, smiling at her as she rounded the desk. The words, that smile, were an embrace, easing the sting of Charlotte's final barb, which was all the more painful for being true. Luce was *not* a Léon by birth. Jean-Baptiste *had* found her while he was at sea: two years old and newly orphaned, the daughter of a Guernsey shipwright. Unable to abandon her to the winds of fate, Jean-Baptiste had simply picked her up and brought her back to Saint-Malo. "Have you had any adventures today?"

Gray threaded his dark hair, and age had weathered his swarthy skin, but it was not difficult to imagine the dashing young corsair he had once been, who had made his fortune through tenacity, daring—and by clinging with a grappling hook to the heaving side of precisely the right ship at precisely the right time. It was this bravery and persistence that had allowed Jean-Baptiste to win the hand of Gratienne, the daughter of a minor Breton noble who, drowning in debt, was not too proud to save himself with Léon wealth.

His gaze flicked to the window and, beyond it, the grounds and the forest, the dusking sea. Looking at him there, trapped behind his desk, overseeing his ships instead of striding across their decks as they stormed into war-torn waters, Luce wondered if he dreamed of taking the helm again. Pushing out onto the night-dark waters of the Manche like a scarred old lion in search of prey. The memory of adventure was on him still.

"None that compare to yours, Papa." Not a lie, but close enough to one that she felt a pang of guilt. What would he say if she told him of her morning? Sneaking from the estate? Pulling a man from the storm-exhausted sea? She went to the window, where her father's globe, a sphere of wonder and adventure in miniature, took pride of place. "Although, I suppose the fishermen bringing us that poor sailor counts as an adventure, doesn't it?"

"I suppose it does." Jean-Baptiste reached for his pipe and tobacco box. The box, carved intricately with flowers and two tiny, roaring lions, was made from the shell of a coconut. As a child Luce had loved running her fingertips over its textured surface, those clever, gleaming lions. "I'm sure it seemed that way to your mother. Has she come down yet?"

Gratienne, exhausted by the day's events, had taken to her bedchamber for the best part of the evening.

"Not yet, Papa."

He chuckled, tamping down the tobacco into the pipe's bowl with practiced care. "I'll never forget the look on her face when they laid him down on that chaise longue. It's hand-painted, you know."

Luce watched him hold a spill to the candle on his desk and use it to char the tobacco, brow furrowing as he puffed. Tiny furrows of red rose and faded in the clay bowl.

"And is our sea-faring guest still abed?"

"I believe he is, Papa." Luce hesitated. "Do you—do you know who he is?"

Jean-Baptiste did not look up from his pipe. "I do."

"And?" She reached out a fingertip, twirling the globe on its axis. Oceans and islands, archipelagos and continents passed in a blur.

Jean-Baptiste was watching her, gray eyes twinkling through a veil of smoke.

"Don't tell me you, too, have fallen under our handsome guest's spell? Veronique has already come knocking: 'Would you like a cup of chocolate, Papa?' Charlotte, too, tried her luck—she brought oranges. Of course, I told them nothing." He chuckled. "Do not look at me like that, mon trésor. I know it was cruel of me. But oh, the expressions on their faces . . ."

Luce cringed. No surprise, then, that Charlotte had been so bitter. Not for the first time, Luce wondered why her father treated her so differently. Was it, as Charlotte had said, because he pitied her? Or did he feel compelled to prove that she was not, as Charlotte had suggested, mere flotsam?

"It would seem the young wolf cub has made quite the impression," Jean-Baptiste continued, leaning back in his chair to enjoy the full effect of his pipe.

Luce frowned. "Wolf cub?"

"The boy is a de Châtelaine, mon trésor."

Oh. She had not expected that. The de Châtelaines were the most influential of the Malouin ship-owning families, their crest a series of white fleurs-de-lis and wolves against an ocean of blue. Castro and Camille de Châtelaine's malouinière, Le Loup Blanc, was set along the banks of the Rance. It was generally agreed to be the largest and most beautiful of the country houses, while their grand town house within the walls of Saint-Malo was the envy of every shipowner's wife.

"Morgan de Châtelaine, to be precise," Jean-Baptiste added. "Castro's youngest son."

Morgan. "Of the sea," the name meant. No wonder it had spared him.

"He was sailing back from Cádiz," Jean Baptiste was saying. "Been living there since he was a boy; learning his family's business, understanding the trade." He sucked on his pipe ruminatively. "I too lived there when I was a youth, you know."

Luce nodded. "I remember."

Many Malouin shipowners sent their sons there to be apprenticed in the intricacies of trade with Spain. Luce rotated the globe until her fingertip rested on Cádiz. As a child she had loved to hear Jean-Baptiste speak of its plazas and markets. It was the oldest city in Europe, he had said. Timeworn ruins sat alongside impressive new buildings, their gardens bursting with exotic flowers brought back by explorers. "That's why we didn't know him."

"Precisely."

There it was, then. The answer to all of Luce's questions. Her sisters' and Samuel's, too.

"Young de Châtelaine was trying his hand at captain for the first time. The *Dauphin* was his father's ship. You remember it?"

"I do." Luce had seen it at anchor in the harbor countless times. It was a beautiful ship.

"He told me they were pursued by two English privateers off Guernsey," Jean-Baptiste said. "They took fire, and the *Dauphin* was damaged. Then the storm rolled in. It prevented the English from finishing the job and seizing the ship and Morgan's crew, but that hardly matters, does it, when it decided to take the ship for itself?"

"What of its ballast?" Luce asked, looking up from the globe. "Were they not carrying storm-stone?"

No sooner were the words out of her mouth than she remembered the stones in the young man's pockets.

"I didn't bother to ask. Assaulted by the enemy and then the weather? The *Dauphin* was clearly unprotected."

Luce frowned. She had no doubt the storm-stones were of the finest quality. She had felt the heavy rumble of their magic as they sank.

"I would have thought Castro would have taken more care," Jean-Baptiste was saying. "It is not as though he can't afford it."

"Indeed," Luce said distractedly. With such stone aboard, and a crew experienced enough to know when to step back from the wheel and simply let the stone—and the storm—run their course, the *Dauphin* and her crew should have been protected against all manner of disaster: mutiny, assault, foul weather. Yet she was lost, her crew still unaccounted for, her captain saved only by chance.

Strange.

"Monsieur de Châtelaine has come back to take his place beside his father and brothers. And itching to try his hand as a corsair." Jean-Baptiste grinned. "I was much the same at his age. Longing for the horizon."

Luce forced herself to smile back. If only she could tell her father that she, too, longed for the horizon. To ask if Morgan de Châtelaine had had the opportunity to travel even *further* than Cádiz. The French Antilles, perhaps? The Spice Islands? The New World? The longing to see such places, to stand in the prow of a ship with spray spilling on the wind, salting her hair—to know that nothing and no one could stop her from seeing the great wide world, was a pain in her heart.

"I sent Jean-Germane with a message for the de Châtelaines this afternoon. Let them know their son is safe in our care." Jean-Baptiste's eyes gleamed with catlike speculation. "It appears my luck has held once more, mon trésor. Castro de Châtelaine's only unwed son washed up like a seal pup—carried under my very roof!—without me having to lift a finger? There has been no marriage between Léons and de Châtelaines for a hundred years. Such an alliance would only be for the good."

Luce frowned. "Then why did you keep his name from Charlotte and Veronique?"

"To increase the appeal, of course! There isn't a man—or woman—alive who's not made more attractive by a little mystery. Although . . . he *is* pretty. Pretty enough, it seems, to intrigue all three of my daughters." Jean-Baptiste tilted his head, considering her. "Veronique's curiosity I understand; she is oft taking an interest in men, and they in her. And Charlotte is always interested in whatever Veronique is interested in. But you, mon trésor . . . I did not expect it."

"Well, he *is* handsome," Luce said lightly, spinning the globe again and trying not to think of Morgan de Châtelaine's lean, muscled back beneath her fingertips. She stilled the globe with a touch and turned to face her father. "To be honest, I was more interested in where he had sailed from. And the fate of the ship, of course. When first I heard of the wreck I feared it was one of yours."

Jean-Baptiste scoffed. "One of *my* ships? Lost almost within sight of Saint-Malo? I think not!"

Luce could not help but smile. It had long been said that, while her father had not inherited the bulk of the Léon fortune, he had certainly received the lion's share of the family's luck. While other shipowners were struck by ill timing or bad investments, Jean-Baptiste's endeavors always flourished. She could not remember the last time he lost a ship. "The lion is a cunning and wily beast, mon trésor," he once told her. "He thinks deeply before he acts. And, of course, he discusses his plans with God."

But even with God's guidance, and the protection of stormstone, such fortune was rare. The sea was notoriously fickle, its moods as changeable as the moon. Every shipowner in Bretagne envied Jean-Baptiste his luck. In reply, he would merely shrug. He had always loved the sea, he told them. The sea simply loved him back.

"In any case, I am happy to hear that you, at least, remain disenchanted by our guest." Jean-Baptiste set down his spent pipe and rose from his chair, joining Luce at the window. The Manche was a wash of distant darkness in the dusk. "I do not think I will ever be ready to part with you." He reached out, touched her cheek. "Although no doubt the time will come. . . . You grow more beautiful every day. More beautiful, even, than Veronique, though I will deny it if you ever tell her I said so." A bittersweet smile. "No doubt some rogue will steal you from me and break my heart."

"Never, Papa." She tried not to look at the globe, at the oceans and the islands, the archipelagos and continents.

4

Prickling

"Let us talk of happier things," Jean-Baptiste said as he returned to his desk and drew a sheaf of papers tied with a soft blue ribbon from beneath a map of the French Antilles. "I have a gift for you."

The memory of Charlotte's cold words and colder eyes chilled Luce's heart.

"Papa, you spoil me," she said uneasily.

"I most certainly do not." He pressed the scroll into her hands, as eager as a boy. "Open it."

The sound of the ship's bell rang twice from the vestibule below.

"Two bells," Luce said. "It is suppertime, Papa."

"Supper will wait." Jean-Baptiste cleared space on the desk. "Lay it here, mon trésor." He turned to her, standing motionless with the scroll. "Why, hurry and open it!"

Slowly, Luce untied the ribbon and smoothed the papers over the desk.

It was a ship. Or plans for one, at least, its graceful lines captured in black ink. A frigate, three masted, many gunned, as beautiful as any Luce had seen.

"What is this, Papa?"

"It's a ship."

"I can see that."

"It's *your* ship." Jean-Baptiste leaned over the plans, pointing. "See?"

Luce took in the plans: the long scooping line of the keel, the layers of deck, all laid out in perfect, birdlike symmetry. And there, at the top of the page, the ship's name:

Lucinde.

It was customary for shipowners to name their vessels after their wives and daughters. Jean-Baptiste's fleet already held the *Gratienne* and the *Charlotte*. The *Veronique* had, unfortunately, been captured by the English Navy the year before. Luce flipped through the pages, pausing at a detailed diagram of the ship's stern and bow. Lush woodwork ornamented the stern and quarter galleries: sea goddesses with shapely arms, their torsos wrapped in cunningly sculpted draperies. Fish pooled about the windows and among the carvings on the taffrail. And the figurehead . . .

It was Luce herself, long dark hair spilling over her bare shoulders, the material of her gown breezing out over the ship's beak and bow, clinging slightly to her legs as though a sea wind dragged it behind her. Her feet, she could not help but notice, were tucked away; hidden beneath the folds of wooden fabric.

"It's been my little secret." Jean-Baptiste beamed at her. "You had no idea, did you?"

"None." She stroked the *Lucinde*'s curving keel, her sails. "She's beautiful, Papa. When will she be ready?"

"She launches in a week or two."

"A *week* or two?"

"I told you—she's been my secret." Proudly. "There is still much to be done, of course. We shall attend the launch. And then the fitting out will take a month or more. . . ."

Luce rolled up the plans and handed them back. Supper, and the rest of the family, would be waiting. "It was kind of you to name her for me, Papa. Thank you."

"Name her for you?" He pushed the plans back to her. "No, no, mon trésor. She is more than yours in name. I am *giving* her to you."

Luce frowned. "You cannot be serious, Papa."

Neither her sisters, nor her mother, had ever received more than the privilege of lending their names to one of Jean-Baptiste's ships.

"It is too much, Papa."

"Not at all."

"She must have cost a fortune."

"She did."

"But—"

"She is yours to do with as you will," Jean-Baptiste said firmly. "Trade, privateering . . . Whatever you wish."

Whatever you wish.

Luce could not take her eyes off that figurehead, face turned to the sea. Fearless. Free.

"Her captain?" she asked. "Her crew?"

"Will be chosen by you."

Luce had heard stories about women—brave women—who took what was forbidden to them. They dressed up as boys and secretly joined crews, went to sea for months or even years, toiling side by side with a ship's worth of oblivious men. They worked as cooks and sailors, or shipwrights. She had even—such stories set a stirring in her heart—heard of women who did *not* hide their true forms. Women like Anne Dieu-le-Veut, whose presence on board was believed to be good luck, and Jeanne de Clisson, the Lioness of Bretagne, who had captained ships and led her own fleet.

Whatever you wish.

"I want to sail her myself." The words were out of Luce's mouth before she could stop them. "I want to take her to Cádiz or Saint-Domingue, or the Americas. Or even further. I want the horizon, Papa, like you." She turned to him, unable to hide her excitement. "Perhaps . . . perhaps *you* could be my captain?"

Her father was staring at her as though he had never seen her before. Of course, he would be shocked. Why wouldn't he? Aside from the color of the figureheads' respective gowns, neither of her sisters had been even *remotely* interested in their nautical namesakes.

"I know this isn't what you were expecting," Luce hurried on. "But haven't we spent years studying charts and maps? Your new ships, your plans for them? Haven't you told me all your sea stories? I want to make my own stories, Papa."

Still, he said nothing.

"I know Maman will not be happy," Luce said, faltering. "But you could convince her, couldn't you? If you talked to her, and explained . . . I'm sure she would let us go."

"I'm sure she would," he said at last, and leaned in to kiss her brow. "And it is a wonderful idea. Truly. But . . ."

Luce's heart sank. "But?"

"Well, mon trésor, the sea is a dangerous place at the best of times. And now, when we are at war with England . . ."

Of course. The Manche was a battleground, English warships and French corsairs waging a war of their own for dominance over the seas. No father would agree to take his daughter to sea with him, now, nor any other time. She had been a fool to suggest it.

"Forgive me, ma chère," Jean-Baptiste said, a look of exceeding pity on his face. "I hate to disappoint you."

"It is not your fault. Perhaps . . . perhaps when the war is over . . ."

There was, of course, no way of knowing when that might be. The fighting had been going for two years now and showed no sign of slowing.

"Perhaps, mon trésor." He took his frock coat from the back of his chair and shrugged it on. "If, of course, we can convince your mother."

"*There* you are."

Gratienne, Veronique, and Charlotte were seated for supper, hands clasped neatly in their laps. Before them, the large, oval-shaped dining table, covered in a spotless white cloth, was crowded with elegant porcelain plateware, glittering glasses, crystal candelabras, and an armory's worth of silver cutlery.

"We were about to send one of the laquais to fetch you," Gratienne said. The men in question—St. Jean, Jean-Pierre and Jean-Jacques (the fourth, Jean-Germane, who had taken word of the wreck to the de Châtelaines in Saint-Malo, was yet to return)—stood to attention near the sideboard, where bottles of wine and fresh glasses waited. All three were impeccable in their matching livery. Before employing them, Gratienne, who insisted upon perfection in her domestiques, had ensured each was of a similar height, and had no qualms about changing his name to one that included 'Jean', in honour of his master.

"No need for that, ma chère," Jean-Baptiste said easily, taking his seat. "Luce was just helping me with the accounts."

"I trust everything is in order?"

"Quite, ma chère." Jean-Baptiste turned to Jean-Pierre, who had materialized at his side, a bottle of wine at the ready. "Ah, Jean-Pierre. Good man. Is that the Bourgogne?"

"It is, monsieur."

"Very good."

"What's that?" Charlotte asked. Luce, who had until that moment been surreptitiously sliding the ship's plans behind a large arrangement of flowers on the room's second sideboard, turned to find all eyes upon her.

"Nothing," she said, slipping her hands behind her back like a child who has been caught at the sugar pot.

At the same moment her father proclaimed, with unmistakeable pride, "*That* is a set of plans."

"What kind of plans, Papa?" Charlotte looked at Luce. "Are you finally giving Luce her own armoire?"

Veronique giggled. "It is a little late, isn't it?"

"Better start stitching, Luce!"

Both Charlotte and Veronique had received their armoires,

impressively grand and ornate, when they were still girls. As soon as they were old enough to sew, they had begun working on their wedding trousseaus in readiness for their marriages. Now, each armoire was bursting with perfectly embroidered sheets, chemises and laces, cushion covers, bed hangings and silks, as well as napkins, tablecloths, nightgowns, and petticoats.

"It is not an armoire, ma chère," Jean-Baptiste said patiently. "It is Luce's new ship."

Silence, of so profound a nature that the sound of red wine slurping into Jean-Baptiste's wineglass seemed loud as cannon fire.

"*Luce's* new ship?" Charlotte echoed.

"Indeed." Jean-Baptiste turned to Jean-Pierre, smiled. "That will do, thank you." He sipped the wine, then sucked it loudly through his teeth with relish. "By God, that's good. See to it that Olivier orders more, won't you?"

"Of course, monsieur."

"You may bring in the soup," Gratienne told Jean-Jacques. "If it hasn't boiled dry in the pot. Jean-Pierre, please help Lucinde to her seat."

All three laquais obeyed at once, Jean-Jacques and St. Jean disappearing through the door leading to the kitchen, while Jean-Pierre slid Luce's seat deftly into place beneath her, then filled her wineglass.

"Luce's new ship? Whatever do you mean, mon amour?" Candlelight played on Gratienne's carefully powdered hair, the diamonds glinting at her ears. "I thought you were to name your next ship *Veronique* to replace the one we lost."

"It is definitely the *Lucinde*," said Charlotte. "It says so on the plans."

Luce, who had been thanking Jean-Pierre, turned to see that her sister had left her seat and retrieved the plans from their hiding place. "It's a much bigger brigantine than the *Charlotte*," she said, casting her eyes over the pages.

"It's a frigate," Luce corrected mildly.

Jean-Jacques and St. Jean returned, each bearing a silver tureen.

"But what about *my* name?" Veronique asked, as the laquais set the soups upon the table.

"You shall be next, ma chère, have no fear," Jean-Baptiste soothed, helping himself to soup.

"A frigate, like Luce's?" Veronique asked.

"Indeed," said Gratienne, with a long look at her husband.

There was a spiky silence. Jean-Baptiste, at last recognizing the effect his announcement was having on his wife and daughters, turned irritably to Jean-Pierre. "Well don't just stand there, boy. More wine."

Jean-Pierre sprang forward, bottle in hand, and filled Jean-Baptiste's half-empty glass. Jean-Baptiste took a generous gulp.

"Am I to have a new ship, too, Papa?" Charlotte asked.

"What?" Jean-Baptiste, spluttering, almost choked. "Good heavens, no!"

"Why not? Why should Luce and Vee have bigger ships than I?"

"Because Luce can tell the difference between a frigate and a brigantine, ma chère," Jean-Baptiste said, not unkindly, dabbing at the spilled wine on his chin with a spotless napkin. "And because frigates are very expensive."

Charlotte did not reply. She was looking right at Luce, her eyes as cold and hateful as Luce had ever seen. Then she looked down at the plans and snickered.

"What is it, Cee?" Veronique was on her feet, rounding the table. She stopped at Charlotte's side, peered down at the plans. "The figurehead? Well, whoever drew this was being kind."

Charlotte giggled. "No feet."

Luce's cheeks burned. She longed to push up from her chair and leave the room, the very *house,* and go out into the coolness of the night. It would be quiet on the shore, and in the cave. There would be no figureheads, or plans, or sisters there. She would miss supper, but there were plenty of oysters on the rocks. She would not go hungry.

She glanced once more at Jean-Baptiste. Her father, however, had seemed to have found something supremely fascinating at the bottom of his soup bowl.

"That's enough, girls," Gratienne said. "Return to your seats at once. Your soup will get cold."

When Gratienne spoke in this way—sharp as a diamond, soft as silk—even Veronique, her favorite, dared not oppose her. The two young women returned to their seats.

When they were settled, Jean-Baptiste looked up from his soup. "So," he said, gazing around the table, one salty brow raised. "Who would like to know the identity of our dashing young guest?"

And just like that, the *Lucinde* was forgotten.

Samuel, as he had promised, was waiting at the cove at six bells. Luce glimpsed his boat through the sea pines as she made her way down to the shore. The *Dove* was a shallow draft lugger, made for moving lightly over the gently sloping beaches near Samuel's home in Dorset, and there were only a few watery steps to take, boots and stockings in one hand, breeches rolled to the knee, before Samuel was reaching down and lifting Luce into the boat.

"Bones isn't coming?" she asked.

"Mind your feet, there." He waited until she had found her balance before releasing her. "And no, he isn't. He accused me of maltreatment, expecting him to go out again so soon after a run. He's still sleeping, the drawlatchet."

Chuckling—Samuel was wont to use the strangest words—Luce moved to the bow as he took up the oars. Compared to her father's ships, the *Dove* was laughably small. Twenty feet in length, it was large enough to cross the Manche, but small enough for Samuel to handle with just Bones's or Luce's help. The amount of contraband it could carry was meager compared to what other smugglers moved in their sloops and cutters, and it required considerable skill, but that was little trouble for Samuel. Aided by Bones, he would deliver the goods to Guernsey, where another boat would pick it up and take it on to England. Sometimes, if the Manche was generous and Samuel was feeling "peart," he would sail all the way to Dorset. The contraband would, after a long and secretive journey on quiet English roads, end up in London, while the profits would be shared among the network of smugglers, with a generous cut for Samuel and Bones. Generous enough, at least, for Samuel to risk attracting the ire of the Manche, as well as the English revenue men's infamous jails. Luce had asked him once if the war had made his life harder. Surely the Malouin merchants distrusted an Englishman in their midst?

"I am no threat to Saint-Malo," he had told her, shrugging off her concern, "and Saint-Malo knows it. I'm just one little cog in a very large wheel."

It made sense, in a way. The war with England had led to an increase in taxes on French goods. The English people, already under pressure from war taxes, relied heavily on smugglers for their tea and lace, their French wines and silks, while the merchants of Saint-Malo—her father among them—were simply happy to keep selling their wares.

With last night's run to Guernsey over, Samuel was wholly focused on storm-diving.

"Did you find out who the sailor is?" he asked, storing the oars.

"I did. He's Castro de Châtelaine's youngest son. Morgan."

They were clear of the rocks framing the cove. Samuel moved to the tiller, taking the mainsheet in one hand. Luce waited for his nod before easing the jib. The sails filled in the breeze and Samuel began to tack around the craggy headland.

"A de Châtelaine, eh?" He whistled, settling back against the *Dove*'s stern. "No wonder he was so pretty."

The sun was rising in earnest, the water around them shining like gold. Luce leaned over the side, her fingertips brushing the water. Here, in the cold, salty wind, the walls of Saint-Malo and Le Bleu Sauvage seemed as distant as the moon. The endless rounds of social events, the pressure to behave as her mother and sisters did, pressed beneath the strictures of corsets and society's will both, was gone. She could be on a frigate in the middle of the Atlantique, with nothing but the horizon and possibility before her. She closed her eyes, breathed deep. Above her, the sails tightened as the wind picked up.

Samuel laughed. "There you go again. Bewitching the wind, or my boat, or both."

Luce smiled. Samuel had always sworn that sailing was smoothest when she was aboard. That she tamed the sea and beckoned the wind into the sails. And, most importantly, that he always found the best storm-stone when Luce was with him.

"Which way do you want to go?" he called, as though sensing her thoughts. She glanced back and saw him watching her, one hand braced on the tiller, the other gripping the mainsheet. Ready to follow her lead.

"Keep going." Sometimes, if the wind was just right and the sea was calm, she could *feel* the presence of storm-stone on the seafloor. She didn't know how it happened; just that the strange tingling against her skin—her prickle, her sisters called it, as Luce herself had done when she was very young—would intensify the closer she came to the stone.

The blueish light of early morning warmed as they passed Fort Guesclin, the rocky little island that lay at the eastern end of the wide sweep of beach where Samuel and the fishermen of Saint-Coulomb moored—or beached, depending on the tide—their vessels. Luce hunched in the prow as they passed a fishing boat, pulling her tricorn low.

"I would have thought a de Châtelaine would have been a better sailor," Samuel mused. "I take it the ship belonged to his father?"

Luce left the prow, gripping the mainmast for balance. She settled herself on the other side of the tiller.

"Yes." She nudged his large, tanned hand away and took the tiller herself. "The *Dauphin.* I thought the same, but then Papa told me that it was his first voyage as captain."

"They were sailing from Cádiz, then?"

"That's right. They got into a scrape with two English privateers, and were limping back to Saint-Malo when the storm finished the job."

"Those cursed English," Samuel said with a grin. "Never trust them, Luce."

The stretch of green water between the fort and the *Dove* was dotted with reefs and rocks; each was reason enough to concentrate on the water ahead. And *not* the memory of Morgan de Châtelaine's pale jaw, the sweep of dark stubble.

"Are you sure we're not wasting our time out here?" Samuel asked. "It doesn't sound like the *Dauphin* was carrying much cloud."

"That's the thing. It *was.* He—Morgan—had ballast stones in his pockets when I found him." She swallowed. "I had to . . . empty them, or risk letting him drown."

"Hmm."

She brought the *Dove* about, heading for deeper water. Vauban's new fort, almost complete, loomed above: a stretch of somber gray wall carving a square into the wild green of the island's crown, topped with cannon, and behind them, towers. All newly built to protect the coast from the English.

"Was there any word on the rest of the crew?" Samuel asked.

"Not yet. But I fear they must have been lost. My father has heard of no other survivors."

"Nor have I." He shook his head. "It's typical, though, is it not? The son of Castro de Châtelaine survives, while the rest of the crew are lost. It seems even the sea can tell the difference between a poor man and a rich one."

Luce frowned at him. "I couldn't tell the difference, and it was *I* who swam out to save him."

"Of course you did. It wouldn't have mattered to *you*." His eyes narrowed as he looked out over the water. "I only hope he deserves your selflessness, Luce."

"You did not seem concerned about whether or not he deserved saving yesterday," Luce said.

"Yesterday I did not know he was a de Châtelaine."

She straightened. "Why does that matter? Does he deserve less because of his name?"

"The question is, does he deserve *more*?"

"More of what?"

"More of everything! Do not tell me any of the de Châtelaines know what it is to be hungry, or cold. Do not tell me they give a thought to anyone who is not as rich, or powerful as they are. They sit in their town houses and country estates while the rest of Saint-Malo is cramped together in filth, letting others do the real work for them. They have so much, and still they take, and take. Wolves, indeed."

Luce stared at him, tiller, reefs, storm-stone forgotten. "My family is not so very different to the de Châtelaines," she said quietly. "Is this how you speak of us?"

"Of course not."

"Would you leave me to drown, then, were it I in Morgan's place, and you in mine?"

"Never," Samuel said, with feeling. "How could you even suggest it? Besides, you are nothing like the de Châtelaines. Or the Léons, for that matter."

You're just another piece of flotsam he brought home when he went to sea. Charlotte's words from yesterday nipped once more at Luce. She gave Samuel the tiller, turned to watch the *Dove* rising over the gentle swell. A flock of silver gulls lifted from the walls of the half-finished fort, wheeling over the water, the sun catching on their foamy feathers.

"Do you truly think the sea could tell the difference? Between a poor man and a rich one?"

He shrugged, laughed. "Who knows?"

"What about the difference between a man . . . and a woman?"

She turned back to Samuel, found him watching her through narrowed eyes.

"What are you trying to say, Luce?"

"Bones and I were talking," she began.

"Oh?" He grinned. "And what wisdom did my dear cousin have to share?"

"He told me about a woman named Hannah Snell. She—"

"I know of Hannah Snell." Samuel's smile had dimmed somewhat. "What does she have to do with you?"

Something in his tone, his face, caused Luce to falter. She plowed on, regardless. "Hannah Snell spent four years at sea, dressed as a man. None of her crew knew she was a woman. She sailed to India, and—"

"Damn my soul," he muttered, with a shake of his head. "Why would Bones fill your head with tales like that?"

"They're not tales," Luce said. "She's a real person. And, well, isn't it obvious? Perhaps *I* could do what Hannah did. Disguise myself, sign on to a crew . . . I could be a cabin boy, or a shipwright's assistant. Bones said that kind of work is easy enough—I would need to make beds and fix meals, clean clothes. . . ."

"Bones said it would be easy, did he?" Samuel turned to the horizon, laughed in a way that was not in any way amused. "I'll kill him. With my own two hands; I'll wring his scrawny neck."

"Why are you so angry?"

"Because this is madness, Luce! *Madness!* Nothing about crewing on a ship is easy. *Nothing.* Do you know the size of a crew on a seventy-four gunner? Six hundred and fifty men, give or take. Most of them are crammed into the gun decks, living on top of each other in between the guns. You'd sleep in a hammock with men a mere handsbreadth away from you. You'd share meals with them, in amongst the gun carriages and the spare sails and the anchor cable. There'd be animals there too, in their pens.

Cows, goats, chickens, pigs. It would be noisy, and filthy, and it would reek of tar and bilgewater. And don't even get me started on how you'd relieve yourself, or keep your body a secret, or survive the work. It's endless, and its backbreaking. Climbing up the ratlines and onto the yardarms in all weathers, hauling on sheets that could break your fingers before you could even think—" He stopped, chest heaving. "It's madness, Luce. *Madness.*"

They stared at each other over the tiller.

Luce opened her mouth to tell him half a hundred different things: That Bones disagreed. That it was not Samuel's decision. That she was not a fool. That *of course* it would not be easy, but it was the only way. The *only* way. She opened her mouth, then closed it again, distracted.

Samuel, watching her, frowned.

"What is it, Luce?"

She glanced at him, at the blue water surrounding them.

"My skin is prickling, Samuel."

"Whoever decided that women were bad luck at sea clearly never sailed with you." Samuel pushed his water-glasses to the top of his head with one hand, while the other gripped the side of the *Dove*. "Did you *see* that cloud?"

Luce, pushing her own glasses off her face as she clung to the boat beside him, nodded. The tide had almost ebbed, and the rocky islets that marked the edges of the reef were becoming more exposed with every passing moment. So too was the wreck of the *Dauphin*. What was left of Castro de Châtelaine's beautiful ship lay broken upon the reef, its hull crushed and gaping, its masts wedged between the rocks. Ship trap, Samuel had called the reef, and it was easy to see why.

"It's almost dead tide," Samuel said. "Perfect time to dive."

Dead tide. The words sent a chill through Luce. The ship was spilling storm-stone ballast onto the sandy seafloor ten meters below them, but she had glimpsed several of the *Dauphin*'s crew among the wreckage, too. The thought of diving once more, to where the *Dauphin*'s gaping wounds loomed out of the murky darkness, made her shiver. She gripped the *Dove* harder. Below her, her petticoat drifted against her bare legs, as pale as the *Dauphin*'s tattered sails.

"Luce?" Samuel was watching her. "Are you all right?"

She had helped him salvage storm-stone before, many times, but never in a wreck so recent. "There are so many of them, Samuel."

"You don't have to do this," he said gently. "You can wait for me on the *Dove*. You'll still get your share."

Samuel always paid her for her help. The jar of livres hidden in the sea-cave did not look like much; even so, Luce cherished it, not least because it was hers. Money she had earned with her own hands, on her own terms. However, it was not the money that gave Luce pause. The memory of his words about Hannah Snell, and going to sea, were still too raw to allow her to give up so easily. She would not give Samuel the satisfaction of being right—of proving that she was too soft, too delicate, to do the work of a man. Besides, they had only half an hour, perhaps a little longer, before the tide turned and the opportunity was lost.

"I'm fine," she told him, pulling her water-glasses down over her eyes. "Let's go."

She was a better swimmer than Samuel, even wearing stays. Diving cleanly, she gripped the weighted guide rope and began to pull herself down. Her petticoats trailed behind her, her dark hair, too, but when she turned her head, she made out Samuel above, and felt the rhythm of his grip as he moved hand over hand down the rope behind her.

Below them, on the sand, the storm-stone thundered gently.

At the bottom, Luce released the rope and swam off to one side, away from the wreck and its grim cargo. Her water-glasses—a clever melding of tortoiseshell, glass, wax, and cord—allowed her to see the shape of the seafloor and the debris strewn across it. She let the prickle lead her, scooping the glittering, palm-sized stones off the sand and slipping them into the satchel around her shoulder. Made of old fishing net, the bag was strong enough to hold the stones' weight while allowing the water to pass through. When it was full, Luce swam back to the rope and dragged herself upward. She glanced back as she went and saw Samuel closer to the wreck, his long, lean torso bare above his breeches, his hands busy sliding ballast into his own satchel.

On the surface, Luce hung the satchel on the side of the *Dove* and grasped another, empty one before diving again, passing Samuel as he ascended, the rope dipping beneath her hands as he swung his own bag onto the *Dove* and dived once more.

And so they went, back and forth, up and down, until the *Dove*'s timbered side was bristling with bags of ballast and the tide began to turn. When the drag of the water became too strong, Luce ascended for the last time.

Samuel was already standing in the *Dove*, dragging the netted stones into the boat. She slipped her bag from around her neck and passed it up to him, then slipped off her water-glasses and clung to the boat, catching her breath. Trying, and failing, not to watch the way the muscles in his shoulders and back moved as he worked, or the water beading on his golden skin. The twin swallows tattooed on his forearms, just beneath his thumbs, and the single star above his heart.

It had begun last summer. They had been out on the *Dove*, on a day just like any other. Until Luce had stood up to untangle some rigging, and everything had changed. Perhaps it was her too-large overcoat; perhaps it was her feet. Whatever the reason, when Luce stretched her hand toward the sail, she lost her balance. Her arms flailed as she struggled to right herself. Her tricorn fell from her head. Her feet scrabbled on the deck as the Manche lurched greedily beneath her. Samuel was on his feet at once, abandoning the tiller, one arm steadying her, the other reaching over her head to secure the sail. For a moment, just a moment, his hand lingered on Luce's waist. She could feel the warmth of him at her back, even through her ridiculous coat. The brush of his hair on her cheek. The strength of his arm around her. It was surprising, this awareness, and completely new. A strange little spark glimmered deep in her belly. Then, as quickly as he had reached for her, Samuel let her go.

"Clumsy as ever, I see," he had teased, moving back for the tiller. As though he had not, for one brief moment, held Luce against him with heart-stopping tenderness. As though he had not, for one brief moment, pressed his cheek to her hair.

5

Storm-Diving

"This was a good start," Samuel said approvingly, looking over their haul. "I'll come back with Bones at the next dead tide, and then again tomorrow. Get as much as we can before someone else discovers it."

"That may never happen." Luce, still clinging to the side of the *Dove*, looked around doubtfully. The wreck was breaking up fast, and what remained was being rapidly swallowed by the reef. At high tide it would be impossible to see.

"Fine by me." He hefted a bag over the side, tucked it away. "I'll head into Saint-Malo when we're done, see if I can't stir up some interest."

"Who do you think will buy it?"

"I wouldn't be much of a smuggler if I named my contacts, would I?" He tossed a piece of ballast playfully in the air, caught it. "With cloud this good, I might even get away with simply selling the location of the wreck. Let some other poor bastards do the diving. It only takes one little rock to start the negotiations."

"And it only takes one little word to a city official to see a storm diver arrested and drowned," Luce said. There were strict laws around the buying and selling of storm-stone in Saint-Malo. Those who did not heed them, and who were caught, were executed by water: secured to stakes below the low water line and left to drown as the tide came in, while the above ramparts filled to bursting with spectators. "Be careful, Samuel."

"Your lack of faith wounds me."

Something brushed against Luce's foot beneath the water. She glanced at the shadows beneath the boat, distracted. "It's not a lack of confidence in you that concerns me. The City Guard will be searching for the wreck."

"The Guard couldn't find their arses in a privy." Samuel left off moving the stones and reached down a hand. "Here, come aboard. You must be cold."

Whatever had brushed against her was larger than Luce had first supposed. She reached instinctively for Samuel as something emerged from beneath the boat.

It was a man. A drowned man, his reddish-colored shirt straining against his bloated body, his face, only inches away from Luce's own as he rolled sickeningly in the water, revealing the empty sockets where his eyes had once been, and the bloody foam leaking from his nose and mouth.

"Jesus fucking Christ," Samuel cried.

Luce stared, and stared, frozen into place. Water pushed the sailor toward her and she lurched back in horror.

"Here, Luce," Samuel said, above. "I've got you."

He gripped her arms, hauling her clear of the water and into the boat beside him. As one, they leaned on the *Dove*'s edge, regarding the man floating below them. Closer to the wreck, Luce made out the form of a second sailor, then a third, bumping gently against the remnants of the *Dauphin*'s hull.

"I'm so sorry, Luce. I never should have let you in the water with me—"

"I chose to help you," she said, trembling. "And it's not the first time I've seen a . . . shipwreck."

"Even so." He reached for a rough blanket, pressed it around her shoulders. "You shouldn't have to see such things."

"Neither should you."

His arms were still around her. So close to him now—his hair dripping on her cheek, his chest before her, water-smooth—Luce had the sudden, treacherous urge to tilt her face to his, shipwrecks and drowned sailors be cursed.

Perhaps Samuel sensed it; he stepped quickly back, letting her go.

"Someone has to make sure my family eats," he said reasonably, turning to the sail. Samuel's father had been killed in a fishing accident many years before, leaving the responsibility of the family resting squarely on his eldest son's shoulders.

"And someone has to help you," Luce said. As though she were not a mess of confusion and longing. Samuel's words seemed to tell her one story, and his body another. Which was true?

"We should head back," he said, reaching for the anchor. He threw her a strained sort of smile. "Wouldn't want you to miss the end of the forenoon watch."

"Of course." She pulled the blanket more tightly around her and gave him a strained smile of her own before moving to the far end of the boat. She stripped out of her wet clothes and stepped into her breeches, drawing on a dry chemise and stays and pinning her caraco into place. Samuel—adhering to an unspoken agreement that had lain between them since the first time they had dived together—busied himself preparing to raise the sails, his back carefully turned.

"It feels wrong to just leave them there like that," Luce said, as they headed back.

"They cast their lots when they boarded that ship," Samuel said, his eyes on the water ahead. "They knew the risks. We all do." For a moment Luce wondered if he would reprimand her for Hannah Snell again. "The sea takes what it will, and she wanted the *Dauphin* and its crew. Its pretty captain, too."

The slightest accusation in his tone.

"I couldn't just leave him there to die," she said, when the silence had stretched on too long.

"I know that. But you stood in the Manche's way, Luce." He

lifted a hand, gestured to the deeps surrounding them. "You took something from her. One day she will want it back."

"She doesn't seem angry." Luce raised her face to the tight sails, the warming sun. She had left her hair loose so that it would dry; dark strands whipped around her, playful in the breeze.

"No," he agreed, watching her. "No, she does not." He tightened his grip on the tiller. "Perhaps I am wrong. After all, the sea loves you, Luce. She always has."

"You don't think she will take my life in Morgan's place, then?" She spoke lightly, trying, and failing, to ease the worry in his eyes. He believed in this; it was more than superstition, more than fishermen's tales. It had been woven into the souls of his people, knots in an endless net, for hundreds of years.

"She will take us all, in the end."

Unlike the ordered tidiness of the little cabinet adjoining Luce's bedchamber—its specimens meticulously classified and labeled in Luce's careful hand, its books on natural history, mathematics, and astronomy arranged in neat stacks—her part of the sea-cave was a riot of textures and color. Every ledge, every crevice, held something different. Glass bottles, unusual shells, mismatched porcelain cups. Feathers of every size, sextants, and spy-glasses.

Fishing nets were strewn from the walls, softening the cave's grim lines, while a handful of ship's lanterns lent light and warmth. There were sailmaker's needles in carved horn cases, bench hooks, mallets, and rigging knives set between drooping silken gowns. Half-finished scrimshaw, wax and twine, glass fishing floats in every shade. Empty casks were arranged around a scarred ship's table, and a canvas hammock swung from two outcrops, soft with blankets and cushions. She even had a dressing table, its drawers only slightly swollen, its triple mirrors glimmering above wooden pots of ruined rouge and spoiled velvet patches shaped like stars, hairbrushes and crab shells, a beautifully tarnished hand mirror, blooms of dried coral, bird bones, shark teeth, and ribbons.

There were dreams and secrets here. Hopes and plans, waiting for their time.

The jar of livres Samuel paid Luce shared space with a salvaged sailor's bag, the rough canvas stained with saltwater and tragedy. Nevertheless, over the past few weeks Luce had been steadily adding to its contents: shirts and breeches, a fid and bodkin, cord, twine and beeswax, a housewife with needles and thread, and a jackknife. All the usual things a sailor carried with him when he rambled through the busy quay, seeking work on a ship.

Luce spent a moment, only, in her cave—she needed to touch the canvas bag, assure herself that her ideas were not, as Samuel had accused, madness—before continuing to help him unload the storm-stone. The area he used was already crowded with casks and crates, packages wrapped in waxed paper. They had almost finished unloading the *Dove* when the sound of the ship's bell drifted down from Le Bleu Sauvage.

"Five bells," Samuel said, into the silence that followed. "Ten thirty. We made good time."

Luce nodded. Her mother and sisters would not wake for half an hour, or more. She considered showing Samuel the sailor's bag and resuming the conversation they had been having when she'd sensed the stone. She was, she realized, still angry at the way he had dismissed her plans. The urge to tell him that he was wrong, that she *could* do as Hannah Snell had done and take her future into her own hands, was strong. The memory of what had—and, at the same time, what had *not*—passed between them on the *Dove*, however, lingered. Far easier to take her leave of him and return to the chapel. To hastily weave the wild, wind-dried tangles of her hair into a rough braid, and brush the sand and salt from her crimson caraco and skirt, the thoughts of Samuel and seafaring and freedom from her mind.

The sound of her family's voices, blended with others she did not recognize, wafted from the grand salon's open doors as she approached. Unusual; her family never received visitors at this hour. Angling across the lawn, she spied an expensive-looking carriage drawn by four handsome grays in the stable yard, the de Châtelaine crest, with its white wolf, emblazoned on its lacquered door.

"Damn my soul," she muttered—one of Samuel's favorites—her belly lurching. It had been a mistake to meet Samuel today. Papa had told her last night that he had sent word to the de Châtelaines. Of course, they would rise early and hurry to Le Bleu Sauvage to reunite with their son.

The sick feeling worsened as she neared the house. Had her family been looking for her? Had they checked the chapel, found it empty? The voices became louder, punctuated by the soft clink of expensive porcelain, the silvery tones of the harpsichord as it woke. A light scale, a tinkering, and then music, sweet and stately. Veronique began to sing. Despite herself, Luce hummed along. Veronique had a lovely voice, and she had always played the piece, one of Scarlatti's, well.

She hesitated at the servants' door, torn. The urge to skulk to the kitchens and hide from their guests, avoid the stilted conversation in favor of one of Olivier's delicious pastries, was strong. It was a good plan. Reliable. She had used it countless times to escape her mother's notice, or whichever torturous social event happened to be transpiring.

And it would be the safest choice today, with Gratienne eager to impress the de Châtelaines, and Veronique and Charlotte wielding every weapon at their disposal: charm, wit, fashion, elegance. The salon would be a battlefield.

And yet. Luce was drawn by a second, no less powerful, impulse: to see Morgan de Châtelaine again. She had not forgotten the taste of salt and life on his lips, the cold touch of his fingertips.

Had he?

In the end, curiosity won the day. Brimming with nerves,

Luce crossed the lawn, mounted the salon stairs, pushed aside the breeze-filled curtains, and entered the fray.

"Lucinde," Gratienne said, from her place on the chaise longue between Charlotte and an elegantly dressed, dark-haired woman Luce knew to be Madame de Châtelaine. "Where have you been?"

Veronique ceased her song as Gratienne examined Luce from the top of her bare head to the tips of her boots. Luce, risking a glance at her reflection in one of the salon's three mirrors, felt her heart sink. Despite her efforts, her clothing was rumpled, her hair—hanging in a thick tail over one shoulder—akin to a milkmaid's. Her complexion was even worse than usual, bronzed by the sun and wind.

"I'm sorry, Maman," Luce said. "I was walking in the gardens, and then I went to the chapel—I did not realize we had guests."

Gratienne frowned. "So it would appear."

A giggle from the harpsichord. With the morning light falling across her rose-colored gown, illuminating her perfect skin, Veronique was raspberry cake and cream.

"Ah, come now, ma chère," Jean-Baptiste said good-naturedly. He was standing near the fireplace with Monsieur de Châtelaine, who was admiring an enormous painting of the *Fleur de Mer* in full flight upon a stormy sea. "Lucinde was not to know. Mon trésor, you remember Monsieur de Châtelaine and his lovely wife?"

"Of course." Luce inclined her head to each of them.

"And this, of course, is their youngest son. Morgan."

He had been gazing up at the painting, hands clasped behind his back, half-hidden by the two older men, but he turned when he heard his name, his dark gaze—curious, warm—meeting hers. Luce's heart gave a strange little stutter. Awake, *aware,* he seemed vastly different to the man on the shore. The rough shadows of stubble on his cheeks were gone. Clean-shaven, he looked younger, perhaps only a few years older than Veronique. His cheekbones were high, his brows and hair as black as ever. Though not as tall as Samuel, he was lean and strong-looking, his sea-green, sleekly fitted frock coat tight across his shoulders, his breeches and stockings revealing muscled thighs and an impressive pair of calves. There was an energy, a quickness, to him. A sense of movement stilled, of energy contained. An impatience in the *tap tap tap* of his well-made shoes, as though their owner wanted nothing more than to spring up, move, be away.

"It is good to meet you, Mademoiselle Léon." A slight bow, a smile. *Oh, that smile.*

"You seem much recovered," Luce said, with a dip of her head.

"Your family's good care has made all the difference."

He was polished, polite. Entirely different to the wild, desperate man who had kissed her on the beach. *That* man had wrapped his fingers in her long hair and drank of her lips, taking and taking, as though he were drowning still and only she could save him. A dark thrill ran through her body. Did he remember?

"I do not know how we shall ever thank you," Madame de Châtelaine said, smiling at each of the Léons. "Without your kindness, I doubt my son would be here with us now."

"And *that*," Morgan said, moving toward the low table at the room's center and sweeping a macaron from a platter, "would have been a tragedy, with macarons such as these."

Everybody laughed.

Over at the harpsichord, Veronique tinkered with a few notes. "Come now, Monsieur de Châtelaine. What of the fishermen who found you? Without them, our care—and our macarons—would mean nothing."

"That is true," Morgan conceded. He took a bite of the light, almond confectionary, chewed blissfully. "I owe those men my life."

Luce swallowed her disappointment.

"Their efforts shall not be forgotten," Castro de Châtelaine said. "Nor will my ship." There was no mistaking the bitterness behind his words. Luce, glancing at Morgan, saw his shoulders, his jaw, tense.

"Has there been any word of the *Dauphin*?" Jean-Baptiste seated himself gingerly on a spindly-legged chair. "Perhaps she could be salvaged . . . ?"

"She is lost," Castro said. "Along with her cargo, and all her crew."

"What was she carrying?"

"What you would expect. Spanish wines, fruits, oil. Goods from the colonies—indigo and wood. A great deal of vicuña wool."

"What of her ballast?"

Morgan, frowning, opened his mouth as though he would say something. After one, swift glance from his father, however, he promptly closed it again.

"We took a risk," Castro said. "Sailed without storm-stone."

"You would not be the first to do so, nor the last," Jean-Baptiste said sympathetically. "I remember a time when storm-stone was as plentiful as sand. Walk upon any stretch of Breton shore, and you would kick your toe on it."

Castro laughed bitterly. "I remember those days. When I was a young captain and in need of a fair wind, I would visit the nearest sea hag and buy one. For a few livres, she'd summon a breeze and wrap it in my handkerchief."

"I, too, bought my share of crone-winds," Jean-Baptiste said. He leaned forward, selected a pastry from the assortment on the table. "We still have a tide-crone here, you know."

"A groac'h? Truly?"

"Indeed. She is shy, and crotchety. But I have seen her in the evenings, in her little witch-boat, or rambling upon the rocks."

"And does she still sell you fair winds?" Castro cocked his head speculatively; wondering, no doubt, if the tide-witch was part of Jean-Baptiste's enviable success.

Jean-Baptiste was no longer smiling. "Not for a long time."

"She will leave like the others, eventually," Castro said grimly. "All of them do, in the end."

A somber silence. It was a matter of great concern, the leaving of the Fae. Not least because their very presence, or lack of it, affected not only the storm-stone quarries, but the existing stone in the ships, buildings, and walls of Saint-Malo. Some blamed the Church, ever set on driving the Fae and superstition out of Bretagne. Others blamed the people who fished and built dwellings on lands where the Fae were known to exist. They had been leaving, slowly and surely, for years. The thought of Bretagne without its magic, without its soul, was a melancholy one, indeed.

"In any case," Castro said, "we did not give the *Dauphin* the storm-stone she deserved. A decision we are paying for, now."

Luce stared at him. How easily the lies fell from his mouth! Not two hours ago she had held storm-stones from the *Dauphin* in her own hands. Felt the low, telling hum of their magic.

"It is truly a miracle that you survived," Charlotte said, gazing admiringly up at Morgan. "To think—you are the only one!"

"Hush, Cee," Veronique said reprovingly. "I am sure Monsieur de Châtelaine does not need *you* to remind him of the perils he has faced."

"Indeed," Castro said, sharp as a blade. "I am certain he will not soon forget them."

There was a loaded silence.

"Does anyone *ever* forget such a thing?" Luce asked. She looked down at the edges of the carpet, the delicate pattern of tangled flowers there, and thought of Morgan's crew, those silent sailors rising from the *Dauphin*'s broken shell. "I do not think it is possible. To bear witness to the fury of the sea, to have your life held entirely in its hands—to live or die depending on its whim—must be terrifying, indeed." She remembered the drowned man, his sightless eyes and bloated limbs. "I can only imagine what those poor men faced before the end. I wish them peace."

She looked up, and immediately regretted her decision to

speak. Every face in the room had turned toward her, displaying various shades of shock, confusion, and disapproval. Only Morgan's dark gaze was free of judgment.

"Do play for us, Lucinde," Gratienne said into the sudden silence. She turned to Madame de Châtelaine. "She has quite a talent for music, you know."

She was not exaggerating. When Luce sat down at the harpsichord or the harp, the mood of the entire household changed. The gardeners stopped in their work and turned their heads to listen. The domestiques trailed aimlessly about the house, polishing rags hanging limp at their sides. The smell of burning wafted from the kitchens. Once, Luce looked up from the harpsichord to find all seven of her father's horses gathered on the steps of the grand salon, ears pricked, huge eyes intent.

Gratienne's pride in Luce's talent, however, was less about the music, and more about leverage. She wanted nothing more than to find perfect matches for each of her daughters; husbands that would enhance not only their social standing but her own as well. In this sense, music was a powerful weapon.

"Yes, Luce, you must play," Veronique said, rising from the harpsichord bench. She, too, was aware of the power of talent, and was not indisposed to basking in its glow. "I cannot hope to perform well when you are near. You so outshine me."

Utter nonsense—Veronique played the way she shone, which was brightly and well. She was, however, already rising gracefully from the bench. Gliding across the room, she took up the platter of pastries and offered it to Morgan with a smile.

"Thank you, Lucinde," Gratienne said gently. Luce, who had long understood that her mother had three sources of pride—the number of domestiques she kept, the cost of her clothes, and the behavior of her children—*and* that obeying her mother now would spare her a great deal of discomfort later, moved obediently toward the harpsichord. At the last moment she changed direction, bearing instead for the harp. Huge and golden, its arched neck as graceful as a swan's, it had been a gift from her father some years ago. Luce ran her fingertips along the strings, wakening them to silvered life, then sat down, arranging her skirts.

The music came, as it always did, from some other place: the air flowing through the salon's open doors, the sunlight pouring against the windows, the sea, hushed and listening beyond the fields and forest. She knew the tune, knew the strings, yet rather than *making* the music, Luce *released* it, allowing it to flow unfettered from her fingers as though it had a will of its own.

"*Upon one summer's morning*," she sang, her voice low and faintly smoky with disuse, "*I carefully did stray down by the walls of Wapping where I met a sailor gay.*"

Conversing with a young lass
Who seem'd to be in pain
Saying "William, when you go
I fear you'll ne'er return again.

The tune, which had begun gently enough, deepened. Luce's voice, clearer now, melded with the harp's notes.

My heart is pierced by Cupid
I disdain all glittering gold
There is nothing can console me
But my jolly sailor bold.

"That is an English tune, is it not?" Gratienne asked disapprovingly as Luce's song, and all its longing and sadness, faded into silence.

"Music cares not for war," Jean-Baptiste said, reaching for a macaron. "It travels where it will, often by ship."

"That is true," Morgan agreed. "I have heard sailors sing that song. I had no idea it could be so beautiful. Your mother did not exaggerate, mademoiselle."

Luce bowed her head to avoid not Morgan's eyes, but Charlotte's. Of all three Léon sisters, only Charlotte was indisposed to music. There had been some ill-fated attempts at the harpsichord in her youth, quickly abandoned when her sisters' talents bloomed. It grated on Charlotte like rough fabric against bare skin. She tried to keep it hidden, but whenever Luce or Veronique played, it sharpened her gaze, embittering her pretty face.

"This talk of music reminds me . . ." Madame de Châtelaine gestured to her laquais, waiting with Jean-Jacques and Jean-Pierre near the door. "Antoine, would you bring it here, please?"

"It" was an envelope of creamy, expensive paper. One word, *Léon,* flowed boldly across its face.

"I know this is most unusual," Madame de Châtelaine said, as Gratienne opened the envelope, "and that etiquette dictates that I send your invitation with the rest next week. However, I could think of no better way to thank you for what you have done for my son."

"Oh, a ball!" Veronique exclaimed, clapping in delight as she read over her mother's shoulder. "To welcome Monsieur Morgan de Châtelaine home. And it's to be at Le Loup Blanc, no less!"

Madame de Châtelaine smiled. "Like you, we have retired to our country home early this season."

"Are we truly the first to receive an invitation?"

"Indeed! You shall have the chance to see the seamstress and the tailor—and all before the rest of the invitations have been sent! Perhaps you will even have time to have something made in Paris."

"My wife has been planning this little soirée of hers for weeks," Monsieur de Châtelaine said fondly. "I do believe she was more concerned about cancelling her plans than Morgan's safety when first she heard the *Dauphin* had gone down."

Madame de Châtelaine slapped her husband with her fan.

"Oh, Maman," Charlotte said, "do read the invitation to us!"

Gratienne did as her daughter bid. "Castro and Camille de Châtelaine are delighted to invite you to a masquerade ball. . . ."

As she read, Charlotte rose and joined Veronique at the back of the chaise longue. They leaned over Gratienne's shoulders, reading along with her and using every fiber of restraint not to snatch the missive from their mother's hands and devour it, ink and all.

"A masque," Veronique sighed, when Gratienne had finished. "How *elegant.*"

Luce, who had been listening to the proceedings with a sense of growing dread, straightened on her stool. A masque would be very different to a regular reception. Faces would be covered, identities hidden. A person who was uncomfortable at large gatherings could remain at the edges of things, confident in their anonymity. No one would question why they chose to refrain from dancing. No one would think to look pityingly at their unfashionable shoes and twisted feet. They would be hidden. Safe.

Unbidden, her fingers moved upon the harp strings in a sweet, excited trill.

"Can we expect a dance with you, Monsieur de Châtelaine?" Veronique asked.

"Of course," Morgan said gallantly. "I would be honored, Mademoiselle Léon." He tilted his head to include Charlotte and Luce. "I should be very happy to dance with each of you."

"Don't bother promising Lucinde," Charlotte said bluntly. "Our sister never attends such events."

"Oh?" His black gaze caught Luce's, held it. "Well. That is a shame."

"I have not yet decided," Luce said truthfully. Emboldened by his smile, she rose from the protection of the harp. "Although, if I *did* attend, I imagine I might have an opportunity to ask about your time in Cádiz. Is it true there are now almost a hundred and sixty towers overlooking the water there?"

Morgan smiled in surprise as she approached. "There are many towers, yes. Although I must admit I have never stopped to count them all."

"And what of the new cathedral? How does it progress?"

"Well, I believe, though slowly. They say it will be Cádiz's crowning glory, but it's the bay that is, in my humble opinion, the city's greatest treasure."

"You mean the Isla de León," Luce said, nodding. "I understand it offers remarkable shelter."

"That it does, yes." His face fell, and Luce wondered if he was thinking of his lost ship, his drowned crew.

Madame de Châtelaine seemed to have the same thought. "I believe it is time we said our farewells," she said, rising.

Gratienne was on her feet. "Are you certain? You are more than welcome to join us for dinner. . . ."

"I would not want to impose upon you any further, Gratienne. And, despite what he would like us to believe, my son needs rest." She smiled warmly. "Particularly if he intends to dance with all three of your daughters."

"Of course."

Farewells were made, gratitude expressed, and wishes for Morgan's continued recovery proclaimed. Morgan's eyes found Luce's among the bustle. One last, heart-thudding smile.

"Oh, may we have new gowns, Papa?" Veronique cried as soon as Jean-Jacques had closed the door behind the departing guests. "Please?"

"Of course." Jean-Baptiste smiled indulgently. "You will each have something new. And shoes, ribbons, fans—whatever you like."

"We shall need masks," Charlotte said practically, taking the invitation from the chaise longue and raking over every word.

"I had planned to return to the city today," Jean-Baptiste said. "I shall ride there at once. I've just received a new delivery from Lyon; you shall have your choice of the finest silks in France!"

Veronique clapped her hands in delight, and Charlotte turned to her mother, insisting that *she*, not Veronique, should have first pick of the textiles.

"Don't be silly, Charlotte." Gratienne sighed of irritation. "There will be plenty for everyone."

"What would you like me to bring you, ma chérie?" Jean-Baptiste asked Veronique.

"I want whatever's fashionable, Papa. Whatever they're wearing in Paris!"

"I will do my best." Jean-Baptiste turned to Charlotte. "And you, my Charlotte?"

"Perhaps pink silk, Papa? Or pale blue?"

"Pink *and* light blue it shall be." Jean-Baptiste gestured to St. Jean. "Have Éliott saddle four horses, St. Jean. One for you, another to carry the fabrics, and one more for Lucinde."

Luce, still thinking of Morgan's last, secret smile, looked up. "For me, Papa?"

"Indeed. We have business at the dockyard."

She returned his grin; they were going to see the *Lucinde*.

"The dockyard?" Gratienne repeated, with a frown. "At Trichet? My dear, is there time?"

"Plenty." Jean-Baptiste kissed his wife's cheek. "We shall be back before supper."

He strode from the salon, eager for the saddle and his ship.

"It isn't fair," Charlotte announced. "Now *Luce* will have first choice of the silks."

"I don't care about that," Luce told her.

"Of course you don't. You don't care about *anything* you're supposed to. Look at how you behaved just now with Monsieur de Châtelaine. Did you *really* ask him how many towers there are in Cádiz? And why do you insist on dressing like that? You look like a governess." She shook her head in disgust. "I think it was better when you *didn't* join us when we had visitors."

"Don't be unkind, Cee," Veronique said mildly. "Besides, it doesn't matter what Luce says to Morgan de Châtelaine. It is *I*, not she, who will be engaged to him by summer's end. Just see if I'm wrong."

She said it plainly, casually; certain in the knowledge that the weapons she had been honing her entire life—beauty, elegance, talent—would make it so. All the hours of practice, of learning how to dance, to sing, to speak courteously, to hold a cup daintily, to dress her hair, manage servants, write beautifully, order the week's menu, and entertain guests had one purpose, and one purpose alone: to find the perfect husband.

What else could there be, for a Léon daughter? For *any* daughter? They could not attend university or be apprenticed in Cádiz, take up administrative positions in Paris or devote their lives to the study of science or music or navigation, or any of the many things a son might have done. The best they could hope for was the freedom that marriage would offer—if sleeping late, spending hours dressing and attending endless rounds of visits, afternoon teas, and suppers—between bearing children, of course—could be called freedom.

Sometimes Luce wondered if her sisters felt the same. If they would choose a different path for themselves, a different kind of life, if they could. If they did, they certainly never said so. Now, as Veronique leaned dreamily on the salon door, watching through the vestibule windows as the de Châtelaine carriage turned gracefully in the yard, Luce wondered what her sister's idea of the perfect husband might be. Luce had always imagined him to be one of the oldest sons of the Saint-Malo shipping families, those fortunate ones who were set to inherit the bulk of their fathers' fortunes. Or a tall aristocrat from Paris, perhaps, willing to ignore Jean-Baptiste's merchant roots for Gratienne's noble bloodline, the Léon wealth, and Veronique's beauty. A charming stranger with grand houses, sleek horses, and the means to frost her sister with jewels.

He was not a youngest son, with storm-dark hair.

He did not come from the sea.

6

All Wild and Beautiful

On horseback, Luce's feet were as good as anyone else's. A touch of her heels, a click of her tongue, and she could be skimming lightly over orchards and fields, through swathes of forest, or along roadways thick with primroses, violets, and wild hyacinths.

Jean-Baptiste was just as fearless, often partaking in the hunting and racing that took place throughout the summer. Side by side, they cantered past farmhouses and the occasional gated drive leading to manors or malouinières, St. Jean jouncing along behind, the packhorse's lead rein clutched in one white-knuckled fist.

Luce heard his sigh of relief when they reached Saint-Coulomb—a clustering of granite houses with the church's spire blooming in their midst—and slowed to a sedate walk.

"I have another surprise for you," Jean-Baptiste said.

"Oh, Papa," Luce said, her heart sinking. "I do not need for anything. Truly."

"I have found a new music tutor for you," he said. "From the Royal Academy, no less. He is due to arrive this week."

The swallows had returned, dipping between the rooftops. Luce barely noticed them. While she understood the gift her father had given her and her sisters by procuring tutors for them over the years—daughters rarely received an education so thorough—those same teachers had become undeniably problematic when Luce began to receive instruction—of a very different kind—from

Samuel. A new tutor would be another obstacle in an already extensive list.

"Did Maman ask you to do this?" she asked carefully. "I know she wishes I'd practice more. . . ."

"I thought you would be pleased," Jean-Baptiste said, looking disappointed. "Monsieur Ferrand is an accomplished composer. He has studied science and mathematics, too. I know you love to learn. . . ."

At the sight of his face, the hurt there, Luce softened. "You are right. I do. It's very generous of you, Papa. Thank you."

With luck this Monsieur Ferrand would be as old as the rest of the tutors—and as willing to sleep late, and nod drowsily over a cup of chocolate in the evenings.

Saint-Malo came into view. Hazy with spray and distance, the walled city clung grimly to its nest of rocks, pushing resolutely toward the sea. It was surrounded by water on three sides: to the north, the Manche; the south, the wide harbor with its dockyards; and to the southwest, the mouth of the river Rance, crowded with ships of every size and description.

The city took shape as they rode closer. The cathedral, its lonely spire rising above the rooftops and towers, and the fortress crouching at the easternmost edge. Islands, reefs, and rocks dotted the water surrounding the city, the largest topped with forts bristling with cannon and mistrust: Fort Royale, Grand Bé, Petit Bé, and La Conchée. They, like the ramparts and walls, were made entirely of storm-stone. Its thundering hum surged in time with Luce's blood, tingling against her face and neck. It was why the city had never been breached, why the Dutch and the English had broken like waves against it, again and again, over the centuries. *Come, then,* it seemed to say. *Do your worst.*

The storm-stone continued to beat silently against Luce's bones as they reached the Sillon, the narrow causeway that, during high tide, was the only means of accessing the city, and fell in with the carts, carriages, and people making their way into the city. To one side, a great stretch of beach, and the Manche. To the other, the inner harbor, the smell of hot tar rising strong from the crews breaming the boats beached on the rough sands like whales.

The fortress perched at the end of the causeway, its high walls manned by soldiers of the garrison, the shoulders and tower of the cathedral watching protectively over all. Jean-Baptiste led the way through Saint-Vincent Gate, and the sun and northwesterly breeze were quickly swallowed by the walls. Tortured little streets wove between crooked stone houses, their rooftops huddling against the sky. Gulls wheeled above, or perched on chimney-pots. They passed a series of shopfronts: sailmakers, linen and cod merchants, wine-sellers, clothing, and ships' supplies. Grease shops oozed with butter, lard, and oil, and pothouses spilled music and rowdy sailors onto the cobbles. Luce's horse shied as a fight erupted close by, two brawny tars swinging drunkenly at each other as their delighted crewmates cheered. Jean-Baptiste turned his horse neatly down the nearest side-street with barely a glance. Luce, following him, could not help but look back. The men were reeling and stumbling together in a clumsy dance, hindered by both their roaring shipmates and the arrival of the City Guard. The result, predictably, was utter chaos. Luce leaned as far back in the saddle as she was able, pilfering every detail of the brawl before her mount's steady pace stole it from sight. St. Jean, rounding the corner behind her, winked conspiratorially.

The pungent scent of the nearby fish market thickened the air, its salty-strong smell a surprising relief; Saint-Malo smelled like the hold of a ship after a long sea voyage: bilgewater, unwashed bodies, and rotting timber.

The Léon home was a tall and stately affair on the corner of Rue Saint-Philippe, beside the wall and Saint Michel's Bastion. Jean-Baptiste had bought the house from the Rivière family near twenty years ago. Four stories of impeccably crafted storm-stone, it overlooked the harbor entrance and, on the other side of the bay, the distant dockyards of Saint-Servan. There was a watch-house built into the steeply pitched roof, where Jean-Baptiste could keep an eye on his forty-nine ships as they entered or sailed from the harbor, and enormous windows able to catch refreshing sea breezes any time of year, or glimpse the tip of the cathedral. Beneath the town house, two levels of cellars and storerooms had been hewn into the rock. Every conceivable luxury was crammed into the cool darkness there: tea and coffee, spices, cacao, printed cottons from India, sugar and indigo from the West Indies, tobacco from the Americas, French silks, wine, brandy, and lace, and Spanish oil and silver.

Inside the gates, Luce unhooked her legs from the side-saddle and slid carefully to the cobbled ground. Two sets of graceful, rounded stairs led from the courtyard to the double glass doors of the grand salon a level above, mirroring each other as they curved to meet at the landing. Beneath them, a set of sturdy doors opened directly into the cellars.

Luce waited while St. Jean lit a lantern for her father, then followed him inside. The air cooled at once, and the sounds of the street, the sea, faded. The rumble of storm-stone, the tingling in her skin, was overwhelming. She closed her eyes, letting herself adjust.

"Coming?" Jean-Baptiste was waiting for her in the corridor, his lantern held high.

"Yes, Papa."

There were ten rooms in all, and Jean-Baptiste knew the contents of each intimately, down to the tiniest box of indigo. (He could also tell you which of his ships had brought the indigo from the French Antilles, and how much he expected to make from it.) To their left, Luce knew, lay the spice room. To the right, Breton linens bound for Cádiz and beyond.

"Here we are, then," he said, leading Luce down the corridor. "The silk room."

St. Jean was already there, lighting the lanterns set at intervals along the walls. Storm-stone walls thick with shelving appeared, and above, a timber ceiling crossed by enormous, rough-hewn beams. Every inch of the time-worn timber floor, made with the salvaged decks of an erstwhile corsair, was covered in packages and sea chests.

"What would you like?" Jean-Baptiste asked, prowling between the chests. "Pink satin? Green silk faille with silver embroidery? Cream silk taffeta?"

The room was brightening with every lantern St. Jean lit, revealing a rainbow of silky color fit to rival the finest mercer or modiste.

Luce, however, was looking longingly through the doorway to the adjoining chamber, where a collection of salty oddments and endings sat rather sadly between packs of furs and crates of tobacco. Too large to be kept in the town house or Le Bleu Sauvage, her father's things—acquired during his years at sea—were infinitely fascinating. Navigational equipment, maps in long canvas cannisters, swords, pistols, and two or three of the hideous-looking grapnels her father used to climb the slippery sides of soon-to-be-captured ships. A ship was considered captured when the boarding crew had seized its colors. There were plenty of those, too, including several faded English ensigns.

"Mon trésor?" Jean-Baptiste was watching her. "What do you think?"

"I hardly know, Papa," Luce said, forcing herself to focus. "There are so many." She had the uncomfortable notion that Charlotte's prediction—that Luce would have first choice of their father's fabrics—had been correct. "Perhaps we should start by finding something beautiful for Charlotte and Veronique?"

"What a splendid idea."

Luce helped her father wade through the glittering sea of chests, opening here, unrolling there, discussing the merits of silver and gold thread, the difference between blue celeste and bleu lapis. St. Jean carefully packed their selections in tissue paper and waxed canvas. And then, of course, came the trimmings: a rainbow's worth of silk ribbons, a garden of silk flowers, miles of silken thread, and a menagerie of feathers.

"That," Jean-Baptiste said, adding the trimmings to the mountain of bundles and giving them a satisfied pat, "should do. Although . . ." He moved back through the maze of chests, opened one, and held up a piece of blue silk, as deep as the Manche on a summer day. "Eh voilà! I saved this one for you, mon trésor."

"Oh, Papa," Luce breathed, despite herself. "It's lovely."

"It is too dark to be fashionable, I know," Jean-Baptiste said, bringing the silk to her.

"You know I don't care about that."

He held it up to her cheek. "It's as I thought," he said approvingly. "The exact color of your eyes. Shall I have St. Jean pack it with the rest?"

The silk glistened in the lanterns' light. It was cool and soft against Luce's hand. Wearing it, she knew, would be like wearing the sea.

"Yes, please," she said.

There were near thirty dockyards scattered across the shores of Saint-Malo, Rocabey, and Saint-Servan. Samuel often said you couldn't walk on the beach without bashing your shins on a pile of timber or getting a face full of tar smoke. The yard Jean-Baptiste favored was half an hour's ride from the gates of Saint-Malo, near Saint-Servan. Reaching it required traveling through the salt marshes of the Talards, with their dockyard, ropeworks, and powder magazine, and around the sweep of muddy beaches littered with fishing boats and drying nets.

Luce recognized the *Lucinde* at once. Of the three frigates resting in the building slips, only one was near completion. Cradled in her stocks, she seemed unperturbed by her layers of scaffolding, or the workmen crawling upon her like hungry insects.

Waiting patiently for her freedom.

Luce followed her father past the timber stores and ropeworks, the smithy and the sawpits, the rigging and mast houses. There were workmen everywhere, hauling timber, tending fires, sawing and steaming and shouting. The smells of smoke and fresh-cut timber and tar blended with the slightly rotten smell of the beach at low tide. Luce breathed it in.

"What do you think of her?" Jean-Baptiste asked, reining in his horse on the beach. Luce did the same, then slipped her feet free of the stirrups and slid to the ground.

"She's perfect." Even without her masts and sails—they would be added once she was safely launched—the ship was beautiful.

"Can we go aboard?"

"Of course."

Leaving the horses with St. Jean, they walked together down the beach. The workers, recognizing Jean-Baptiste, nodded respectfully as he passed. One of them, an older man who was clearly in charge, raised a hand in greeting.

"Charles Le Page," Jean-Baptiste said quietly to Luce, as the man hurried over. "Master shipwright." He greeted the shipwright warmly and gestured to Luce. "Allow me to introduce my daughter—"

"Lucinde," Le Page finished, with a smile. "Forgive my familiarity, mademoiselle. But we have met before, you know."

Luce frowned, confused. "We have, monsieur?"

"Indeed." He pointed straight up, to where the prow of the *Lucinde* loomed against the sky. There, affixed to the beak and the knee of the head, was the ship's figurehead. "Would you like to meet her?"

They followed the shipwright along the slip, and up the ramp to the scaffolding.

"You will need to climb, I'm afraid," Le Page said, slipping through a break in the planking. "Here, allow me."

He helped Luce into the belly of the ship. It was dim and cool, stripes of dusty sunlight cutting through the shadows.

"The decks are fully planked and ready for caulking," Le Page said, leading them up a steep set of stairs. "And the stern gallery and rudder have been fitted."

"I would like to see them," Jean-Baptiste said.

"Of course."

Luce trailed behind the men as they crossed the upper deck. Even unfinished, with gaping holes where her masts and capstans would soon be, it was hard not to imagine that the deck was moving gently. That the *Lucinde* was running before the wind and the stars.

"I know what you are thinking," Jean-Baptiste said, squeezing her hand. "It is impossible not to imagine her on the fly, no? Come. See your figurehead."

Construction on the prow had only recently ended. The smell of timber, freshly cut and caulked, was strong, the scaffolding surrounding the beak and prow still in place.

"I don't have to tell you to be mindful," Le Page said, helping Luce onto the platform skirting the prow.

"There's no need to worry about this one," Jean-Baptiste said proudly. "She knows her way round a ship. Now, about that rudder . . ."

Luce was already edging around the *Lucinde*'s hull as the men's voices drifted away. The wind, which had seemed gentle enough on the beach, clawed at her bergère hat. She gripped the wide brim with one hand, used her other to keep her wide skirts from catching on the rail. *Perhaps,* she thought, thinking of one Samuel Thorner, *if women were not compelled to wear such ridiculous clothing, they would be better at moving about on ships.*

At last she reached the figurehead.

There were countless mirrors at Le Bleu Sauvage—only Claudine, who was responsible for covering each one during thunderstorms, would know the exact number. In the vestibule and dining room, the bedchambers and salons. Even the servants' entrance contained a small, pitted rectangle of silvered glass.

Because of this, Luce knew her own countenance well. Its shape and expression. The precise color of her eyes and hair (blue and black, respectively). It was, however, something else entirely to see herself carved in oak, and painted in remarkable detail.

Freckles dusted the figurehead's nose. Her hand, resting against her brow as she surveyed the horizon, was identical to Luce's own: long-fingered, browned by the sun. Her black hair was loose, flowing over the prow. White lace, cleverly carved, foamed at her elbow-length sleeves and bodice. Her dress was a deep, rich blue. Like her hair, it ruffled and snapped in an imaginary wind, coming to an abrupt end just below her thighs, as though she were emerging from the ship's timbers: half within, and half without.

No feet, Charlotte had giggled as she looked over the plans at supper, and now Luce understood why. The figurehead's legs, knees, and feet disappeared completely beneath the folds of carved blue timber. The old shame gnawed at her, as well as . . . something else. She ran a hand over the figurehead's hip, feeling for the exact place her body ended and the ship began. The feeling of freedom, of movement, was gone; she seemed trapped, bound tightly by wood and iron. Compelled, through no choice of her own, to follow a course charted by another.

"I take it you're not happy with the craftsmanship, Mademoiselle Léon?" came a smooth voice from the deck above.

Luce looked up.

Morgan de Châtelaine was leaning on the bow rail, smiling down at her.

"What are you doing here?" she demanded, too surprised to be polite.

"The same as you, I imagine." He leapt lightly over the rail and onto the scaffolding. (Oh, how she envied him the quickness of his step, his casual, easy grace!) "Admiring your father's new ship."

He looked exactly as he had only hours before, in the salon at

Le Bleu Sauvage. Paler, perhaps, and a little out of breath, though he was trying to hide it.

"It's *my* ship," she said, rather rudely. He had startled her, after all.

Morgan raised a doubtful eyebrow. "Yours?"

"Yes."

A brief look of confusion. Then he nodded in understanding. "You mean she's named for you."

"No. I mean she's *mine.*"

"I thought she was your father's."

"She is. But he is giving her to me."

"I see." Both eyebrows lifted this time. "Quite the gift."

"My father is generous."

"Lucky you." He looked away from her, out over the yard, and leaned his elbows on the makeshift railing. "Would that I could say the same."

Luce remembered the tension between father and son earlier that morning. "I take it your father is not pleased about the loss of the *Dauphin.*"

"That's one way of putting it."

He was quiet for long moments, shoulders hunched, his gaze roving moodily over the dockyard. Luce wondered what to say. For the first time in her life, she wished she were more like Veronique. Her sister, with her grace and charm, would know exactly how to speak to the man beside her.

"I am surprised to see you here," she said awkwardly. "Your mother said you needed rest."

Grace and charm, indeed.

"My mother says a lot of things. It doesn't mean she's right." He straightened, looked at her—and at the figurehead behind her. "Good God! You weren't lying when you said the ship was yours, were you?" He stepped closer to the carved-Luce, taking in her face, her hair, her bare arms. "It looks just like you."

The sight of him so close to the figurehead, face upturned,

his lips mere inches from her curving wooden ones, put Luce strongly in mind of what had passed between them after the storm. She cleared her throat. "I suppose it does."

"Come, you must give credit where it's due. The likeness is remarkable."

"I suppose so," Luce said doubtfully. She wished he would move away from the figurehead. Seeing herself rendered so, and his witnessing it, was discomfiting, indeed.

"Quite the gift," Morgan said again, softly. "And what will you do with your ship, Mademoiselle Léon?"

"I do not yet know."

He moved along the scaffolding, narrowing his gaze as he took in the ship's prow, her hull. He ran a hand over her timbers, inspected the caulking. "Perhaps she will take you to Cádiz?"

Luce stared at him. "Cádiz?"

"Of course." His dark eyes were kind, interested. "You spoke of it today with such interest. It obviously intrigues you."

"Intrigues me?"

"Yes, the—do you intend to repeat everything I say, mademoiselle?"

He really was handsome—disarmingly so, with his black hair ruffled by the wind and his wide, warm smile. Luce looked away, her cheeks burning. "No."

His smile widened. "Well, that *is* a relief. It would be a rather one-sided conversation, otherwise. Me talking, you repeating things. It is often the way with young women, I find. But you . . . I feel as though *you* might actually have something to say."

At that moment Luce could, of course, think of nothing to say. He was very near, close enough that she could have reached out and touched his hand. The thought made her heart quicken.

"And so, here we are," Morgan said, leaning against the figurehead companionably, his dark eyes twinkling with mirth. "Together with so much to say."

"Well, I *did* want to ask you . . ." *Do you remember who saved you on the beach? Do you remember that kiss?* "What happened? To the *Dauphin*, I mean."

A cloud passed across his face, and she regretted her words at once. "I'm sorry," she said hastily. "I should not have asked you that."

"Two English frigates came upon us as we passed the Îles de la Manche," he said quietly. "One on one they would have had no hope against us—but the two of them . . ." He shifted against the figurehead's blue skirts. "We managed to get away, despite the damage, but the storm finished us off. The *Dauphin* was to be my first command. I had planned to go raiding, make a name for myself." He shook his head. "It doesn't matter now. The *Dauphin* is gone, my crew lost—along with my father's trust in me."

But how? Luce longed to ask. *How did you lose the ship when she was carrying such powerful stone? And why did your father lie about it?*

Morgan was quiet. Thinking, no doubt, of the *Dauphin* heaving herself to pieces, listless and defeated. "Sometimes I wonder how I was the only one to survive," he said softly. "Why no one else made it to shore. My mother calls it a miracle, my father a curse. He says it is his duty to punish me. That, as captain, *I* was responsible for every soul aboard. Not to mention the—" He shook his head, helpless. "He has refused to furnish me with another ship—or the coin to secure one."

"For how long?"

A bitter laugh. "For as long as he sees fit." He straightened, sighed. "I heard your family speaking of you, you know. You hear such things, when you are abed in an unfamiliar house."

Luce winced. "What did they say?"

"Your mother did not seem pleased with you. She said you were never where you were supposed to be. And that your collection of sea shells was making the entire house smell."

Luce smiled. "That's probably true."

His gaze traveled over her, rested on her face, her hair. "It is not seemly for a lady to keep such things, she said. Even if your father *does* bring them to you. People, she said, will talk." His voice softened. "Between you and me, I wondered if she should not be more concerned about people suspecting you of being a seamaid."

Luce's heart hammered in her chest. She thought of his lips on hers, the salt-kiss on the beach. Did he remember?

"You've seen one of the sea-folk?" she asked.

Every seaman had his tale. A green-haired woman combing her hair before a storm, or diving alongside a ship, or gazing at her reflection in a hand mirror. A fisherman who ensnared a seamaid in his net and, despite the maiden's pleas, refused to set her free. Injure or anger a seamaid and she would raise a storm. Placate her and you would have good luck. Some old shellbacks told of kindly seamaids who offered stricken sailors help; others described monsters who lured men to their drowning deaths, ornamenting their gardens with their salt-washed bones. These tales, and a hundred more, Luce had heard.

"Of course," Morgan said. "Haven't you?"

Luce shook her head. "There are no sea-folk in Bretagne anymore. Though Samuel swears—"

"Samuel?"

Damn my soul. "One of the fishermen who delivers to our kitchens at Le Bleu Sauvage," she said hastily. "He swears that he once saw the shimmer of a tail and the gleam of pale skin beneath the waves off his bow." *And don't even* think *about saying I only saw it because I was half-seas over, Luce. I know what I saw.* "Most people believe the sea-folk have moved on to wilder shores. They do not like ships, or people."

"I have heard the same," Morgan said.

"Did you see them in Cádiz, then?"

"The French Antilles." His voice was softer still. "I will never forget it. And when first I saw you . . ."

Luce could scarce breathe. She waited for him to say more, but

Morgan was gazing out over the dockyard, a faraway look on his face. *Ask him.* The words were dancing on the edge of her tongue, yet still she hesitated. *God alone knows how long he was drifting, cold and exhausted,* Samuel had said. *It will be a miracle if he remembers anything at all.* Perhaps it was for the best if Morgan *had* forgotten. Well-behaved young women did not swim in their chemises and drag sailors from the sea. They did not allow said sailors to wrap their cold arms about them and steal their souls away.

And yet. She needed to know.

"When . . . when first you saw me?"

He turned back to her, blinked. "Yes—today in your father's salon. You had the look of the Fae about you." He smiled shyly. "All wild and beautiful. And everything I had heard them say, the way they spoke of you, made sense. I wondered about you."

I wondered about you.

All wild and beautiful.

"Well, I *do* have too many sea shells," she said lightly, as though his last words were not echoing in her bones.

He was watching her. Waiting, she realized, for her to say more.

"You will think me strange, I fear."

"Never." He raised a hand to his heart, all theatrical earnestness, and she laughed.

"Very well. I am interested in the history of things. The sea, its creatures. How it came to be, what has shaped it."

"I knew it," Morgan said, sliding closer. "I knew you would be fascinating. Tell me, then. Is it just the shaping of the sea that intrigues you? Or do you wish to sail it, too?"

A stab of sudden guilt. Luce had only ever spoken of sailing with one other person. It was *Samuel* who had taught her how to sail the *Dove.* How to read the wind and chart a course. How to tack, and prepare for bad weather. Sailing was *their* secret. But Morgan was here, now. Morgan, who thought Luce had the look of the sea-folk, all wild and beautiful.

"I *long* to sail," she said. "If it were possible, I would command my own ship—*this* ship. Sail to Cádiz and the French Antilles, as you have done. Find those wild places where the sea-folk still exist."

She waited for him to laugh.

He didn't. "Why isn't it possible?"

"You know why." She gestured at herself. "Look at me."

"Oh, I am."

Luce could not help it; she blushed.

"There is nothing strange about wanting those things," Morgan said, leaning closer still. He smiled, the corner of his beautiful mouth lifting as though she were his secret, and he hers.

It was all Luce could do to stop herself from reaching out and touching him. That sea-green sleeve, resting so close to hers on the rail, perhaps. Or his hand. He was like storm-stone, tingling against her skin, calling her closer.

"Do you know," he said, thoughtfully. "That my father has a collection of curiosities? It is very large and wondrous. And, in my humble opinion, rather disgusting."

Luce laughed. "I have heard of it."

Who had not? It was common knowledge that Monsieur de Châtelaine had the most impressive collection of oddities and artifacts in Bretagne. Luce's father had spoken of it with awe and more than a little envy—his own collection paled into insignificance. Luce had longed to see it for as long as she could remember.

"What would you say, then—" Morgan's face was a mere handspan from Luce's own, now. She could smell the pomade in his hair: almonds and cloves, bergamot and musk. "—if I stole you away at the ball and gave you a tour of the collection? You could poke and peer at my father's rare sea shells to your heart's content."

He traced the inside of Luce's wrist with his fingertips. Back and forth, burning a path across her skin.

"I'd like that." Impossible to say more; she was wordless, boneless.

"Good."

"Lucinde?" Her father's voice floated down from the forecastle deck. Luce scrambled away from Morgan, her feet jarring painfully, as Morgan stepped neatly back, pressing himself tightly against the figurehead, whose flowing skirts hid him from view.

"Are you ready, mon trésor?" her father called down. "We must leave now if we are to return in time for supper."

"Yes, Papa." Luce edged back along the scaffold, squeezing past Morgan. They grinned at each other as she passed, that wonderful, secret smile.

A brisk wind blew in from the northwest as she rode back to the malouinière with her father and St. Jean. It cut across the Manche and the fields, creeping with insistent fingers along the back of her neck. She hardly felt it. Morgan's warm touch, his shadowed glance, remained.

7

Preparations

Preparations for the ball began swiftly and with violence. It came as no surprise to anyone that Veronique and Charlotte both coveted the same piece of fashionable Rose Pompadour silk taffeta for their ball gowns. The malouinière became a battlefield, filled with shouting and tears, professions of life-long hatred, promises of eternal vengeance. Its rooms were strewn with fashion plates and feathers, discarded swathes of silk taffeta, cloth of silver, and floral silk brocades. Fashion dolls dressed in miniature ball gowns lay like fallen soldiers among ribbons, rosettes, and lace. Luce picked them up whenever she passed, straightening their little gowns, fixing their tiny wigs. The brave and glorious dead.

To escape the fray, Luce spent as much time as possible at the sea-cave. She left the house early each morning and returned just before noon, then spent the afternoons in the gardens or her little cabinet, looking over the *Lucinde*'s plans or reading. The very act of sitting down to the harp or the harpsichord was a risk, as there was no telling when her sisters might charge through the room in the midst of some terrible skirmish. Sometimes, one or both of them tried to force Luce into the fray, begging her to take a side. More often, they left only moments after entering, a trail of insults and ill will in their wake. Mealtimes had become intolerable, each service of Julien's delicious dishes served with lashings of her sisters' fraught silences, bitter exchanges, and icy rejoinders as intricate and subtle as one of Olivier's remarkable chilled mousses.

After three days of collective suffering, Gratienne interceded.

"Veronique will wear the Rose Pompadour," she announced, calmly spooning extra crayfish coulis over her roast chicken.

"But Maman!" Charlotte cried. "You cannot mean it!"

"I most certainly do," Gratienne said. "That pink does nothing for your complexion, Charlotte. I have laid out three colors that will suit you better. After supper you will choose one."

"But—"

"Maman is right, Cee," Veronique said sweetly. "If you do not hurry up and decide we won't have our gowns made in time. We shall lose our advantage."

Charlotte glared at her, seething.

"I have already sent for the tailor," Gratienne said firmly. "Monsieur Briard will be here tomorrow." She glanced at Luce across the table. "Will you be attending the ball, Lucinde? You will need to select your fabric, if so."

"I have already made my choice, Maman."

"So, you *are* coming." Luce winced at the venom in Charlotte's voice. "I was sure you would not."

"Why?" Luce asked, curious.

"Because you do not like receptions, Lucinde," Charlotte said, rolling her eyes. "We all know it. What is different about this one?"

"Madame de Châtelaine delivered the invitation to us herself. It would be rude to not attend." Luce turned her attention to scooping more of the gratin of oysters—thick with parsley and golden butter—onto her plate. It was best to say as little as possible when Charlotte looked at you that way.

Her sister, however, would not be dissuaded. "And what color did *you* decide upon?" she demanded, cutting into her fricandeaux with vehemence.

"Blue."

"Blue? What kind of blue? Is it fashionable? Madame de Pompadour prefers a very light shade, you know."

Luce, disliking her sister's demeanor more with every passing moment, glanced at her father. Surely he would say something? *Do* something to quell the tide of bitterness rising around his elegant dining table? Jean-Baptiste, however, was tucking heartily into his second serving of roast lamb. Did he never wonder about the feelings of his wife and his daughters? Did he never think that a different kind of life—one in which they could somehow be *more* than just wife, mother, or daughter (or more than rivals bickering over silks)—might have benefited them? Her father merely glanced up at Jean-Germane, hovering near the sideboard. "Are there more oysters?"

Disappointment bowed Luce's shoulders. She finished her food and pushed back her chair. "Papa, may I be excused?"

"Are you sure, mon petit oiseau chanteur?" he asked, not looking up from his near-overflowing plate. "You will miss the second and third services."

"I am sure."

"Very well. But come, come." He waved her over jovially. "Give your papa a kiss before you go. And it is almost dark. Remember—"

"I know, Papa. I won't brush my hair."

The following morning brought little relief. Uncertain when the tailor would arrive, Luce remained at the house. Her mother and sisters rose earlier than was their custom, and a tense morning of chocolate-sipping and door-watching ensued. Six bells had rung, then seven, then eight—the end of the Forenoon Watch—before hooves sounded in the courtyard. Veronique and Charlotte leapt to their feet at once and pattered excitedly to the vestibule, breathlessly throwing open the front doors.

"Good day, mademoiselles."

The smiling young man Luce glimpsed over her sisters' shoulders was not Monsieur Briard, master tailor. *This* man was much younger, straight-backed, with white, neat teeth. He removed his tricorn, revealing thick, curling caramel-brown hair tied at the back of his neck.

"You are not—" Veronique began.

"Indeed," the young man interrupted, with an apologetic smile. He drew a folded document from within his waistcoat. "But I have a letter here from him, explaining the circumstances in full. I assure you, I shall do my best to serve you in his stead."

"I suppose you will have to do." Veronique barely masked her disappointment as she drew wide the door, waving away the laquais hurrying to help her. "Fetch Maman, won't you, Jean-Pierre?"

"Is your father within?" The young tailor tucked his hat beneath one arm and entered the vestibule. He carried a rough-looking leather satchel over one shoulder, and his breeches and stockings were covered with dust. Charlotte, noting these details at the same time as Luce, met her eyes, her brows raised.

"Papa?" Veronique frowned. "Why on earth would we need *him*?"

The young man looked bewildered. He went to open his mouth, but was prevented from saying further by the arrival of Gratienne, her embroidery hoop in one hand, a long trail of pale silk—a nightgown for Veronique's armoire, perhaps—sweeping her skirts.

"You are not—"

"He has a letter, Maman," Charlotte said, gesturing to the missive.

"It will explain everything, Madame Léon," the young man said, offering it to her. Luce, noting the flush to his cheeks, the slight shake in his hands, could not help but pity him. "I assure you, I am more than qualified."

Gratienne waved the letter away. "Indeed. I trust Monsieur Briard implicitly. If he believes you are capable of replacing him, then it shall be so. What is your name?"

"Monsieur Briard. . . . ?"

"No, *your* name," Gratienne said impatiently.

"Gabriel," he said. "Gabriel Daumard."

"I take it you studied in Paris?"

"I did, Madame Léon."

"Then let us begin."

She turned and led the way into the grand salon, her daughters falling into step behind her. Luce, the last to go, noted that Monsieur Daumard hesitated before he went, glancing at the open doors as though he were considering walking back out of them. At last, he followed.

"We shall begin with Charlotte," Gratienne said, sinking onto the chaise longue, her floral robe à la française fanning gracefully around her. She set her embroidery upon her lap and calmly resumed stitching.

"*Charlotte*?" Veronique echoed.

"*You* got the Rose Pompadour," Charlotte told her, all but running to stand before the young tailor. "*I* get to go first."

Gabriel Daumard took in the fabrics and trimmings flung over the furniture, the fashion plates and puddles of lace, the neat bundles of fabric—rose-pink for Veronique, pale blue for Charlotte, and Luce's own dark silk, wrapped in layers of tissue for the journey to the tailor's. He looked at Charlotte, standing expectantly before him, and reddened.

"I'm afraid I do not know where to begin."

"Where to *begin*?" Charlotte wadded her hands on her hips. "You have a measure, don't you?"

"Oh. Well, yes. Of course." He rummaged in his satchel, suddenly eager. "I always carry one with me. One never knows when one might need to take of note interesting specimens . . ."

"Interesting *specimens*?" Charlotte muttered, incredulous.

"Indeed." Monsieur Daumard produced a measuring ribbon. It was not, as Luce had expected, one of the paper measures favoured by Monsieur Briard—he had one for each of the Léon women, their names inked neatly on one side, their waists and shoulders and chests marked in a confusing code of cut-out shapes. *This* measure was rough, and small. A beaten metal case housing a frayed linen ribbon, wound snail-tight. Luce, who kept one just like it in her cabinet, knew at once that it was designed to take measurements of a more robust, scientific nature. She looked again at Monsieur Daumard, his satchel and dusty breeches, his straight back and ink-stained hands, the unmistakeable terror in his eyes . . .

Charlotte was frowning at the measure. "That does not look correct."

"It doesn't?" He turned it this way and that. "I assure you it is accurate." He pulled the end of the measure from its worn casing, smiled helpfully down at Charlotte. "What would you like me to measure, mademoiselle?"

"*Me!*" Charlotte spat.

"Oh." The young man's gaze moved over Charlotte—over all the places she might be measured—and the color drained from his face: pink to bone-white in moments.

Luce stepped forward quickly, her suspicions confirmed. "You are the new tutor Papa sent for, aren't you?" she said. "Not the tailor."

A sidelong glance, the measure frozen in his hands, as though the smallest of movements was certain to bring about catastrophe. "I am so sorry, mademoiselle. I did not want to cause offense—"

He got no further. At the expression of woe on his face, the outraged horror on Charlotte's, Luce burst into laughter. It rippled from her chest, relentless as the tide, worsening every time she looked at her sister, or the measure. Veronique tittered, bringing a hand to her mouth before exploding into giggles. Charlotte, unable to help herself, joined her.

Mortification melted into mirth, until she was laughing so hard that she bent at the waist, clutching her belly. Even Gratienne's shoulders shook, her embroidery hoop cast aside on the longue.

Finally, Gabriel began to chuckle, too.

That made them all laugh harder, so loud and so wild that the tension of the previous days, the rivalry and pettiness, vanished. Their laughter rose, and rose, until several of the domestiques were hovering concernedly at the door, watching their mistresses spilling about the room in gales of laughter with a strange young man chortling in their midst.

Jean-Baptiste arrived next.

"What in God's name is going on here?" he demanded.

"The new tutor has arrived, Papa," Luce said, wiping her eyes. "See?" Fresh laughter bubbled out of her; she hid her face in her hands, unable to go on.

"Monsieur Léon," Gabriel said, gathering himself with some difficulty. "May I introduce myself? I am Gabriel Daumard—"

"Papa!" Veronique cried, tears running down her cheeks. "We thought he was the *tailor*!" She diminished into fresh giggles, collapsing face-first on the chaise longue and snorting into a cushion.

Gabriel was fighting hard against laughter. He took a deep breath, managed to contain it. "It is good to meet you, sir."

Jean-Baptiste was not smiling. "You are not Monsieur Ferrand."

"Oh, of course." Gabriel waved the letter he had tried to give Gratienne in the vestibule. "I'm afraid Monsieur Ferrand is unwell, Monsieur. He sent me in his stead."

"Unwell?" Jean-Baptiste frowned.

"Yes, monsieur. He is not . . . as young as he used to be. There was concern the journey from Paris would be too much for him."

"I see." Jean-Baptiste took the letter. Read. Luce's laughter faded, along with her sisters', until a heavy silence cloaked the room.

"It says that you studied music at the Royal Academy."

"Yes," Gabriel said. "I also studied science and mathematics at the Academy of Sciences. Monsieur Ferrand told me knowledge of both music and science was important to you."

"It is." And yet there was no pleasure in Jean-Baptiste's eyes. He folded the letter crisply, pocketed it, and scraped his gaze over the younger man in such a way that Luce wondered if he would set him back on the road to Paris.

"Monsieur?" Gabriel was no doubt fearing the same. "I trust all is in order?"

Jean-Baptiste glanced at his daughters, his wife, and gave a long sigh. "It would seem so. Have you much baggage?"

"No. I sent all my books and scientific instruments by post."

"They should arrive in a year or two, then." Jean-Baptiste smiled at last, deftly leading the young tutor from the room and calling for Claudine. There was a moment of confusion in the vestibule as the *real* tailor arrived, just as the ship's bell struck the next watch. During the commotion, Gabriel Daumard smiled warmly at each of the women through the open doors. Perhaps it was the shuffling in the vestibule, the upheaval caused by the meeting of the tailor, who had brought his large dogs with him, and Claudine, who had a tremendous terror of dogs. Or maybe it was simply the hurry of the laquais to reach the sandglass and the bell at the right moment. Whatever it was, Luce was certain Gabriel's gaze lingered longest, and warmest, on Charlotte.

Once every month, after attending mass in Saint-Coulomb, Gratienne took Luce to bathe her feet in the sacred fountain at the nearby Saint-Vincent's church. Like the storm-stone quarries of the coast and the standing stones of Bretagne's interior, fountains were places of great power, offering a range of cures: those who longed for a child, for example, might bathe at the Fountain of the Virgin, while the sacred waters of Sainte Anne were known to cure madness. The water at Saint-Vincent's was reputed to heal ailments of the legs and feet.

"Must I, Maman?" Luce asked as the carriage rolled to a stop before the little church. "Surely if the spring was of any benefit, we would know by now?"

They had been completing the ritual for years—since the healers had given up on Luce's ever-worsening feet—with little results, despite the water's miraculous reputation. The most Luce had ever received was a sharp nip or two from the belligerent water-fae who inhabited the spring. It was not like the sea, which never failed to ease the pain. (After all these years, Luce was still without a reasonable explanation for that; she could only surmise it was the salt.)

"Luce is right, Maman." Charlotte, sitting across from the carriage, drew her shawl around her shoulders. "I am cold just *thinking* about that water. And those dreadful creatures . . ."

"Who are we to question the workings of the Fae?" Gratienne said quietly, with a furtive glance at the church. The pastor tolerated visits to the springs—and the pagan beliefs at their source—but even so, such visits required discretion. She squeezed Luce's hand. "It would be lovely for all three of you to dance at the de Châtelaine ball, would it not? We must do all that we can to ensure that Luce has that chance."

"I suppose so," Charlotte said doubtfully.

"We are here now," Luce said with a sigh, stepping down from the carriage. "We may as well finish it."

She did not wait for her mother and sister to join her. Neither of them could abide the slippery little waterae, their sharp teeth and wicked grins.

The fountain was located a short walk from the chapel, in a rather grim patch of forest. It had been revered for time untold—long before the church had dampened the people's belief in the old ways—and the twisted path was well-worn. The forest was still, the ancient trickle of water and the slow, quiet green of the trees as they breathed were the only sounds.

She soon reached the glade where the spring lay. Stone steps dropped to a mossy pool, with dappled light and a few listless leaves moving upon its surface. Newish-looking statues of saints gazed disapprovingly into its dark depths.

When Luce was young, and the pool still held some hope, it had been enough for her to sit on the edge with Gratienne, a blanket and her mother's arm around her shoulders, her little legs dangling in the water. As she had grown—and Gratienne's faith in the waters dwindled—she had encouraged Luce to go further, and then further. It was nothing, now, to strip down to her chemise and plunge into the pool, eyes closed, hair drifting, body tensed at the unforgiving cold.

It was not like swimming in the sea. The water was eerily still, and when she held her hands out before her, she glimpsed little more than a pale suggestion of them in the thick water.

A stone bench had been carved into the pool's edge. Luce made her way to it, drawing her thighs against her chest and laying her head on the twin islands of her knees. Cold water rarely bothered her, but here, sitting in perfect stillness, surrounded by stone and shade, she invariably began to shiver. She closed her eyes, tried to distract herself with the sounds of the birds in the trees above, the burble of water rising from the underground spring.

"Thievery." The barest whisper of a hiss, a rippling of water against stone.

Luce opened her eyes.

The faery in the water beside her was no larger than a newt, with a newt's slender, earthen-colored body and tail. Its face was oddly human, sharp and shrewd, with pointed ears and too-large, too-strange eyes. "*Thievery.*"

"Calm yourself," Luce said mildly. "I've no plans to steal anything from you or your kin."

It was always this way. Spring sprites were a shadowy sort, inclined to mistrust and accusation, and fervently protective of their home.

"Thievery," the little creature said again, skittering up the pool's stony edge on its four, clinging feet.

"Thievery," lisped another, floating near Luce's elbow.

"Thievery!" From the shoulder of the nearest saint, the alcove protecting the mouth of the spring, the cow parsley near the path: a chorus of low, angry voices. More appeared, skimmering and slipping into the water, sliding from between the stones.

"*Thievery!*"

Luce flinched as one of the creatures clawed its way up her shin, perched on her knee. "Thievery!"

"I *told* you," Luce told it. "I'm not here to take anything. How many times have we had this conversation?"

The fae only stared up at her, flicking its long, black tongue between its teeth.

Luce poked out her tongue.

"Luce?" Charlotte was coming down the path. The sprites scattered, the creature on Luce's knee digging its claws into her thigh in one final insult.

"Everyone wants a bite," it hissed as it slither-dived out of sight.

"Are those little devils here?" Charlotte carried a bundle of woolen blankets and dry underclothes, which she placed at the spring's edge. "Honestly, Luce, I don't know how you stand it."

"The sprites or the cold?"

"Both." Charlotte peered into the water, to where Luce's feet rested on the stone seat.

Luce fought the urge to draw her chemise over her toes. At last Charlotte moved away, seating herself on the edge of the pool.

"Oh, stop it," Charlotte said, swiping at a sprite as it lunged at her, baring its teeth. "You really think we've come to steal your slimy rocks? Go away."

Luce rested her head on her knees again, watching her sister. At times like this, when it was just the two of them, she adored Charlotte. Her quick wit, her fierce cleverness, her mischievous laugh. They were close in age—only a year apart—and as children they had devised games together, practiced the minuet and the allemande. Luce's feet had not hurt so much when she was young, and she had loved to dance, spending many a happy summer day turning and scooping, bowing and parading, while someone—usually a governess or a tutor—had accompanied them on the harpsichord. Charlotte's eyes had sparkled on those days, sweet and brown. Her laugh had been—still was—addictive.

The sweetness, however, always soured. It could happen instantly: A disagreement over a step in the gavotte, or the appearance of Veronique, whose presence never failed to change everything. (Three is a cursed number for children, for mustn't there always be someone left out?) A visitor's comment on the beauty of Veronique's hair, or Luce's voice. The gift of a feather.

"Your poor feet," Charlotte said. "What makes them that way, do you think?"

"I hardly know." Luce watched an oak leaf flutter to the pool's surface.

"Will you be able to dance? At the ball, I mean."

Luce shrugged. It was unlikely, and they both knew it. Dancing was its own, special kind of agony.

A wren chittered a sweet little song in the trees above, the leaves swaying gently in time. It was old, this place, far older than the little granite church and the stern-faced saints. It was not the sea, it was true, but Luce had to admit it had its own kind of beauty.

"What think you of Monsieur Daumard?" Charlotte asked suddenly.

"It is too early to have a true opinion of him," Luce replied. "But he seems pleasant enough. He plays beautifully. And yesterday we had a fascinating discussion about molluscs." The new tutor had only been part of the household for a few days, but he had already corrected her fingering for the new harp piece she was learning and insisted they ask Papa for permission to mount a scientific expedition to the cove, where, chaperoned by Jean-

Pierre, they had examined the rocks and weed, the shells and shore lichens. He was far more enthusiastic than her previous tutors. Quicker to smile, too.

"Hmm."

"Papa has invited him to attend the ball with us," Luce said, watching her sister.

"That was kind. I suppose it will be a treat for Monsieur Daumard, attending such a grand gathering." Charlotte toyed with the ribbons on her hat.

Luce smiled. "He came to us from Paris, Cee."

"Yes, but before the university he lived in Touraine. His father is an *attorney*." Her nose wrinkled in distaste.

Luce raised her head. "How do you know all this?"

Charlotte flicked a shoulder. "I asked him." She rose abruptly, brushing at the leaves clinging to her skirts. "I was thinking I could help with your hair before the ball. Have you given any thought as to how you will wear it?"

Luce, taken aback at this unexpected generosity, shook her head. "I was going to ask Nanette what she thought."

"I have some new fashion plates from Paris. We could read through them, look for something together? Your hair is very long—too long, really—but I'm sure we could come up with something."

"I'd like that," said Luce, touched. Charlotte usually guarded her fashion plates jealously, refusing access to anyone but Nanette. "Thank you."

Charlotte reached for the blanket and shook it out. "We'll be representing Papa at the ball. We *all* need to look our best." She sniffed. "Not just Veronique."

Luce hid a smile.

"And now," Charlotte said, holding out the blanket. "Time to end this torture."

"Maman likes me to stay in as long as possible. . . ."

"Well, there's no sign of Maman, and your skin is turning

blue," Charlotte said practically. She leaned down, offered Luce a hand. "You're no use to anyone like that."

The harpsichord at Le Bleu Sauvage was a thing of true beauty. It was painted a gentle gray, overlaid with delicate flowers in pinks, blues, and creams. Luce was seated at it, working on one of Bach's concertos under the guidance of Monsieur Daumard, when her father entered the room.

"That was much better," the tutor was saying, as Luce finished a particularly difficult section. "See the difference that fingering makes?"

Luce nodded, intent on her fingers again and again over the black and white keys, memorizing the new movements.

"Try again," he instructed. "Just the beginning of the allegro movement, this time."

The shimmering tones of the harpsichord filled the room, elegant, rapid, and bright.

"Wonderful," Jean-Baptiste said, when Luce was done. "I see now why Monsieur Ferrand sent you to us, Daumard. Although, I'm sure you're aware of the rare talent my Lucinde possesses."

"I am, Monsieur Léon," Gabriel said. "Indeed, all three of your daughters are remarkably accomplished."

Jean-Baptiste beamed with pride. "I *had* come to speak with you about the *Lucinde,*" he said, flicking up his coattails and sinking into a chair. "After hearing you play just now, however, I think it would be far wiser to let you continue your lesson."

"The *Lucinde*?" Luce straightened on the bench. "But what were you going to tell me, Papa?"

He smiled. "Monsieur Le Page assures me it will be ready to launch next week."

"Next week?" Luce's fingers lifted from the keys, Bach's notes forgotten in her excitement. "Then we have much to discuss!

Have you given any more thought about who might be best to captain her?"

"A little," Jean-Baptiste said. He settled back in the chair with a sigh. "There's still plenty of time to decide. Will you play that lovely piece by Scarlatti for me, mon trésor? You know the one."

Luce did. Scarlatti's 208 Sonata was her favorite, too. Still, it was not thoughts of Scarlatti that raced through her mind, but ships' masts and furnishings. Captains, and crews. She had so many questions. Her father, however, had already rested his head against the chair's back and closed his eyes.

She raised her hands to the keys, pushed down her disappointment, and began to play, her fingers moving slowly over the first halting notes. The music grew in strength and smoothness, rising tide-like, until the notes cascaded downward again in a fall of quiet silver.

"Lovely," Jean-Baptiste said.

A commotion in the vestibule caused Luce to stop playing and look up, alert to the possible resumption of the war between Veronique and Charlotte. It had been a week since the Battle of the Pompadour Rose had ended—a week since Gabriel Daumard had joined their household—but that was no guarantee that some new, equally dramatic conflict had not begun.

The palaver grew in intensity. Veronique squealed in delight, and Charlotte fired a series of rapid questions. Gratienne was there too, her low, strong voice failing to quell the rising excitement.

"That must be the tailor with the new gowns," Jean-Baptiste said wearily, pushing himself out of his seat. "Come, mon petit oiseau chanteur, Daumard. Let us see."

8

A Sliver of Ocean

Veronique was in the vestibule, pink-cheeked and shining with excitement.

"Our gowns have arrived!" she announced, leading Luce, Jean-Baptiste and Daumard into the grand salon. She paused in the doorway as they filed obediently past, leaning back to call back up the staircase. "Anna-Marie! Hurry and bring the dressing screen from my chamber!"

At that moment Charlotte entered the room, her wide skirts bumping into Veronique's. They struggled comically before Charlotte managed to squeeze past, followed by Nanette, her arms loaded with two large, narrow boxes. Jean-Pierre came in behind her with a third box, followed by Anna-Marie and St. Jean, Veronique's dressing screen hoisted between them. At last, Gratienne swept in, her maid Madeleine hurrying behind.

"Saints preserve us," Jean-Baptiste muttered.

There was a pause while the boxes were laid carefully out, and the two laquais and Gabriel Daumard politely retreated, closing the double doors behind them. Jean-Baptiste threw them an envious glance.

Expectation settled over the room. Gratienne paced before the chaise longue, hand raised, floating over first one, then another of the sumptuous boxes. At last, it came to a stop. "I think we'll open this one first, Madeleine."

It was, of course, Veronique's gown that swept into being from between the layers of expensive tissue. She hurried forward, scooping up the gown and disappearing with it behind the dressing screen. Luce bit her lip, cast a sideways glance at Charlotte. True to her word at the spring, Charlotte had shared her precious fashion plates with Luce, helping her decide how to style her hair. Now, watching her sister wait her turn yet again, Luce felt a pang of sympathy. She reached out, squeezed Charlotte's hand.

At last, Veronique emerged. Despite the Léon wealth and Gratienne's skillful styling, the grand salon would never equal the magnificent salons of Paris. Yet when Veronique stepped out from behind the screen, it seemed as fine as one of the rooms in the palace of Versailles—and Veronique, as beautiful as the famed Madame de Pompadour herself.

The luxurious robe à la française was the color of early roses, or the last pinkish blush of the evening. Its half sleeves were thick with ribbons and gold lace, its skirt a shining mass of silk, the thick pleats of the back panels sweeping the carpet. Every inch of it had been embroidered—thousands of roses in golden thread on stomacher and sleeves, skirts and petticoat. It glittered like the dawn.

Veronique turned slowly, admiring herself in the long mirror above the fireplace.

Gratienne sighed in contentment. "Oh, my darling," she said.

"I do not think I shall be able to pass through the door," Veronique joked, turning this way and that. "It is very wide, is it not, Maman?"

"It is perfect."

"It *is* lovely," Luce added, meaning it. She could all but smell the first blush of spring roses.

"Thank you, Luce." Veronique tilted her head, waiting for Charlotte's compliment.

"Yes," Charlotte said flatly. "Maman was right about that color suiting you better."

While Veronique preened in the mirror, Gratienne selected

another box from the chaise longue. This time, a gown of palest blue silk taffeta appeared. As Nanette lifted it out, visibly straining under the weight, Luce saw that the robe and underskirt were as heavily embellished as Veronique's. Bluebells, daffodils, clouds, and bumblebees meandered in silver thread across the skirt and matching petticoat. The stomacher was festooned with row upon row of silver bows, and silver lace rippled at the sleeves.

"Oh, Cee," Luce said, when Charlotte was standing before the mirror. "It is beautiful. Like the sky at twilight."

Charlotte smiled at her. "Thank you, Luce. I like the color, too."

Veronique, watching her reflection in one of the windows, mumbled something that sounded like, "Yes, yes. It's wonderful."

"I still prefer the cream silk." Gratienne came to stand behind Charlotte, head tilted thoughtfully. "Or the lilac."

Charlotte tensed.

"Still, it will suffice," Gratienne added, nodding to herself. "Especially with your mask and jewels."

"It's Luce's turn," Veronique said, dragging herself away from her reflection. "Here, Nanette; let us see what she chose."

"Yes." Charlotte, still at the mirror, looked over her shoulder and smiled. "I want to see, too."

Nanette threw Luce a grin of her own, small and secret, before she lifted away the box's lid.

The silk was even darker than Luce remembered: a sliver of ocean at night. But for a few layers of black lace sewn into each half sleeve, the dress was completely unadorned; no embroidery, buttons, or bows. Nanette took hold of its shoulders, lifting it from its nest of tissue. It rose easily with her, falling like water.

"Hm," Gratienne said, a sharp little sound that gave nothing away. "It is darker than I would have chosen for you, Lucinde, but I suppose it will have to do. Help her try it on, please."

Luce stepped behind the screen, and Nanette and Anna-Marie gathered around her, their practiced hands moving quickly. There were no embellishments for them to navigate, no ribbons to flounce. The stomacher Nanette pinned over Luce's stays was smooth and plain. And yet, when she stepped out from behind the screen . . .

"Heavens above, mon trésor," Jean-Baptiste said. "You are a vision."

"It's so plain," Veronique added, perplexed. "There is no embroidery, no trimming. And yet . . . my goodness, Luce. You look *beautiful.*"

Luce gazed at herself in the mirror. She had always thought herself too tall, too thin, too dark to be truly beautiful, yet she could not deny that the new gown, though almost painfully simple, looked . . . well on her. Her eyes seemed bluer. Her black hair shone. The silk was like a live thing, lustrous in the sunlight slanting through the salon doors, causing her skin to glow. Would Morgan notice her in a dress the color of the sea? Would he remember what had happened after the wreck? A delicious little thrill ran through her at the thought.

Jean-Baptiste came to stand behind her. "Perhaps I should have chosen a different color for you, mon trésor," he said gravely, regarding her reflection over her shoulder. "It seems very likely that my worries will come to pass, and that someone will indeed try to take you from us."

"Don't be absurd, Papa," she said guiltily. "It is only a gown. Only a ball."

"The color *does* suit her, I suppose," Gratienne said grudgingly. Her eyes flicked from Veronique to Luce and back again. As though it were her eldest daughter, and not Luce, she found wanting.

"I had no idea you were so lovely," Veronique said, stepping closer. "Your skin—it's like honey. And your hair . . . so beautiful and dark." She reached out to touch a strand. "My goodness, Luce."

Luce turned to Charlotte, eager to see what she thought, whether the hairstyle they had planned would be suitable—and felt a familiar, sickening dread. Charlotte was utterly still, her gaze hard and unsmiling.

"Shall we try on our masks?" she said coldly, turning away.

Luce's unease grew as Nanette tied the ribbons of her mask, a simple eye-covering of black silk. Veronique's mask—a concoction of powder-pink satin and gold netting—sprouted a cluster of ostrich feathers, powdery and exotic, above her head. Charlotte's, a blue and silver butterfly, arched its wings over the sides of her face. When each was secured, her sisters joined her before the mirror.

"Breathtaking," Jean-Baptiste said, as he beheld his daughters. His gaze returned, again and again, to Luce, until it was plain that, of the three of them, it was *she* who drew the eye. Too tall, too thin, too dark, she might be; but in that moment, she outshone her sisters like a single star in a velvet sky.

Any pleasure she felt was short-lived. Charlotte's masked gaze was fixed upon her in the mirror, all trace of warmth and sisterhood gone.

Jealousy had returned, as it always did, and hardened her heart.

It was never wise to be caught outdoors after dark in Bretagne. Eldritch things wandered the night. Night screamers and the brous, who rampaged through the forests and thickets, devouring small creatures that strayed across their paths, or the feared Lavandières, the Night Washerwomen, who cleansed the graveclothes of the dead at the water's edge. Seeing them was to be feared, indeed, for doing so foretold one's own death.

The Bugul Noz, too, rode at night. Luce had seen his tall figure moving through the dusky landscape several times. He had even spoken to her once; whispered that she lingered too long outside after dark. Many had been drowned for the same offense, but the Bugul Noz had only lurched away on his hideous, shadow-hoofed horse. The sound of his whistling voice, the glowing embers of his eyes, had pierced her with terror.

There were hours yet before nightfall, but she walked as quickly as she dared. It had been a week since she had last been to the cove. Preparations for the ball, and the presence of the new tutor, had made escape impossible. A pity, to say the least. Since the arrival of the new gowns, Charlotte and Veronique had resumed their rivalry, bickering in front of the shoemaker one day, and freezing the house with icy silence the next. There was, of course, no silence cold enough to quell the stream of bitter insults Charlotte threw Luce's way. The shoemaker's visit, however, had been worse than any of her sister's barbs. The look of pity he had given Luce when she removed her slippers haunted her still.

Tonight, however, was the last before the ball, and the Léons had supped and retired early. Unable to resist the call of the sea—and the opportunity to bathe her aching feet—Luce had waited until the house was quiet, then stolen away. No sooner had she reached the

the cliffs and spied the Manche, calm and gray-green in the evening light, all thought of insults and shoemakers alike faded.

On the beach, she gathered driftwood and stacked it on the sand near the cave, then ducked through the long passage, emerging with a lantern and tinder box, blankets, part of an old sail, and a battered little knife. She spread the sail upon the sand and heaped the blankets upon it, then built a fire, feeding it until flames the color of lavender danced against the dusk.

The water beckoned.

A silver gull wheeled overhead as she plunged into its cool folds. Cradled in its gentle arms, face upturned to the first of the night's stars, she was weightless. Thoughtless. Free. The pain in her feet disappeared, washed away by cold and salt. To prolong the feeling as long as possible, she padded slowly out of the water and across the wet sand, then wrapped herself in a blanket and watched the fire.

She was almost dry when the faint sound of music drifted to her from around the headland. She tilted her head, listening. A fiddle, a bombarde, a veuse, and a drum. Not the jetins out playing their wild, fey little songs to the moon, then, but a group of fishermen, or folk from Saint-Coulomb. Her heart skittered at the thought. Might Samuel be with them? It had been days and days since they'd gone storm-diving at the wreck of the *Dauphin*. She had left a note for him in the wall near the chapel, where a loose stone provided the perfect place to store secret messages.

New tutor, she had written. She had almost told him of the ball, the appointments with tailors and the shoemaker, but at the last moment had decided against it. *Will leave word when I can get away.*

In reply, he had left her a drawing of a swallow, capturing the angle, the flight, in a few clever lines and reminding Luce of his tattoos. She dreamed of them, sometimes. Of him. Of running her fingertips, her lips, over the ink on his skin. Would it feel as smooth as it looked?

Luce got to her feet, threw off the blanket, and pinned herself hastily back into her bodice and skirts—she had not bothered to dress in her men's clothes so late in the day—and pulled a shawl around her shoulders, tucking the knife into her pocket. She climbed onto the rocks shielding the cove from the east, scrambling to the highest point.

Away from the shelter of the cave mouth, the music was louder. Voices floated over the water. And there, upon the next headland, the glow of a large fire.

She narrowed her eyes as the breeze tugged at her shawl, her hair. The headland was higher and wilder than the one she stood upon. Instead of pines, it was covered with gorse, the branches fizzing with yellow flowers. People had gathered on an expanse of rock jutting out over the water, seated themselves on stones among the gorse and sea thrift, their faces golden in the fire-glow as they shared food and drink. Some of the younger fisherfolk, perhaps, and servants from the surrounding farms, manors, and malouinières. No doubt a few shipwrights, too. They gathered, sometimes, to tell stories, sing and dance. Faint echoes of their conversation, their laughter, drifted across the water.

Luce imagined the warmth of that fire, the glow of such companionship, and felt a stab of inexplicable loneliness. She sighed, and the water beneath her rippled in sympathy. The ripples spread, growing in strength, crossing the water and breaking against the rocks.

A lone figure drew away from the rest and walked to the cliff's edge. Luce recognized the shape of his shoulders, the way he thrust his hands into the pockets of his overcoat.

She smiled.

As though he had heard his name, Samuel looked her way. She saw the moment he saw her, the lift of his shoulders, the tilt of his chin. Watched him walk away from the gathering and onto the path that led to Luce's cove. In the space of a breath or two he was hidden by the sea pines lining the gently-curving cliffs.

Luce, meanwhile, lingered on the rocks, prising oysters from their ribs. Returning to the cave, she stretched out the sail to make more space, then settled against the blankets to crack open the oysters and wait.

"I thought you were the tide-crone, when I saw you just now," Samuel said, crossing the sand. Luce grinned when she saw that Bones was with him, carrying cups and a bottle. "Bones stole us some cider."

"That's right," Bones said good-naturedly. "Blame me, as always."

He flopped down on one side of Luce while Samuel took the other, stretching his long legs out toward the fire, and poured out three cups.

"Thank you." Luce took a sip. Apples and spring. "There's oysters if you want them."

Both men eagerly obliged her, tilting their heads back to slide the salty-fleshed creatures down their throats. Luce had already eaten her fill.

Samuel took a long swallow from his own cup, then raised an eyebrow at Luce's damp hair.

"Been swimming?"

"Hmm-mm."

"It's late in the day for that, isn't it?" He glanced mistrustfully at the brooding expanse of the Manche, the silvery water lapping against the rocks. "You don't know what's lurking out there."

Luce shrugged. "Tide-crones, apparently."

"And other things, besides," Bones added.

Samuel took another sip of his cider. "Things have been busy at the malouinière, then?" he asked. "What was it you said? A new tutor?"

Luce nodded. "Monsieur Daumard. He has come to distract me with music and natural history." She had chosen the words—*distract me*—as a jest, only. Nevertheless, something about it snared at her.

"You've had tutors before," Samuel said idly. "It never stopped you from sneaking out."

"There are also . . . other things afoot." She glanced at him, considering. He had made his feelings about the de Châtelaines more than plain, that morning on the *Dove*, yet that was not the only reason she found herself hesitating to tell him about the ball. For the first time since they had met, the differences between them—in family, and in wealth—seemed important. Samuel was well aware of the way the Léons lived. The lavish suppers, the extravagance. He had even been inside Le Bleu Sauvage and seen it all for himself. It was entirely natural for Luce to want to attend the ball at Le Loup Blanc. So why did it feel like a betrayal?

"*I* know what's afoot," Bones said, sliding more wood onto the fire.

"Oh, you do, do you?" Samuel raised a brow.

"That's right. Luce is going to the de Châtelaines' ball tomorrow night."

Luce glanced at him, surprised. "How do *you* know the de Châtelaines are having a ball?"

"I try to keep a weather eye open," Bones said solemnly.

"Christ," Samuel muttered.

Bones ignored him. "It'll be, by all accounts, a grand affair."

Luce, biting back a smile, nodded. "Most certainly."

"New dress?"

Another nod.

Samuel snorted. "You must have *loved* that."

"It was not so bad," she admitted. "Papa found some silk for me. Dark blue. It's beautiful."

"I can imagine." Samuel took another sip of cider, his gaze on the fire.

"What of your sisters?" Bones inquired. "New dresses, too?"

Samuel frowned at him. "What in God's name is *wrong* with you?"

"What?" Bones asked, defensive. "I'm interested."

Luce chuckled. "Veronique and Charlotte both wanted the same fabric for their gowns. Rose Pompadour," she added.

"Ah," Bones said sagely. "A popular choice this season."

"Indeed. The house has been a battlefield. I comfort myself with the knowledge that by this time tomorrow we will all be at Le Loup Blanc, and my sisters will be too busy enjoying themselves to do battle."

"I have no doubt they will," Samuel said wryly. "The de Châtelaines, after all, are very good at enjoying themselves. Some of them more than others."

"What do you mean?" Luce asked.

"Nothing." He sat up, reached for more driftwood. The sun had made its final descent beyond the horizon now, and the air was cooling rapidly. "Though while we're speaking of the de Châtelaines, I should tell you we've had several offers for the stone."

"So soon?" Luce sat up straighter. "Have you even finished salvaging?"

He laid the wood on the fire. "We've emptied the hold and brought up as much from the seafloor as we could find."

"Already?"

"We had some assistance. I don't like bringing in extra hands—the more people who know, the more who might talk—but it could not be helped."

A shiver ran down Luce's spine at the thought of that shadowy wreck, the looming darkness. "Where is it now?"

He tilted his head toward the cave. "Where do you think?"

"My God, Samuel." She should have known. The telltale tingling on her skin was subtle, but unmistakeable. "Is that safe?"

The cave was well hidden, protected by the groac'h, and her father's presence, both. Even so, the thought of so much stolen storm-stone sitting a few steps away was . . . worrying.

"You've never been concerned about us storing cloud here before," Samuel said, watching her.

"You never stole it from the de Châtelaines before. Who else knows it's here?"

Bones raised his hand. "Guilty."

Samuel ignored him. "Only the three of us." Satisfied with the fire, he flopped back against the cushions.

Luce frowned. "I should tell you—Castro de Châtelaine lied to my father when he asked about the *Dauphin*'s stone."

"What did he say?" Bones leaned forward.

"That he took a risk. Sailed without storm-stone. I knew, of course, that he was lying."

"What of his son?" Samuel asked. "What did he have to say?"

"He said nothing."

"Interesting."

Luce waited while Bones refilled her cup. "Why would they lie, do you think?"

"You tell us, Luce." Samuel held his cup out to Bones, firelight catching on the gold in his hair.

"Well, there are two reasons I can think of," Luce said. "The first is pride. No one wants to lose a ship, but the loss is decidedly less shameful if it was unprotected. Or if everyone *believes* it was so."

"True. What's the second?"

"Security. By claiming the *Dauphin* carried ordinary ballast, they'd protect it from storm divers."

Samuel grinned. "Also true."

"Which is it, then?"

"I'd say both. The de Châtelaines are proud. They'd do anything to protect the family's reputation. And with stone like that in the hold, something must have gone very, very wrong aboard that ship."

Luce, remembering the set of Morgan's shoulders as he leaned on the *Lucinde*'s scaffolding, the pain in his eyes, nodded. "But what?"

"I'll tell you," Bones announced. "Rather than trusting his crew and his ballast, de Châtelaine took the wheel himself. Stormstone only works in weather like that if you let the ship run—the cloud will take over, keep it safe. Anyone with experience knows that. And our brave captain was far from experienced."

Luce frowned. Morgan was inexperienced, it was true; but that was hardly his fault. "What about you?" she asked Samuel. "Do *you* think he ran the ship onto the reef himself?"

Samuel shrugged. "Such behavior requires a certain amount of arrogance. And the de Châtelaines are rather good at arrogance."

"That's not fair," she said. "Neither of you have even *met* Morgan de Châtelaine."

"I don't need to," Bones said mildly. "I know his kind well enough."

"And you agree, I suppose?" Luce raised an eyebrow at Samuel.

He shrugged. "It's hard not to. And it's not as if de Châtelaine is going to *admit* to any of this, is he? He's already lied about the storm-stone being on board. What else isn't he saying?" He tilted his head back, admiring the early stars glimmering over the Manche. "To get back to your second reason, Luce . . . I've no doubt Castro meant to protect the wreck. Or that he has men out looking for it. He'll want that stone back. It's too valuable to lose." He threw her another grin. "Why do you think I moved so fast, and brought in extra help for the salvage?"

"I hope the extra 'help' can be trusted." If Castro de Châtelaine was willing to punish his son so harshly for losing one of his ships, what would he do to a storm diver who stole his stone?

"They'll all get a cut of the profits—plus a little extra to ensure their silence. As will you, of course."

"I didn't do much." Compared to what Samuel and the rest of the men had done, the meager amount Luce had salvaged seemed immaterial.

"You found the wreck," Samuel said firmly. "You'll get a cut, the same as always."

"Thank you."

Bones poured what remained of the cider into each of their cups.

"What do you do with it?" Samuel asked Luce. "The money, I mean?"

Luce glanced at Bones. "I'm saving it."

"For what?"

She straightened her shoulders. "For when I go to sea. It—it will break my father's heart, when I go. I won't take his money as well."

Bones suddenly lurched to his feet, brushing the sand from his breeches. "We, good people, are out of cider," he said hastily.

"Time for old Bones to rejoin the festivities." He tottered across the sand, waving in vague farewell.

"Coward," Samuel said grimly, watching him go.

Luce looked sideways at him. "This doesn't have anything to do with our conversation on the *Dove*, does it?"

"You mean the conversation when you told *me* that my fool of a cousin told *you* that disguising yourself as a boy and signing on to a ship was a splendid idea?" Samuel drank deeply of his cider, wiped his mouth angrily on his sleeve. "Of course not."

"He was only trying to help."

"He was only trying to get you killed. Or worse."

Luce sighed. "You're being dramatic, Samuel."

"Dramatic, is it? Because I refuse to let you throw yourself into a life of unimaginable hardship? Of disease, and danger, and violence, and . . . *debauchery*?"

"Debauchery?" Luce could not help it; she laughed.

"Christ." Samuel wiped his palm wearily over his eyes. "You don't have the slightest notion what I'm talking about, do you?"

Luce wondered if the cider had gone to her head. "Debauchery," she repeated, giggling.

"At least promise me this." Samuel set his cup in the sand and reached for her hand. "If you *do* decide to go ahead with this madness, tell me first."

"Why?" Luce had stopped laughing. Samuel's hand was rough, and warm, around hers.

"Because I'm going with you."

"Don't be absurd. What of the *Dove*? Your family?" It was up to him to provide for his mother and younger siblings. "You can't drop everything and leave."

"They'll manage without me. You won't."

Luce bristled. "I'll manage just fine," she said, pulling her hand free of his.

"You might." Samuel lazed back on the cushions, arms bent behind his head. "Until your crewmates discover you're a woman."

"They won't—"

"They will, Luce. They always do. The ship, the sea—it betrays them, every time. And it always ends the same way."

"How?"

A muscle in his jaw flickered. "Badly."

Before his father died, Samuel had worked on privateers and merchant ships out of Portsmouth and Weymouth. He had never told her how many times women had joined his crews, or the details of those "endings." In truth, she wasn't sure she wanted to know.

"Not every tale ends as well as Hannah Snell's," he said, in a gentler tone. "She was the exception, not the rule."

"Let's not discuss this now," Luce said. "After all, it is not as if I'm leaving tomorrow."

"No. Tomorrow you'll be dressed in a blue silk gown, dancing with Morgan de Châtelaine."

"You know I won't be dancing."

He made no reply, staring up, watching the stars as they bloomed.

"Samuel?"

"Hmm?"

"Do you ever feel as though you are not where you are supposed to be?"

He snorted. "All the bloody time. I'm a seaman, which, depending on who you talk to, means I'm neither reckoned among the living nor the dead, on account of my life being in danger every time I push my tub out from the beach. I'm an Englishman who spends most of his time in France, and we're at war. I'm a smuggler, constantly moving from one shore to another, doing my best to avoid the Royal Navy and the revenue men. I'm a storm salvager, under water as often as I'm on top of it, breaking the law every time I meet a potential buyer in the back of some dingy, disreputable pothouse." He shook his head, chuckling. "I spend every day of my life where I'm not supposed to be." The laughter faded from his voice. "Even now, I'm not where I'm supposed to be. A lowly smuggler, sharing cider with the daughter of one of the grandest shipowners in Saint-Malo. And me a fisherman's son from Lulworth." He shook his head ruefully. "What would your father say if he knew you were here with me?"

"I'm not really a Léon," Luce said. She had not meant to say it; perhaps it was the cider, or the way Samuel looked in the firelight. Either way, the words had slipped from her mouth of their own accord.

"I beg your pardon?"

"You didn't know? I thought everyone knew. My father found me in Guernsey when I was two years old. Rescued me, really. My parents had died of typhus and I was all alone."

Samuel had unusual eyes, storm-gray and flecked with gold. Right now, they were wider than Luce had ever seen them.

"You're jesting, surely?" he said.

"Not at all. They were from Bretagne. My parents, I mean. My father made enquiries." Luce glanced up at the sail, white against the blue of the sky. "He was a shipwright, my father. My *real* father, I mean. He'd worked in the dockyards in Brest for five years before traveling to Guernsey with my mother."

"A shipwright . . . ?"

"He repaired fishing boats, for the most part. He fished as well, of course. Maybe even smuggled."

Samuel was still staring at her. "How have you never told me this?"

"It never seemed important." She raised one shoulder, shrugging his gaze away. "Why are you looking at me like that?"

"I'm sorry. I'm just . . . shocked, that's all." He shook his head, looked out over the Manche. "A shipwright's daughter, living under the roof of Jean-Baptiste Léon."

"Perhaps he's not as heartless as you think."

A movement, out on the gloaming water. Luce narrowed her eyes against the fire's light.

"Samuel," she hissed. "*Look.*"

He followed the line her pointed finger made. Swore softly as he focused on what Luce could already see: the black shape of a small boat entering the cove. It moved against wind and tide, smoothly, slowly, the sinister shape of a solitary woman at its tiller.

"Witch boat," Samuel murmured. And then, as the vessel drew nearer: "Is that *her*?"

Luce nodded. She would recognize that tall silhouette, that long pale hair, anywhere. "Yes."

He pushed himself hastily up, grabbed at the blankets. "Should we—"

"She won't trouble us," Luce said. "She knows we mean no harm."

Samuel watched the little boat scrape upon the sand, its lone passenger step out. She looked up the beach, toward the fire, the tusks curling from above her top lip glittering silver in its light.

"Are you entirely certain about that?" Samuel asked uneasily.

"Entirely? No." The Fae Folk were unpredictable. They could be recklessly cruel or sweetly benevolent on the turn of the tide. "But she's never done more than glance this way. She keeps to her cave, and we keep to this one. I don't know why she'd want to harm us now."

Tide-crones were notoriously solitary, much opposed to noise and disturbances. Even the brazen band of jetins kept their distance. Luce watched as the crone made her way up the beach, to where her own cave lay beneath the darkening cliffs.

"It will be dark soon," Samuel said, getting to his feet and brushing the sand from his breeches. "We should get you home."

"Don't you want to return to the gathering?"

"There will be other gatherings." He held out a hand, helped her to her feet. "Let's go."

9

Needle and Bough

Without the fire's light the beach seemed suddenly dark, the narrow strip of lantern light on the sand and the sliver of the rising moon doing little. Luce knew a surge of regret—she should not have stayed so long. Down at the water's edge, the witch-boat was gone. Further out, the horizon softened as a sea fog rolled in to the coast.

"Come on." Samuel, too, seemed edgy. He led the way to the cliff path, then helped Luce up the steep, rocky trail.

"I can manage the rest of the way," Luce said when they reached the top of the cliffs. "You don't need to walk with me."

"I know." He stiffened as the wind lifted from the Manche, ruffling at his hair. "But that's a strange, ill-omened sort of breeze, don't you think? And that fog . . . I have a feeling tonight is no longer a good night to be out of doors."

He fell in behind her as she resumed her walk along the path. There were tree roots and slippery sections of gravel to manage, and she was careful to take her time.

"She spooked you, didn't she?" Luce asked. "The groac'h."

"She didn't spook you?"

"No more than usual."

They followed the winding path along the clifftop. Below and to their left the shore ebbed and flowed, its sands pale in the moonlight, its coves and rock-spills velvety dark. The fog had drawn closer, shrouding the water and the deeper rocks. It was eerily silent.

Luce stopped at the place where the path veered off through the woods toward the malouinière.

"I'll be fine from here," she said. "You really don't have to come the rest of the way—"

"Do you see that?" Samuel was looking out over the shore, eyes narrowed. "There. On the sand. There's something moving."

"You are being ridiculous," Luce said, shoving him slightly to hide her growing unease. She could feel it, too. The sense that all was not right with the world. "Come, Samuel. Let us go."

"Hush," he hissed. He reached for the lantern in her hand, extinguished its glow. "They'll see us."

"Who . . . ?"

She peered along the dusking shore. Was that . . . ? Yes. There *was* something moving down there. Something the size and shape of a man, but moving like something . . . else.

"There are more of them," Samuel whispered. "Look."

Luce let her gaze relax, let the shapes and shadows of the beach speak for themselves, rather than what her eyes assumed them to be. Samuel was right. The narrow cove below, the stretch of open beach beyond, was scattered with the same dark, lumbering forms. The shallows, the water . . . they were there, too. Walking out of the foggy sea, stumbling on the sand. Moving up the beach. Toward the forest.

"Drowned men," Samuel muttered, swallowing hard. "Or their lost souls, at least."

Luce nodded. She had heard the tales—stories of the sea's unclaimed dead walking the shore, the land, at night, though she herself had never seen them before now. From the look on Samuel's face, neither had he.

"Papa always says the dead never hurt the living," she whispered.

"Is he sure about that?"

They exchanged a glance.

Samuel moved first, dropping the lantern and grasping Luce's hand. He sprang toward the forest path, his long legs fast and sure over roots and stones, needle and fallen branch. Sparks of discomfort rose in Luce's feet as she followed him, a prickling that she knew would soon worsen into real pain. She tried to ignore it, tried to keep up with Samuel, swift and surefooted beside her.

"Samuel," Luce panted. "My feet . . ."

"I know. I'm sorry. But if we don't move fast they'll cut us off."

He ran harder, pulling her with him. She did her best to ignore the pain stabbing into her feet, shooting into her legs. Just when she thought she could go no further, Samuel stopped, chest heaving. Following his gaze, Luce saw the sea mist wending pale tendrils through the pines and oaks on either side. And, between it, dark, lumbering figures, their ragged clothing hanging off them in tatters. Looking back, she saw the path behind them was lost in a wash of sea fog, the lurching movements of the drowned men moving eerily in its depths.

"Keep going," Samuel breathed. He broke into a run once more, Luce's hand gripped in his. Luce tried to keep up but lost her footing on the slippery path. She stumbled, fell to one knee. Samuel barely broke stride. He slid one arm beneath her knees and another around her back, hauling her against him as he straightened.

"Hold tight," he breathed.

Luce threw her arms around his neck, clinging to him as he rushed along the path. Her fall, however, the extra moments it had taken for Samuel to scoop her up, the slower pace he could not help but keep now that Luce was in his arms, had cost them. Three dark figures loomed out of the fog ahead, blocking the path.

"Christ," Samuel gasped, chest heaving as he slid to a halt. He whirled around. In every direction, mist. And moving through it, slow and hideous . . .

Luce waited for the sea-dead to spy them. To change their staggering course and come ever closer.

They only lumbered through the woods, silent, slow.

"They're barely looking at us," she whispered. "Do you see? It is like . . . it is like they cannot see us at all."

Samuel swallowed. "What are you implying?"

"I think we should stop. Be still. Let them pass."

He met her eyes, torn. The urge to flee was strong in him still. Luce did not blame him. There was nothing she would have liked more than to be away from the eery, silent woods, the strange fog and its unnatural presences. To be safe within the high walls of Le Bleu Sauvage.

"We can't be certain they won't hurt us," Samuel whispered. "We don't know what they'll do, what they want . . ."

The sailors drew closer, fog swirling around their sloping shoulders and dripping clothes.

"To Hell with it," Samuel muttered. He stepped off the path, moved deeper into the woods.

When there was nothing but fog and pine trees in the darkness around them, he set Luce on her feet. She glanced round, searching for somewhere to hide. An old maritime pine, easily the largest tree in the woods, loomed before them. She dragged Samuel toward it.

No sooner had they reached the trunk than the dead men appeared, trudging through the night. Pushing her back against it, Luce seized the lapels of Samuel's aged overcoat and drew it up to his face, pulling him in close. Perfectly still, perfectly quiet, the rough, brown folds of the coat melding into the bark, they would look, she hoped, like part of the tree.

"Shhhh," she breathed, as the sea-dead shuffled and creaked in the woods around them.

Samuel, eyes glinting in the dark above her, nodded.

As the sound of that slow, morbid shuffling increased—more and more sailors were passing through the forest now—Samuel drew even closer, pinning the edges of his cloak to the bark with his forearms, sealing them both in the darkness. He was nervous. Luce heard it in his rough breath, felt it in the set of his wide shoulders. She smelled his scent, salt and leather, the sweet afterthought of cider. A set of footsteps shuffled closer, and closer. Samuel reached down to slip his knife from his belt, and part of the coat slipped away from the tree.

Luce flinched as a pale, rotting face appeared beside her, so close she could have touched it. A pale, rotting face with empty sockets where eyes had once been. And below it, a tattered, reddish-colored shirt.

She whimpered, her body straining of its own accord, desperate to be as far as possible from that awful, bloated face, familiar despite the ravages of saltwater and decay.

"It's all right." Samuel lifted the coat to the tree once more, hiding the dead sailor from her sight. "I've got you, Luce."

Panic consumed her, stealing reason and sense. She clung to him, pressing her face into the worn linen of his shirt.

"It's the sailor from the wreck," she breathed. Rolling hideously in the water beside her, bloody foam leaking from its nose. "From underneath the *Dove.* This is the *Dauphin*'s crew—"

"I know."

"He's—it's—right there, Samuel," she hissed. "Right next to us."

"It's not." Samuel released the other side of the overcoat, slipping his arm around her, cupping the back of her neck with astonishing tenderness. "It's already moved on. You were right, Luce. They're not interested in us."

She turned her head, expecting to see that face staring sightlessly back at her. Instead, she glimpsed, through the sliver between coat and bark, empty forest, swirls of fog.

"See?" Samuel's palm moved up and down her back, infinitely soothing. "They're leaving."

She nodded against him, unwilling to let him go. "Why are they here?"

"Who knows? I have never seen anything like this before. I already believed something terrible must have happened aboard the *Dauphin*. Now, I am certain of it."

The last of the footsteps in the undergrowth faded. The night settled around them, releasing its dusky breath.

"They're gone," Samuel murmured.

Luce waited for him to release her. Silently ordered herself to release *him*. The *Dauphin*'s haunted crew, the aching in her feet, faded from her mind. She was intensely aware of all the places Samuel's body touched her own: his hand at her nape. His fingers in her hair. His cheek against her brow. His arms, chest and thighs.

She could smell the sea in his hair.

Samuel bent his head still lower, and she felt the scrape of his lips against her neck. A thrill of desire ran through her, but she kept herself perfectly still. Terrified, aware that even the smallest movement might startle him and shatter the spell that had settled over them both. Like the sea mist still drifting through the woods, it was delicate, fragile. The barest breath of wind could break it apart.

Those lips of his touched her neck again and her skin burned deliciously. He nuzzled in deeper, breathing in, she realized, the scent of her hair. She tilted her head back, letting him in, hope and desire and something more, something nameless and wordless, rising within her.

An explosion of stars glimmered through the murky-white pine needles above. Slowly, slowly, Luce ran her hands down Samuel's chest, slipped them beneath his shirt. Found the smooth, bare skin of his chest, the hard muscle beneath.

He drew back and looked down at her, eyes glinting in the half-dark. For one sweet moment Luce thought he would press his mouth to hers. She had imagined kissing him a hundred times. Had dreamed of it, and more, waking in a storm of confusion and longing, her sheets rumpled, her nightgown askew, one hand between her thighs.

Surely he could see it in her face? Surely he knew?

And then, "I'm sorry," Samuel muttered hoarsely. "I can't . . . We can't do this, Luce."

A brisk salt breeze rose up from the Manche, pushing through the trees, catching at that delicate sea mist where it clung to needle and bough, to starlight and dream, ripping it to shreds.

Night had cloaked the malouinière in velvet darkness when Luce returned, the house still and dim.

"Go lightly, tall one," the lutine murmured sleepily as Luce passed. "'Tis quite the risk you take."

Luce nodded grimly and crept across the lawn, careful to avoid the gravel as she rounded the house and came to the servants' door. It was, thankfully, still unlocked; her father's valet or the maids were no doubt still awake, working over last-minute alterations for the ball. Quietly, quietly, she slid into the dimness of the domestiques' hall, closing the door behind her with a melancholy little *click*.

Her face gloomed out of the shadows as she passed the mirror hanging near the coat-hooks: a pale oval, tear-smudged and grim beneath the wild black tangle of her hair. She sighed at the thought of leaving her hair in such a state till morning—it was too late to brush it now—pausing at the bottom of the servants' stairs to remove her shoes. Sand scattered over the worn timber, and she brushed it hastily away, catching at her skirts and climbing the narrow, winding stair to the first floor.

As it turned out, her efforts to remain quiet, and leave the stairs tidy, were entirely wasted.

Gratienne was sitting in a chair on the shadowy landing outside her daughters' bedchambers, a candelabra blazing on the lacquered table beside her. She had been embroidering, her hoop resting in her lap.

Luce's belly iced with dread.

"You are home late," Gratienne said. Candlelight played upon the ruffles of her peignoir, catching at the embroidered butterflies and roses. Her blonde hair, glimmering with strands of silver-gray, was loose. She had been beautiful in her youth, the most beautiful young woman in Saint-Malo, and the shadows smoothed her age away, playing on her fine cheekbones and long, elegant neck—so similar to Veronique's.

"I am sorry, Maman."

"Where were you, Lucinde?" Gratienne rose from her seat, setting her embroidery hoop beside her. Her worried gaze roved over Luce, from the top of her damp, disheveled head to her sandy hem, missing nothing.

Honesty, then.

"I was at the cove, Maman."

"The cove?" Gratienne frowned. "At this time of night?"

"I was swimming, Maman."

"*Swimming?*"

"Yes. There had been a lot of pain since the shoemaker's visit"—*not entirely untrue*—"and I thought the water might help."

"Ah, yes. Your feet." Gratienne glanced down at the offending limbs as though they too were guilty. "How did you get out?"

The time for honesty was over. She could not, would not, reveal the chapel's secrets.

"I climbed over the wall," she lied.

"You *climbed*?" Gratienne's voice rose an octave. The closest door—Charlotte's—opened a crack.

Luce nodded. "It was not so very hard."

"I heard music on the headland," Gratienne said. "Did anybody see you?"

"No, Maman."

"What would people think, Lucinde?" Gratienne demanded. "What would they say if they saw the daughter of Jean-Baptiste Léon wandering about in the dusk like a common fishwife? And let us not even mention what might have happened if someone *had* seen you—this countryside is full of rough people—fishermen and smugglers—ill-mannered men who would take one look at you and . . . and . . ." she trailed off, uncertain. "It is not *safe*."

What would your father say if he knew you were here with me?

A second door clicked open. Veronique, her hair like spun gold in the candlelight. Like Gratienne, she was careful not to touch it, adhering to Jean-Baptiste's unswerving rule.

"I'm sorry, Maman," Luce said. "It's just—I cannot bear to be contained all the time. I need to be outside. I-I cannot help it."

"You must learn to help it," Gratienne said, not ungently.

Veronique and Charlotte were no longer attempting to hide their eavesdropping. They had opened their doors wide and were gaping at Luce from behind their mother's back.

"You are no longer a child, Lucinde," Gratienne said. "Your father spoils you, it is true, but at some point you must understand that every poor decision you make reflects badly upon him. Upon *all* of us. Think of your sisters. If word of such unseemly behavior was to get out, it might affect their chances of securing advantageous matches. Everything we have worked for, planned for, trained for, will be undone."

Luce looked guiltily down, her gaze resting on the garment in her mother's hands. It was not, she realized, a new piece, but one she knew well. The baptismal gown was Gratienne's most beloved possession. Small and creamy-pale, it had been worn by Gratienne herself, and her mother, and *her* mother before her, a long line of noble women held safely in their mother's arms while they received the water of God. Veronique and Charlotte had both worn the gown for their baptisms, while Luce, of course, had not. As children, her sisters had taunted Luce about this fact. Indeed,

Charlotte had done so with particular vehemence, so much so that even now the sight of the tiny white gown filled Luce with remembered loneliness and shame.

"It hurts me to do this," Gratienne said. "But I fear I have no choice. You must be punished." She took a bracing breath. "When we attend the ball at Le Loup Blanc tomorrow night, you shall stay behind."

The silence that followed was a plunge into a sea of ice.

"*Maman!*" Veronique exploded at last, as though bursting, lungs screaming, to the surface. She stared between her mother and Luce, horrified. "You cannot mean it! It is too cruel, too—"

"I do not make this decision lightly, Veronique," Gratienne said wearily. "You must think of what might have happened, who might have seen—"

"But Maman," Veronique said again, one final valiant effort. "Luce's new gown. It is so beautiful. She *must* wear it!"

"The ball is all anyone will be talking about for months," Charlotte added. "You cannot expect her to miss it."

"I have made my decision," Gratienne told her daughters. "Luce will not attend. Now, please. Return to your beds."

There was a creak and groan as Jean-Baptiste's door opened. He stepped onto the landing, the floral brocade on his dressing gown lustrous in the candlelight.

"What is all the commotion about?" he roared. "Can't a man rest in his own house?" He glared at all four women. "And did I just hear someone say that Lucinde will not be attending the ball?"

"I am astonished, Luce," Veronique whispered. "Truly. You climbed the *wall*? Whyever would you *do* such a thing?"

"*How* she could do it is the question you should be asking," Charlotte, pressed close between her sisters, hissed. She glanced pointedly at Luce's feet. "Climbing a wall that high would be difficult for anyone, much less—"

"Hush, Cee," Veronique cautioned. "Maman's getting very angry now . . ."

All three sisters, clustered against their mother's chamber door, stilled. Jean-Baptiste's voice, a low, displeased rumble on the other side of the gold-edged oak, faded as Gratienne cut across him.

"She is wild, Jean-Baptiste. Wild and wilful. Wandering down to the shore alone and coming home in the dark without a care in the world—"

Luce, her face pressed close to the cool wood, might have laughed had circumstances been different. If the terror of the *Dauphin*'s ghostly crew, and the confusion, the hurt at . . . at what had happened after were not still so raw.

"What if someone had seen her?" Gratienne demanded. "What would they have thought?"

Lucinde imagined her father's shrug. "The girl loves the sea. And why should she not? Hasn't it given us everything? All that you hold dear has come by its grace. Besides, you said it yourself—no one saw her. She got home safely. I'll have the portier inspect the walls, patch up any weaknesses. It will not happen again."

"You have spoiled her for too long," Gratienne said. "No good will come of it."

"I hardly think—"

"You cannot tell me that you deem it appropriate for Luce to be out alone at night?"

"Of course not, but—"

"You are too soft on her," Gratienne said. "Indulging her whims, bringing in tutors, filling her head with nonsense. And now this ship you have gifted her—why, Jean-Baptiste? You know as well as I that it will never truly be hers. You are allowing her dreams and hopes that can never be—you are leading her toward disappointment."

Jean-Baptiste was silent.

"I know you love her," Gratienne said, softer. "But you know as well as I that Lucinde must marry. Must find her match and do her duty, as Veronique and Charlotte must do. As we *all* must do." Was that a trace of bitterness in Gratienne's voice? Had she once dreamed of something more? Something of her own? "It is her duty as your daughter. As a *Léon*."

"And who are the Léons? Royalty?" Jean-Baptiste scoffed. "We are merchants, Gee. Traders and sailors. It was generations of hard work that got us here, not blood or lineage. Never forget that."

"Speak for yourself!" Gratienne seethed. "*My* father was a baron. And I expect at least one of our daughters to make a match worthy of him!"

Luce winced. This difference in opinion—her mother's staunch pride in her nobility, her father's steady faith in his roots, in hard work, in risk and daring—was a tender spot between her parents.

"Worthy of his high blood and low means, you mean. Do not forget why your father was so quick to agree to my marrying you, Gee," Jean-Baptiste said coldly. "A title does not equal a fortune."

"I am doing *everything* I can to ensure our daughters secure good, strong marriages," Gratienne cried. "Just think of the damage Luce's behavior tonight could do to their prospects! What if someone had seen her?"

"No one did," Jean-Baptiste repeated patiently. "And I told you, I will speak to Luce. In the meantime, you will not punish her this way. Let her go to the ball, mon amour. Perhaps attending such a gathering, in such fine company"—there was the barest hint of derision in his tone—"would be beneficial to your plans."

"Perhaps," Gratienne said grudgingly. She sounded calmer now, and Luce wondered if the danger might have passed. But then . . .

"And what of *your* plans?" Gratienne demanded. "Do you not

wish to see *all* your daughters wed? Your line secure? Your fortune in trustworthy hands?"

"I wish to see my daughters happy," Jean-Baptiste said. "Their happiness is more important to me than any marriage, any line. And I do not think this constant obsession of yours—this competition you have fostered between them—is doing any of them good."

Gratienne's voice was deathly quiet. "What do you mean by that?"

"Well, just look at Charlotte," Jean-Baptiste said.

Luce felt her sister tense beside her.

"That girl's jealousy will be her undoing," Jean-Baptiste continued. "You want to worry over one of our daughters? Worry over *her.*"

"Charlotte has done nothing wrong!"

"She pecks at Luce like a crow at a baby mouse. Always has. I may have spoiled Luce, but she has a soft heart. She does not deserve such treatment."

"There you go again. Taking Luce's part, as you always do!"

"Someone has to," Jean-Baptiste roared. "Why, between the three of you, she is poked and prodded mercilessly. It is jealousy, nothing more."

"Jealousy?" Gratienne, too, was furious.

"Indeed. Luce cannot help being beautiful."

"*Beautiful?* I hardly think—"

"She is," Jean-Baptiste said firmly. "She is more beautiful than Charlotte, more beautiful than even Veronique. She cannot help being the loveliest, any more than Charlotte can help being the plainest."

Charlotte went even stiller, if such a thing were possible. Luce felt a surge of overwhelming sadness for her sister. By chance or choice, Charlotte was never first. Never the eldest, never the youngest. Never the most beautiful, never the most intriguing, never the most talented. Her voice was not the sweetest, her skin—with its smattering of freckles—was not the purest, her waist was not the smallest. She was favored by neither her father (that being Luce's privilege) nor her mother (Veronique's). She was always, to put it quite simply, in the middle.

"We should go," Veronique whispered, her face troubled. She reached for Charlotte's sleeve, tugged it gently. Charlotte ignored her.

"You spoil Lucinde!" Gratienne's rage seeped through the keyhole and beneath the closed door, as relentless as water in a sinking ship.

"I do not."

"You do, and you *know* it!"

"Very well then," Jean-Baptiste said, his voice frighteningly soft. "I *do* spoil her. And why shouldn't I? You weren't there, Gee. You didn't see her on that God-forsaken beach. Everything she knew, everything she loved, taken from her. No child should have to endure what she did. From the moment I scooped her into my arms, I swore I would do everything in my power to ensure her happiness. In truth, it means more to me than—"

"Your other daughters' futures?"

Most men would have demanded their wives' silence long before, stifling conversations like this—filled with honesty and judgment—as a captain might order his crew to strike a sail. Luce's father had been an exceptional captain, but he never was, and never would be, like most men. Even so, she wondered how far his patience would stretch.

"I'll speak to Luce, Gee. I *promise*," was all he said. "But make no mistake, I will not stand by and see her punished. She has suffered enough."

He moved, slippers scuffing gently as he neared the door. At once the sisters broke from their places, hurrying toward their bedchambers. Luce slipped into hers, but not before she glanced back and saw the look Charlotte threw her before she did the same. A look so cold and hateful it sent shivers up her spine.

10

Shallows

Luce was in Veronique's bedchamber, bathing in the huge copper tub—brought to the first floor, with no small amount of difficulty, by the laquais—when Veronique swept into the room, effervescent with excitement.

"I was thinking I could help with your hair tonight, Luce," she said. "If you'd like." The events of the night before had taken no toll on Luce's oldest sister. Perfumed and powdered, she was as fresh and pink as a rose in her chemise and pink-ruffled peignoir as she happily checked her reflection in one of the three mirrors, festooned with an alarming amount of pink silk taffeta, on her dressing table. "Morgan promised to dance with all three of us tonight. We must look our best."

Morgan. The very sound of his name conjured a confusion of thoughts and emotions, each one warring against those that arose whenever she thought about what had passed between her and Samuel in the woods the night before. The memory of his rejection of her, the shame of it, was like a knife to her heart.

Instead, she focused on Morgan, his cheek pale against the *Dauphin*'s shattered hull as she swam out to rescue him. The dark gleam in his eyes as he leaned against the figurehead on the *Lucinde*.

His long finger, slow and luxurious against her wrist.

Her blood surged at the memory.

She stood up in the bath, the silky water pouring from her skin and hair as Nanette took a towel from the stand before the little fireplace and wrapped it around her shoulders.

Veronique grinned. She turned to Nanette. "Go and help Anna-Marie, won't you, Nanette? She's bringing fresh water for Charlotte's bath." She gazed about the room, small hands bunched on hips. "Where *is* Charlotte? I've not seen her all afternoon."

"I'll find her," Nanette said with a sigh, taking up an empty pitcher and leaving the room.

Veronique helped Luce into her undergarments and peignoir, then sat her before the sunny window and brushed out her hair.

"What kind of style woud you like?" Veronique asked, running her fingers through the long dark lengths.

"I really don't know," Luce said. "Charlotte was going to help me. But now . . ."

"Don't let her ruin this for you," Veronique said firmly. "You are coming with us tonight, and that is that."

The warmth of the sun, the rhythmic slosh of falling water as Anna-Marie and Nanette tripped back and forth with hot water for the bath, and the delicious tickle of Veronique's hands on her scalp and shoulders as she lifted Luce's hair this way and then that, muttering to herself about curls and ribbons, hair powder and pins, soon caused Luce to relax. Her uneasiness returned, however, the moment Charlotte came into the room.

"Where have *you* been?" Veronique demanded.

"I went for a walk," Charlotte replied.

"You will make us late."

"You and I both know it will be *you* who does that, Vee." Charlotte waited patiently while Nanette helped her undress, then stepped into the bath.

"Your hair really is too long, you know, Luce," Veronique mused. "Perhaps we should cut it? It would make drying it so much easier."

"I'd rather we didn't," Luce told her sister warily. She was fond of her hair, the dark, thick waves that fell to her hips. Unbidden, the memory of Morgan's fingers, buried in the long, wet strands as he kissed her, sprang into her mind.

Did he remember that kiss? Would he want to kiss her again?

She wanted very much to know.

"Whatever you prefer," Veronique said good-naturedly. "That's as dry as we're likely to get it, though. Let's put it up." She led Luce to the little stool set before the dressing table, its lacquered mahogany bristling with Veronique's expansive collection of powders, perfumes, and pots.

"You have sand in your hair, mademoiselle," Nanette said, as she lathered Charlotte's hair.

"Do I?" Charlotte glanced at the pink-framed mirror, met Luce's eyes in its reflection. "It was windy on the headland." She tilted her head, inspecting what Veronique had done with Luce's hair. "That's too high, Vee. Here, let me . . ."

She finished her bath, dressed in her underclothes and morning gown, and took the brush from Veronique's hand. "You need to do it like this, see? Luce and I had it all planned."

She twisted and looped Luce's hair, creating a glossy black construction at the back of her head. "Voilà!"

Veronique nodded her approval. "That is perfect, Cee. How clever you are."

Nanette stepped forward, pins at the ready.

"Thank you, Cee," Luce said to her sister's reflection.

Perhaps Charlotte had forgiven her, after all.

Late in the afternoon, when the sisters had finished powdering their faces and pinning their hair (or, in everyone but Luce's case, powdering both face *and* hair) and stepped into silk stockings and ribbon garters, petticoats, panniers, and stays, they assembled in Gratienne's bedchamber, where the ball gowns, freshly pressed and readied that morning, were waiting. One by one the maids brought them out from the dressing room: rose-pink, sky-blue, and . . .

"But where is your dress, Luce?" Veronique asked.

Luce peered into her mother's dressing room. Nanette was rifling through the gowns hanging in the enormous armoire, her face a picture of confused dismay. "It's not here!"

"Not here?" Veronique, already lacing her pink underskirt, came to look. "Whatever do you mean, Nanette? How can it not be here?"

"It's gone," Nanette said in despair. She met Luce's eyes. "I swear, Mademoiselle Lucinde, I put it right here this morning . . ."

"It's all right, Nanette," Luce said, squeezing the maid's hand. "I believe you." A cold kind of knowing was seeping into her, darkening her heart. She glanced at Charlotte. Her sister was carefully arranging her pale blue underskirt over her panniers, her face impassive.

"It is not all right!" Veronique was holding her arms behind her as Anna-Marie helped her shrug into her open dress. "A dress does not simply disappear." She twisted her shoulders, allowing the heavy silk to fall into place. "Go and find Maman, Anna-Marie. Quickly."

Luce glanced again at Charlotte. She had hung her gown on Gratienne's silk dressing screen and was arranging the long pleats at the back. "Don't just stand there, Nanette," she said to the stricken maid. "Come and help me. There is no point in all three of us standing about."

Luce's parents came into the room, with Anna-Marie and Madeleine close behind.

Gratienne had already donned her silver-gray gown, and powdered her cheeks and hair. A glorious silver feather arched above her head, its base nestled in a clutch of large diamond-studded hair pins. "The dress is missing, you say?"

"It is gone, madame." Nanette wringed her hands helplessly. "I cannot explain it."

"Well, find it!" Jean-Baptiste was wearing a powdered wig and his best suit, a sleek affair with lashings of golden embroidery, and a lace jabot and cuffs. At his tone, the three maids burst into action, rifling through the dressing room with renewed vigor. Gratienne took over from Nanette, pinning Charlotte into her dress. Veronique, her stays peeking out between her unpinned gown, helped.

"Careful, Vee!" Charlotte snapped. "You will pin me instead of the stays!"

"I found the shoes," Nanette said, emerging from the dressing room with a pair of deep blue slippers. "But the gown is still missing, Monsieur Léon."

"How can a dress go missing?" Jean-Baptiste was growing angry. "What do I pay you domestiques for, if not to keep order in my house? Find it—or you will be paying for it yourselves. And mark me, it will take you a long, *long* time to make good your debt."

Luce looked at the crestfallen Nanette, at the other maids, desperately searching. Her disappointment, bitter though it was, was as nothing compared to what they would endure—the terrible burden of a debt they could never hope to repay, or, even worse, the loss of their position completely.

"It was me," she blurted.

Seven faces turned to her in shock.

"*You?*" Veronique demanded.

"Yes." Luce fumbled for a reasonable-sounding story. "I took the dress out this morning to—to admire it." She glanced at her mother's face, dark with disapproval, and an idea came to her. "But my hands were dirty—I'd been looking at soil—"

Charlotte made a face. "*Soil*?"

"Yes. Monsieur Daumard and I had been discussing the relationship between plants and the way different soils help or hinder their growth. His microscope has finally arrived from Paris, and I wanted to fetch some samples for our next lesson." It was only half a lie. Monsieur Daumard *had* been teaching her about soils just yesterday, when he mentioned the arrival of the microscope. "And I . . . I ruined the dress—marred it with my hands. I felt so terrible, I hid it."

Below, the old ship's bell clanged.

"Well, fetch it," Veronique said. "It is almost time to leave!"

"It is too late for that," Gratienne said wearily. "We cannot clean and press the dress now. There is no time."

"Well, fetch another gown, mon trésor." Jean-Baptiste looked distraught. "Surely there are others? What is the point of trading in silk if my daughter has nothing to wear?"

"Luce can wear one of mine," Veronique offered.

"Or mine," Charlotte added.

"That is kind of you both," Luce said, nodding gratefully. She wanted more than anything to go. To see the gardens at Le Loup Blanc, the steps leading from the house down to the Rance, glimmering with starlight and torches. To hear the music as she stepped from the carriage, and see Morgan de Châtelaine in his finery, greeting his guests, handsome as the night. Wearing one of her sisters' gowns would not be the same—not at all—but it was far better than missing out completely.

"What of your mask, mademoiselle?" Nanette asked in a small voice.

"Is it not there, Nanette?"

The chambermaid shook her head. She looked as though she might cry.

Luce went to her mother's dressing room and riffled among the thick swathes of skirts hanging to the floor. There was no sign of the mask.

"Surely we have others?" Jean-Baptiste asked of his wife, his daughters. "This is hardly the first masque to be held in Saint-Malo."

Veronique shook her head. "Anna-Marie always pulls my masks apart and uses the feathers and jewels for other things."

"And mine are all back at the town house," Charlotte said.

"As are mine," Gratienne added, with a sigh.

Disappointment was a stone on Luce's chest. That finely crafted sliver of satin was the only reason she had been bold enough to attend the ball at all. Without the anonymity it would afford her, she would be terrifyingly visible—especially as every other face would be hidden. Tears tightened her throat, but she forced herself to speak lightly. "Well, that settles it. I really shall have to stay behind."

"Stay . . . *behind*?" Veronique repeated the words slowly, as though Luce had spoken in a foreign language.

"You cannot be serious, Lucinde," Charlotte said.

"I cannot attend a masque without a mask," Luce told her reasonably. Would Morgan notice that she was not there? Would he be sorry he could not show her his father's curiosities? "In truth, I would prefer to stay here."

"*Prefer* it?" Veronique looked like she might be sick. She turned to her mother, appalled. "Maman, make her stop!"

"I find I am in no mood for balls, or people, now," Luce lied smoothly. "Besides, you will all be late if you do not leave at once."

"Oh, let her stay, if she wants," Charlotte said, impatient. "She will only hide in a corner all night, anyway. It's not as though she will *dance*."

There was an awkward silence as the weight of Charlotte's cruel words settled over the room. Luce looked at the blue silk slippers lying forlorn on the carpet, and blinked away her tears.

"Well?" Charlotte said, defiant. "We were all thinking it."

When the sounds of the carriage finally faded down the drive, Luce burst from the house and into the chapel, throwing the battered overcoat over her peignoir and pulling on her hat and boots. She hurried towards the comfort of the cove, her stockingless feet burning in the rough leather of the boots, the bones shrieking in protest at the pace.

The pain rose with every step, a storm against the earth.

Even so, she did not slow until she reached the edge of the cliffs, catching at a pine to steady herself while she caught her breath. Below, the beach, empty but for hulking lumps of rock, dark with lichen, and a smattering of pebbles and weed.

And there, drifting in the cool, greenish shallows, easing gently back and forth in its own dreamy dance, was her blue gown.

Charlotte's last words, her coldness and cruelty, came back to Luce in a rush. She had disappeared that morning, and said she had been walking. Nanette had found sand in her hair, and she had looked up, met Luce's eyes in the mirror.

Could she . . . could she have taken the dress?

Her sister could be harsh, it was true. Jealous and quick to anger. But was she truly capable of this?

Luce slipped and scrabbled down the rocky cliff path, nearly falling to her knees as the slope gave way to sand. A cloud of sea campion nodded their white-petals at her sadly as she pushed herself up, not caring that her tricorn had fallen from her head, and her hair, so carefully arranged, had come loose. That the shimmering pink powder Veronique had smoothed across her cheeks, the red paste she had dabbed so carefully upon her lips, was brushing away. She stumbled down to the water, knelt in the shallows, and cradled the dress in her arms.

How could Charlotte have done such a thing? Did she truly care so little?

Luce cried, then. Held the dress against her while the gray-green water lapped consolingly over her thighs. Her mask, too, was there, the ribbons floating sadly in the shadows A silver gull flew overhead, its wretched cry echoing across the water. As though it, too, felt her pain.

When Luce's tears were spent, she wiped her ruined face and slumped back in the water, her morning gown floating around her.

Just a dress, she told herself, taking a shaky breath. *Just a silly dress. Pieces of silk sewn together, lace and trim and lining. The loss of it doesn't matter.*

But the loss *did* matter.

Losing *Charlotte* mattered.

"What's this? A little seamaid crying in the shallows?"

Startled at the sound of a voice close by—Luce had thought she was quite alone—she looked up.

The groac'h stood on the beach behind her.

This close, the tide-woman was much younger than Luce had supposed; younger, even, than Gratienne. Her hair was as long as Luce's and just as wild, a shade of blonde so pale and silvery that it glowed like the moon. She wore a ragged chemise, its sleeves rolled up to her elbows, with a bodice made of what could only be fishes' scales—thousands of them, sewn cunningly together. Her rust-colored skirts were tattered, overlaid with swathes of ruined fishing net cinched roughly around her waist with a piece of old rope. Her feet were bare. Yet it was her face that caught Luce's gaze and held it. Her eyes, glinting like the silver coins she had once found on the beach after a winter storm. Her mouth, where two of her front teeth jutted from between her lips, great curving shards of bone like walrus tusks.

"I'm sorry," Luce sniffed, brushing at her tears on her cheeks. "I did not mean to disturb you." Out of respect, she had always kept as much distance as possible between herself and the fae woman, avoiding the entrance to her cave and the patch of sand where she was wont to rest her little witch-boat. She glanced again at those extraordinary teeth and went to rise. "I will go."

"There's no need." The groac'h stepped into the water, her bare feet, sun-browned and rather small, surprisingly ordinary. "And you did not disturb me."

Her voice was gentle, despite those eldritch tusks. Luce half expected her to reach out and help Luce to her feet. Instead, the fae sat down in the water beside her, careless of the cold and her rust-colored skirts.

Luce stared at her, mouth hanging open.

". . . You will get cold." She finally managed to say. "And wet."

The tide-woman tipped her head back and laughed, a beautiful, liquid sound. "Late to be worrying about that, isn't it?"

Despite herself, despite everything, Luce smiled. "I suppose it is."

"And too late for this, too." The shore-woman reached out, touched the blue silk, drowned and mournful in Luce's arms, with a gentle hand. "*This* was not meant to be ruined by salt and water. This was meant for candlelight and dancing. For hope, and jealous glances, and joy. What thievery has taken place, that it has instead been lost to the sea?"

Jean-Baptiste had oft said that the groac'h was as wild as she was dangerous. She would sell a sailor a fair wind in one breath, and in the next sink her terrifying tusks into his flesh, dragging him to the bottom of the Manche. Or, perhaps worse, into the cold, dank recesses of her cave. Luce tried to reconcile this image with the eloquent shore-woman sitting beside her, and failed.

"Perhaps it made someone *too* jealous," she said.

"I see." The groac'h was quiet a moment. "You meant to wear it to the gathering at the white wolf's house this night. Yes?"

Luce glanced across at her. "You know about that?"

"My child, *everyone* knows about that." A sideways glance from those storm-silver eyes. "I take it you still wish to go?"

Luce glanced at the floating dress. It was spectacularly ruined, well beyond the point of salvage.

"The dress is spoiled," she said slowly. "It cannot be saved."

"It is," the shore-woman said reasonably. "And yet, I ask again: Do you still wish to go?"

"Is that . . . is that even possible?" Of all the fae folk on the shore, the tide-woman was said to be among the most powerful. She could pluck a wind from nothing with a flick of her wrist; she could summon a storm for spite. But what else was she capable of?

"Anything is possible when sorrow meets sea."

Luce frowned. "When sorrow meets sea?"

"Your tears." The groac'h gestured to Luce's red-rimmed eyes, then the water. "Your tears fell into the sea. There is magic in such meetings."

Something flickered in the air, in the water. A low thrum of promise, of magic.

"I will ask you one more time. Do you wish to go? Or . . ." The fae woman pursed her lips. "Perhaps you'd prefer to stay here. Light another fire, and wait for the storm diver to find you?"

"No," Luce said, too quickly. Samuel's rejection in the woods was a constant sting in her heart. And now Charlotte had betrayed her, sharp as a blade in her back. Beneath the pain, beneath the loss, something else simmered.

Why shouldn't Luce have a little happiness?

Why *shouldn't* she go to the ball?

"Thank you," she said firmly. "I would like to go to the ball. Very much."

She pushed herself to her feet, ignoring the pain, thinking only of Morgan de Châtelaine's black eyes, his wicked smile.

"It's decided then," the groac'h said. She, too, rose water shimmering in her bodice of scales, at the ends of her silvery hair. "We must move quickly. The tide is about to turn."

Luce was suddenly nervous. "What must I do?"

"Take off that overcoat, for one."

Luce shrugged out of the sodden coat, and gave it, dripping and awkward, to the tide-woman.

"And the pretty robe."

Luce slipped out of her peignoir, handed it over, and stood uncertainly in her underclothes. The blue gown floated still in the shallows, its skirt brushing her ankles.

"Should I—"

"Hush now, child," the shore-woman said. She closed her wondrous silver eyes. "Tears and blue silk," she murmured. "Tears and blue silk."

The sun was low, the world silvering toward sunset. A trio of gulls flew overhead, farewelling the day. Luce, shivering, began to doubt her recent choices.

"Perhaps I—"

"There." The shore-woman opened her eyes and smiled approvingly. "Hold your breath, child."

A moment of panic. Those strange, silver eyes, those outlandish teeth—

No time to finish the thought; the groac'h seized Luce by the shoulders and pushed her backward into the sea.

PART 2

This done, she gave her a pair of glass slippers, the prettiest in the whole world.

—Charles Perrault, "Cinderella"

11

Sea Slippers

The world spun hard on its axis, whirling like the globe in Papa's study used to when Luce, too young to understand its worth, sent it spinning. At the same time—absurdly, impossibly—time itself seemed to stop. She was falling backward, arms flailing in panic, dream-slow. Her hands became a child's again, small and plump, though now there were strange webs of fragile skin glowing between her fingers. Beyond them, the sky was moving rapidly, turning and turning, although it wasn't the sky anymore. It was her father's globe: islands and sea serpents, archipelagos and continents, a blur of ancient color beneath the endless wheeling of the stars.

The water, when she finally hit it, stole her breath. She gasped, tried to right herself and stand, but there was no longer sand beneath her. The water was suddenly, unreasonably deep, and she was sinking like a stone, black hair trailing through splayed fingertips.

Silence, and softness. She heard singing, low and sweet, a tune she did not recognize. Light and dark at once. And still she sank, down and down. Fear caught her in its teeth. She struggled against it, against the relentless weight bearing her down, and felt something soft beneath her. Silk billowed, rippling like water.

The blue dress.

It cradled Luce as gently as a mother. Folded her unto itself, held her in its cool embrace. And still the groac'h sang, gentle as a lullaby.

Time ceased to be of consequence. How long had she drifted in blue, caught between the surface and the seafloor? How long had it been since she had breathed? Minutes? Hours? Her eyes fluttered open, realization causing the last of her breath to bubble out of her lungs. The surface seemed too far, the distance too great, the weight of the blue dress dragging her down, down, toward the deep.

A hand broke the surface above. Luce reached up, grasped it. The sea surged at her back, lifting her, pushing her. She stumbled onto the shore, gasping. The beach, the Manche, the sky—even the groac'h—looked exactly as they had when she had fallen into the water. Luce, however, was utterly dry. Her hair, her skin, as fresh and clean as if she had just bathed in scented oils and powdered herself in the sun. She looked slowly down. In place of her sodden underclothes, she wore a gown of blue silk. It too was dry and shining-smooth, as though Nanette or Anne-Marie had pressed it only moments before.

She croaked, a wordless little sound of shock. Struggled to make sense of what she was seeing.

It was the blue gown. And yet, it was not. *This* gown was darker, like the Manche at midnight. Pricks of silvery thread glimmered across its wide skirts like stars. Engageantes of black lace stitched with silver swung from its elbow-length sleeves, catching at the last of the day's light. The stomacher shimmered with scallop shells and fine, black pearls. Indeed, the entire dress was pearlescent, shining subtly like the inside of one of the rare seashells in Papa's study, pink, mauve and gleaming sea-green.

It was magnificent.

"What did you—how did you—?" Words had abandoned Luce.

"Tears and blue silk," the shore-woman said. She tilted her head, considering. "You need shoes."

"What?" Luce squiggled her toes in the dry sand, found that they were quite bare. "Oh. I suppose I do." Her heart sank. She was yet to forget last week's torturous appointment with the shoemaker. Veronique and Charlotte had confidently bared their feet, discussing the latest designs, the daintiest dancing steps. Luce's feet, however, had produced a predictable reaction from the shoemaker: revulsion, quickly followed by pity.

"May I see them?" The groac'h's voice was gentle.

Luce bowed her head, shame rising as the fae woman knelt in the sand before her, her moon-colored hair gleaming in the fading light. She pushed Luce's heavy skirts back, ran long, cool fingers over her feet.

"What have they done to you?" she whispered.

"I cannot help it," Luce said hastily. "I know they're ugly. . . ."

The tide-woman straightened, met Luce's eye. "Not ugly," she said, gesturing to her tusks. "Just different. Is there pain?"

Luce nodded. "Though . . . they hurt less when I swim in the sea."

"Then you shall wear the sea."

She began to hum. A spiral of seawater rose from the shallows, glittering and swirling. The song changed, and the water broke into two, snaking around Luce's feet, coiling and twisting like twin serpents as they took on familiar shapes: a delicately pointed toe, a graceful arch, a plump little heel. Luce rose slightly as an invisible force lifted her gently from the sand. And then the water hardened, clinging to her skin, as smooth and shining as glass.

"There," the groac'h said, with a satisfied nod.

Luce held up her skirts. The slippers shone mirror-bright, like diamonds or ice. And yet they were quite comfortable—it barely felt as if she were wearing shoes at all. She took a tentative step, and then another.

"No pain?" the groac'h asked.

Luce shook her head in wonder. "No pain." She took another step, savoring the marvelous, cloud-soft comfort. She would be able to walk gracefully into Le Loup Blanc tonight and move about with elegance and freedom. She would be able to dance.

What would you say if I stole you away at the ball?

"How?" She stared at the groac'h, as grateful as she was bewildered. "How did you do this?"

The tide-woman only smiled. "We should hurry," she said. "The tide has found its rhythm. It will not wait."

She began to sing again.

The sea was waiting this time, tense and expectant. The sea birds had stilled. Even the stars, early and earnest, seemed to halt their shining.

Luce sensed it before she saw it: a rumbling in the seafloor, a disturbance beyond the rocks edging the cove. The water there foamed and roiled, growing more and more agitated, as though a serpent of mythic magnitude was rising from the depths, unfurling its great scaled body, churning the sea with its tail.

The tide-woman's song grew in strength, reaching notes Luce had never known existed. Jagged shadows breached the water's churning surface. A mast, stark against the violet sky, and the broad, curved sweep of a ship's shattered hull, blackened with age. A hunk of ancient deck floated in the chaos of its counterparts: a cracked forecastle, a slab of stern, its cracked timbers gaping like broken teeth.

"Damn my soul," Luce breathed.

The original wreck had been a caravel; a pretty little Spanish ship, all dashing curves. As Luce watched, the pieces of wreckage began to *move,* shards of sea-worn timber clipping and catching. Assembling themselves into something *other,* something new and darkly beautiful.

A black boat, unlike anything Luce had ever seen. Long and low, with inky sails and an elegant little cabin, its seats covered with cushions of midnight velvet. Inky draperies flowed gently in the evening breeze, glittering as though they had been embroidered with stars. Luce was reminded of the river barges she had seen in old paintings; sumptuous vessels made for royalty. A queen of stars and dreams, she thought, might sail in something like this.

"It will take you to the Le Loup Blanc," the groac'h said.

Luce shook herself. She was asleep, surely; had drifted into the exhausted slumber that comes when tears are spent. Even now she lay on the sand, wrapped in the ruined silk dress. Any moment, now, she would wake, cold and disoriented, and begin the long, slow trudge back to the house.

"You are not dreaming," the groac'h said mildly. "And now, are you ready? The tide will not wait."

Luce regarded the beautiful boat before her. The de Châtelaine estate was set high upon the banks of the Rance. To get there, she would need to sail past Saint-Malo and Saint-Servan. The waters surrounding both would be crowded with moored vessels of every size, as well as seamen rowing to and from the quays.

"Won't people see me?"

"Not if you don't want them to."

It would be dark soon. Only a fool or a Malouin would dare to enter the port at night, Papa often said.

"But will it be safe?"

"There is nowhere safer. But heed me, now." The tide-woman grew serious. "When the tide reaches its peak and turns, the magic will fade. That is when you must return."

Luce looked at the water, the color of the lichen on the rocks, the impressions in the sand. The tide had turned half an hour ago, perhaps less, at almost the same moment she had heard the ship's bell toll the end of the evening's second petite watch. An hour of daylight yet, and five hours more before the tide reached its zenith. "That will be more than enough time." Her heart pattered at the thought of seeing Morgan again. "The tide will be highest two hours after midnight. I shall leave before then."

The groac'h nodded. "Make sure that you do." She raised a hand, and the sea surged forward, bringing the little black boat close to the sand. A neat ramp appeared, and Luce stepped aboard.

"Why are you helping me?" she asked. She knew the way of such things—had heard the stories of those who had been foolish enough to take gifts from the Fae without understanding the risks. There was always a reason. Always a cost.

"I know what it is to cry and have no one but the sea there to listen," the fae said quietly. "And because too much has been stolen. Something must be given back. It is the tide's way."

Luce frowned at the mysterious words. "What do you mean?"

"No time, no time," the groac'h said, pushing the little boat smoothly out into the water "The faster it ebbs, the quicker the magic will weaken. You must not linger." She pursed her lips, and blew gently through her tusks. A night-charmed wind billowed in the black sails. "I will ask the wind to watch over you."

"And I you," Luce said. "I—thank you."

The shore was slipping away, fading into the shadows. A moment of panic as the night swept its cool arms around her.

"Do not fear the darkness," the groac'h called. "It will show you the way."

Luce stood in the stern, watching as the cove, the lone figure of the fae, melded into the hazy smudge of the coast. She had questions, and plenty of them. Reservations, too. She had sensed no evil in the shore-woman, no ill intent. If anything, she had seemed more human, more gentle, than any of the fae creatures Luce had met. She wondered anew why her father and the fishermen feared her so. Perhaps it was because they had never deigned to speak with her. Perhaps they saw her tusks, her sea-foam hair and strangeness, and had decided for themselves that she was dangerous and cruel.

It would not be the first time men had judged a woman so.

A silvery hand mirror, its twisted handle dark with age, and a half-mask—cleverly made of black lace, dark pearls, and the same silvery shells as the dress's stomacher—lay on a cushion inside the barge's little cabin. Curious, Luce settled herself and raised the mirror to her face. A stranger looked back. The woman's dark hair was piled atop her head and adorned with ropes of fine, black pearls, while a thick, elegant curl trailed over one shoulder. There were more pearls at her throat and her wrists, and the iridescence of seashells shone on her eyelids and cheeks, her shoulders and collar bones. She looked otherworldly; a princess of the old tales, her blue eyes rimmed in black, her lashes long and thick.

Luce set the mirror down, ran her fingers once more over the wondrous gown: dark as the deepest sea, and shining with the light of distant stars. Sky and sea, reflected.

Saint-Malo came into view, thrust out upon the rocks. The cathedral with its spire, the walls and bastions lent the city an ancient air; it seemed to be born of spray and rock, as old and formidable as the sea itself. At night, however, it shimmered like a city of old. Countless candles lit its many windows, and the street lanterns turned the stone a buttery gold.

True to the groac'h's word, the boat remained unseen as it passed the city's necklace of island forts. It passed the entrance of the harbor, the forest of masts within, and swept into the mouth of the Rance. To Luce's left the lights of Saint-Servan glittered, the tall shape of Solidor Tower standing sentinel over the shadowy dockyards and bays. A few frigates lay at anchor, lights swinging gently. She heard the soft slap of water against wooden hulls, snatches of a lonely ballad from a sailor on watch, a brief, low argument on deck about which Saint-Malo bawdyhouse had the most competitive rates.

The splash of oars, and a pair of ship's boats, brimming with sailors, pulled toward the town. They passed so closely that Luce could have stood and brushed the men's shoulders with her fingertips, had she chose.

Not one of them noticed the little black boat as it passed by.

Night was falling over the river. Music drifted across the water, muted and broken.

Luce recognized the elegant strains of Vivaldi's Allegro in E from "La Primavera". The music grew louder as Le Loup Blanc came into view, the malouinière standing grandly atop its hill, creamy light spilling from its many windows, hundreds of torches illuminating the paths and gardens and woods sloping down to the banks of the Rance. Guests strolled along the ordered paths, and gathered before the house, their laughter drifting over the glittering, gold-stained water.

A thread of uneasiness wound itself around Luce as the boat edged toward the de Châtelaine's private dock. Several boats were there already, finely dressed gentlemen helping their wives, sisters and daughters, in their precarious gowns, safely onto dry land. What if Luce stumbled and fell? What if everyone saw her, flumsing and flooming in yet another ruined gown, struggling up the muddy bank?

"Take hold of yourself," she muttered sternly. "You can do this." She slipped the half-mask onto her face, tied the satin ribbons behind her curls with trembling fingers. Then she leaned down to the little boat and whispered, "Let them see us."

At once the lanterns affixed to the mast and four corners of the black-canopied cabin brightened. On the dock, the other guests stopped and stared. Luce did her best to look regal as the glittering barge, shimmering like starlight on seashells, drew smoothly alongside the dock.

There was no need to have worried about falling: three young men had left their gaping partners and were hurrying to make fast Luce's boat; to set the little carpeted gangplank into place; to reach down and help her ashore.

"May I be of service, mademoiselle?"

". . . Magnifique."

"Here, allow me. . . ."

Despite her jangling heart, the sudden, stifling closeness of the blue-black gown and stays, Luce smiled beneath her mask.

She had arrived.

Music floated across the grounds, enticing Luce and the other guests up the long, winding path to the house. Elegant torches set into the grass lit the way, assisting the gentlemen and their teetering mademoiselles. Their flames were warm on Luce's cheeks as she passed, head high, her enormous dress, as heavy as the sea around her waist, sweeping the gravel with each step.

A set of grand stone stairs loomed ahead. Luce climbed them easily—painlessly!—, her skirts held carefully before her, her seawater slippers chiming against the stone.

More people came into view as she neared the house, strolling across the sweeping, lantern-lit lawns, or admiring the gardens. Fountains splashed and shimmered. Elegantly liveried laquais handed out glasses of champagne. Luce took one, nodding her thanks and sipping nervously.

The guests ahead of her flowed through an alley of cleverly shaped hedges and sweet-smelling roses, the air between them thick with the strains of Vivaldi. Following, Luce beheld a magical sight: an outdoor ballroom, packed with masked dancers performing an elegant minuet, the patterns of the dance echoed in their gorgeous gowns and splendid suits. Festoons of greenery, flowers and tiny lanterns stretched over the dancing, and between the branches of the oak trees ringing the floor.

There were hundreds of guests. Many danced, but even more crowded the edges of the floor, or gathered around the little tables and chairs perched on the lawns. The musicians, impeccably attired in matching suits and buckled shoes, had arranged themselves beneath the sparkling trees. Nearby, long tables sheathed in crisp white linen and fresh flowers held mountains of food: mousses and macarons, shellfish and soufflés, pastries and petit fours. Enormous candelabras towered over the array of delicacies, their lights glistening on a series of magnificent ice sculptures. The very air tasted of flowers and starlight.

It was spectacular.

It was utterly terrifying.

Luce paused uncertainly on the edge of the dance floor. It seemed that everyone knew each other, despite the glorious masks—butterflies and birds, constellations and animals—concealing their faces. They seemed to know the evening's intricacies—when to move, when to stay still, how to greet and compliment and enchant, as though such things were merely steps in a complicated dance. A dance, Luce now realised, that everyone knew the steps to but her.

Even worse, people seemed to be noticing. They were turning from their conversations, from their chaperones, from their dance partners, even, to stare at her. An old madame, glittering with jewels—she had clearly taken the masque as an opportunity to wear every item of value she owned—went to bite a macaron and, when her gaze snagged on Luce, crunched it against her heavily powdered cheek instead. A group of young ladies arranged like a box of colorful bonbons watched her with unconcealed curiosity.

Luce blushed beneath her mask. Had she made a terrible mistake? She searched for her own family among the throng and saw Charlotte and Gratienne on the other side of the dance floor, gazing at her in surprise, and, in Charlotte's case, envy. They took in Luce's dress, her hair, her mask without an ounce of recognition.

They don't know, Luce thought, relieved. *They don't see* me.

It was an intoxicating thought, as bubbly and delicious as the wine. She took another sip, opened her fan with an elegant flick—shoulders back, arms held out from her wide skirts in the way her sisters' dancing masters always insisted upon—and dropped into the deepest, most elegant curtsey she had ever performed, her fan fluttering gently against a sea of shining silk.

"Who is *that*?" someone whispered, close by.

"Do we know her?"

"Is she from Saint-Malo? I've never seen her before . . ."

The muttering continued, until one of the young men approached. His hair was powdered, his frock coat of green velvet embroidered with roses. A golden mask covered half his face.

"Mademoiselle," he said politely. "Would you care to dance?"

Luce forced herself to nod.

He led her out onto the floor, her dress a glittering shadow among the sweet pinks, yellows and creams. A new dance was about to begin, a minuet, and Luce's heart thrilled.

She knew this dance, had learned it along with Veronique and Charlotte years ago, when her affliction had been milder. As Luce had grown and the condition worsened, she had been forced to stop those lessons and watch her sisters take part instead. Now, with the sea-glass slippers shimmering at her feet, she found she remembered the intricate little steps, the required lightness and the grace. The swirling pattern of the dance, in which she met her partner, turned to dance with another and then circled back to her partner once more, came as naturally to her as though she had danced it a thousand times before. Her back was straight, her arms floating at her sides, her fan swinging delicately from her wrist. And her feet. . . . free from the pain, there was nothing to hold Luce back. Nothing, but the joy of moving to the beautiful music, of glimpsing her extraordinary gown as it glittered and swirled like some iridescent creature beneath the sea. It was wonderful indeed to dance beneath the stars; to be part of something so grand and so beautiful.

One dance became two, and two became three. Luce was asked to dance by more young men than she could count. They trailed after her, arguing over who would fetch her more wine, or a slice of blancmange with wild strawberries, or iced cream flavoured with honey and notes of lavender and rosemary. Luce, eager to escape their attentions and find Morgan, looked out over the dance floor.

And there he was. In his dark, sleekly-fitted suit and black mask, Morgan de Châtelaine cut a dashing figure. He was dancing a gavotte with a young, golden-haired woman, a smile on his handsome face as he flowed through the dance's light and elegant movements. His partner, Luce could not help but note, danced beautifully. Indeed, she was light and graceful as an angel. . . .

Luce went very still. Morgan was dancing with Veronique.

A strange, icy sensation stole through her. She looked at the obscene amount of food her admirers had heaped on her little plate, and pushed it onto the long table beside her. She felt crowded, of a sudden. Her gown too hot, her stays too tight.

"Here, mademoiselle," one of the young men murmured, his fingers brushing Luce's wrist. "You must try the rose-water meringues. They are almost as exquisite as you."

"Thank you, no," Luce muttered, drawing away. She hurried along the path to the house, eager for fresh air and solitude, but hampered in her efforts to find them by her wide skirts and would-be dance partners, who followed enthusiastically. All but running, she pulled ahead, then swung tightly around the shadowy trunk of a horse chestnut. It worked—Luce heard her admirers crunch on toward the house. Congratulating herself, she rounded the tree, only to find herself facing yet *another* young man. Luce went to dodge away, an irritated apology already spilling from her mouth. The young gentleman, however, only smiled.

"Finally," Morgan said, his black eyes twinkling behind his mask. "I've got you alone, Lucinde Léon."

12

Of the Sea

Of everyone at the ball, Morgan was the only one who knew Luce for who she truly was. Even her own father, a masked Gabriel Daumard looking rather dashing at his side, was looking at Luce as though he had never seen her before.

Won't people see me?

Not if you don't want them to.

It was just as the groac'h had said. Luce's will, her willingness to be seen, dictated who might recognize her. And Morgan . . . Morgan had seen her because she *wanted* him to. A strange little shiver, at the thought.

Dancing with Morgan was not like dancing with the others. The air around them was heavy with more than just the scent of flowers and fire. Magic had settled over the dance floor, polishing the stars, gilding the night. And all the while Morgan was sweeping around her, his fingertips touching hers, his hand brushing her waist, his eyes fixed only on hers.

"You were dancing with my sister, earlier," Luce said airily, as the music drew him close. "Veronique."

"Your sister?" He frowned, as though trying to remember. "Ah. Yes. Politeness dictates that I dance with *all* the young ladies here tonight."

Relief, double-edged. On one hand, that her beautiful sister was simply another young lady. On the other, disappointment that he would soon part with her. Several young women were already watching Luce enviously, clustered on the edges of the dance floor like waiting gulls.

"And will you?" she asked.

"Absolutely not." He turned her smoothly. "I intend to enjoy three dances with you. Perhaps four. And then"—his voice lowered to a whisper as he circled her, his breath warm on her neck—"I intend to steal you away. If, of course, your father doesn't see and call me out."

"My father doesn't know I'm here," Luce said quietly. "None of my family do. There was a . . . misunderstanding today over my gown. As far as any of them are concerned, I am at home. It is, of course, the advantage of a masked ball. I would be grateful if you kept my presence here to yourself."

Morgan gave a wicked grin. "Of course." His fingertips trailed down the inside of Luce's arm as he placed it atop his own for a graceful promenade. Sweeping to a stop, he moved lightly away, spiraling through the other dancers. Luce turned to curtsey to another gentleman, his appreciative glance sweeping over her as he raised his palm to hers. Behind him, the guests lining the dance floor looked on.

"Who *is* she?" a young woman asked her maman. Her pink lips were puckered in frustration. "She has had three dances with Monsieur de Châtelaine now. *Three!*"

Luce swept back into the dance, and found herself with Morgan once more.

"Everyone is staring at us," she told him worriedly.

"Are they?" His gaze swept over her appreciatively. Her blood, her body, warmed in reponse. "I'm almost certain they're looking at you, not me. Not that I blame them; you *do* look awful."

Luce laughed. Around them, the rest of the couples stilled as the music drew to a graceful close.

"That was three minuets," she reminded Morgan.

"Was it?" He lifted her hand to his lips, unperturbed by who might see. "That's my limit, I'm afraid. Come. Let us see if we can elude the gulls."

Luce giggled.

Morgan placed her hand casually in the crook of his arm and led her off the floor.

"Where are we going?" she asked.

"Didn't you want to see my father's cabinet of strangeness?"

They moved toward the gardens, swiftly falling in with a group of guests about to take an admiring turn through the topiaries.

The gardens, like everything else at Le Loup Blanc, were magnificent. Gravel paths meandered through elaborate parterres, the boxwoods within carved into patterns and spirals as delicate as Gratienne's embroidery. A pond shimmered out of the darkness, reflecting the lights from the house. Benches rested among beds of roses and lavender, while sculptures edged the path. The most beautiful of these depicted the four seasons. Luce was admiring the flowery wreath adorning the youthful head of Spring when a familiar voice caught her attention. She left Morgan contemplating Old Man Winter and followed the sound, arriving at a small wood at the far edge of the garden. More than one young couple was strolling dangerously close to its shadowy depths.

One of them was Charlotte and Gabriel Daumard.

At the sight of her sister, Luce's hurt and shock at Charlotte's betrayal lost some of its power. There was something in the way Monsieur Daumard bent low to hear Charlotte speak. In the way Charlotte looked up at the young tutor . . .

"Someone you know?" Morgan enquired, appearing at her elbow.

"No," Luce said quickly, turning him toward the house. "For a moment I thought it was. I was mistaken."

She followed him along a path heavy with the scent of magnolia, resisting the urge to go back. To step between her sister and Daumard and warn them that the way they were courting scandal of the most spectacular kind. To remind them that aristocratic young women like Charlotte did not allow their tutors to court them. Morgan's presence, and the look of happiness on her sister's face, stopped her.

Besides, Charlotte was not the only one drifting too close to the shadows this night.

"The domestiques are all busy with the party," Morgan said, opening a small, plain door that was obviously meant for the servants. "We shall not be disturbed."

Luce nodded, suddenly nervous. Other than Samuel, she had never been alone with a man in this way.

She followed Morgan inside, skin prickling at the sudden presence of the storm-stone in its walls, then halted, frozen by the sound of her glass shoes upon the flagged floor. Each step was like a cannon blast in the dark, echoing through the shadowy house.

"God above," Morgan muttered, glancing down. "What . . . ?"

"My shoes," Luce breathed. A winding stair of dark wood loomed in the shadows to her right. Servants' stairs, narrow and steep. She edged toward them and sat, her gown foaming around her, then bent, raising the hem of her skirt. Moonlight spilling from the landing above illuminated her feet, glittering like diamonds on the seafloor.

"Are they . . . made of glass?" Morgan's voice was soft with awe.

A groac'h shaped them from the sea. Right before she sent me to the ball in a witch-boat. Luce tried, and failed, to imagine his reaction to the truth. "I shall have to take them off," was all she said.

She waited for Morgan to look away, step back courteously, as Samuel always did. *Samuel.* Guilt rose in her at the thought of him, sudden and painful. What was she *doing*?

Take hold of yourself, ordered a small, stern voice deep within her. Why shouldn't she be here with Morgan if she chose? *Besides,* the little voice reminded her, *Samuel doesn't want you. Hasn't he made that clear?*

The pain Luce had tried so hard to ignore, to push beneath the shifting waters and swirling sands of her mind, rose to the surface. It stayed with her as Morgan knelt before her, slowly reaching for her hem.

Luce drew away instinctively. Her fine silk stockings ended above her knee. Even so, she did not want him to see her feet. "Morgan . . ."

Of the sea, the word meant. An image of him on the beach, his cold hands, his warm mouth. *He* had wanted her.

"Let me help you, Lucinde." Her name, the three beats of it, sweet and soft against his lips.

"But . . ."

It was too late. He had already laced his fingers about her foot. Luce could scarce breathe as he slipped the shoe free and held it up. Light glittered on its curves as he turned it this way and that. "Exquisite."

He looked about for a place to put it, then, with a slight shrug, slipped it into his coat pocket. Luce peered over her skirts, saw that, in moonlight and silk, her foot looked no different to any other woman's. When Morgan reached for the second shoe, she let him.

"We should go," she breathed, when the second shoe was safely stowed in his coat.

Morgan's hand, however, remained on her foot, his fingers running lightly over her ankle.

"Do you remember," he said, quietly, "when we first met? On the beach?"

There, in the darkness, Luce's heart hammered and leapt. "You *do* remember."

"Of course I do." He looked up, moonshine shadowing his cheekbones, playing in his hair. "The most beautiful girl I ever saw, saving me from the sea. How could I forget?"

Oh, how her heart beat. Harder and harder until it must surely burst through her ribs.

"Why . . ." She swallowed. Tried again. "Why did you kiss me?" Her voice was but a whisper.

Morgan ducked his head. She was certain, even in the darkness, that he was blushing. "Oh, Lucinde. Do not make me say it."

"I want to know, Morgan." Just the two of them, here, face to face in the shadows. "Please. Tell me."

Music wafted from the ball, a distant quadrille.

"Please, Morgan."

"There are two reasons," he said, at last. "The first is that . . . I kissed you because I could not help it, Lucinde. I had nearly died. And you looked so . . ."

"So?"

"So wondrous. In truth? For a moment, I believed you were a seamaid."

Fire burned through silk as he stroked her ankle again. His fingers skimmed over her calf. Luce could barely breathe.

"And what was the second reason?" she managed.

"Does it matter?" Both hands on her calf, now, smoothing the silk. Soft as a butterfly, barely touching, as though it were not a touch at all, but merely the *thought* of a touch. Harmless. Inconsequential.

"Yes." Even as she said it, Luce was struggling to remember just what it was she had wanted to know. The air around them had thickened and slowed, water-soft. Part of her wanted him to move away, stand up and help her to her feet. But another, darker part of her longed for . . . something else.

When Morgan's hands slid over her silk-clad knee to the ribboned garters holding the silk to her bare thighs, however, the spell broke. As much as Morgan's touch thrilled her, Luce was all too aware there were certain things respectable young ladies simply must not allow.

"Morgan . . ."

His eyes gleamed hungrily for a heartbeat or two. Then he smiled, releasing her.

"Come," he said, rising and reaching down a hand. "The oddities await."

Morgan led Luce through the silent rooms of the malouinière, the sea-glass slippers clinking softly in his pockets. Monsieur de Châtelaine's cabinet was on the far side of the house, furthest from the river and the ball, and the rooms surrounding it lay in shadow. A single candelabra glistened on a side table near one of the enormous salons, and Morgan scooped it up with one hand, using the other to open a nearby door with a flourish. "Voilà!"

The room beyond was large, and very dark. Luce stayed close to Morgan as he prowled effortlessly through the shadows, lifting the candelabra high.

"Can we be expecting your father any time soon?" she asked.

"I doubt it." A pool of golden light rose around him as he lit a pair of candles in a sconce set into the wall. "My mother will expect my father to do his duty and remain with our guests tonight. I cannot guarantee he won't come in, though; he does love to show off his collection. It is, of course, the reason he keeps it. What better way to remember his adventures? To reveal the marvelous scope of his empire?"

Luce nodded. Her father had a similar, smaller, cabinet in the town house in Saint-Malo. He was not, however, the collector that Castro de Châtelaine was. This room was known to be the finest cabinet of curiosities in all of Bretagne, its wonders and marvels a spectacle for the senses. At the thought, she ceased following Morgan and came to a standstill in the center of the room, closing her eyes.

"You sound as though you would like to do the same," she said.

"I suppose I would." Morgan's voice faded as he moved further away from her. "If I was perfectly honest."

"And will you?"

"I will try."

"*Try?*" She managed, with some difficulty, to keep her eyes closed. "It seems to me that you will have little need for such efforts. Isn't it your destiny to be free, and to do as you please? To go to sea, and travel and trade?" She could not keep the envy from her voice.

"I suppose it would seem like that to you." More light, pinkish gold against her eyelids. "But I am not as free as you might think."

Luce huffed a bitter little laugh. "I doubt that."

"It's true. I'm the youngest son. The barest sliver of my father's wealth will trickle down to me. I must make my own fortune, find my own way. I thought I had begun, too. I had the *Dauphin*, and my father's support. But now . . ." Even with her eyes closed Luce knew his thoughts had turned once more to the ill-fated *Dauphin*. What had happened aboard the ship that stormy night? Was it as Bones and Samuel had said? She thought again of the wraith-like forms roaming the shore in the sea fog. Sightless, lost. She longed to ask Morgan what he remembered of the wreck, but found she lacked the courage to do so.

"And what would you do if you were truly free?" she asked instead.

"Truly? I would go raiding—like Surcouf, and our fathers, and the other great men of Saint-Malo. I would chase glory and greatness to one horizon, then turn my ship and chase them to another."

Luce said nothing. His words had woken a longing in her, a wanting and an ache so bright and true, they burned her soul. She, too, longed for adventure, to see the seas, to sail into the horizon.

"And if I had to marry," Morgan said, his shoes whispering across the polished floor as he came back to her, "I would choose someone who longed for adventure as much as I. Someone who would sail beside me, towards distant shores, without fear, or doubt. Someone . . . brave." He was very close to her now. "Why are your eyes closed?"

"I'm waiting."

"For what?" She felt him smile.

"For the light."

Morgan leaned in, filling the space between them with the scent of clean linen, his earthy-sweet pomade. in his hair. She felt his fingers in her hair. Felt the mask fall away from her face.

"Open your eyes," he whispered.

The cabinet of curiosities was easily thrice the size of her father's own, and far grander. Every surface—from the walls to the ceiling to the specimen tables set neatly out about the room—was covered with preserved fish, stuffed animals, strange and beautiful shells (some of which Luce recognized and some she did not), plants, and dried flowers. There were bookcases, too, but unlike her father's shelves, they were bursting with specimens: dried corals, stones, feathers, and minerals. The walls teemed with flocks of stuffed birds, wings outstretched.

"See the alligator?" Morgan said, pointing above Luce's head. He had removed his own mask, and was all cheekbones and dark eyes, thick hair falling across his forehead. She dragged her gaze away from him and looked up, flinching at the sight of an enormous, scaled creature, murky green and forbidding, its long snout opened to reveal rows of greenish, pointed teeth. "Papa brought it back from the Americas. Isn't it hideous?"

He trailed Luce as she walked slowly through the room. Starfish, crabs, seahorses, and shells. Sculptures and paintings, ancient jewelery, coins, and fossils of every description. Clocks and scientific instruments, their brassy surfaces glinting among antlers, insects, shark teeth, and beads. There were even pieces of sea-silk, the rarest and most valuable textile of all. Woven from the long, silky fibers of rare deep-sea molluscs, they shone like watery rainbows, pearlescent and tinged with magic.

A painting caught Luce's eye: Gradlon, king of the famous

drowned city of Keris, sacrificing his daughter, Ahez, to the sea. Keris, a beautiful city that had once existed off the coast of Saint-Malo, was built on land stolen from the Manche. To keep the waters at bay, Gradlon's forefathers had constructed a complicated series of water-gates, which he controlled with one single, masterful key. Keris had prospered for centuries, rich in trade and fishing, until Gradlon's wayward and spoiled daughter, Ahez, stole the key and—persuaded by her lover—used it to unlock the sea-gates. The ocean reclaimed Keris at once, flooding its streets and markets, its gardens and cathedrals. Gradlon and Ahez escaped on the king's mighty steed and rode hard for the shore of Bretagne, the churning waves threatening to overtake them. The horse, however, soon struggled under the weight of two riders, and Gradlon pushed his beloved daughter from the saddle and into the waves, saving himself.

"Do you know what they say about Ahez?" Morgan came to stand behind Luce. He looked up at the painting, his breath warm on her neck.

Luce shivered. "What do they say?"

"They say she was a harlot, full of lust, and that she lay with as many men as she liked, as often as she liked." He stroked the black ribbons on Luce's mask, still in his hands. "They say that when she tired of them, she bade them wear a black satin mask, which was specially designed to poison them. When they were helpless, she would strangle them with the ribbons and toss them from the walls of Keris into the sea."

"Morgan!" Luce giggled, shocked.

He laughed, too. "Forgive me."

"Do they . . . do they say anything else?"

Morgan grinned. "They say that she did not drown at all. That when she fell into the sea, she grew a tail in place of her legs, and became a seamaid. From then on, she used her wiles and her beauty to lure unlucky sailors and fishermen to their deaths in the drowned city. Just as she had when she lived there before."

"I would like to hear *her* side of the tale." Luce walked on, browsing a lifetime's worth of collecting, from countless trading voyages and privateering runs. Oh, to visit such places! To see such wonders alive, and whole. She could not deny that the sight of them, lifeless and still, filled her with an aching sadness. It was, after all, collection of death, of wild and beautiful creatures stolen from their lives and fixed with hook and pin. Trapped, sightless, joyless forevermore. The groac'h's words on the beach came back to her. *Too much has been stolen.*

She had reached a series of jars, some small, some as long as her arm. Inside, floating in a viscous, murky fluid, were a multitude of unsettling specimens—foetuses, brains, and organs. One item, however, caught her attention more than the rest. It was a human hand, cut off at the wrist. Its liquid bath was dim and cloudy, but Luce could see that the fingers were webbed, semi-circles of skin stretching from finger to finger, like a seal's flippers.

"Ah." Morgan came to her side. "You've found the seamaid's hand. Father's favorite."

"A seamaid?"

"Of course. Have you never seen one?" He bent down, examined the jar. "Vain, useless creatures, by all accounts. Spend most of their time gazing at their reflections and combing their hair. See the webbing between the fingers? Very helpful in the water, I imagine."

"One would think so," Luce said faintly.

Morgan was already moving. "There's a unicorn horn and some phoenix feathers, too, if the mystical interests you. And over here . . ."

But Luce had had enough of the cabinet and its grisly contents.

"Morgan . . . do you think we might go back and dance, instead?"

He smiled, offering her his arm. "What a charming idea."

It was a relief to be out of the house and back in the beautiful gardens. Morgan helped Luce to a bench, then knelt before her and drew the sea-glass shoes from his pockets.

"May I?" he asked softly.

She nodded, deliciously, dangerously wordless as he lifted first one foot, then the other, slipping the glittering shoes into place.

"Extraordinary," he murmured. He raised himself on his knees, until they were face to face. Luce could barely breathe as he smoothed her mask back over her eyes, tying it deftly into place, his fingers lingering in her hair. Her heart quickened as he leaned forward, his lips almost brushing hers.

"Do you know," he murmured, "how often I think of that kiss on the beach?"

Intention was writ upon every part of him; his eyes, his hands, the angle of his jaw. Luce leaned forward, ready to meet his lips with her own. So close, they came; so very close. And then a sudden sense of loss, of *failing*, swept over her, from the crown of her head to the tips of her toes. Like a sail emptying of wind, or the last moments before the setting of the sun.

The tide had turned.

The tide will not wait, the groac'h had warned. *The faster it ebbs, the quicker the magic will weaken. You must not linger.*

Luce leapt to her feet. She glimpsed Morgan's confused face as she picked up her skirts and dashed away. Down the magnolia-scented path, and the secrecy of the woods; past the fountains and the roses, the stony faces of the four seasons looking on in blatant disapproval. She dodged parterres and skirted topiaries, her feet in their enchanted slippers light and strong, the rapid pace of Bach's Paris Concerto urging her on.

Morgan caught up as she burst onto the crowded dance floor.

"Wait!" he cried. Luce, weaving between the rows of dancers, risked a backward glance. He was surrounded by a gaggle of young, masked women, his mother striding accusingly toward him. Luce plunged on, a trail of missed steps and broken poses strewn in her wake. On, past the musicians and the laquais with their sparkling wine. On, down the long, winding path to the river.

No time, no time.

She was almost at the river when Morgan reappeared, a dark silhouette before the oak trees and their festoons of light. He left the path and dashed across the wide, rolling lawn, meaning, she had no doubt, to cut her off before she reached the Rance.

You must not linger.

Luce gathered her skirts against her and ran, her slippers clinking on the path, her breath aching in her chest. Her right stocking was slipping—her garter must have come loose—and she hitched at it clumsily, losing precious moments. Somehow, she reached the stone stairs leading to the river. Somehow, she made it down them without falling and breaking her neck.

The dock was blessedly empty. She ran toward it, past a single laquais dozing against a bollard. Onto the sea-washed timbers, the Rance waiting in the dark.

Hurry, hurry, it sighed. *The tide will not wait.*

"Lucinde!"

Hurry!

She had moments, only, before Morgan reached the dock. Luce clattered along it, near-tripping as her loose stocking caught on the heel of her other shoe. Silk ripped as she stumbled, righted herself, ran on. One sea-glass slipper lay on the timbers in her wake.

Hurry, hurry . . .

The witch-boat was nosing its way toward her. Luce ran along the dock to meet it, her bare foot whimpering with pain, her heart thudding in time with her steps and the frenzied pace of Bach.

"Lucinde!"

Morgan was on the dock, his buckled shoes clattering like ballast in a storm, waking the sleeping laquais. He, in his turn, startled so violently that he lost his balance, slipped off the bollard, and toppled backward into the Rance. Morgan slowed, distracted, and Luce seized her moment. She gathered her wide skirts and ran off the edge of the dock, landing rather gracelessly on the witch-boat's deck.

"Hide me, please," she gasped. "And take me home as quickly as you can."

The boat obeyed, turning for the open water as though a storm-wind filled its sails.

Luce peered over the stern. Morgan had run to the edge of the dock, the very picture of confusion as he scanned the seemingly empty water. In his hand, glinting like a star, was Luce's lost slipper. As she watched, he yelped softly in surprise and looked down, eyes widening as the shoe turned to water in his hands. He clutched at it desperately, to no avail: there was nothing left but sea-water running through his empty fingers.

She saw no more then, for the little boat was skimming over the smooth, dark water, starlight glimmering in its wake.

They were sailing along the coastline of Clos-Poulet when the lanterns hanging from the canopy above Luce's head began to gutter. The sails slackened and the boat slowed, its timbers creaking wearily.

"Please, keep going," Luce whispered. She could see the cove ahead, a pale blur beneath the cliffs. Onward went the little boat, shuddering with effort, its sails ruffling sadly as the magicked breeze died.

Luce's dress began to change. Silk lost its shine. Threads unraveled. Her hair fell from its bindings as the pins disappeared; her mask turned to sea mist on her face. She watched sorrowfully as the remaining slipper melted from her foot.

And still the little boat sailed valiantly on. Its mast teetered and fell, slipping beneath the waves. Its deck began to shudder. Yet onward, it plowed, and on, until water clawed between the planks, soaking Luce's skirts, rising to steal her bodice, the lace at her sleeves, the pearls at her throat. Returning them to the deep, one by one, until she was clad in her underclothes once more, the same chemise, petticoat, and stays she had worn when she had cried salty tears into the sea, mourning a lost gown and sister, both.

A watery glint caught Luce's eye. The groac'h's mirror, bright as the moon against the sinking velvet. The thought of such a lovely thing returning to the cold dark of the sea-bed caught at Luce, would not let go. As the boat's broken keel scraped against rock and the last of the deck howled its demise, she snatched up the trinket and dived. Starlight lit her way as she swam for shore, the final, eerie moans of the caravel as it returned to its grave loud in her ears.

Luce staggered onto the sand, panting. Looked out at the water, the stars, the memory of the wondrous night. Then she turned and trudged up the beach, feet already protesting, body shivering beneath its sodden clothes. Her tricorn and overcoat were waiting for her, completely dry and folded neatly atop a bank of sea thrift. She put them on, slipped the mirror into her pocket, and limped home.

13

Uncomfortable Conversations

The clang of the ship's bell woke Luce far too soon. She blinked, rolled over and was brutally assaulted by the sunlight streaming through her open curtains.

"Damn my soul," she groaned, burying her face in a pillow.

The bell continued its violence, sounding six times more before it fell into blessed silence. Luce cracked an eye. The sun, her enemy, was too bright for it to be the morning watch. The forenoon, then.

She had slept the entire morning.

Veronique's sleepy voice wafted across the hall, followed by Charlotte's low reply. Unbidden, the events of the previous day came back to Luce in a rush: the ball and the witch-boat and Luce's slipper, falling like water through Morgan's hands. His gentle grip on her stockinged calves. Their near kiss. *Of course I remember.* The tide-woman's kindness, and her strange, confusing words. *I know what it is to cry and have no one but the sea there to listen.* Luce's ruined gown floating mournfully in the shallows, and Charlotte's cold carelessness as she arranged her own beautiful dress.

Luce knew her sister could be jealous. Difficult. Even so, the wound her betrayal had caused seemed fresh and painful as ever. Unable to bear it another moment, Luce climbed from her bed, threw on a peignoir, and padded to Veronique's room.

Her sisters glanced up as she appeared in the doorway, but did not halt their conversation.

"I look as though I am a thousand years old," Veronique said, seated before her dressing table. She turned her face this way and that, frowning at her reflection. "I do not understand why balls must go all night. Surely three in the morning would suffice?"

"Don't be a goose, Vee. That was when the fun was just beginning." Charlotte lounged on a chaise longue. Her soft brown hair was loose, her freckles stark across her nose.

"Was it?" Luce came into the room and sank into a velvet-covered armchair.

"Yes," Charlotte said, throwing an arm over her eyes dramatically. "They served the most delicious supper. Outside, you know. There were hundreds of candles-you could see the Rance from the dance floor. It was breathtaking."

"It sounds wonderful," Luce said. "And the music?"

"The usual," said Charlotte, still burrowed beneath her forearm. "Vivaldi, Bach. A little Purcell. Minuets, mostly. The occasional gavotte and cotillion. I danced so much my feet feel like I have stepped on knives all night."

"Really?" Something in Luce's tone made Veronique look up from her mirror for the first time. "It must be awful to feel such pain."

"It is. My head is throbbing, too, and my belly aches. The price we pay for all that good wine and food, I suppose."

Veronique was still watching Luce in the mirror. "How are you feeling this morning, Luce?"

"I am as well as can be expected."

Charlotte removed her arm from over her face and gave Luce an appraising look. "You slept late," she remarked. "Anyone would think you actually *enjoyed* your evening at home."

"It is not as though I had a choice," Luce said frostily. If she had hoped that her sister might show signs of regret over her actions, she would be woefully disappointed.

"You had a choice," Charlotte pointed out. "You could have

borrowed one of gowns, or Vee's. Do not blame me because you were too proud to share."

"Too *proud?*" Luce gaped at her sister. "Is that why you think I'm upset?"

Charlotte shrugged. "Isn't it?"

"Is that truly all you have to say, Charlotte?"

"What more *is* there to say?"

"You could *apologize*!" Luce cried. "You could be gracious and brave enough to admit that taking the dress from Maman's room was childish and wrong, and that you feel terrible about doing it!"

Charlotte sat slowly up on the chaise. "I didn't take the gown, Lucinde," she said. "I would never do such a thing to you. Indeed, I cannot believe you would even consider it."

"Then who did?"

"How should I know?"

"Do not look at me," Veronique said quickly, raising her palms. "*I* had no reason to take it."

Charlotte glowered at her. "And *I* did?"

"Well, you *did* seem rather angry after the dress fitting," Veronique said with a shrug. "And you had barely been speaking to Luce . . ."

"So you agree with her?"

". . . No," Veronique said thoughtfully. "No, I don't. But I can see why Luce would blame you."

Charlotte flopped back on the chaise longue with a weary sigh. "Believe what you want, the both of you. But I didn't take the dress."

Silence.

"If you insist," Luce said wearily, getting to her feet.

"I do." Charlotte threw her arm over her eyes again. "I suggest you speak to the domestiques."

Luce remembered Nanette's horror when she discovered the dress was gone. "It was not the domestiques," she said firmly.

"Then I don't know what else to tell you."

"Well, if *that* uncomfortable conversation is finally over," Veronique said, opening a little pot of face cream while she watched Charlotte slyly in the mirror, "I suggest we begin another one. Tell me, Charlotte, how many times you danced with our very own Monsieur Daumard last night?"

"What do you mean, Vee?" Charlotte did not remove her arm, but there was a definite edge to her tone. Luce, remembering what she had seen in the gardens at Le Loup Blanc, sat back down.

"You know precisely what I mean,' Veronique said, applying the cream to her cheeks. "You danced together so many times I thought you might have gotten your fan stuck on his coat buttons."

"*Vee!*" Charlotte removed her arm and sat up once more, throwing her sister a furious glare. "You must not speak so!"

"Why shouldn't I? You *did* dance with him often. Too often, truth be told." Veronique smoothed the last of the cream over her skin. "They'll be whispering about you all over Saint-Malo this morning."

"Not as much as they will be talking about Morgan de Châtelaine and that mysterious woman," Charlotte countered.

"Which woman?" Luce asked, innocently.

Charlotte smirked. "Oh, just some woman," she said blithely, watching Veronique's reflection in the mirror. "She was masked, like us all, but even so you could tell she was *beautiful.* And did I mention her gown? I have never seen anything like it. Black, it was, and yet it shone like the stars. Her hair was black too, and she wore the most beautiful slippers. Silver, they were."

"They were not," Veronique said, too quickly. "They were clear. Like . . . like glass."

"*Glass* slippers?" Charlotte made a face. "Surely not! Why, they would crack in a moment! It is impossible."

"They were made of glass," Veronique insisted. "I heard them clicking on the dance floor. I heard them plain as day." She tapped one impeccably-shaped fingernail on the dressing table. *Tap. Tap. Tap.* "Just like that."

Charlotte shrugged. "In any case, I have never seen shoes like them. Clearly Monsieur de Châtelaine had not, either. He could not take his eyes off that dark-haired woman. Danced at least three dances with her and did not leave her side all night."

"He danced with others, as well." Veronique scowled. "Including *me!*"

"He was smitten with this woman, whoever she is," Charlotte told Luce confidentially, ignoring her sister. "My word upon it." She collapsed back on the chaise longue with a satisfied *whump.*

"Goodness," Luce said. Charlotte's words had set a ringing in her heart, a thrill of delight through her body.

"Well, *I* heard Maman speaking most highly of you to the Vicomte de Talhouët-Foix," Veronique told Charlotte smugly. "He seemed inclined to listen, too. I would not be surprised if he called upon you this week."

"Ugh." It was Charlotte's turn to scowl. "He is three times my age and his breath smells! Maman insisted I dance with him, too. Why must she thrust us into the path of such men?"

"Because he is a vicomte, obviously."

"He is a bore! I would sooner marry one of the laquais."

The tension between the sisters evaporated as all three of them burst into giggles.

"Charlotte, how can you say such things?" Veronique said, wiping her eyes. "Truly, I am astonished!"

"I mean it!" Charlotte declared. "St. Jean would do nicely, I think. You must agree he is the most handsome of the four."

Veronique turned on her seat to face her. "Nanette would certainly agree with you," she said slyly. "Why, just yesterday I saw her kissing him on the servants' stairs!"

"You did *not*!" Charlotte hissed.

"There was no mistaking it," Veronique said sagely.

Luce tensed. She had been aware of Nanette's dalliance with the laquais for some time, but had been careful to keep the knowledge to herself. Such secrecy was not without its benefits. As Luce's chambermaid, Nanette could not help but notice things like sandy petticoats and sea-dampened hair, or comings and goings at odd hours of the day. The two women had long ago come to a quiet understanding, guarding each other's secrets as closely as they guarded their own.

"You won't tell anyone, surely?" Luce asked. Such behavior would be more than enough to warrant Nanette's immediate dismissal.

"Of course not," Veronique said. "I like Nanette."

"I certainly won't say anything," Charlotte agreed. "Nanette's the only one who knows how to curl my hair the way I like it. Where is she, anyway? I'm hungry."

As though she had heard her name, Nanette appeared with a tray bearing porcelain cups, a silver pot, and a plate of pastries.

"We shall need another cup for Luce, Nanette," Veronique told the maid. "And more pastries, too. Are there any more of those little caramel ones Olivier made yesterday?"

"I did love those shoes," Charlotte said thoughtfully. "I wonder if I can get a pair made in Saint-Malo?"

Veronique's reply was sullen. "Try Paris, Cee."

The question of who had destroyed the blue dress haunted Luce for days. Despite her earlier misgivings, she believed her sister. Who, then, had taken it? There was, quite simply, no reasonable explanation for what had happened.

She was soon too busy to give the matter much thought. Between her lessons with Monsieur Daumard—who remained as pleasant and professional as ever, even when Charlotte happened to pass through the room in which he and Luce or Veronique were working—and helping her father plan the imminent launch of the *Lucinde*, there was barely time to steal away to the cove. Even so, she managed it, rising early day after day and waiting near the groac'h's cave.

She had never dared approach the tide-woman's dwelling before. However, it seemed only fair that Luce make an effort to thank the fae properly for her help on the evening of the ball, and to return her beautiful silver hand-mirror. (There was also, of course, every possibility that the groac'h knew who had thrown the blue dress into the Manche.) Day after day Luce waited near the tide-woman's cave, watching for her little witch-boat on the water and thinking of Morgan de Châtelaine. His black eyes, his wicked smile. The feel of his body pressed against the folds of her skirts as he removed the sea-glass slippers. *I would choose someone who longed for adventure as much as I. Someone who would sail beside me, towards distant shores, without fear, or doubt. Someone . . . brave.*

Day after day waited, and day after day the groac'h did not appear. At last, Luce left the mirror on the rocks near the cave, her questions unanswered.

Though she never admitted it to herself, there was someone else Luce watched for at the cove. She had seen no sign of Samuel, or Bones and the *Dove*, since the night before the ball, and could only surmise that they had gone on a run to Dorset. The hurt and shame Luce felt whenever she thought of what had happened in the woods—*we can't do this, Luce*—warred with her worry that Samuel had been caught up in something dangerous—plucked from the sea by a revenue clipper and thrown into a filthy cell in Poole or Portsmouth, perhaps, or detained by the City Guard in Saint-Malo for his connection to black market stone. Despite her lingering embarrassment, she hoped, fervently, that he was well.

One evening a week after the ball, Luce threw her coat over her woolen dress and went down to the cove once more. Her father had gone to Saint-Malo to see to one of his ships, while her mother and sisters were dining with the Fontaine-Roux at their nearby malouinière. Luce had shrugged out of her coat and tricorn, and was watching the water, half expecting to see the *Dove* scrape onto the sand and Samuel come loping toward her, when footsteps crunched upon the cliff above. She turned.

It was not Samuel, but Morgan de Châtelaine—incongruous in frock coat, breeches and shining riding boots—scrambling down the path. Above him, at the edge of the woods, Luce made out the pale shape of a gray horse in the twilight.

"Good evening, Mademoiselle Léon."

"Good evening, monsieur."

Oh, but he was handsome. Treacherously so. One glance from those dark eyes, one smile, and Luce felt as though all that tethered her to the world had frayed, and that she was drifting, rudderless.

"I wanted to see you again," Morgan said.

She gestured to the cliffs. "Clearly."

A slow grin. "My family is dining with the Fontaine-Roux tonight."

"As are mine."

He nodded. "Yes. When I saw that you were not with them, I made my excuses and rode straight here. I hope you don't mind. I thought, after the storm. . . . Well. I hoped I might find you here."

She nodded, suddenly shy.

"My family have been pestering me relentlessly, desperate to know who I danced with so often at the ball. I did as you asked and refrained from telling them your name."

"Thank you."

A flicker of a smile as he looked at her. "This is where I washed up, isn't it?" he said, glancing around. "Where you saved me."

"Yes." She gestured to the water's edge. "It was just over there."

He looked at the damp sand, the clear, calm water, rippling gently, and a shadow passed over his face.

"What happened that night, Morgan?" Luce asked quietly. "Your father said the *Dauphin* carried no storm-stone. But I-I saw it in your pockets that day. I emptied them, in truth; it was the only way I could get you to shore."

Morgan looked out over the water. Swallowed. "The *Dauphin* did carry stone," he said. "Good stone, too. My father bade me lie about it to keep the salvagers away." His expression darkened. "Those vultures catch the mere *scent* of a wreck and they'll swoop in to pick the bones."

Luce kept her face carefully calm. "But how did the *Dauphin* go down?" she asked. "If you had the stone—good stone—she should have prevailed. . . ."

"I made some . . . poor decisions."

"Oh," Luce said, realizing what he meant. Storm-stone ballast, like all storm-stone, was not infallible. The finest stone in the world would not keep a ship from sinking if an inexperienced captain or pilot took the wheel, as it were, into their own hands.

"I blame myself entirely for what occurred," Morgan said. "I was arrogant. Foolish." He shook his head again. "All those men. All those families. Lost because of me."

"The weather was treacherous that night. . . ."

"You are kind." He gave a rueful smile. "My father has recompensed each of the families generously, and if any of them should have need, they know they can call upon our family. My father did it gladly, but even so . . . I had hoped to make it right with him, somehow. The *Dauphin* was gone, but the stone could still be saved; I knew that finding it would go a long way toward earning his forgiveness. We found the ship a week after she went down. A total wreck, of course. But when our men searched the hull, they found it empty. The stone had already been salvaged. *Stolen*."

Morgan ran a hand through his hair, long dark strands breaking loose from the ribbon tying it at his nape. "That stone was worth five of the *Dauphin*," he said darkly. "If I could have saved it, I might have had a chance of redeeming myself." He glanced at her. "I don't have to tell you how precious storm-stone is. It gets harder and harder to find every year. The *Dauphin*'s ballast was part of my father's most prized stock. He is furious with me. Even now he will barely speak to me."

An oily heaviness settled in Luce's chest. Guilt, she realized. She had led Samuel to the wreck. Had helped him take the stone. *Pick the bones.* What was worse, the entirety of the *Dauphin's* storm-stone was, at that very moment, only steps away in the sea-cave. She could *feel* its presence prickling against her face and neck. She could *see* the cave's entrance, disguised by shadows and rocks, over Morgan's shoulder.

"What will you do?" she asked softly.

"What I must: find the stone. I cannot see another way of winning back my father's favor. He has left its recovery entirely in my hands. Another means, he says, of testing my suitability."

"Suitability for what?"

"For being a de Châtelaine, of course," he said bitterly. "What else? I cannot let my father down again, Lucinde. I have already made enquiries. Saint-Malo is a small place, when all is said and done. People talk, even storm divers. I'll find the stone soon enough. And then I'll see that justice is served to those who stole it from me."

Luce's mouth went dry. It was taking every shred of willpower she possessed not to look at the narrow opening in the cliffs where the storm-stone lay hidden.

"But enough of such things," Morgan said, reaching for her hand. "I hear your new ship is to be launched."

"Yes. In two days. We're going to Saint-Malo tomorrow so we can be there, and then staying for the Blessing of the Sea."

The Blessing was one of the most important of Saint-Malo's annual celebrations. It always began with a Mass in the cathedral, after which the priests led the townsfolk in a grand procession down to the quay. There, they blessed each and every Malouin ship—the fishing fleet, the corsairs, the frigates and the smaller merchant vessels—asking for prosperity and safe passage for the coming year.

"Then I shall see you there," Morgan said.

"You shall."

He glanced regretfully at the sky. "I had best get back before I'm missed."

Luce nodded, forced herself to relinquish his hand. "You had best go, then."

"Yes." But he lingered, and lingered, dragging his fingertips from hers as he started up the beach.

"I will see you again soon," he promised. "You have my word, Lucinde Léon."

"I will hold you to it."

He moved fast, so fast, covering the distance between them, catching her fingers and drawing her close.

"I rather hope you do." He murmured the words, his mouth so close, so very close to Luce's own that her breath, her heart, her entire body fluttered.

Then he pulled away with a grin.

"Until we meet again."

She watched, attempting, and failing, to collect herself, until he was no more than a cliff-top silhouette against the sky. When he was gone, she turned back to the water and saw the *Dove* coming in. Luce waved in greeting. Bones raised a hand in return, but Samuel did not respond. He was watching Morgan riding against the dusk, his face grim, his eyes hard.

"I leave you for a few days," he said, "and the wolf comes prowling."

The tide was low and falling with every exhalation, the lugger's belly rasping against the shore. Samuel stowed the oars and leapt into the shallows, Bones close behind. As one, the two cousins hauled the boat up onto the beach.

"Was that Morgan de Châtelaine?" Samuel asked, wedging the anchor into the sand. It was clear from his tone that he knew precisely who Luce's visitor was.

He sounded so unlike himself that Luce hesitated. "Does it matter if it was?" she asked at last, glancing questioningly at Bones. "I know you don't care for the de Châtelaines, but—"

"Why was he here? Alone with you on the beach?"

Bones looked between them, brows so high they all but touched his hairline, before reaching into the boat and unloading several watertight bundles. Wools and textiles from England, Luce knew from a brief glance. They *had* made a run, then. Bones bundled the packs hastily in his arms and headed toward the cave. "I'll see to these," he announced, throwing an apologetic glance at Luce as he passed. *Good luck.*

"For heaven's sake, Samuel," she said, when Bones had gone. "You and I are alone on this beach all the time and it never worried you."

"I am not *him.*" Samuel was watching her, his face uncharacteristically stony. "Is he calling on you, Luce? Is that what this is?"

Is it? She wasn't entirely sure what Morgan was doing. Or what *she* was doing in return. He had danced with her more than anyone else at the ball. He had removed her slippers, run his hands up her legs in a way that still gave her shivers. He had kept her secrets. Ridden here specifically to see her. And he remembered, just as she did, that kiss right there on the sand.

"What if he is?" Luce demanded. There was a possessiveness in Samuel's tone that she liked not at all. After all, hadn't he pulled away from her, *rejected* her, in the woods? "I am allowed a suitor, am I not?" The words lay unspoken between them, as baldly as if she had shouted them in his face: *it is not as though* you *wanted me.*

"Not *that* suitor," Samuel all but spat. He was angry, truly angry, the muscles in his jaw clenching.

"Would you prefer someone else, then?"

He swallowed. "I'd prefer anyone but him." He turned back to the *Dove,* heaved it higher onto the beach. "Mind your feet," he warned, as Luce stepped around the anchor.

"Is that it, then?" she asked, watching him. "'Mind your feet'?"

She watched him gather the remaining contraband against his chest, reach for his hat, his coat, his boots.

"Samuel?"

He only strode up the beach to the cave. "I need to sleep, Luce," he said, not looking back. "We've been on the water all day. I'm hoping you won't mind if we bed down in the cave."

"I *do* mind," she said, following him. "As a matter of fact."

"Of course you do," he muttered.

"I want to know why you're being like this."

"Being like what?"

"So angry and harsh. I don't deserve it, Samuel."

"No," he said, slowing. "I suppose you don't."

"If anything *Morgan* should be angry, not you. After all, *we* stole the storm-stone from *him* . . ."

"The *Dauphin* was wrecked, the stone fair game." He stopped, turned to her. "It's the law of the sea, Luce. You know it as well as I."

"He knows the wreck's been salvaged, Samuel. He wants the stone back."

"Well, a man can want something as much as he likes. It doesn't mean he'll get it." He was angry again, striding for the cave. "And what I do—what *we* do—has never bothered you before."

Luce had no answer for that. Up until now, the stone they found in wrecks had been just that—stone. Adrift, ownerless. But after speaking to Morgan, learning of his guilt, his pain . . .

"Does it ever bother you?" She had never thought to ask him if he felt remorse for the things he did. Breaking rules, avoiding the law. "The stealing, I mean?"

"Guilt is a luxury I can scarce afford." Samuel reached the cave, tossed his belonging onto then sand. Behind him, light glowed faintly from its depths—Bones had busied himself lighting Luce's lanterns, storing the packages of English wool.

Samuel sighed wearily.

"How well do you know de Châtelaine?" he asked, gentler now. "How often have you met with him, I mean."

"What?" Luce frowned, confused by the change of tack. "This was the first time he'd come here. Apart from when I found him after the storm, of course."

"Ah," Samuel said, disagreeably. "Of course. How could I forget?"

"But we have met at the house, and the dockyard." She plowed on, uncertain. "And at Le Loup Blanc . . ."

"That's right. The grand and glorious ball. You actually went, then?"

Luce considered telling him everything—of the tide-woman's help, the exquisite gown and shoes, the witch-boat. The hardness in his eyes stopped her.

"I did. And, well, I very much enjoyed it, Samuel. The entire evening was like something from a story. We danced outside—"

He frowned. "*You* danced?"

"—and there were ice sculptures, and so many candles, and flowers . . ."

"A ball from a story, eh? I never received my invitation. It must have gotten lost."

Ordinarily Samuel's jests made Luce laugh so hard her belly ached. But the way he spoke now, so angry and bitter, made her tense.

"So that's what you want, then, it is? Balls and flowers and ice sculptures." He gestured to the top of the cliffs. "Fine horses and frock coats."

"No," Luce said, hotly. "No, that's not what I want. Not at all."

No sooner were the words out of her mouth than she wondered if they were a lie. *I rather hope you do.* Morgan's touch, his words, still glowed like embers.

"It doesn't seem that way."

"That's not fair, Samuel. You are misjudging me. And Morgan, too. He—he is not what you think he is. He feels terribly about what happened to the *Dauphin*."

"I'm sure he does," Samuel said wryly.

"He is a person, the same as you and I. With . . . with thoughts, and feelings." She faltered, unable to withstand the look Samuel was giving her. "He cannot help that his family is wealthy."

"Indeed. It must be a terrible trial for him."

She bristled. "He is just as trapped as the rest of us!"

"I doubt that very much."

"He cares for me!" Luce was truly angry now. How dare he speak to her this way?

"The de Châtelaines care for no one but themselves," Samuel snarled, fast and hard, as though he could no longer contain himself. "I hear the stories, Luce. The talk. Castro and his sons have always been . . . wild. But Morgan's exploits put them all to shame. He's the talk of the docks, of the warehouses, of the taverns. He made quite the name for himself in Cádiz, by all accounts, and seems intent on making one here as well. From the moment he recovered from that wreck he has made it his purpose to conquer every brothel and bawd from Our Lady's Gate to Saint-Servan."

A heavy stone had settled upon Luce's chest. "Why are you saying such things?"

"Because they are true. Had I known he had set his sights upon you, I would have said them sooner."

"You cannot know if they are true. These could be merely stories, or speculation. It is not as though young gentlemen do not frequent such, such . . ." She felt herself blush. "He would not be the first, is all I am saying."

Samuel gaped at her. "You're excusing such behavior?"

"Of course not. But . . . for God' sake, Samuel! Madame de Pompadour is at this very moment the most fashionable, the most desirable, woman in all of Paris—in all of France! The king's *mistress.*" She shrugged. "Such things are to be expected, when men are of a certain . . ." She foughtbto find a word that would not insult him.

She failed.

"I see," Samuel hissed. "And I suppose the ribbon garters he is said to steal from his conquests do not concern you, either? Word is he has a collection so mighty it requires its own valet."

"You're lying!"

"I would never lie to you." Samuel bent wearily and picked up his things before heading into the cave. "I only wonder if Monsieur de Châtelaine can say the same."

14

Launches and Lessons

It was as though every man, woman, and child of Saint-Malo had turned out to see the *Lucinde* greet the sea. They crowded the beach and clustered between the workshops, perched on piles of lumber and equipment. Children ran on the sand, shoes and hats discarded. The men of the dockyards perched high on the bones of the half-finished ships, chattering like the gulls. On the water, vessels of every size—from jolly-boats to frigates, their ratlines and footropes crowded with watching sailors—bobbed expectantly.

The day was fine, the sun warm, and the *Lucinde,* festooned with flags and flowers, gracefully awaited her debut. Behind her, across the harbor, the stone battlements of Saint-Malo wavered, as beautiful as a mirage.

Luce held her breath as the priests completed the blessings. The larger the ship, the greater the risk of mishap on its rapid, backward slide into the water, and she knew that most of the people assembled secretly hoped for the spectacle and excitement of disaster. A fouled slipway, perhaps, or a dramatic sideways topple. The ship might survive the launch, but then list, or take on water, or crash into another vessel.

The possibilities were endless.

Luce clutched her father's arm as the men knocked aside the shores and stanchions holding the *Lucinde* in place. The slipway had been liberally coated with soap and tallow before the tide rose, and the vessel began to slide at once with alarming speed, entering the water moments later with a mighty splash that soaked the onlookers on the nearest ships and boats. As the *Lucinde* settled back into the water, all those who had hoped for her shocking, embarrassing demise gave a deafening cheer, waving their hats and clapping.

"She made it," Jean-Baptiste crowed, kissing Luce's cheek. "She made it."

"Of course she did." Luce sagged against him with relief. Even without her masts and rigging—they would be added later, along with her guns and ammunition—the *Lucinde* was magnificent. "How could she not?"

"May we go soon, Maman?" Veronique sounded infinitely bored. "It's hot here. And dirty."

"You may wait in the carriage, if the dockyard is not to your liking," Gratienne told her. She glanced around, wrinkled her nose. "Where *is* your sister?"

Luce, who had seen Charlotte moving through the crowds in the moments before the launch, her hand resting on Gabriel Daumard's arm, said nothing. Luce liked the young tutor; he was intelligent. Kind. Why shouldn't her sister steal a little time in his company, if it made her happy?

"I have no idea," Veronique said, with an irritable wave of her fan. "Come, Maman. She will find us at the carriage easily enough."

"Would you like to go aboard?" Jean-Baptiste asked Luce, when they were alone.

"I thought you'd never ask."

They were not the only ones. The decks of the *Lucinde* were crowded with admirers. The scents of tar and fresh timber were strong, even with the breeze kicking over the harbor.

"Another beauty for your fleet, Jean-Baptiste," Monsieur Fontaine-Roux said, shaking his head. "I don't know how you do it."

"The luck of the lion," Jean-Baptiste said, with a grin.

"What will you do with her?"

Jean-Baptiste glanced at Luce. "We have not yet decided."

"I had great success in the African trade before the war," Monsieur Fontaine-Roux said. He looked around at the *Lucinde* thoughtfully. "She is the perfect size for a slaver."

Luce stared at him, appalled. It was no secret that many of the shipowners of Saint-Malo invested in the trade of people as well as goods. They would leave port loaded with textiles, guns, ammunition, and sail to the Slave Coast of Africa, where they would trade the items for people, taking them to the French colonies in the Caribbean—Martinique or Saint-Domingue—to be sold to the owners of sugar and indigo plantations. The ships then returned to Bretagne loaded with sugar, coffee, and indigo. The entire, appalling trip took a year, more or less.

"Risky, but highly profitable," Monsieur Fontaine-Roux said. "With the right crew, and the right captain."

Bones, who had once worked a slave ship—*once,* he had said significantly, being more than enough—had described its horrors to Luce. The vessels were cramped, rough, and rife with disease as well as unspeakable cruelty and sorrow. A good slaver captain was generally agreed to be one who used violence to keep his "cargo" in check, without damaging it.

Popular opinion held that the slave trade was beneficial for the very people it abused, those who were stolen from their homes and forced into a life of servitude, because it enabled the light of a Christian God to shine upon their souls. Privately, Luce thought that reasoning simply a means of helping slavers, investor and shipowners sleep at night. Both Samuel and Bones, who avoided any interaction with captains and shipowners in the trade, agreed.

"I would rather," she declared, "see the *Lucinde* at the bottom of the Manche. If you'll excuse me, Papa."

She made her way back along the deck, keenly aware that both her father and Monsieur Fontaine-Roux were watching her go, the latter frowning in disapproval, the former hiding a smile.

Luce climbed carefully up the narrow stairs to the quarter deck. It was quieter there, the freshly planked passageways and cabins deserted. In the captain's quarters the large windows were bright with sky and water, the distant shape of Saint-Malo hazy through the glass. The spacious cabin was empty, but would soon contain a large desk and table, bookshelves, and storage for maps and equipment. The urge to see it completed, to imagine her own belongings there and in the adjoining berth, was an ache in Luce's chest.

"There you are." Morgan stood in the doorway. "I saw you come down here from the deck. I hope you don't mind my following."

"Of course not."

Why was he here? Alone on the beach with you? Samuel's rage—his *worry,* Luce now realized—came sharply back to her. She looked again at Morgan's black eyes, tried to read what lingered, hidden, in their depths.

I would never lie to you. I only wonder if Monsieur de Châtelaine can say the same.

"What are you doing down here?" Morgan asked.

"Nothing, really." She reached out to touch the fresh paint coating the window frame. "Just imagining."

"Imagining." He smiled as he stepped further into the room. "Tell me what you see."

"My books will go here." She pointed to the empty shelves. "My seashells and feathers, here."

"I see."

"Navigational equipment and maps here, of course."

"Naturally."

"Desk, table . . ." She moved through the cabin, painting her dreams to life with her hands.

"There is one problem with all of this, of course," Morgan said.

"There is?"

"Well, this is the *captain's* quarters. So if you were to live here, you would be sharing the space with him."

Luce sighed. "It is only a dream, Morgan."

"What if it didn't have to be?"

He had removed his tricorn, and was leaning against the paneling, watching her.

"I want to marry you, Lucinde," he said. "I want to go where you go. Sail where you sail. If we were together, *all* of this could be ours. I could captain the *Lucinde.* You could live in these rooms with me. *Sail* with me." He pushed off from the wall, strode toward her. "I know it's fast. I know we have only just met. But I don't care. I can see your dreams. They are the same as mine."

Could this truly be happening? Luce's heartbeat was like thunder in her ears. The sun was filtering through the windows, catching on the angles of Morgan's face, illuminating hints of red in his dark hair. He was so beautiful it hurt. And his words, his *words . . .* She could *see* the life they were weaving for her. *I can see your dreams. They are the same as mine.*

He took her hand, skimmed her palm with his lips. "Besides," he whispered, leaving a trail of delicious warmth over the inside of her wrist, "I cannot deny there has been something between us since the morning after the storm. Can you?"

Luce's heart beat even faster, if such a thing were possible. *I kissed you because I could not help it, Lucinde.* She remembered the heat of his touch through her stocking, the hunger in his dark eyes. Fire and silk.

All this time, she had thought she had stolen Morgan from the sea; plucked him out of its cruel arms and back to shore, to life.

But what if she had been wrong? What if the sea had *wanted* her to have him?

"We could build something together, you and I," Morgan whispered, his fingertips leaving Luce's wrist and stroking her jaw. "With your ship and my stone, we could be unstoppable."

Luce frowned as the spell he had woven around her shattered. "*Your* stone?" she repeated. "I-I thought you said the *Dauphin*'s stone had been stolen."

He laughed a little, wounded. "Is that all you can say? I have just bared my heart to you, and all you can think of is ballast?"

"I'm sorry," Luce said, carefully. " But . . . surely we cannot make plans—marriage or otherwise—without it?"

"Have no fear," Morgan said grimly. "The bait has been set. It is only a matter of time."

Luce's heart quickened for an entirely different reason. "You . . . know who has the stone?"

"Not yet. But I will, soon enough. And when I do, you can be certain they will regret stealing from me."

Luce slid out of his arms.

"You have flattered me greatly with your offer, Morgan," she said. "In truth, it's overwhelming. And there is much for me to consider. . . ."

"Of course. Please, take as much time as you need." He crossed to the cabin door, pausing to look back at her. "I will say nothing of this to anyone until you have made your choice."

It was the middle of May, and the sun's heat relatively mild, but Saint-Malo was already working itself up to an impressive stench. A latrine by the sea, Samuel called it, and it was hard to disagree. The trick to avoiding the worst of it was to venture out of doors in the early morning or late in the evening, when a veil of cool, fresh air was wont to draw itself over the city. With this in mind, Luce spent the next morning in the town house with Monsieur Daumard. The family had returned to the city for a few days only, to attend the *Lucinde*'s launch and the Blessing of the Sea, and all three of the sisters' lessons were continuing as planned. Today, however, it was Luce who was playing the tutor. Monsieur Daumard had developed a keen geological interest in storm-stone, and was eager to learn more about its properties.

"So what you're saying," he said, gesturing to the three granite samples on the desk in the smaller of the town house's three salons, "is that the storm-stone"—he pointed to the middle piece, its gray undulations rippling with telltale shards of lightning—"is different to these others because it is somehow *imbued* with the magic of the . . . the Fae Folk? Seamaids and tide-women and . . . and *korrigans*, and such?"

"Yes," Luce replied. "Although . . . all three of these samples are storm-stone."

He frowned. "They are?"

"Mm-hmm." She pointed to the middle piece. "This one is obvious—see how it glitters. But *this* one"—she pointed to the piece on the left—"is of better quality."

"Better? It looks like ordinary granite to me."

"Storm-stone is like any stone. No one piece, no one quarry, is the same. You can tell this one by its sound." Luce picked up the stone, offering it to Gabriel. "Listen. Do you hear thunder?"

He pressed the granite to his ear, concentrating. "I do!" he exclaimed, grinning. "It is like holding a shell to your ear and hearing the sea."

Luce returned his smile. "Precisely."

"Extraordinary." Gabriel replaced the stone and pointed to the third sample. It was the least impressive, its texture a homely gray. "What of this one?" He raised it to his ear, looked at Luce questioningly. "I don't hear anything. And it does not sparkle like the others."

"And yet, it is the most powerful." Luce took the stone from him, hefted it in her palm. "This is Léon storm-stone. Straight from my father's ballast stores, if I'm not mistaken."

Gabriel nodded. "He was kind enough to offer me some samples for our lesson." He smiled sheepishly. "Well, *my* lesson. Tell me, how did you recognize it?"

"There is an energy to it. A very faint rumbling, the kind you feel in your bones when thunder is nearby."

He hefted the stone in his palm. "I don't feel anything."

"Not everyone can." She considered telling him about the prickle, and decided against it.

"Do you feel it now?" he asked.

"Of course. This entire house is made of the finest storm-stone."

"There must be some scientific reason for all of this, though." He looked sidelong at her. "You don't truly believe that the fairies are the only source of the stone's power?"

"Why shouldn't I believe it? I have seen nothing to suggest otherwise."

"But, *fairies*, Mademoiselle Lucinde?" He raised his brows meaningfully. "I would be laughed out of Paris if I were to suggest such a thing."

"What are you suggesting?" Charlotte swept into the salon. "And who is laughing?"

At the sight of her, the tutor's face, his whole body, lit up.

"Monsieur Daumard does not believe in the Fae Folk," Luce said, watching her sister's reaction carefully. "Or that they are the reason we have storm-stone."

"I thought you were more intelligent than that, Monsieur Daumard," Charlotte said, stopping at the harpsichord and throwing him a smile. "Everyone knows how storm-stone is made."

"And how, pray tell, is it made?"

Charlotte tinkered a few notes. "By the Fae, of course."

He grinned. "By the korrigans?"

"*Yes*, by the korrigans. Among others. Houle fairies, tide-crones, cave wights. What you call them hardly matters. What matters is that they live in sea-caves up and down this coast—and out on the Storm Islands, of course—and that their very presence changes, for want of a better word, the nature of the granite."

"Making it resistant to bad weather," Gabriel finished.

"Storms are much more than simple weather," Luce told him. "They can be an act of violence, an attack. A castle may be stormed, for example, or a city."

"A storm can be emotional, too," Charlotte added. "An outpouring of temper, a commotion, a disagreement."

"Storm-stone protects against all of these," Luce said, nodding. "A city with storm-stone in its walls, like Saint-Malo, will never be breached. A ship carrying it as ballast will be safe from tempests, but also from mutiny and unrest among its crew."

Monsieur Daumard looked between them. "You don't truly believe this?"

"Look around you, Gabriel," Charlotte said, and Luce's gaze snapped to her sister's face at the casual use of his first name. "Look at my father's house, at this street, at this city. It was a fishing town once. Now it is one of the most powerful port cities in France, with trade connections all over the world."

"The Malouin corsairs are the bane of the English, amassing untold wealth, stealing countless ships," Luce said. "We should have weathered assault after assault for all that we have done, and yet the city has never been breached. You think the gentlemen of Saint-Malo have been blessed with such good fortune for nothing?"

"Your father is a clever man," Monsieur Daumard said, with a shrug. "Daring, too. With great risk comes great reward."

"There is more to this than risk," Charlotte said firmly.

"Perhaps we should visit one of these magical quarries," he mused. "See the fairies for ourselves. We could gather samples, take notes and sketches. Make a proper lesson of it."

"We can't," Luce said.

"Oh? Why not?"

"Because there *are* no quarries," Charlotte told him. "Not anymore."

Monsieur Daumard frowned. "Whyever not?"

"Because most of the Fae have left Bretagne," Luce said quietly. "Sometime in the last thirty years they began to slip away. There was nothing to be done."

"That is . . ." The tutor's mouth twisted thoughtfully. "For some reason that makes me rather sad."

"It is sad," Luce agreed. "The quarries closed, and the shores fell silent. We still have the existing stocks of stone, of course. And the presence of the remaining Folk keeps it strong."

"Why do you think Papa insists the kitchen maids leave treats for the lutins at Le Bleu Sauvage?" Charlotte asked. "Or the people in the city leave food and gifts outside the walls? They *want* the tide-crones or korrigans or mari-morgens—whatever is still about—to stay."

"Mari-morgens?" Monsieur Daumard repeated. "You mean . . . seamaids?"

An image of that graceful webbed hand, fingertips outstretched in the specimen jar's syrupy liquid as though it beckoned for help, wavered in Luce's mind.

Charlotte shook her head. "Mari-morgens have legs, not tails. You should be wary if you ever see one, Gabriel. They will lure you into the waves with their sweet singing and tear you apart."

"There are no mari-morgens, or seamaids, in Bretagne anymore," Luce said, sliding a reproving glance at her sister. What was Charlotte about, addressing their tutor with such intimacy? "They left before the swell fairies."

"Why?"

Luce shrugged. "No one knows. All that's certain is that more of the Fae leave Bretagne every year, and when the last of them go there will be nothing, and no one, to strengthen the stone."

There was a long, sad silence.

"Whatever brought on this depressing conversation?" Charlotte inquired.

"We were talking about storm-stone," Monsieur Daumard said. "Mademoiselle Lucinde was explaining its properties. She surprised me by saying this house is constructed of the stone. That you and she both can hear its presence in the walls."

"Can't you?"

"I'm afraid not."

"Here, then," Charlotte left the harpsichord and went to the tutor's side. "Let us see if we can remedy that."

And then, as though it was nothing at all, Charlotte took Gabriel Daumard's hand. Luce watched, breath held, as the young man got to his feet, allowing her sister to lead him to the nearest wall.

"Beneath all of this," Charlotte said, waving at the wall paneling, the gilded sconces, the paintings, "there lies a wall of stone."

"Really?" Monsieur Daumard's eyes widened in mock disbelief. "I had no idea!"

Charlotte ignored that, lifting his hand and holding it to the paneling. "Close your eyes," she said softly. "Listen."

A delicate hush descended over the room. Luce all but blushed at the look that passed between her sister and Gabriel Daumard before the latter closed his eyes.

"I hear nothing," he said, after several moments of concentration. He opened his eyes, bewildered. "Do you?"

Charlotte sighed. "That was terrible, Gabriel," she said matter-of-factly. "Try again."

Luce, feeling more and more like an intruder, watched as they moved around each of the salon's four walls, pausing to close their eyes and listen. Each time Monsieur Daumard was disappointed, and Charlotte offered him a new insult. Until they reached the final wall.

"That's strange," Charlotte said, pausing before a large painting hanging over a lacquered side table. "I don't hear anything here, either."

Luce frowned. "What do you mean?"

Charlotte smoothed her hand over the oak paneling. "I can hear stone here . . ." She swiped along the wall until she reached one corner. "And here." Leaving a point near the middle, she grazed her fingertips along the other side of the wall until she reached the opposite corner. "But there's nothing here."

"Could it be an old doorway?" Monsieur Daumard asked.

"Perhaps," Charlotte said. "Papa bought the house from the Rivières when we girls were very young. There's no telling what was done to it before then." She glanced at Luce. "Come then, Luce. Test your prickle."

Monsieur Daumard looked bewildered. "Her . . . prickle?"

"Luce didn't tell you?" Charlotte grinned. "Storm-stone makes her skin prickle."

"It does?"

"Mm-hmm," Charlotte said, her eyes shining. "We're not sure why."

"Hush, Cee," Luce said, stifling a giggle.

"Fascinating," Monsieur Daumard muttered. He watched with scientific interest as Luce stepped up to her sister's side, ran her own hand over the empty space.

"I feel nothing," she said.

"No prickle?" Charlotte asked solemnly.

"No prickle."

"Strange, indeed," Monsieur Daumard said. He seemed to realize just how close he had drifted to Charlotte, and stepped hastily away. "But not at all surprising in a house as large as this, I suppose. Now, if you'll both excuse me, I must oversee Mademoiselle Veronique's harp practice." He smiled at both sisters. "I thank you both for your thorough instruction. If I ever come across a marimorgen, I will not hesitate to run."

He bowed slightly and left the room.

"He doesn't believe a word of it, you know," Charlotte said. She traced her fingers over the granite samples the tutor had left.

"Perhaps when he begins to hear the storm-stone himself he will change his mind. That's what usually happens with newcomers."

"What are you doing, Cee?"

"Hmm?"

"The way you speak to him, look at him. The way you say his name—"

"*Hush,* Lucinde." Charlotte's hand abandoned the samples and clamped hard over Luce's own.

"You're not going to deny it?"

"Deny what?"

"That there is—" Luce glanced around the salon, lowered her voice. "That there is something between you and Monsieur Daumard."

"How imaginative you are, Lucinde," Charlotte said tightly. "Anyone would think you read too much."

"I saw you with him," Luce said. "At the—at the launch. I've seen the way you look at each other. I've no wish to hurt you, Cee, or see you hurt. I am only saying this because I am worried for you. And for him. Such a match—you know it cannot be. You are a Léon. He is a tutor."

"And what of it?" Charlotte hissed. "Why should my name and his profession keep us apart? From the moment we met—when he stepped into the salon with that ridiculous measure—we knew that we were meant to be together. It's as simple as that. And I'm not sorry for it, Luce. I won't be. You're not the only one in this family who longs for something more. Who longs to be free. Why shouldn't I take happiness if it's offered to me? Why should I deny it, deny him, and let Maman and Papa parcel me off like a prize mare?"

The words sparked against Luce's soul; a sudden, nameless longing.

"Gabriel loves me, and I love him," Charlotte said. "And I won't give him up. Not for anyone."

Luce stared at her sister as though she had never seen her before. "This is madness, Cee."

"I know." Charlotte smiled then, so radiantly that Luce felt any further protestations die on her tongue. "Promise me you won't tell anyone, Luce."

"Of course," she said, squeezing her sister's hand. "I won't say a word."

15

Darkness

Strange dreams haunted Luce that night. She was on a ship—the *Lucinde*—but instead of being fresh and new, its beautiful timbers were black with rot. It was sinking in a terrible storm, and she could see someone huddled at the wave-battered prow.

It was Samuel.

She struggled to get to him, pushing across the broken foredeck, wading through the seawater rushing over the side—but the ship was breaking apart. She fell into the water, kicking, fighting against the waves. At last she reached the bow. Samuel was struggling to hold on as the waves surged over him, threatening to drag him into the furious water below. Luce lunged across the deck and caught his hand, pulling him to safety. They clung to each other as the ship wallowed and wailed, moaning in its death-throes. At last it broke apart, pieces of deck spearing the stormy sky before sinking beneath the surface.

Samuel was pulled roughly away, sucked down into the swirling depths. Luce dived after him, again and again. Each time she came up empty-handed, her panic rising, her terror, too. At last she saw him, draped lifeless over a slab of wreckage, face pale, eyes closed.

"Samuel!" She swam for him, as hard and fast as she could. When she reached him, however, he was gone.

Morgan was in his place.

Luce lurched away, panicked, pawing the churning water. "Samuel!"

"Don't bother," Morgan said softly. His eyes were open, his beautiful face serene. "I told you I would find the one who stole from me, didn't I?"

Something gripped Luce's ankles in the dark water below. She lashed out, kicking, but it was no use. Water flooded her mouth, her nose, as she was pulled down.

"Do not fear the darkness," Morgan crooned. "It will show you the way."

The last thing Luce saw before she was yanked beneath the surface was Morgan's beautiful smile.

Luce jolted awake, chest heaving with tattered, drowning breaths. Moonlight fell across the bed, cutting across her waist, her legs. The ship's bell never rang the night watches—there was, after all, only so much shipboard routine a household could be expected to endure—so there was no way of knowing the hour. The malouinière was utterly silent, no hint of movement from above or below.

"Just a dream," she whispered, flopping back on the pillows. "Just a dream."

Sleep, however, eluded her. She could not unsee Samuel's face, the horror of watching him slip beneath the waves. Morgan's proposal, too, weighed heavy on her mind. He was offering her a life aboard the *Lucinde*. The horizon. *Freedom*. It was everything she had ever wanted, laid neatly before her like one of her father's maps.

Just waiting for her to reach out and take it.

She rolled over in her bed, sighed. Of course, she would be an utter fool *not* to accept him. Morgan was all that a young lady could wish for. Handsome. Charming. Ambitious. And there was no denying the attraction that had bloomed between them since that morning on the beach. Indeed, she could not deny that a part of her had longed ceaselessly for Morgan to kiss her so again.

Sleep, she told herself firmly. *Sleep.* The minutes passed, and the night settled further into its shroud, yet there was no stilling the dark spiraling of her thoughts. The sense of unease, of foreboding, her dream had awakened was gone. Instead, her night-mind, curious now, latched onto the memory of Gabriel's lesson that day, and the patch of emptiness in the salon's stone walls. Doubtless the tutor had been right, and the hole was nothing more than an oddity of the house. Whoever built it could have run low on storm-stone and decided to miss a section. Or, they could have simply stolen it. Such theft was not uncommon.

"Damn my soul." Curiosity had chased sleep away entirely. It nudged at her, a hungry cat, forcing her out of bed. It purred happily as Luce carried it down the looming stairs and through the silent vestibule, the ship's bell glinting in the glow of her candle. Twitched its ears and flicked its tail as she crept through the grand salon and into the adjoining room, where the harpsichord crouched in the shadows beside a wall that should have tingled on her skin, but did not.

Luce set the candle on the side table, careful to keep the flame from touching the fresh flowers arranged in a brilliantly glazed porcelain vase, and stepped up to the wall.

Moonlight cast its beams across the carpet, lapping at her toes. She closed her eyes, listening. There was no sound but her breathing, and the shallow exhalations of the sleeping Manche.

She ran her hands over the wall, feeling the edge of the silence. It aligned, she realized, with the largest of the room's paintings: a sea scene, her father's three favorites—the *Fleur de Mer,* the *Lionne,* and the *Thétis*—plowing with stately magnificence through turbulent waters. Running her fingers around the painting's gilded frame, her fingernails caught on something hard. Taking up the candle and peering behind the frame, she discerned a small, iron latch.

Luce pressed it.

There was a sharp *click,* and the painting, the wall itself, shuddered. Luce pushed tentatively against the paneling, and the painting, the entire *wall,* swung away from her, as though on an enormous hinge. Within, a set of impossibly narrow stone stairs curled into the inky blackness above.

A hidden door.

A hidden door, and secret stairs.

Luce knew a flicker of fear. They were dark, those stairs. Darker than the night, or the deepest secrets of the sea.

Do not fear the darkness. It will show you the way.

Morgan had spoken the words to her just now, in her dream. But surely Luce had heard them before? She clutched at the memory, caught it: the groac'h, pushing the little witch-boat out into the star-stained waters of the Manche.

As though it, too, remembered the tide-woman's words, the Manche—which had been slumbering beyond the city walls—awoke. Luce heard the slap of its breath, felt it wait for her to take up the candle and climb.

And so, she did.

The stairs were even narrower than they appeared, steep and rough. Her feet protested sleepily as she moved higher and higher into the twisting dark, her nightgown flowing behind her, the candle lighting her way. It was grimly cold, the stone untouched by sunlight or the warmth of a chimney for who knew how many years. The walls squeezed around her, tighter and tighter.

At last she came to another door, small and plain. She reached for the handle, twisted.

An ominous, ancient-sounding creak, and candlelight spilled, a circle of gold, onto a floor of bare timber. Raising the flame, Luce saw a tiny chamber, perhaps half the size of her own. She paused, confused. Where was she? She had not known such a room existed. Indeed, she was certain *no one* in her family knew. Her father had purchased the town house—all sixty rooms and four and a half stories of it—from the Rivières almost two decades ago; had this chamber lain forgotten since then?

She stepped further into the little room, holding the candle high. It was not unlike the storerooms far beneath the house: dusty floorboards as wide as her foot was long, and walls of rough stone. Iron sconces dripped with the hardened wax of long-ago candles. But for an old sea chest shoved against one wall, the room was empty.

A shiver of unease in the darkness. How many secrets did the town house keep?

Her gaze came to rest upon the sea chest. It seemed no different to any other—oaken, squat and sturdy, with thick iron strapwork and a heavily embellished lock plate. Someone, long ago, had left it here. But why? She crouched before it, setting the candle on the floor.

The elaborate lock was a ruse, designed to fool a would-be thief. The real lock, Luce knew, would lay hidden in the intricate ironwork laid along the chest's rounded lid. She ran her fingers over it, flinching as she felt the unmistakeable shape of a key.

It couldn't hurt to look, could it? Whoever owned the chest—some long-dead Rivière, no doubt—was nothing more than dust.

Luce turned the key.

There was a rusty clunk as the complicated lock sprang into action after so long without use, and then it opened with a satisfying *click*. Breath held in anticipation, Luce cracked opened the lid.

The chest was empty. Utterly, disappointingly, empty. Apart from a decorative silver back plate depicting fae creatures that were half horse and half fish, there was nothing of interest in its woody depths.

Unless . . .

Luce seized the candle, angled it to better examine the smooth timber of the chest's bottom. And then she saw it—a small wooden box, unadorned and unassuming, affixed in one corner.

The real treasure, her father always said, *is not always the most obvious.*

Excitement thrilling through her, Luce opened the box.

Inside lay a tightly coiled ball of ocean. *No,* she realized, reaching down to pull it free. Not ocean, but silk.

Sea-silk.

It was blue as the ocean on a summer day, yet green and silver, too. Subtle hints of gold and rose shimmered in the candlelight. Luce got to her feet, and it unfurled like water beneath her: as long as her body and half as wide, luminous as the moon. Enchanted, she pressed the silk to her cheek, meaning to breathe in its scent and feel its softness. No sooner had it touched her skin, however, than a strange shiver passed over her. She could have sworn she heard the sound of distant thunder. Beyond the city walls, the Manche broke its watchful silence and exhaled, a breath of wondrous cold in her soul.

Luce knew, down to her bones, that there would no returning the sea-silk to the chest. To return it, so rare and beautiful, to the cold and the dark seemed an act too cruel to contemplate. Instead, Luce closed the empty chest and turned the key, tucked the silk into her nightgown, and crept back down the winding stair. She closed the secret door behind her and wended her way through the darkened house, not stopping till she reached her own chamber.

Secrets. Secrets in the dim.

The family always rose earlier than was usual on the morning of the Blessing of the Sea, taking their morning cup of chocolate together before walking the narrow streets to the cathedral. An air of excitement hung over the city ahead of the feasting and dancing that would follow the religious formalities. By nightfall, bonfires would light up the quays and the beaches, an ancient homage to the Fae the priests had never quite managed to stamp out.

Luce walked with Charlotte, noting the careful distance her sister kept from Gabriel Daumard, and the dutiful way the tutor walked alongside her father, listening carefully as Jean-Baptiste explained the origins of the Blessing.

Charlotte, of course, was not the only one keeping secrets. Luce had lain awake for what had seemed like hours after returning from the hidden chamber, wondering if she should tell her father of her discovery. After all, the town house—and everything it contained—belonged to him. And yet, the silk was so rare, so precious, that she could not help but fear that he would be compelled to take it from her. To sell it, perhaps—she had no doubt of its value—or, even worse, display it among his curiosities, within, and yet wholly without of, Luce's reach. In the end, she had decided to keep the silk a secret, tucking it within her chemise that morning to prevent Nanette finding it when she tidied Luce's bedchamber. For reasons she could not explain, she felt compelled to keep it near.

"The Church is the problem," her father was saying to Gabriel. "It is crushing the Old Ways, strangling the belief in the Fae. We should all dance drunkenly around fires more often, as far as I'm concerned. Not only is it good fun, but it's excellent for business."

"And does everyone take part in these celebrations?" Gabriel inquired.

"What?" Jean-Baptiste said. "God, no, Daumard. The Blessing is no place for ladies when the sun goes down."

Not everyone was welcome around the fires. While Luce and her mother and sisters—and the rest of the well-bred ladies of Saint-Malo—would be welcome at the markets and festivities for the afternoon, in the evening they would all be expected to make their graceful apologies and "leave the men to it."

Luce smiled secretly. Unbeknownst to her family, she had spent the last two Blessings in the thick of the celebrations with Samuel and Bones, hidden by her breeches and tricorn, coat-collar pulled up high around her face. Indeed, it was only Samuel's boorish behavior of late that was keeping her from doing the same tonight. She had seen neither hide nor hair of him—or

Bones—since their argument on the beach after Morgan's visit, and doubted that would change any time soon.

They soon reached Saint-Vincent's. The stained-glass windows, with their tones of green and blue, threw ripples of light down upon the entering congregation. It looked, Luce had always thought, as though the cathedral's great stone pillars and soaring arches were part of some wondrous, underwater city.

The other ship-owning families were there, sitting in their accustomed pews. The Fontaine-Roux, the Béliveaus, and the Desailles. The Landais, the Rivières, and the Gaultiers. The de Châtelaines entered last. As the mass began, Morgan slid his gaze across the aisle to Luce. A hint of that wolfish smile.

Luce wondered how it would feel to stand before the altar with him, before her parents and the other Malouin families, and say her wedding vows. Would they celebrate with a wedding feast, or simply set sail in the *Lucinde*? Either way, it would be a charmed life. She would want for nothing, need for nothing.

Unbidden, an image of Samuel appeared in her mind, the wide blue sea behind him, water streaming from his shoulders as he pulled himself onto the *Dove*.

She looked away.

When the mass was over and the congregation milled about in the square, waiting for the procession to begin, Charlotte and Veronique dragged Monsieur Daumard toward the cathedral's bell tower. Two of the laquais followed obediently to chaperone, their shoulders slumping at the thought of facing the cathedral's notorious, winding stairs. Luce, watching them go, fought down a pang of envy. As children, her sisters had climbed the tower often. Each time, Luce had remained in the nave, pretending she did not care about the wondrous view Veronique and Charlotte would soon be enjoying at the top of the tallest building in Saint-Malo. Nowhere else could one see so much: the harbor, the Rance, all four of the forts, and, beyond them, the wide blue sweep of the Manche. On such days, Luce's heart had near burst with longing. She never wished to be rid of her aching, ill-made feet so much as when she was trapped in the nave, and her sisters were climbing those stairs without her.

Thankfully, the bishop and his priests were soon ready to lead the congregation down to the quay. . Charlotte, Veronique, and Monsieur Daumard, flushed and out of breath, returned just as the family joined the procession flooding the cobbled streets. Beyond Our Lady's Gate, the tide was in, and the harbor was full and blue. The quay was lined with frigates, luggers, ship's boats, and everything between, masts festooned with colors, splendid in the sun.

Crowds flocked to the waterline as the bishop threw spring flowers onto the water and blessed each of the ships. Afterward, the family walked along the quay, where stallholders hawked oysters and pancakes, cider and wine. Second-hand clothing flapped in the breeze beside stalls selling fine Bretagne lace, sea chests, soap, and pastries.

Charlotte came to Luce's side. "I bought you a madeleine," she said, slipping the biscuit into Luce's gloved hand. Beneath the elegant curves of her bergère hat, Charlotte's face was troubled.

"I also want to say that I'm sorry, Luce," she said quietly. "I know that I have not been kind to you, of late. That I have been prickly, and jealous. You are Papa's favorite, and Vee is Maman's, but they have always loved me too. Very much." Charlotte swallowed, dipped her head, and Luce wondered if her sister was about to cry.

"Is everything well, Cee?" It was not like her sister to so. Charlotte *was* rather prickly and jealous, and it was these sentiments that seemed easiest for her to express. But she was capable of deep kindness and affection, too, which, when all was said and done, made the rare moments when she revealed them to be all the more precious.

"Of course." Charlotte raised her head, smiled. "Everything is wonderful. I just—I just wanted you to know."

"Very well," Luce said, bewildered, but grateful all the same. "I love you too, Cee. I always have. Even when you were prickly and jealous."

They walked arm in arm through the stalls, pausing now and then to watch the wrestling competitions and dancing, the games and musicians. A troupe of actors performed a dramatic play about Keris, the drowned city. Luce's mind turned at once to the painting of the same scene in the de Châtelaine's cabinet of curiosities, and, of course, to Morgan's proposal. She wondered if she should confide in her sister. Tell her everything, from the wreck of the *Dauphin* to the launch of the *Lucinde*. At that moment, however, the audience gave a collective screech as a wall of "ocean" (shredded fabric in varying shades of grimy blue) crashed over the theatrically painted "walls" of Keris. The actors playing Gradlon, Ahez, and their horse leapt into action. Breaths were held and encouragement shouted as the trio raced for the safety of the coast, and there were wails of dismay when Gradlon pushed his daughter into the sea to save himself.

"Do you think Papa would have done the same, had that been one of us?" Charlotte murmured, when the show was over.

Luce squeezed her hand. "Of course not."

In the early evening the Léons, along with the Gaultiers, Fontaine-Roux, and the Béliveaus, returned to the town house on Rue Saint-Philippe for supper. Afterward, the women of the families would spend the evening together enjoying coffee and petit fours while the men returned to the festivities.

Over supper, the men discussed the possibility of England attacking Saint-Malo. Rumors were swirling up and down the coast—the English king was planning to retaliate for the damage the Malouin corsairs were doing to his shipping and trade. The Marquis de la Châtre, charged with the command of the city, had ordered extra troops to be stationed at the forts, while Monsieur Mazin, Chief Engineer, was ensuring the strength of its defences.

"They will not come here," Monsieur le Fer sniffed. "They

wouldn't dare. An English fleet would break itself against our walls, as they have before."

"They will move against Brest, not Saint-Malo," agreed Monsieur Fontaine-Roux. "If they even bother to drag their cowardly tails across the Manche."

Luce excused herself at the earliest opportunity. To her surprise, Charlotte rose at the same time, claiming a headache.

"Are you sure you're quite well?" Luce asked her sister, as they climbed the stairs to the first floor. It was not like Charlotte to retire early.

"Of course. It is just a headache." Charlotte reached her door, hesitated. "Good night, Luce."

"Good night, Cee."

Some time later, as Luce lay in bed reading, she heard the softest of footsteps on the landing. Curious, she rose and cracked the door.

Charlotte was creeping down the stairs, wearing her plainest dress and traveling cloak, its hood drawn up over her hair. She carried her favorite bergère hat and a bulging leather portmanteau under one arm. Alarmed, Luce padded from her chamber and leaned over the balustrade. She was just in time to see her sister slip through the enormous front doors and out into the night.

Luce stood frozen on the landing. Where was Charlotte going? And why was she dressed for travel? There was no denying that her sister had been behaving strangely. There was the expression on her face, when the actor playing King Gradlon pushed his beloved daughter into the waves—*do you think Papa would have done the same, had that been one of us?* And she had retired early, though she had seemed well enough throughout supper, if a little quiet. Luce's hands tightened on the banister as she remembered Charlotte's words at the Blessing. Her apology, as sweet as the madeleine she had pressed into Luce's hand. *I know that I have not been kind to you, of late. That I have been prickly, and jealous.*

It had been, Luce realized, a farewell.

"Damn my soul!" The words were a strangled hiss as Luce dashed back into her chamber. She kept a second set of men's clothing at the town house, and she wasted no time, yanking the breeches on over her nightgown, throwing on the tattered overcoat, and grabbing her tricorn and boots. She did not bother with stays, merely slipped a knotted kerchief around her neck as she hurried down the servants' stairs and through the—blessedly empty—kitchen, ignoring the startled bleating of her feet as she slipped onto Rue de Toulouse.

Was she too late? Was Charlotte already lost to sight? Peering up and down the street, Luce made out her sister's small, hooded form nearing the corner of Rue de Dinan. She hurried after her, then froze, throwing herself into the shadows beside the servants' door.

Jean-Baptiste and the rest of his male guests were about to return to the festivities at the quay. Gathered in the town house's courtyard, and clearly visible through its high gates, they gamboled like colts, eager to stretch their legs.

Charlotte, meanwhile, would soon be gone.

There was nothing for it. Luce plunged onto the cobbled street, sinking into the distinctive, swinging gait of a sailor. She passed the gates to the town house, forced herself to look ahead, to scrunch her shoulders and bow her legs. Waiting for her father to recognize her, to seize her shoulders and push aside her hat, his face furrowed with worry and confusion.

It did not happen. No sooner had Luce passed the gates than her father and his friends wandered out of them. They traveled east behind her for a few moments, then turned toward the cathedral, their low talk and laughter bouncing against the high, stone houses.

Up ahead, Charlotte turned the corner and disappeared.

Luce hurried after her, feet braying, until she reached the corner of Rue de Dinan.

A small, slightly shabby carriage—no doubt hired—waited near the Dinan Gate. As Luce approached, she discerned a familiar form, shoulders hunched and furtive, speaking to the driver.

Luce broke into a run, heedless of the pain, and reached the carriage just as Gabriel climbed inside. He was leaning out to close the door when Luce skidded to a clumsy stop, meeting his horrified eyes. Behind him, in the carriage's candlelit gloom, was Charlotte.

"What are you doing, Cee?" Luce blurted. A foolish question; it was appallingly obvious. The little carriage was packed with Charlotte's and Gabriel's belongings, his precious scientific equipment nestled at their feet.

"Luce? What are you doing here?" Charlotte demanded. She blinked. "And what in heaven's name are you *wearing*?"

Luce stared at her sister, torn between bursting into tears and pulling her bodily from the carriage. "What are you—how could you—? You're *leaving*?"

"Gabriel and I are running away," Charlotte said, with a determined set to her jaw. "We love each other, and we want to be married."

Luce stared at her sister. Was she truly willing to risk everything—her relationship with her family, her good name, her future—this way?

"There will be no coming back from this, Cee," she said. "Once this carriage leaves the gates, once Maman and Papa discover what you have done, there will be no way to undo it."

"Good," Charlotte said flatly. "For I do not *want* it to be undone. You know as well as I what would have happened had Gabriel asked Maman and Papa for permission. They would have refused him, dismissed him, shunned him. They would have been furious that he had even *considered* himself worthy of me."

Samuel's face, Samuel's words, rose unbiddenechoed in Luce's mind. *What would your father say if he knew you were here with me?*

"It would not have mattered that Gabriel is good and kind, and that we love each other," Charlotte said. "Maman and Papa believe there is only one way for you and Veronique and me to be happy—we must marry a certain way, *live* a certain way. But that's not true, Luce. It's not. All the money in the world won't make us happy if we must live without love, and freedom. I don't want anyone but Gabriel. If I stay, Maman will shovel me onto some impoverished old noble in need of Papa's money. She values our good name, our connections, above our feelings. I have no choice. Don't you see?"

So that's what you want, then, it is? Balls and flowers and ice sculptures. Fine horses and frock coats. It was Samuel's words, Samuel's hurt, that Luce was seeing, and hearing. Could it be . . . could it be that he *did* care for her, and had kept her at arms' length because he, like Luce's parents, believed that she should live a certain way? She looked again at her sister, at the way she held tight to Gabriel's hand, risking everything to begin a life with him, no matter his place in society. Charlotte, she realized, was braver than Luce had ever imagined.

"Yes," she said quietly. "I *do* see."

"Then . . . you won't tell your family you saw us?" Gabriel asked warily.

She shook her head. "No. I won't tell."

Charlotte leaned forward, hugged her. "Thank you."

Luce held her sister so tight she feared she would not be able to let go. "Are you certain, Cee?"

"I've never been more certain about anything in my life, Luce."

"Then I am happy for you. Truly."

Gabriel's voice was soft with regret. "Charlotte, we must go . . ."

"Yes, I know." Charlotte was trembling with excitement or fear, or both. "I won't say where we're going, Luce—it's better you don't know."

Luce nodded. Her tricorn had fallen off; it didn't matter.

"You cannot judge a man, or anyone, on their place in society. Remember that, Luce. Don't be afraid to fight for what you really want."

Gabriel's touch, light on her sister's shoulder. "My love, it's time to go."

Luce drew back, wiped away her tears. "Go," she said, her voice cracking. "Quickly."

"Be brave," Charlotte told her, before Gabriel closed the door, smiling at Luce in farewell. "Be free."

Gabriel signaled to the driver, and the carriage rolled into motion. Luce watched it pass beneath the gates and out of the city, Charlotte's words ringing in her mind.

Be brave.

Be free.

16

Barnacles and Shadows

Luce found herself walking behind her father and the other gentlemen as she made her way to the quay. The men moved at a leisurely pace through the lantern-lit streets, their ranks swelling with every elegant town house they passed.

The de Châtelaine brothers, Morgan among them, fell in with the gentlemen at the Place du Pilori. Luce could not help but envy their easy confidence. Not for them the confines of the salon. They were free to move as they pleased, to walk without fear through the unruly streets and celebrate late into the night. And why shouldn't they? Weren't they the gentlemen of Saint-Malo? Most of the ships in the quay, newly blessed, belonged to their families. The ocean and its horizons lay open to them in a way that Luce had only ever dreamed of. The familiar ache, the wanting—the endless blue horizon, the lure of distant ports, awoke in her, stronger than ever.

Be brave.

Be free.

She walked on.

They soon left the wealthier part of the city behind, turning toward its older, darker interior. The cathedral spire appeared above the rooftops, its storm-stone stonework gleaming softly in the moonlight.

The tide had retreated now, and the Malouin ships lay on their sides on the wet sand of the harbor like beached leviathans.

Bonfires had sprung up around them, and the crowds ebbed and flowed between, drinking and dancing, talking and laughing. Music rose from at least five different places, the tunes clashing and melding in turn. Jean-Baptiste and the older men seemed content to wander the quay, watching a group of dancers twirl fire and throw it high in the air, but the younger men flowed down the sea-steps and onto the bustling sands. It would be safer, Luce knew, to stay near her father, or even Morgan. Saint-Malo at night was rough, and dangerous, at the best of times. Yet it was not her father she had come to find.

Be brave.

Hunching deep into her overcoat, her tricorn pulled low, she descended the sea-stairs.

The celebrations on the harbor-floor were always wildest, as though the revelers were worshipping the sea itself. Luce half expected to see the groac'h moving slowly through the dancers, her tusks glinting with wild magic, or the jetins dancing merrily around the fires.

She pushed through the crowds, boots sinking in the watery sand, until she came to the place where she, Samuel and Bones had enjoyed the festivities during the last Blessing. There had been a crepe-seller set up beneath one of the ships, and they had gorged themselves on the thin pancakes, sipping cider and watching the dancing.

A knot of men—sailors, from their weather-beaten faces—came toward her, loud and drunken. She swerved to avoid them, her foot catching on a half-submerged rock. Pain shot through her foot. She stumbled, threw out a hand.

"Easy there, lad." A gnarly old tar caught her shoulder, righting her. "Can't hold your liquor, eh?" He laughed toothlessly and slapped her on the back, so hard she lurched straight into a crowd of people gathered around a large bonfire. Annoyed shouts, and spilled cider. Someone caught her arm, steadied her.

"*Luce?*"

It was Samuel.

"What in Christ's name are you doing out here?" He pulled her into the shadows beneath a stranded frigate, then looked her over, incredulous. "Are you *alone*?"

"I can take care of myself," Luce snapped, wrenching her elbow out of his grasp.

Bones and a handful of Samuel's smuggler friends lounged on crates and casks around the fire. Their voices bounced off the frigate's barnacled hull, mingled with the music rising from a fiddle, a bombarde, a veuse, and a drum. Someone was frying fish over a flame; the scent of its cooking, of smoke and the unmistakable tang of the exposed sea-floor, was heavy on the air.

"I never said you couldn't," Samuel said quietly.

They had not seen each other since their argument at the cove. The memory of it lingered between them, tainting the very air its with awkwardness. Luce stole a look at him. He was slightly disheveled, as always, his hair escaping its tail at the back of his neck, the collar and top buttons of his shirt laid open. There was a drink in his hand, and salt in the creases of his overcoat. He looked like nothing so much as a smuggler; good-for-nothing, and utterly dishonorable.

Then why did her heart quicken so?

"Can I walk you back to Rue Saint-Philippe?" Samuel asked.

"You just said . . ."

"I know what I said. But Luce, you shouldn't be out here. This particular gathering is not . . ."

"Not what?"

"It's not for you, that's all."

Luce gestured to crowd around the fire. "There are lots of women here."

"Ye-es, but . . ."

She looked closer. Some of the women were dancing, their skirts hitched high, their feet bare as they skipped across the sand. Others lingered with the men, perched on a knee or an upturned cask, stockings peeping from beneath grimy petticoats as they drank and flirted brazenly.

"Oh." She blushed.

"As I said." Samuel refrained from looking at her. "Not for you."

Luce watched the dancing. There were no courtly bows and curtseys, no rules and patterns to adhere to. The men grasped the women around their waists, their bodies scandalously close. They messed up the steps, laughed, spilled their drinks, and crashed into each other.

She stifled a giggle.

Nearby, a sailor thumped his drink upon a rickety crate and burst into song:

"*So up the stairs and into bed I took that maiden fair. I fired off my cannon into her thatch of hair—*"

"Christ," Samuel muttered.

"He has impressive diction," Luce said solemnly.

Samuel snorted.

More sailors joined the first, loud and bold and drunk.

"*I fired off a broadside until my shot was spent, then rammed that fire ship's waterline until my ram was bent.*"

Shouts, close by, loud and rageful. Two men were brawling, punching and swinging and cursing. Everyone stopped what they were doing to shout encouragement.

"Right," Samuel said firmly, tossing back what remained of his drink. "That's more than enough for one night. I'm taking you home."

Charlotte's voice whispered in Luce's mind. *Don't be afraid to fight for what you really want.*

"You didn't seem to mind me being here last year, or the one before," she said. "What's changed?"

He considered her. "I suppose I figured you'd still be angry with me for what I said to you at the cove. Couldn't imagine you wanting to spend the Blessing with me, after that." He swept a hand over the fires, the ships. "And I can't just let you wander off on your own. Christ knows what might happen to you."

"So home it is."

"That's the conclusion I've come to, yes."

"There's another option, Samuel."

He sighed. "Of course there is."

"You could apologize to me."

"For what?"

"For how you treated me at the cove. And for all the awful things you said about Morgan."

He leaned against the ship's hull, arms crossed. "Very well. I'm sorry for the way I spoke to you, Lucinde. You didn't deserve it. But I'll be damned before I apologize for what I said about de Châtelaine."

"You still believe it's true?"

"I *know* it's true." His eyes narrowed. "Why does it matter so much to you?"

"It doesn't matter to me."

It was true; it didn't. She had decided already that she would not, could not, marry Morgan. Not when she felt the way she did about Samuel. She had come here, to the Blessing, to discover if her feelings for him were returned. To be *brave.* The stubborn set of his jaw, however, told her that achieving her aims might require some added . . . encouragement. She shrugged weakly, as though his opinion of Morgan *was* the most important thing in the world to her—and she was trying to hide it.

Samuel took the bait at once. "Why does it matter, Luce?"

"Because Morgan asked me to marry him." *There,* she thought. *Let's see what you make of that.*

"He *what*?" Samuel drew back as though she had bitten him. "And what did you say?"

"I've said nothing, yet." She looked back at the dancing. A woman swirled by, her partner holding her close. "I told him I needed time to think."

"Time to think?" His eyes narrowed. "So you're considering it."

"Of course I am. If I married Morgan, I could go to sea with him on the *Lucinde*."

"The *Lucinde*? Isn't that your father's new ship?"

"She's my ship. Papa is giving her to me."

"I see." Samuel nodded grimly to himself. "Now it all makes sense."

He pushed off the ship and strode away from her, into the shadows of a second frigate looming in the darkness.

"What is *that* supposed to mean?" Luce followed him.

"Word in Saint-Malo is that Castro blames his son for the loss of the *Dauphin*," Samuel said over his shoulder. "Morgan wants to captain a corsair, go raiding, but Castro refuses to give him another ship. Seems as though he means to take yours."

"He would not be *taking* it," Luce said. She did not want to marry Morgan, it was true. Even so, she did not like the thought of him using her for his own ends. He cared for her. Didn't he? "We would sail it together."

"How romantic." Samuel stopped, turned. "I thought the plan was to join a crew. Go to sea on your own terms."

"And *I* thought you said that was madness!"

They were at the center of the ship. The broadest part of the hull, thick with barnacles, loomed over them, its masts and rigging sweeping the night sky.

Luce looked into Samuel's face, searching for a sign that he cared. That she had not imagined what had passed between them on the *Dove* and in the woods. He glanced away, unwilling to meet her gaze, and the rejection of it, the stubborn set of his mouth, filled her with sudden anger.

"What would you have me do?" she demanded, balling her fists. "You and I both know that dressing in breeches and joining a crew was never really an option for me. No, let me speak. You've seen my feet. And you've worked on enough ships to know that

I would never manage. I would never be fast enough. Never be able to go aloft or keep my feet on a pitching deck." She had never admitted this before, not even to herself. Her heart clenched with grief and regret. "Going to sea with you was a childish dream, nothing more. And as for Morgan . . . well, at least he was brave enough to tell me how he felt, and what he wanted. I would be a fool not to consider him. Even if—"

"Even if what?"

Even if I don't love him. There were limits to one's courage, it seemed, and Luce had reached hers. The words stuck to the roof of her mouth, refusing to budge.

"He's *brave,* is he?" Samuel asked, low and angry. "And what about . . ." He shook his head, swallowed.

Luce shifted her weight. "What about . . . ?"

"Nothing. It is nothing."

But it *was* something. Luce could feel it in the darkness between them. "Samuel?"

"You are right," he said at last, stepping away from her. "It was a dream, nothing more. Foolish." The light of the fire was the barest glow on the side of his face. The music, the sounds of the Blessing, seemed very far away.

"I never said that," Luce said.

"You never had to. I've always known it."

I've always known it.

He was no longer speaking about Morgan, or going to sea. He was speaking about what lay between *them.* The unvoiced, unacknowledged awareness that had begun when Luce had tripped over her feet on the *Dove* and he had steadied her.

"Just as I've always known that . . . that someone like de Châtelaine would come along, and . . ."

"What are you saying, Samuel?"

"I'm saying it should have been me, Luce. *I* should have been the one to kiss you on that beach."

Luce's heart trilled, three notes quavering, both at his words, and the look upon his face, all hunger and beauty. Then . . . "You saw that?"

"Of course I saw it. In truth I cannot *unsee* it. It is there every time I close my eyes." The careful distance Samuel had been maintaining between them crumbled. He reached for Luce, pulled her hard against him, pushed away her hat, his own. His breath was warm against her lips. "I should have kissed you, so many times."

The fire, the dancing, the sparks flying into the dark sky, the looming ships, the drums and the fiddle and the pipes disappeared. There was nothing, no one, but Samuel.

"On the *Dove*," he murmured. "In the woods that night." He smelled of the sea; of salt and wind. His heartbeat was rapid as the drums. "I've regretted it every day. Every hour."

The tide was coming back in. Luce could feel it in the air, in the sand beneath her boots. Even now it snaked back along the sand, reaching, eager to reclaim what it had lost. In a few hours the fires, the dancing, the music would be nothing more than memory, lost beneath dark water.

There was only this moment.

There was only now.

"You definitely should have kissed me, Samuel," she whispered. "Every day. Every hour."

He did kiss her then; his mouth, his body, crushing hungrily against hers. Luce, for her part, was already raising her mouth to his, arching her body to welcome him. She wound her arms about his neck, drew him close. Closer. She had dreamed of this moment so many times. He flicked his tongue lightly against her own, deepening the kiss, and her legs, her body—the deepest, hidden parts of her—melted with desire.

It was too much. It was not enough.

How easy it was, to push the coat back from those broad shoulders and slip her hands inside his shirt, against his bare skin. To run her fingers through his sea-gold hair and taste the salt on his neck, his chest. To guide his hands along her thighs and wrap her legs around him as he hauled her off her feet, bracing her against the hull.

"Are you all right?" he muttered against her mouth. "The fouling—"

"I can't feel anything but you."

It was true. The roughness of the timber against her back, the pain in her feet, were as nothing compared to the feel of him against her. Chest to chest, hip to hip, mouth to mouth. He slid a hand beneath the soft cotton of her nightgown, touched her bare waist . . . And stilled.

"You're not wearing stays?"

She shook her head. "I left in a rush." She sucked his bottom lip between her teeth, guided his hand higher. He groaned softly, and desire coiled itself low in Luce's belly, rippling through her as Samuel's lips grazed her neck, her collarbone, his hand sliding over the swelling softness of her breasts.

"Christ, Luce," he said, ragged. "This is madness."

"Do you want to stop?" A moment of real fear; would he draw away, leave her again?

"God, no." He laughed against her neck, tickling her in a way that was so wicked, so delicious that her fears were forgotten. "Never again, Luce," he muttered. "I'll never stop again. I swear it." He was the one thieving kisses now, taking Luce's heart, her soul, along with them. "I'm yours, Luce. Yours."

I'm yours.

She was burning for him. *Burning.* And, by the way he was moving his hips against her, so was he. Some wildness, some instinct, took hold of her. She reached between them, for the laces of his breeches, and clawed them free. Felt the sudden, silky hardness of him against her fingertips.

"Christ." Samuel groaned against her mouth.

He was working at her laces, too, one large hand bracing her hip. She gasped as the laces loosened, as he—

"Samuel, you grumpy bugger!" Bones's voice, cider-loose, cut abruptly through the cocoon of warmth and want; Luce tensed in Samuel's arms. "Where have you slunk off to? Oh. Is that—? *Oh!* Jesus-fucking-Christ-I'm-sorry!"

"I'll kill him," Samuel muttered against Luce's shoulder. "I will fucking kill him."

Luce giggled.

A nervous-sounding cough from the stern. "Er, Samuel?"

"Still here, cousin," Samuel said, with the air of one who has suffered long and well.

"The only remaining question is, why are you?"

"We need to talk."

"*Now?*"

"'Fraid so."

"No," Luce whispered, clinging to him. "No, no . . ."

Samuel sighed. "I'm so sorry." He kissed her once more, long and full of promise, before setting her gently on her feet. "Mind the fouling."

He left her to rearrange her clothing, reaching down to scoop both their tricorns from the damp sand before joining Bones. Luce, pushing her tricorn firmly onto her head and arranging her kerchief, watched Bones grin and nod toward Luce, then raise his hands defensively as Samuel no doubt repeated his earlier threat. Sobering, Bones leaned in, muttering something in Samuel's ear. Luce saw Samuel frown, throw a quick glance around the crowded sands, and clasp his cousin's shoulder in thanks before hurrying back.

"As fun as it's been," he said, taking her hand. "We need to go."

"Is everything well?" she asked, as they wended through the knots of dancing and fires crowding the expanse of sand before the quay.

"Of course." He slid her a smile and brushed her fingertips with his. "Why wouldn't it be?"

"You look worried. What did Bones say?"

"No more than his usual ramblings."

He stepped around a drunken man sprawled and snoring on the sand, then returned to her side.

"Do you remember the last thing you said to me when we argued at the cove?" Luce asked. "'I would never lie to you.' That's what you said, Samuel."

"Fine." He stopped in the middle of the crowds to face her. "Bones told me that while you and I were . . . talking"—his mouth twisted a little, barely containing his grin—"that a certain someone came poking around the gathering, looking for me."

"Looking for you? Or looking for the *Dauphin*'s ballast?"

"Both."

"Was it the City Guard?" she asked.

"No. Bones suspects it was someone looking to claim the reward de Châtelaine has offered for information leading to . . ." He shrugged. "You know how it goes."

A knot of worry coiled in Luce's belly. "I should have told you earlier," she said. "Morgan is determined to get the ballast back. He told me that . . ." She frowned, remembering. "'The trap has been set'. He believes it is only a matter of time before he finds the one who stole the stone and ensures they regret what they've done."

"Much luck to him, then," Samuel said wryly. "He isn't the first to say such things, and he certainly won't be the last." He tilted his head, considering. "Although, he may be the most dramatic."

"That man just now knew your name," Luce warned, "which means that Morgan probably knows it, too." The knowledge, and the memory of Morgan's face when he had spoken of seeing the thief punished, set an icy chill around her heart. She could not help but glance toward the city, where the long wooden stakes where storm-stone smugglers were punished sat exposed on the sand. "I think . . . I think you were right about him, Samuel. I think he's been interested in nothing but his own ambitions, and the *Lucinde*, from the start." And she, fool that she was, had been too enchanted to see it. "I should have listened when you warned me about him."

"You're not the only one who should have done things differently." Beneath the cover of their wide sleeves, he took her hand. "If I hadn't been pushing you away, he might not have turned your head."

Luce frowned up at him. "Why *were* you pushing me away?"

He glanced around them. "Is now the best time for this conversation?"

"No, it's not," she conceded. "Every moment we linger here we risk being seen by whoever is looking for you."

"Off we go, then."

He led her through the crowds, ducking and weaving, cutting a crooked path toward the quay. At one point a pair of seamen burst at them, rolling and fighting and swearing, and Samuel gripped Luce's waist, swinging her smoothly out of the way. At another, a woman in grubby velvet stepped into Luce's path, latching on to her arm. "How's about you and me go somewhere more private?" she slurred in Luce's ear. "I'll make you a man, my boy, just see if I don't." She winked at Samuel. "Your fine tall friend can watch us for free, and then—"

Samuel cleared his throat, pulled Luce away. "You're very generous, madame," he called back. "But we have business elsewhere."

The woman raised one painted brow. "Like that, is it?"

Luce was still giggling when they reached Our Lady's Gate, which were no less chaotic than the quay. Crowds of people flowed between them, spilling into and out of the seething pothouses and cabarets, or loitering at tables sticky with drink.

"Keep moving," Samuel said quietly, leading Luce through the melee. "And watch your pockets."

Luce should have been nervous. The streets around the docks were notorious at night, rife with drunks, thieves, and cutthroats. She should have been wary, too. Morgan knew Samuel's name, had sent men out to search for him. Every moment they spent in Saint-Malo increased the risk of his being caught. And yet, joy walked at her side, obscuring the filthy roughness of the cobbled streets, the stench of bodily fluids and rotting fish from the nearby market. Even her feet hurt less than they should. She grabbed Samuel's hand, pulled him into a narrow side street where the shadows were good and dark. He came with her eagerly, pressing them both into the dimness as though he had been wanting Luce's mouth as much as she had been wanting his. The unexpected strains of Vivaldi wafted from an establishment further along the street, winding around them.

"Look at you," Luce panted between kisses, "allowing me to throw myself into a life of debauchery."

"At this point, I think it's safe to say I'm throwing you in myself." His mouth was on her neck, his hands loosening her kerchief, the ties of her nightgown. "And myself right behind you."

He cupped her breast, trailed kisses, and then his tongue, over her skin. It was unbearable, the want. Luce arched against him. "I'm yours, Samuel," she murmured. "Yours."

He raised his head, to speak, or kiss her, Luce could not say. Before he could do either, Vivaldi's music grew louder. Light spilled through an open door, illuminating a swarm of glossy, well-dressed young men tumbling out onto the cobbles.

Samuel pulled Luce's coat gently closed before leaning casually on the wall beside her, hands deep in his pockets. She mimicked him as best she could.

"That right there is the Convent," he whispered. "One of Saint-Malo's more refined pleasure houses. Hence the fine music and discreet entrance."

"Debauchery indeed," Luce muttered, and caught the pale flash of his smile in the dark.

She kept her head down as the men drew near. There was every chance some of them knew her father, had supped at the town house or Le Bleu Sauvage. She watched, curious, from beneath the edge of her tricorn as they passed, then caught a sharp breath as she spied Morgan and three of his brothers.

"Is that . . . ?" Samuel winced as Morgan tripped on the uneven cobbles. Two of his brothers caught him, scrubbing at his hair, squeezing his cheeks.

"Had a pleasant voyage, did we?" one of them teased.

Morgan pushed them off. "No more than you, you pair of fucking ferrets."

"A pair of fucking ferrets or a fucking pair of ferrets?" They crowed with laughter.

"Did you get your trophy, then?" another of Morgan's companions asked.

Morgan grinned. "Do you doubt me?" He fished in his pocket, and a tangle of garter ribbons spilled to the cobbles, blue, pink, and green. The young men wasted no time, pouncing upon them greedily.

"What's *this*, then?"

"A veritable treasure trove!"

"Saints preserve us! How many did you tumble, Morgan?"

"Only one tonight." He pointed to a band of vibrant red. "The others were already in my pocket."

"This one's got words embroidered on it," one of the men was saying. He held the ribbon toward the Convent's lanterns. "'I die where I cling,'" he read.

Someone guffawed. "This one says 'Rubicon.'"

More laughter.

There was a low whistle, and someone held up a ribbon that caused Luce to gasp in recognition. Samuel glanced at her.

"Look at *this* one," the whistler said. "This one's not like the others!"

The ribbon was made of blue silk so dark it seemed black. It glimmered in the lantern light like a sky full of stars. A row of fine, black pearls were stitched about each edge.

"Fancy," someone commented.

"No message?"

"Not this one, no. She's *mysterious.*"

Luce could barely breathe. She remembered Morgan's touch on her knee when he took off her shoes, the way her stocking had slipped down again and again as she had run to the dock.

Samuel touched her hand, a silent question.

"He stole it from me at the ball," Luce whispered, a bare breath of sound. "I—I never even knew."

Samuel, his gaze fixed squarely on Morgan, said nothing.

"Who's this fancy stargazer, then?" one of the men asked, waving the ribbon under Morgan's nose.

"She's no stargazer," he said roughly, snatching the ribbon back. "And I'll thank you to keep a civil tongue in your head." He held out his hand, and the ribbons were dutifully returned.

"Let's get another drink," someone suggested, and the men set off once more, passing so close to Luce and Samuel that they could have reached out and touched them.

And then, to her horror, Samuel *did* reach out and touch them. Luce could only gape as he lurched drunkenly into the group, hands pressed to his mouth, his belly as though he were battling violent nausea. He crashed headfirst into Morgan, gripped him like a man drowning. There was a scuffle, and much swearing and clamoring before the men shoved Samuel away. He fell to his knees, pretending to retch.

Luce watched from beneath her hat, doing her best to look manly, drunk, *and* benign as the men debated whether or not to kick Samuel to death. In the end it was only Morgan who acted, striding to Samuel and slamming his boot so hard into his belly that Samuel keeled over on the cobbles, gasping and retching in earnest.

"You drunken shit," Morgan spat, seizing Samuel's collar and jerking his face toward him. "Keep your filthy fucking hands off your betters."

Luce froze, stunned by the rage, the hatred, in Morgan's face.

"Temper, temper, Morgan," one of the older de Châtelaines said soothingly, tugging Morgan away. "Save it for the English if they ever arrive, eh? Come on. Let's get that drink."

Morgan glared at Samuel as his brothers pulled him away, only turning from him when the group rounded the corner and disappeared.

Luce crashed to her knees beside Samuel.

"What in God's name was *that*?" she demanded.

He groaned as he rolled over. Held up a fist full of ribbons, one of them a sliver of glimmering night across his knuckles.

"You already risked your soul to save that arrogant bastard," he rasped. "Now he wants the *Dauphin*'s ballast, the *Lucinde, and* Lucinde." A pained, though triumphant grin. "May the Fae take me if I let him have your garter ribbon, too."

17

Thievery

The following morning when Luce woke it was to hear not the quiet, sleepy conversation of her sisters in the next room, but cries of alarm. Rapid, panicked footsteps in the vestibule, on the landing and the nearby bedrooms, and what could only be described as wailing.

She rose quickly, threw on her peignoir, and hurried down the stairs.

Her mother was pacing the vestibule, wringing her hands, her cheeks streaming with tears. Veronique, also in her peignoir, stood at the bottom of the stairs, her arms folded tightly across her body, like a frightened child. Jean-Baptiste was in the grand salon. Luce knew this because her father was shouting, not in joy or excitement, but in pure, predatory rage. She peered into the salon and saw the domestiques huddled before him, their heads bowed.

"Charlotte has run away," Veronique whispered to Luce. Her eyes were wide with horror, her face ashen. "With *Monsieur Daumard.*"

Gratienne gasped, as though hearing the words spoken aloud was a knife thrust to her heart. "How shall I bear this?" she moaned to nobody in particular. "We shall be ruined. *Ruined!*"

"God above," Luce said, doing her best to look shocked. "When did this happen?"

"Last night. It seems our clever tutor knew precisely when to steal our poor sister away, with father and most of the domestiques at the festivities and the rest of us busy with our guests."

"Thank God none of them know," Gratienne croaked. She was unable, it seemed, to cease her relentless pacing. "Thank God we did not discover this—this *aberration* until this morning!"

"Poor Charlotte," Veronique said with a mournful sigh. "To be so disgraced . . ."

"It is not only your sister who is disgraced," Gratienne spat. "We will *all* suffer for this!" She glanced at Luce. "Your father is speaking to the servants. Seeing what they know, if anyone saw Charlotte and—and *him*—leave." She stilled suddenly, looked again at Luce, as though seeing her youngest daughter for the first time. "What of you, Lucinde? Did you hear anything? See anything?"

"No, Maman." Luce swallowed.

"I trusted him," Gratienne wailed. "Trusted him with my *daughters!* He is a fox! A wily, cunning fox!"

Jean-Baptiste strode out of the grand salon. "Very good," he said, his gaze, black with fury, roving over his family. "I am glad to see that only *one* of my dear daughters was stolen from me this night."

"Did you learn anything from the domestiques, Papa?" Veronique asked. "Did anyone see them go?"

"No one saw a thing," he said. "Not that it matters. They will have gone to Dinan or Rennes, and from there to Paris. I must go at once, see if I can't track them down."

Charlotte's expression as she had watched the play at the Blessing rose in Luce's mind; the way her sister had paled when King Gradlon pushed his treacherous daughter into the sea. *Do you think Papa would have done the same, had that been one of us?*

The domestiques trailed miserably out the grand salon, shoulders bowed as though they were somehow responsible for the misfortune that had befallen the family.

"I will go with you," Gratienne said, scrubbing away her tears.

She waved at the groom, the coachmen, as they filed toward the servants' stairs. "Ready the carriage, Elliot, Alexandre. Quickly." She gripped her maid's arm. "Madeleine, pack my things."

"No, no, ma chère," Jean-Baptiste said soothingly. "It will be far better—faster—for me to go on horseback. I'll take two of the laquais with me."

"And what am *I* to do?"

"Take Veronique and Lucinde back to the malouinière, and wait there for my word," he told her. "Say nothing of this to anyone, ma chère. If you receive visitors, have the domestiques tell them that sickness has come over the household. No one can discover what has happened. Not until we know more."

Gratienne burst into fresh tears. "How could she do this?" she cried. "The scandal, Jean-Baptiste, the *scandal*!"

Jean-Baptiste held his wife tenderly until his valet and the laquais were ready, three horses waiting in the courtyard. There was barely time to bid him farewell as he rushed from the house and into the saddle. There came the sound of hoofs scattering gravel, the sad creaking of the gates.

"We are ruined!" Gratienne moaned into the silence, sinking onto the stairs. "*Ruined!*"

The events of the Blessing shook Luce for days. Charlotte's departure alone would have been enough to do so, but Samuel's confession—and all that had passed between them in the shadows of the frigate—also played its part.

And then, of course, there was Morgan.

There was no denying that Samuel had been right about him. About his selfishness, his callousness. And Luce had never imagined that he could be so rageful. So *cruel*. His violence toward Samuel appalled her, even more so because, in that moment, Samuel had been no more than a stranger to him. What would Morgan have done, had he known who Samuel really was? Had he known that it was *Samuel* who had salvaged the *Dauphin*'s storm-stone? The very thought made her shudder.

"I already told you," Samuel said, when they were out on the *Dove* three days later. "I'm not concerned. The stone is well hidden, and I've been careful."

"Not careful enough."

They had headed east when they'd left the cove, tacking along the coastline, the waves slapping against the hull, and the wind snapping in the rigging. It was bliss to be on the water once more, far from the shroud of worry, sorrow and shame that Charlotte's absence had drawn over Le Bleu Sauvage.

Gratienne, Veronique and Luce had done what Jean-Baptiste had commanded before he left: returned to the malouinière, stayed indoors, and avoided socializing with the other ship-owning families. If visitors called, the laquais sent them away with claims of sickness in the house. Without an endless supply of afternoon teas, suppers, and receptions to plan and attend, Veronique and Gratienne had taken to going to bed, and rising, earlier. Until yesterday, of course, when four cases of fine new wines from Bourgogne had arrived. Thanks to the wine's generous consolations, Gratienne and Veronique had tottered to their chambers far later than Luce had expected, allowing her to leave a note for Samuel in the chapel, then rise early, tuck the sea-silk into her chemise, and make her escape.

The *Dove* entered a sheltered bay between two ragged, rocky heads. The water was marvelously clear, as pure and shining as Luce's glassy slippers. Glancing over the side, she could see straight down to the reef below.

"Whoever came looking for you at the Blessing knew your name, Samuel," she said, turning back to where he sat at the tiller. "If they know it, there's every chance Morgan does, too."

"It is just a name. A name doesn't prove anything." He pointed to the sails. "We might strike the sails, do a little fishing."

Luce waited for Samuel to turn the boat into the wind, then

lowered the jib while he handled the mainsail. "You should have waited," she said, when they had finished. "Let a few months, a year, pass before you opened negotiations."

"I'm not doing this for fun, Luce," he said, dropping the anchor. "It's not a game."

"No, it's not," she agreed pointedly.

"If I don't do this, my family doesn't eat."

"And your family certainly won't eat if you're tied to a post beneath the ramparts of Saint-Malo, watching the tide creep up your neck." It was warmer now, the morning sun strong. She pushed the long sleeves of her coat up to her elbows, irritated. "Only a fool would remain in Saint-Malo now. There is every chance Morgan and his father know your name. *And* he saw your face at the Blessing, when you stole those ribbons."

"He stole them first," Samuel said reasonably, returning to the bench in the stern. "You can't steal something if it never belonged to you."

She glared at him, feet bare, shirt sleeves rolled high, his tanned face turned up to the sun. "You know, just once I'd like to go sailing without having to dress as though I'm about to commit highway robbery."

He shrugged. "Then don't."

Luce looked around them. There was no other vessel in sight. But for the swallows nesting on the cliffs high above, they were alone.

"You should go home to Dorset," she said, shrugging out of the heavy overcoat. "Even for a week or two. Fish. Mend nets. Do whatever you must to keep yourself safe."

"And leave the stone unprotected? Leave *you* unprotected?"

"The stone will be safe enough in the cave. And *I'm* not the one who needs protecting. Damn my soul, why is this so difficult?"

"What's wrong?"

"This cursed *coat*—"

It was caught on something. An oar, perhaps. She twisted around awkwardly to free herself.

"Here, let me . . ." Samuel got to his feet. "What's upsetting you?" he asked, laying a hand on her squirming shoulder. "It's not just the coat, or the sun, is it?" He leaned close, brushing his lips across the soft skin beneath her ear. "Are you worried about me, Luce? Is that it?"

"*Somebody* has to be," she grumbled.

He chuckled. "Stay still. I'll get you free. . . ."

At that moment a stiff breeze gusted over the water, catching at the boat. Luce stumbled, wincing as her foot twisted painfully. She reached for the side of the boat to steady herself, missed, and lost her balance entirely.

"Watch yourself," Samuel warned, too late. Before Luce knew what was happening, she was tumbling into the sea.

"*Luce!*" She heard Samuel's cry before she hit the water, before all became a blur of bubbles, cold and breathlessness. The overcoat was instantly drenched, its weight dragging her down. Panicked, she struggled out of it, went to kick for the surface, and found that she could not.

Her legs were tangled in the coat.

She pulled at it desperately, sculled for the surface, and only sank further, the weight of her clothing forcing her down. A trail of bubbles rose above her, drifting toward the rounded bottom of the *Dove,* which was growing smaller and smaller the further she sank.

She tore at the coat with clumsy fingers, finally tugging herself free. Lungs near bursting now—there had been no time to take a breath—she kicked for the surface again. Again, she failed. She struggled and fought, but her legs were still tangled, somehow, her movements awkward. Terror, heavy as a stone, pulling her down. She tried again, felt the last of the air leave her lungs as panic overcame her. Something was wrong with her legs. Something was—

There was a disturbance above, and Samuel was coming for her, slicing through the water with strong, smooth strokes. She flailed and kicked, reached up as he reached down, wrapping his arm about her waist and dragging her toward the surface.

Luce clung to him as he hauled her back to the *Dove*, leveraging himself against its side and hoisting her into the boat. She fell heavily into the bottom, a spluttering mess of limbs and wet clothing, one of Samuel's discarded boots digging painfully into her shoulder. That nightmare of a coat was gone, drifting somewhere below the boat, and yet there was still something wrong with Luce's legs. She coughed against the oiled timber. Felt the boat sway and right itself as Samuel hauled himself out, rolled into the boat beside her, panting.

Luce struggled to sit up, pushing her wet hair back from her face. She glimpsed Samuel through the strands, heaving himself to his knees, white shirt clinging to his chest, breeches dripping. She tried again to sit up, and found that she could not. Her legs—there was something very wrong with her legs.

Beside her, Samuel froze.

"Jesus fucking Christ," he said in English.

Luce looked down.

Her legs, her breeches, were gone. And in their place, shimmering and strong, covered in a thousand scales of green and blue, pink and silver, was an enormous fish tail.

"Damn my fucking soul," Samuel breathed. He scrambled to his feet, slipped, and crashed to the floor of the boat. "Luce? What the . . . ?"

"I don't know," Luce whispered, trembling. She reached for the side of the boat, tried to pull herself up. Her hands, too, seemed different. They gripped the edge of the timber easily, absurdly strong, and strangely opalescent. Stretched between her fingers, knuckle to knuckle, were fine, flesh-cloured webs.

"Fuck," Samuel said, gaping at her. "*Fuck.*"

At the terror in his voice, Luce panicked. The great tail lifted and thumped against the planks, its long trailing fins, fine and shining as gossamer, flinging water everywhere. It hit Samuel's discarded boots and coat, sent them skidding across the boards.

"Jesus," Samuel whispered. He crabbed backward as Luce flailed against the side of the boat, desperately trying to escape her own body.

"What—" she said, teeth chattering, jaw locking with shock and fear. "What—"

"You're a fucking seamaid!" Samuel yelped. "Luce? *A seamaid!*"

"N-no," Luce said, shaking her head. She released the rail, collapsed back into the prow, shivering. *No, this could not be.* And yet, here she was, lying in the bottom of the *Dove,* with a tail. *A tail.* She forced herself to look down.

The top of her body—chest, arms, belly, waist, looked as they always had. Longer, perhaps. Lither. Her skin, like her hands, glittered faintly, as though she had rolled in the silvery powder Veronique sometimes puffed upon her hair. Her caraco was waterlogged, while her thigh-length chemise—which had been tucked into her breeches—clung wetly to the place where her hips ended. Fingers trembling, Luce gingerly peeled the chemise higher. Tiny, silvery scales shimmered beneath her belly button and over her hips, melding gradually into larger, thicker scales. They shone like overlapping jewels in the sun—dusk-pinks and sea-greens, moonlight-silvers and sunset-golds, winter-blues and storm-grays—all the way to Luce's feet. *No, not feet.* Enormous fins, curved like half-moons, glimmering as they caught the light, their diaphanous edges trailing the entire length of the *Dove.* A shudder of revulsion passed through Luce as her fingers brushed against those scales, against the cold, wet otherness of the—of *her*—tail.

She flung herself away from Samuel, and vomited what was left of her morning meal.

The boat rocked as Samuel inched closer. "I'm coming over, Luce. All right? I'm going to move very slowly, very carefully."

She barely had time to nod before another wave of nausea surged through her body. She leaned over, utterly wretched.

A tentative hand laid itself upon her back. Another caught her long hair, scooping it over her shoulder. "Are you all right?"

"Absolutely not." She wiped the back of her mouth with her webbed hand.

This can't be happening. It can't—

Samuel's hand remained on her back, moving in long, gentle strokes. "I take it," he said, carefully, "that this has never happened before?"

"Never," Luce whispered. She was shaking, her teeth chattering. "I'm frightened, Samuel."

"Honestly? So am I." Regardless, he settled himself beside her. He had brought his coat with him, and he tucked it around her, drawing her against his chest. Luce leaned into him, comforted immeasurably by his warmth, his calm.

"Look at your tail," Samuel's voice was soft with wonder. "Look at your *tail,* Luce."

"I don't know how this happened, Samuel."

"We'll find out," he said, stroking her damp hair. "We'll find out."

Luce must have dozed. Exhausted by the changes to her body, by shock and fear, and lulled by the warmth of Samuel's arms and the gentle rocking of the *Dove.* She opened her eyes, instinctively scanned the sky for the angle of the sun.

"It's fine," Samuel said, the words rumbling against her ear. "It's the morning watch, yet."

She nodded against him. Realized she was no longer cold and wet, but dry and warm. She pushed the coat away.

Her legs were back.

"It happened a few minutes ago," Samuel said apologetically. "I didn't want to wake you. . . ."

"... How?"

"You dried," he said simply.

"I didn't feel it."

"No. It was fast. I barely saw it."

Luce sat up. She had never thought to miss the tortured bones and gnarled, misshapen skin of her feet, yet she ran her hands eagerly over every familiar knot. Then her shins, her knees, her thighs. "Thank God."

"I've been thinking, while you slept," Samuel said. He sat up, too, rubbing at his shoulder, no doubt cramped after being bent up in the prow. "Turning what happened over and over in my mind. Trying to remember everything I've been told about the sea-folk."

The sea-folk. The half-fish, half-human fae had always seemed more myth than reality. They belonged to a different time, before Luce was born, when magic was still rife and Bretagne untamed. Long gone, they existed only in the stories told by old seamen on stormy nights. They were beautiful, the stories said. Beautiful, but unpredictable. In some tales, seamaids were merciful and generous: they aided shipwrecked sailors, brought winds to becalmed vessels, and granted wishes to people who helped them. In others, they were malevolent and dark, luring unwary sailors to their deaths with their beautiful voices, bringing down storms, supping on the bones of the drowned.

A shiver of unease. Which of the tales was true?

"Did you mean it, Luce?" Samuel asked. "When you said this had never happened before?"

She nodded. "Never."

"And you had no notion it *could* happen?"

"It was as much a shock to me as it was to you, believe me."

"That's the thing, Luce—I am not so very shocked." The *Dove* lolled slowly on the water. A gull sawed by.

She looked up at him. "You're not?"

"No. I think you've always been . . ." He gestured to her legs. "*This.*"

"Why?"

"Well, you are always on the shore. As though you know, in your heart, that you belong there. You're a wonderful swimmer, and a better diver than me. The sea seems to calm when you are around, though there's always wind for my sails. Then, of course, there's your prickle—the way you always know where the storm-stone is. You are the only person I know who can do that. And your voice—I've never heard anyone sing as sweet as you. And, well, you're . . . you're." He shrugged. "The tales always say that seamaids are lovely. That their beauty as well as their voices lead men to their delight. Or their doom."

Delight or doom.

Luce blinked at him. "You are being very calm about all of this."

"I've had time to think about it. And I've told you before—you are not the first seamaid I've seen. Though of course," he added, gesturing at Luce's bare legs, "I've never seen one *this* close."

Luce's belly roiled again. She drew her knees to her chest and hugged them. "Oh, my God."

"The tales say that a seamaid may shed her tail and walk as women do," Samuel mused. "Some have a little cap that allows them to move between land and sea. Some carry a magic comb. The selkies up north take off their skins and slip them on again when they want to return to the waves. I don't know what happened to make you change the way you did, but . . ."

And all at once, Luce knew. She raised her head from her knees, reached into her bodice, and drew forth the sea-silk. It was, she realized with a jolt, almost the exact color of her tail. "Perhaps it was this."

Samuel stroked the fabric with gentle fingers. "Is that sea-silk?"

"You've seen it before?"

"Only once. It had been harvested off the coast of Corsica, from the molluscs that grow there. This piece is *far* finer. Someone with a rare skill indeed must have woven it." He tore his gaze from the silk, met Luce's eyes. "Where did you get it?"

"There is a secret chamber within the walls of the town house. I found it in there in an old sea chest."

"A secret chamber? How did you find it?"

"My prickle. It didn't *feel* like the rest of the house. I was curious . . . afraid, too. But I had dreamed . . . and the groac'h told me not to fear the dark . . ."

For the first time that morning, Samuel looked truly frightened. "You spoke to the *tide-crone*?"

"She's younger than we thought," Luce said defensively. "Kind, too."

He scoffed. "Of course she is."

"It's true. She helped me get to the ball. Gave me a gown, and shoes, and a boat to get there."

He was staring at her. "Three gifts, eh? And she asked for nothing in return? No bargain, no price?"

She shook her head. "She saw me crying and wanted to help."

He blew out a long breath. "Anyone else would have given away their right to live by accepting such gifts. But not you." He shook his head as though he did not know whether to be fearful or impressed.

"Perhaps she knew," Luce said, gesturing to her tail. "About . . . all of this."

"Perhaps." He nodded thoughtfully. "We should find her. Ask her."

"Yes. But first I need to get home." It seemed ludicrous to think, after all that had just happened, the most worrying matter was that her mother and sister would discover she had gone. With Papa away, however, and Charlotte gone . . .

She got to her feet, quickly realising that she could not go home in such a state: her thigh-length chemise was all that covered her bare legs. There was spare clothing in the sea-cave, of course; but first, they had to sail there. She leaned over the side and looked down. Her breeches were a shredded, tattered mess floating near the *Dove*. Her overcoat, however, was clearly visible on the sand below, sleeves outstretched, eerily human.

Samuel joined her, peering into the water. "Man overboard. Are you going to rescue the unfortunate fellow, then?"

Luce hesitated. Any other day, she would have relished the chance to dive off the *Dove* and retrieve her clothing. For the first time in her life, however, she was afraid of the sea.

Samuel, perceiving it, stripped off his shirt and dived cleanly over the side. Luce watched him scull for the bottom, grab the coat, and drag it up to the surface.

"This was not," he huffed, shoving the sopping mass over the side where it squelched at Luce's feet, "what I expected to be doing with my day."

"Are you disappointed?"

He grinned up at her, clinging to the boat, water streaming over his bare arms. "Far from it."

Late that evening, when Gratienne and Veronique had retired, Luce met Samuel at the cove once more.

"How can you be certain she'll come?" Samuel asked, as they built a fire and settled themselves around it.

"I can't," Luce told him. "But this is the time of day that I most often see her."

It was an in-between time, when the world was half tilted between night and day, moon and sun. If ever there was a time to meet with a groac'h, it was now.

An hour they waited, and then another. The gold-blue shadows lengthened, and the gulls became still, waiting for the moon. The little band of jetins stopped to throw rocks at Samuel before marching over the headland, but of the groac'h there was no sign.

Pale stars were blooming in the sky when Luce went down to the water. She threw every sense she could out into the waves, willing the little black witch-boat to appear, its dark sails defying the breeze.

The cove remained stubbornly empty.

When the moon rose, and the bluish-dark of dusk threatened, Samuel came down to the water.

"We should leave," he said quietly. "The sun will set soon. And I for one do not intend to take a stroll alongside the *Dauphin*'s crew again."

Luce nodded. They had agreed to wait for the groac'h until dark, and no later. "Have you seen them again?"

He shook his head. "But I have spoken to others who have. They rise from the sea most nights, now."

Luce shivered. "Why? What are they searching for?"

He shrugged. "Maybe it's not *what* they're searching for, but *who*."

The dusk deepen around them, heavy with foreboding.

"Morgan," she said.

Samuel raised one shoulder. "I've asked about. Shared a drink with an old salt or two. They all said the same thing: that a crew betrayed by its captain will walk the shore at night in search of him."

"Betrayed by its captain?"

"Abandoned. Forsaken. We both know that cloud is the highest quality. There was no reason for the *Dauphin* to founder with it aboard—unless someone, through inexperience or arrogance, say—refused to give up the helm." Samuel narrowed his eyes, looked out over the quiet Manche. "You told me Morgan's pockets were full of storm-stone when you found him. What if Bones was right? What if Morgan doomed the *Dauphin* himself—drove it onto the rocks—and then filled his pockets with stone and abandoned ship?"

Luce remembered the look on Castro's face when he regarded

his son in the grand salon that first morning. He would know the worth, the strength, of his own ballast. Had he known what Morgan had done? Had Luce seen not been anger in his eyes, but shame?

"It would be another reason to lie about the ballast," Luce said quietly.

"Yes," Samuel agreed. "It would."

Luce watched the Manche shed its colors in the last of the light. "Why won't the groac'h come?"

"Perhaps she's gone," he said quietly. "I have not seen her, or her little boat, since the night we first saw the *Dauphin*'s crew."

Luce nodded. She herself had not seen the water-witch since the night of the ball, just one day later. The thought of her leaving, silently bidding her stretch of shore farewell and sailing into legend, was unbearably sad.

"There is someone else who might be able to help us," Samuel mused, as they left the shore.

Luce smiled. *Us.* As though he were with her in this, absolutely. The two of them together, no matter what might come.

"Who?"

"Mother Aggie." He shortened his strides to keep pace with her as they neared the cliffs. "The oldest, wisest person I know. Her father was a fisherman, and his father, and his before him . . . some say that Aggie herself has salt in her blood—that one of her forefathers took a seamaid to wife, and birthed a line of sea children, gifted with visions." He helped Luce up the rocky cliff path. "If anyone can give us answers, it's her."

"Then we must go to her. Now. Quickly."

Samuel laughed as he jogged up the path behind her. "Easy, Luce. Mother Aggie lives in Lulworth, same as my family. She's English."

Luce's heart sank. Lulworth was on the other side of the Manche. In England—France's, and Bretagne's, enemy. It may as well have been the other side of the world.

"I can take you," Samuel said, following her into the gloaming woods. "You could make a run with Bones and me. We'd be gone for much longer than a morning, though. Two days, perhaps longer. It'd be dangerous, too. We would need to make the crossing at night to avoid the English Navy, and the revenue cutters. Say the word, though, and we'll go. Tonight, if you want. The tide is perfect now, the moon all but dark."

Luce's heart almost breached clear out of her chest. She imagined the crossing, being there as Samuel and Bones set the sails, caught the wind. The longing to go with them was a physical pain in her chest. But . . .

Two days. Her family would be distraught if she went missing, especially now. She had told Samuel of Charlotte and Gabriel's decision—were they well? Married? Happy? She fervently hoped so—and her family's resulting misery. As it was, her mother could barely eat.

It was impossible.

"I cannot go with you," she said, biting back her disappointment. "I do not think my mother would survive if another of her daughters disappeared."

"We'd make your sister look better, though, wouldn't we?" Samuel smirked. "A tutor is always preferable to a smuggler."

Luce glanced at him. Saw, beneath his smile, the pain.

"There's nothing stopping *you* from going to Dorset," she said with forced cheer, taking his hand. "You could see Mother Aggie in my stead, and then spend some time there. Your mother would no doubt love having you home for a few weeks, or months. . . ."

"A valiant effort, Lucinde," Samuel said, slinging his arm around her. "But unless you're coming to Dorset with me, I'm staying here." He leaned down to her, his whisper tickling her hair. "But leave word for me at the chapel if you change your mind."

18

Crossing

Morgan came to the house the next day. Dread squeezed Luce's chest as she heard the sound of hooves in the courtyard, the polite greeting of St. Jean as he opened the front door. She leaned over the banister on the first-floor landing, and glimpsed a slice of dark hair, a handsome, angular face above a stylish frock coat.

Relief, as St. Jean launched at once into the well-rehearsed apology. *Afraid the family is unwell. Unable to receive visitors at this time.*

Luce waiting for Morgan to retreat. She had been on her way to her cabinet, where a copy of Louis Renard's *Poissons, Ecrevisses et Crabes* lay open on her desk. She had done nothing but read, it seemed, since Charlotte and Gabriel had gone. Her mother glared at her every time she touched the harp or the harpsichord, as though the very sound of music reminded her of their erstwhile tutor. But Luce had used the time well, poring over each of the books in her own collection, as well as her father's—*Systema Naturae*, Newton's *Philosophiae Naturalis Principia Mathematica*, Chambers's *Cyclopaedia*—in search of information about the sea-folk. Renard's work was the only one to feature drawings of a seamaid, her long tail sweeping behind her in shades of green and blue. Before St. Jean could close the door, however, another voice rose from the vestibule, soft and curious.

"Who is it, St. Jean?"

Veronique emerged from the grand salon, embroidery in hand. "Oh. Monsieur de Châtelaine."

"Bonjour, Mademoiselle Léon." Morgan removed his tricorn. He ignored St. Jean, who had stepped out of the way, his hand still on the door, and gave Veronique his most charming smile. "Do forgive me—it was not my intention to intrude. I was riding nearby and thought I'd call on the family who cared for me so well after the *Dauphin*'s loss."

"That's very kind of you." Luce heard the indecision in Veronique's voice. Even from this height Luce could see the pink staining her sister's cheeks, the sparkle in her eye. "We are not currently receiving visitors."

"I see."

"Although . . ." She glanced upstairs, caught Luce's eyes. Luce shook her head—*no, don't invite him in*—but it was too late. "Maman is resting upstairs, but I myself am much recovered, as is my sister Lucinde. I do not see how a turn around the gardens could hurt anyone?"

Morgan tilted his head, meeting Luce's eyes.

"What a charming idea. I have heard the roses at Le Bleu Sauvage are among the finest, and sweetest, in all of Clos-Poulet." That dark smile. "I trust you will join us, Mademoiselle Lucinde?"

"Of course she will." Veronique took up the lace shawl and bergère hat she had left on the side table that morning. "Come, Monsieur de Châtelaine. There is much for you to see! And it has been so long since we had any visitors. . . ."

Veronique's arm rested on Morgan's crooked elbow as she led him through the roses and the lavender, the boxwood hedges in their intricate curving broderie, the parterres of grass and gravel framed by jonquils, tulips, and lilies. Luce followed them in silence.

"Maman oversees these gardens herself," Veronique told Morgan. "See the tulips? Papa brought the bulbs for her from the Netherlands."

"They're lovely," Morgan said admiringly. He was so courteous. So charming. Nothing like the bitter, rageful man who had kicked Samuel on the cobbles after the Blessing. *Keep your filthy fucking hands off your betters.*

"Beware, tall one." The whisper came from the low branches of a horse chestnut. Luce looked up. The rose lutine was clinging to a cluster of creamy flowers, her tiny face tight with misgiving. "This one is not what he seems."

Luce gave her a reassuring nod.

"Is that a dovecote?" Morgan asked, pointing across the lawn to a squat, stone building shaded by an enormous elm tree.

"An icehouse," Veronique said proudly. The status of such an item was not lost on her; only the wealthiest of wealthy households could afford such a luxury.

"Truly?" Morgan looked at the building. "My family keeps ice in the cellars beneath the kitchens. May I?"

"Of course!" The look on Veronique's face, so sweet, so eager, was difficult to bear. Luce had no doubt her sister was as taken with Morgan as Luce herself had been, before her opinion of him had so dramatically changed. She could hardly blame Veronique; Morgan was undeniably dashing in his blue frock coat and cream-colored breeches, his calves shapely in elegant white stockings. Beneath his beauty, however, lay something dark and treacherous.

Veronique, oblivious to the danger, led the way to the icehouse, chattering happily as she unbolted the door and stepped inside.

At once, Morgan took Luce's elbow and hurried her around the building's curved wall.

"I had to see you," he muttered. "Have you given more thought to what we discussed?"

"I have, as a matter of fact."

He raised his brows, expectant. "And?"

Though overwhelmed and flattered by your generous offer, she longed to say, *I'm afraid I must enthusiastically decline.*

"It depends," she said instead.

"On what?"

"On whether you're any closer to finding the storm-stone." It did not sit well, this deception, this falsity, but if it meant keeping Samuel safe . . .

His eyes glittered. "What a wicked creature you are."

She gave a bored shrug. "You said it yourself, Morgan. My ship, your stone. Have you found it yet?"

"I am close."

"That's what you said last time. I need more than that if I am to make my decision. You promised me the horizon. How can I be certain you will give it to me?"

A wren trilled somewhere in the chestnut trees, as sweet as falling water.

Morgan sighed. "I have it on good authority that the stone was salvaged by an English scoundrel named Samuel Thorner. He has proven to be elusive so far. Mark me, though, Lucinde—"

"Are you two coming inside or not?" Veronique appeared, frowning at them. "We mustn't leave the door open."

"Of course." Morgan hurried to Veronique's side, casting a meaningful glance at Luce before he ducked his head and followed her inside.

Luce remained where she was, barely aware of the cool stone at her back, or her sister's muffled chatter. All her worry, all her caution, was completely founded. Morgan knew Samuel's name. It was only a matter of time before the City Guard closed its fist around him. Her blood chilled at the thought of those sea-worn stakes buried in the sand beneath Saint-Malo's ramparts, their rusty chains swinging in the breeze. She must warn Samuel; leave a message at the chapel, tell him to leave for Dorset at once.

She looked up, distracted, to see her mother hurrying across the lawn, skirts clutched in one hand. In the other, held triumphantly aloft and fluttering like a ship's ensign, was a letter.

"Veronique!" Gratienne cried. "Lucinde! Your father has sent word! He's found—" She saw Veronique and Morgan emerging from the icehouse, visibly fumbled for her next words. "—the new sideboard we have been searching for!"

"He found it?" Luce echoed.

"Yes! In Nantes!" The delight and relief shining on Gratienne's face was sunshine after days of rain. "And even better—he has found it with another. Two pieces!"

"Are they . . ." Luce searched for a way to ascertain whether her sister and Gabriel had achieved what they had set out to do, and married. ". . . a matched pair?"

"Yes!" Gratienne screeched.

This was good news. The scandal would be considerably less if Charlotte and Gabriel were married. There would be no hiding from the fact that one Léon daughter had married down, it was true, but, once the talk had died down, Veronique and Luce would remain unscathed.

"Oh, Maman," Veronique gasped, clapping her hands. "This is wonderful news!"

"I *know*!" Gratienne seemed to remember Morgan was there. "Apologies, Monsieur. I'm afraid we must away. My husband has sent word—we are to travel to Nantes at once."

"For a side table?" Morgan asked, bewildered.

"Maman is very particular about her furnishings," Veronique told him, with an apologetic shrug.

It was a day for deceptions.

First Morgan, then Veronique, happily oblivious to what was transpiring between Luce and Morgan at the icehouse. The last of the lies was the most important, and the most difficult.

Gratienne had always been near impossible to deceive.

Even so, Luce put her plan into motion as soon as the women

farewelled Morgan and returned to the house. Instead of helping Nanette pack her things as her mother had bid, Luce laid herself on her bed and did her very best to look wretched.

"Lucinde?" Gratienne frowned when she came to the door a few minutes later. She was dressed for travel, eager to be away. "Why have you not changed?"

"Oh, Maman," Luce said. "I feel so unwell. I do not know what has come over me. . . ."

"Lucinde," Gratienne said, with a heavy sigh. "If you didn't want to come to Nantes, why didn't you simply say so?"

Luce blinked. It was a trick, a clever ploy to catch her out. "Maman?" She gripped her belly, willed her face to pale, her skin to sweat. "I think it would be best if I stayed behind. . . ."

"Oh, very well," Gratienne huffed. "I do not have the time nor the patience to argue with you, Lucinde. Your father has organized a belated wedding breakfast for your sister and her new . . . *husband* in four days' time. Perhaps something can still be salvaged of this . . . disaster. We must leave at once, or risk missing it."

"Are you not coming, Luce?" Veronique, also dressed in a traveling gown and hat, paused in the doorway. "We are to go shopping after the wedding breakfast. You will miss it!"

Luce tried to look disappointed.

"I can *feel* your devastation," Gratienne said drily. "Come, Veronique. There's no time to waste. I leave the household under your care while we are gone, Lucinde. The responsibility will no doubt do you good. Nanette will stay behind to help you."

Luce winced. The maid would be disappointed to miss a trip to Nantes. It was the wealthiest port city in Bretagne, and the most fashionable.

But, "I don't mind at all, mademoiselle," Nanette said, when Veronique and Gratienne had bundled into the carriage with Madeleine and Anna-Marie. Both coachmen and the postilion were going with them, as well as Jean-Pierre. The remaining laquais, St. Jean, would also remain at the house.

"Really?" Luce raised an eyebrow. "You don't mind?"

"I grew up in Nantes," Nanette said. "I can still feel its filth on the inside of my nostrils. I have no wish to return." She looked sideways at Luce. "Besides, St. Jean will be here too. . . ."

Of course. Luce had all but forgotten about the attachment that formed between Nanette and the handsome laquais, both of whom, she now realized, seemed nothing short of delighted about the sudden change in their circumstances.

"I see," she said, hiding her smile. Then, "Nanette? Perhaps you and I can *both* benefit from the situation we find ourselves in."

It was the first honest thing she had said all day.

That night, as a sliver of moon rose, Luce stole down to the cove.

The *Dove* rocked companionably as Samuel took Luce's pack and helped her aboard, then showed her where to sit among the packages of silk stockings and lace, the casks of spirits and brandy that crowded the boat.

"Glad you could join us after all," he said, fingers grazing her cheek before he turned to help Bones ease the lugger into deeper water.

"You can thank my sister," Luce said. She told them both of her father's discovery of Charlotte and Gabriel in Nantes, their marriage, and her mother and sister's journey to meet them. A pang of regret, at the thought of missing Charlotte and Gabriel's wedding breakfast. Who knew when next Luce would see them? Her mother had read aloud Jean-Baptiste's letter, had said that Gabriel and Charlotte were planning to settle in Paris. Luce could almost hear the relief in her voice.

"I'd pay a pretty penny to have been there when your father found them," Bones said, taking the tiller. "I don't know the tutor, but I can't help but feel sorry for him."

Samuel laughed softly in agreement as he readied the mainsail.

"My father isn't the one you should be worried about," Luce told him. "Morgan came to see me this morning."

Samuel stiffened. "And?"

"It was as I said in my note." The message Luce had left at the chapel after her mother and sister departed for Nantes consisted of just two lines: *Morgan knows it was you. We sail tonight.* "He has your name, Samuel. He's looking for you as we speak."

"Much luck to him, then," Samuel said. "Unless he's planning on looking for me in England." The sail unfurled beneath his hands, billowed as it caught the breeze. Luce twisted in her seat, eager, despite her worry for Samuel, her guilt at leaving Bretagne under the cover of darkness, to feel the first rush of the Manche as it opened out before her. Was she really doing this? Crossing the Manche with only Nanette's word to protect her? As thanks for the precious time with St. Jean Luce's absence would afford her, the maid had promised to maintain the illusion that Luce was unwell and abed, delivering bowls of broth and pots of tea to her empty chamber. There were risks to such a plan, of course, but Luce had the distinct impression that Nanette, who of all people would notice Luce's wet hair and sandy clothing, had been well aware of her secret outings for some time—and had kept the knowledge to herself. Comforted by the thought, Luce turned her face to the north, where England waited, her pale cliffs and pebbly beaches ready to take delivery of Samuel and Bones's French contraband. And, with luck, to answer Luce's questions.

The *Dove* was not the only boat making the crossing this night. As the hours passed Luce caught sight of other vessels—luggers, small fishing boats like Samuel's, and larger ones too, slipping into sight upon the dark water and disappearing just as quickly. Their number grew when they passed Guernsey, though no lights glimmered, no voices echoed across the water. The sea, the dark moon, the pale light of the stars were the smugglers' loyal companions.

"You should sleep," Samuel said, when the islands were dark

shapes against the darker sky behind them. "We've hours ahead of us, yet."

Luce had been trying to ignore the burning in her eyes, the nodding of her head.

"I'll wake you if anything exciting happens," Samuel promised. He had taken Bones's place at the tiller an hour before, and he leaned toward her, holding out a woolen blanket. "You won't miss a thing, I swear."

"Do you promise?" She was already laying her head on a package of silk, throwing the blanket over herself, drawing it tight over her shoulders. The last thing she heard before she drifted into sleep was Samuel's low voice.

"I'll always keep my promises to you, Luce."

When she opened her eyes again, the stars were fading and the first faint, gray blush of dawn was staining the eastern horizon. It was cold, the still air over the water crisp and winter hard. White cliffs loomed out of the darkness above.

She sat up at once.

"There's food, here," Samuel murmured. "Bread, cheese. Some water." He was still seated in the stern, his hand at the tiller, though Luce assumed the two men had taken turns throughout the crossing. They looked tired and disreputable, hunkered in their heavy overcoats, their tricorns pulled low against the chill. Unlike Luce, they had not had the luxury of a few hours' sleep. But they smiled at her, all the same.

Luce reached for the food. "How much longer?"

"Not far now."

They tacked alongside those breathtaking white cliffs until they reached a bay, perfectly round and glimmering like a mirror in the darkness. A rocky shore edged it, waves slapping against stone. High above, the looming paleness of more white cliffs.

"What is this place?"

"Lulworth," Samuel said quietly. "Home. The water is clear, and the bottom sandy. Perfect for sinking casks of brandy."

"Is that what we're going to do?" Luce's tiredness was rapidly fading. She was away—far away—on another shore.

"Not this time. I've silk and lace, not brandy. And you can't sink silk." He made a tack, bearing away from the beach.

They sailed toward a rocky headland, the absence of stars and the pale foam of waves breaking against its base the only sign that it was there. Luce waited for Samuel to skirt the headland and move further out to sea, allowing her to drink in more of those spectacular, ghostly cliffs, but he only drew closer and closer, until the sound of breaking waves was loud in her ears, and the little boat began to toss and roll. The darkness loomed, the outline of rocky cliffs huge and forbidding against the night.

"Samuel," she said, uncertainly. "Are we not very close to those rocks?"

"We are."

"But . . ." She clung to the boat's edge as the *Dove* rolled sickeningly. "Samuel . . ."

"Do you trust me, Luce?"

She tore her gaze from the impending rocks, looked at him. "Yes."

"Then trust me now."

She managed a nod, held grimly to the side of the boat as Samuel and Bones maneuvered them closer and closer to the headland. The sun was considering rising now, the first grayish light edging its way up above the sea to the east. In its early light she could see enormous rocks sitting at the headland's base, as though they had been ripped from the cliffs above and cast down by some ancient sea-god. A leviathan, perhaps, thrashing its enormous tail into the cliffs, or a kraken. Between the rocks the sea sucked and plunged, gurgling and muttering, as though it, too, wished to wreak its violence upon the land.

"Samuel . . ."

"Trust, Luce. I'll not let any harm come to you." He spoke firmly, rapidly, on the edge of distraction—he was using all his strength to keep the *Dove* from the rocks. Luce clung to the side, kept her mouth closed, letting him and Bones work. And then, just when she thought the little boat would be thrashed to splinters on the cliffs, it was swept *inside* them. Luce cried out in fear, her knuckles aching.

"Hold fast," Samuel muttered.

The little boat spun and dipped, and then with a terrifying lurch, surged into darkness.

Luce could see nothing. She felt the boat moving, rolling forward with the movement of the sea as it surged into the depths of the headland. The sound of water rushing against rock was deafening. And then, as suddenly as it had begun, the *Dove* drifted into stillness. Luce sensed, rather than saw, the rocky walls open up around them. The air was fresh, salt-tinged and cool.

"Still with us, Luce?" There was a smile in Samuel's voice.

She nodded, realized they could not see her, and managed a croak.

"You did well," said Bones. "I all but soiled my breeks the first time."

The snap of a flint being struck sounded in the dark. A lantern flickered into life, illuminating Bones's face. He hung it on the mainmast and the pool of golden light widened, lapping against dark water. Beyond the light's edges, the unmistakable sheen of damp rock.

"What is this place?" Luce asked.

"You'll see." Samuel steered the *Dove,* still moving with that final push of the sea, toward one rocky wall. Rough steps had been cut into the stone, rising into darkness. Two lines of thick iron rings had been embedded on either side of the stairs, one above the other, higher and higher, until they too were lost to the shadows.

The *Dove* came to rest alongside the rock. Samuel got to his feet, taking down the lantern as Bones secured the boat to the rings.

"Wait here," Samuel told Luce, stepping onto the rough-hewn stairs and climbing out of sight. Bones went with him. Moments later another light appeared in the murkiness above, and then another, until Luce saw that they were in a sea-cave. A sea-cave as grand and beautiful as the crossing of the cathedral in Saint-Malo, stony buttresses soaring above a vast pool of dark water.

"Not bad, eh?" Samuel came back down the stairs.

"It's magnificent. I never dreamed such a place existed." She frowned at him. "You never told me!"

"Wouldn't be much of a smuggler if I told you all my secrets." He took her hand. A thrill of warmth shot through her at the touch of his calloused palms. "Come. I'll show you."

The stairs were not as slippery as Luce had expected. Looking down, she saw that small grooves had been cut into the stone, which was clear of weed and shellfish.

"We scrub them," Samuel said, seeing her glance. "Well, my cousins do. It's the least they can do, with Bones and I out risking our necks." He led her up, and up, until the stairs opened out onto a large, smooth rock platform, perhaps a dozen paces wide and the same deep. On one side, the rock wall continued, grooves and indents in the stone creating a series of shelves where all manner of casks and water-tight packets were neatly stowed. Above, a rocky ceiling protected the entire cave from the elements.

"It's always dry here, no matter the tide," Samuel said, holding the lantern high so Luce could see. "And the entire cave is hidden from the land—if you didn't know it was here, you'd miss it entirely. Brandy, silks, lace, tea, coffee, playing cards . . . all the luxuries of the Continent, hidden right beneath the revenue men's noses."

"Where will it all go?"

"To London, mostly. Bones's brothers will see that it gets there safely. They'll be along later to collect it."

He sat the lantern on one of the shelves and led Luce to the edge. Below them, the *Dove* rocked gently at its moorings. Luce peered into the shadows and saw the narrow entrance Samuel had used to bring the boat into the cave.

"It's as wide as the *Dove*," Samuel said, watching her. "Or rather, the *Dove* is as wide as the passage."

"How deep is it?" It appeared endless, lantern light glimmering and rippling on its black surface.

"Not as deep as you think. The bottom is sandy, too. You'll see when the sun rises." He released Luce's hand. "Speaking of . . . we had best unload."

"I'll help you."

"No need. Bones and I will manage." He cleared his throat. "There's a passage, over there . . ." He pointed. "It leads to a small outcrop on the headland. It's hidden. Private, I mean."

"Thank you," Luce said, torn between laughing at his discomfort, and blushing. She took up a lantern and made her way to the passage. It was dark and close, but she soon felt fresh air on her face. Keeping the lantern low, she crept out onto a narrow, scrubby ledge overlooking the sea and, as Samuel had said, completely hidden from the cliffs behind the headland. Gathering her skirts, she crouched on the sandy ledge and sighed in relief as her bladder—which felt as though it was very near to bursting—was finally able to empty. When she was done, Luce cast one wistful look at the still-dark coast before returning to the cave.

Samuel and Bones spoke quietly as they unloaded the *Dove*, their voices echoing slightly off the walls. When they were done, Bones shrugged on his coat, winked at Luce, and left the cave through another, wider passage.

"He's going home to get some sleep," Samuel said.

Home. Luce had never heard Samuel use that word. This was his home. His family was here, his mother and sisters.

"Don't you want to do the same?"

"Not sure what my Ma would say if she found me with a seamaid in my bed." He grinned, then yawned magnificently. "I'm well enough here. It is not yet dawn—too early to knock on Mother Aggie's door—and my eyes are set to burn themselves out of my head. What would you say if I closed them for a few moments?"

"I would say nothing at all, lest I wake you."

"That's the spirit."

He set about stacking packages of silks and lace into a makeshift bed, then slid out of his coat and lay upon it, kicking off his boots and stretching out with a sigh. "I won't sleep long. Just a few moments."

"I'll be here when you wake."

He mumbled something incoherent in reply, his body softening as his breathing slowed. Luce's heart gave a little squeeze of affection before her own fatigue called. As quietly as she was able, she slipped off her boots and curled against Samuel's side. He rolled in his sleep, arm slipping around her, tucking her close. In moments, she too was asleep.

19

Delight or Doom

Luce woke to find Samuel gone.

Weak sunlight filtered through cracks in the stone above her, slanting through the cave. Its texture told her it was midmorning.

"Samuel?"

"I'm here."

His voice came from below. She moved carefully to the platform's edge, peered down.

And caught her breath.

Sunlight streamed into the sea-cave—great golden swathes of it illuminating the sea-pool below. The water was a startling blue-green, glimmering as if a thousand candles shone beneath its surface.

Samuel, standing in the *Dove*, and winding a rope in his hands, looked up at her, grinning.

"I knew you'd appreciate it." He finished with the rope, stowed it neatly away, and hopped from the boat to the stone stairs, climbing toward her.

"It's wonderful," Luce breathed. The bottom of the pool was covered in pale sand. The water so clear, she could its ripples and undulations, the occasional crab or shell.

It was infinitely inviting. Part of her longed to leap from the platform and feel that wondrous water on her skin. The rest of her shuddered in terror. She slipped a hand into her pocket, felt the sea-silk there, and quickly withdrew her fingers.

"You *really* should have told me about this place," she said accusingly as Samuel reached the top of the stairs. His hair, she saw in surprise, was wet, his shirt clinging to his broad shoulders.

"You swam?"

"Did I wake you? I tried not to splash." He tousled his hair, and droplets of seawater flicked onto Luce's cheek. She reached up quickly, wiped them away, distracted, for a moment, by the desire to run her fingers across his damp skin.

"No." She dragged her gaze back to the water. "No, I didn't hear you."

She felt him regarding her.

"Would you like to swim, Luce? I'd understand if you were afraid . . ."

"I'm not afraid." She spoke too quickly, dishonesty shining through her words like the sun on that rippling sand below. She *was* afraid. The feeling of her legs being bound, useless, the failure of her body to save her from the water as she sank deeper and deeper, was impossible to forget. But she was curious, too. And in this place, with such water, and such *light*. . . . Surely there was no better time to try?

"I'm going in," she said. "With the silk."

He nodded. Swallowed. "All right."

"I cannot swim in my clothes."

He swallowed again. "No. Of course not."

"I was thinking, if I wore my stays and kept the silk inside them . . ."

Samuel nodded.

"And if you turned away, when I first dived?"

"Of course."

Luce took a breath. Released it. "Very well. Go back down to the *Dove* and close your eyes. You can open them when you hear a splash."

She watched him move back down the stone stairs, heart pounding with nerves. She undressed quickly, before she could change her mind: untying her breeches, unpinning her caraco and stomacher, unlacing her white stays. She peeled off her chemise, stockings, and garters and then, completely naked, reached for her stays. She drew the bony, satin-covered wings of them around her body, tightening the laces with practiced fingers, bottom to top, waist to breast. She unpinned her hair—it fell down to her hips, long and thick and black—and tucked the sea-silk within the top of the stays, against her skin.

Below, on the *Dove,* Samuel was quiet as midnight.

"Dear God," Luce whispered. *Does God listen to seamaids?* She padded to the edge, peeked over. "Are your eyes closed?"

"They are."

At the sight of him, Luce almost lost her footing. Samuel was naked from the waist up, his vest and shirt draped over the tiller, his arms raised, his hands covering his eyes.

She had seen his body before, of course. But always in glimpses and glances, secret and stolen. Now, completely unhindered, she looked and looked and looked. At his chest and shoulders and back, all sun-browned and smooth. At the muscles curving in his arms and cutting across his belly. At his narrow hips, and the twin creases of muscle disappearing into the top of his breeches.

Dear God.

He must have sensed her gaze. "I thought I'd best prepare, as well," he said. "In case you . . . needed me."

Remembering, no doubt, the way she had panicked and sunk that first time. Fear traced its cold claws down her back at the thought. She looked at him, standing in the *Dove*—with her, unquestioningly, as he always was—and felt a surge of gratitude.

"Thank you."

There was nothing for it. She could stand there, naked and nervous on the ledge.

Or she could dive.

Freefall, and then the sudden shock of the water's embrace. She felt the change this time: the magic slicking over her, head to toe, as cool as the green-blue sea. She dipped her head, arched her spine, rolled her hips, adjusting to her new body.

It knew what to do. Her tail flicked of its own accord, and she surged through the water, faster and stronger than she had ever thought possible. She flicked it again. Opened her eyes and found that she could see everything—ripples in the sand, a few stray fish, a scattering of shells—in glorious detail.

Luce propelled herself across the pool, moving sure and smooth, sinking into her new rhythm. She rolled, swam smoothly back, beheld her tail, its glorious fins like tendrils of brightly-hued ink in the water, blues and greens, silvers and pinks, shimmering like a dream. High above, the *Dove*'s hull, bubbles trapped against the wood, each plank plain. And a watery shadow that could only be Samuel. He was leaning over the side, watching her. The whiteness of his teeth, his broad, excited grin.

In a burst of sudden joy Luce turned her body and aimed for the surface, swimming hard.

It was easier than walking or running or dancing had ever been.

It was easier than breathing.

She cut through the water, sliced for the surface, impelled by the force of her tail.

She dived into air, soared over water, dripping and shimmering. She heard Samuel's joyous whoop, sensed him leaping with her, before she arched her back and—fingertips first—slipped back into the sea. An explosion of color and light and water—here and then gone again, the water parting smoothly to admit her once more.

Welcoming her home.

"Having fun?" Samuel leaned on the Dove's bow, grinning and dripping.

Luce had dived and leapt and dived again, over and over,

splashing the boat, drenching the sails, the stairs, and Samuel too. Now, there was nothing to do but drift lazily on the surface; to flow along the *Dove*'s side, barely touching the boat. There was no need to reach for it, or to cling to its side while she rested. She was light as air, strong as the tide.

"Look at you," Samuel said. His voice was low, his sea-gray eyes dark as a coming storm. They drank her in, those eyes, from her dark hair, trailing across the surface, to the shimmering tendrils of her tail.

Luce, too, was looking. He gleamed with salt and water, his damp hair curling at the nape of his neck, tattoos stark against his bronzed skin.

Elation became something else entirely.

She drifted to the *Dove*'s bow and reached up a hand to him, the way she always did when they were diving and she needed him to lift her back onto the boat. And as *he* always did, Samuel leaned down, trusting and steadfast, and gripped her arm.

It was startling, how easily he fell over the side. His eyes had widened as he felt Luce tense, as the boat rocked and swayed in warning. And then he had simply . . . fallen, as though he had *wanted* it to happen. There was a rush of bubbles and limbs, fins and hands and mouths, and then Luce crushed herself against him.

His mouth opened beneath hers, heedless, wanting. She could hear his heartbeat, feel it through the layers of her stays—silk, whalebone, and ribbon—separating them. He was larger than she, greatly so, and yet here, in the water, she felt his powerlessness, his fragility. She could wrap herself about him, tangle her hands in his hair, her tail around his legs. She could steal his kisses and his breath, and give them back to him.

He took them willingly.

They broke the sea's skin as one, snarled together, mouths and lips, tongues and hips. Sculling for the sea-stairs, the sturdiness of rock.

Half in the water and half without.

Luce let him press her against the salt-stained stone. Ran her hands over his chest, his belly, slipped her fingers across his back, downward, beneath his breeches, across the curve of muscle and bare skin.

The kisses deepened, a delicious sliding of tongues and teeth.

Samuel's hands were roaming, too. They knotted in Luce's hair, tilted her head back against the stones so he could trail his tongue up her neck, his fingers over her curving, silver-scaled hip.

"Luce . . ." He drew back from her. "Is this what you want? What you truly want?" She knew what he was asking. Had not forgotten his words in the shadow of the ship at the Blessing, the doubt in his eyes.

It was a dream, nothing more. I've always known it.

Someone like de Châtelaine.

I've regretted it every day. Every hour.

Luce had always believed in the law of the sea—that what you found on its shores was undeniably yours. That every shell, every relic, every oddity washed upon the sand—and into her path—had drifted there of the sea's accord.

"You found me on the shore," she said. "That night when you ran from the jetins, remember?"

A half-smile. "How could I forget?"

"Sea law says I'm yours."

"It's not the sea's opinion that worries me."

"Whose, then?"

He sighed. "We are from different worlds, Luce."

She glanced at her tail, glimmering in the shallows between them. "Clearly."

"That's not what I mean. How . . . how could I possibly make you happy? After living as you have for so long? I cannot give you such a life."

"Good. Because I don't want it." Luce guided his hand to the top of her stays, curving his fingers around the ribbons.

He hesitated. Then, "Delight, or doom, the tales always said," he muttered. "I understand it now."

He drew upon the lacings, hooking his fingers between, loosening the silky panels. Each brush of his knuckles against her bare skin was a flame; her very bones were melting by the time he pushed the stays away. The sea-silk was all that lay between them now, pooled against Luce's breasts.

"So beautiful," Samuel murmured, his gaze, his hands, stroking every part of her—breasts, hips, the sudden, smooth length of her thighs. He stowed the silk within the stays and pushed them onto the stairs above their heads. At the sight of him stretched above her, one long, browned arm gleaming with seawater, Luce was near undone. She arched her back toward him, wrapped her arms around him, kissed him deep as the sea.

"Delight it is," Samuel whispered. "And perhaps my doom, as well." His hand slid between Luce's thighs. "Let it be so."

He trailed kisses down her neck, across the swell of her breasts, tasting and savoring. All the while his fingers stroked and circled, quickening in a way that was so startling, so *delicious*, that she could barely breathe. The *Dove* rocked beside them, the water lapping at their legs, as though the sea was listening, was just as hungry and desperate. Luce would surely die from this. Would surely, *surely* die . . .

Then Samuel's fingers stilled.

"Don't stop . . . ," Luce begged.

"Patience," he murmured, easing downward, his kisses moving from breast to belly to thigh . . .

The touch of his tongue against her was so shocking, so unexpected, that Luce opened her eyes.

"Samuel?"

"Do you trust me, Luce?"

She managed a nod. Barely.

His mouth was upon her again, his tongue flickering, faster

and softer at once. Luce arched against the stairs. A tide was rising within her, quick and strong. She could not stop it now. No one could. She clung to the stairs as though her life depended upon it, desperate, gasping, drowning in a sea of stars.

And then, salvation. Samuel was lying over her, naked, cradling her in his strong, steadfast arms. She felt his wanting against her, tilted her head to watch him gently, slowly, ease within her, utterly lost in the pleasure and the fullness and the wonder of it. She had thought herself sated, but now her body rocked eagerly in time with his, ebbing and flowing in a rhythm as ancient as the tide, or the spiraling of the moon. Half in the water, half without—water and stone, stone and water—her legs entwined with Samuel's, her body at one with his, Luce found a haven at last. Shelter from the storm, light in the darkness. Home.

"Well, I suppose that settles that," Samuel murmured, some time later. "We know how the magic works."

Luce nodded against his chest, where his heart beat sounded, steady as the tide. "We do."

They were lying together in the bottom of the *Dove*, in a nest of blankets and nets Samuel had hastily thrown together when the cold and discomfort of the stairs had become, in his words, "fucking unbearable."

"I'm a seamaid, Samuel."

"Yes," he said calmly.

"Fae."

"Yes."

The force of that one word—*yes*—and the certainty that the sea-silk could indeed do what they had suspected and turn Luce into a creature half woman and half fish, as strange and magical as the serpents painted on the surface of the globe in her father's study or in the pages of *Poissons, Ecrevisses et Crabes* was so shocking that it all but took Luce's breath away. She held tight to Samuel, concentrated on the steady beat of his heart.

"I thought you might drown me, at first," he said. "When you pulled me off the *Dove*."

"The thought did cross my mind."

"Christ." He flopped one arm across his eyes, wincing. "And *I* thought loving the daughter of Jean-Baptiste Léon was the most reckless and foolish thing I could do. Turns out it's far, far worse."

Luce went very still. Some words, she had found, were more important than the rest. They stood apart from their counterparts because they gleamed like stars in the night sky. There was one word, in what Samuel had just uttered, that was shining so hard and so beautifully bright she feared she might be burned.

Samuel, too, had stilled.

Silence yawned between them, a darkling sea.

"Reckless?" Luce said at last. "Foolish?"

"Your father is a dangerous man," he said, gratefully taking up the line she had thrown him. "There's not many who would willingly cross him."

"You think him dangerous? Why?"

"For lots of reasons. He's rich, for a start. That means he's powerful. He's wily, too—he knows his business, the difference between a solid venture and a risky one. He was a fine captain, in his day, and he knows ships. People, too. There's not a man, woman, or child in Saint-Malo unknown to Jean-Baptiste Léon. He knows every crew, every vessel, who mans her and what they're carrying. He understands the importance of investors, of sharing the risks. Stand by him, earn his trust, and he'll be loyal as the day is long. But cross him and, well . . ."

"What?"

"I've heard it said that betraying your father is like prodding a hungry lion. He might lie quiet, or . . . well . . . you might turn around one day to find him quietly stalking you. By then, of course, it's too late. There is nothing to be done but hope the end comes quickly."

A chill ran up Luce's spine.

"I can't say I'm overfond of the idea of your father knowing what I've been doing with his daughter in my boat." Samuel spoke lightly, but Luce sensed the truth beneath the words. "I'd be torn to shreds in a matter of moments."

"I would never let him do that."

"They say a lion knows nothing of pity, Luce. I fear you'd not be able to stop him." Samuel touched her hair again, ran it through his fingers. "It would be worth it, though."

"Don't say such things." She drew him close. They were wrapped in the thick blankets Samuel always carried in the *Dove*, yet she was suddenly cold.

"It's true." His voice had lost its playfulness now. "All I ever wanted—all I ever wished for, since first I saw you in the water at the cove—was you."

They had come back to it at last, that word. Its brightness and its softness. Its warmth.

"And I you," Luce said, pressing her forehead to his. "And as much as I'd enjoy staying here and doing things with you in your boat, I want to know more about what I am. I need answers, Samuel."

"Then let's find them. Mother Aggie's house isn't far. I'll take you to her now." The purposeful words were completely at odds with the wanderings of his hands, his mouth. "There's just one very important thing *I* need to do first. . . ."

He raised himself over her, his lips, his hair, trailing over her breasts.

"Oh," Luce said with a sigh. "*That* important thing."

"Very, *very* important . . ."

Later, they climbed from the sea-cave into the brightness of the day. A magnificent headland rose beneath their feet, challenging the sea, while the wild, windswept curve of the coast peeled back to watch. Pale cliffs, a perfect, startling white, rolled one after the other, hazy with salt, spray, and distance. The wind was strong, tugging at Luce's hair, loosening the hasty plait she had woven. She held it back from her face, drinking in the sight.

"The entire coast is made of chalk," Samuel said, pausing on the barely discernible path through the thick, waving grass. "All the way to Kent," he added, pointing. "And east, to Lyme."

"It's beautiful."

They followed the narrow path east, until Luce saw a village sheltering in the curve of a cove far below, its thatched rooftops warm against gray stone. Mother Aggie's tumble-down cottage sat away from the other houses, closer to the sea. The garden was scattered with treasures: old fishing nets, glass floats, and dried seaweed. There were shells in the crevices between the cottage's stone walls, hanging from strands of fishing line tied to a large piece of driftwood fixed above the single, crooked window. They chimed softly in the morning breeze. Unlike the ordered gardens of the nearby cottages, Mother Aggie's garden was thick with wildflowers. Sea thrift foamed in shoals of pink and mauve, along with wild clary, sea holly, and campion.

Samuel led Luce through the rickety driftwood fence and along a path made of sand and crushed shells.

"Are you ready?"

Luce nodded, swallowed. "Yes."

Samuel knocked gently on the faded door. A faint shuffling from within, and then the door opened, revealing an old woman with white hair so long and thick it trailed almost to her knees. Her dress was rough, patched in faded squares of fabric Luce suspected had washed up on the beach after storms: grays and blacks and washed-out blues, silken reds and faded pinks, even a salty gold.

"Well then," Mother Aggie said, in English. "There's a handsome smuggler at my door." She squinted up at Samuel, who towered over the little woman, his shoulders filling the doorframe.

"Hello, Aggie," he said easily.

Mother Aggie peered around him, her gaze catching—and holding—on Luce. "And what have you brought me, rogue?"

"This is Lucinde," Samuel said. "A friend of mine. We were hoping you could help us."

"Of course. Come in, come in." The little woman ushered them inside, and they were immediately folded into the scent of damp and brine, the after smoke of cooked fish. Samuel was forced to duck his head to avoid bumping it on the low ceiling, but even so the house was brighter and more comfortable than Luce had first supposed, with two small windows opening onto the cove and a fire burning in a stone hearth. A sleeping space was half-covered by a faded curtain; four stools set around a little table, a bowl crowded with shells, sea glass, and interesting stones at its center.

"Sit," Mother Aggie said, gesturing to the stools. Luce did as the old woman bid, tucking her dark woolen skirts beneath the table. Beside her, Samuel folded his long legs with difficulty. "Tea?"

"Yes, please," Samuel said, and Luce nodded eagerly. They had eaten the last of Samuel's bread and cheese on the walk across from the headland, but the thought of hot tea made her belly grumble happily. Mother Aggie poured fresh water into a pot, swung it over the open flames.

"How would you like to begin?" Samuel asked Luce softly in French.

Luce shrugged. "I hardly know."

Mother Aggie's ears pricked up. "You are from across the Channel?" she asked Luce, in smooth French.

Luce nodded in surprise. "Yes," she said, in English. "From Saint-Malo."

"Saint-Malo? Gah," Mother Aggie spat. "That hornet's nest. Bane of the English Navy, and the king himself. Long have I wished to see it. Tell me, are the ramparts as impressive as they say? And are they truly made of enchanted stone?"

Luce grinned. Mother Aggie was like the rare shell in her father's study, seeming at first one color, one texture, then, when turned a different way, becoming another. "We do. The city has never been breached. Not even when the Dutch tried in 1694." Luce could not help the pride in her voice. Her father had read to her of the raid when she was a child. The Dutch and English together bombarded the city for four days, damaging some of the buildings and even the cathedral. Even so, the city had prevailed.

"It will fall one day," Samuel said. There was a hardness to his tone that caused Luce to glance at him, surprised. "All cities must, in the end."

"Perhaps. Perhaps not." Mother Aggie shifted in her seat, her eyes, beneath the fall of white hair, sparking, shrewd. "But you did not smuggle Lucinde across the Channel like fine French silk to speak of walls. Why have you come to visit me?"

"We were hoping you might be able to tell us about this." Luce reached into her pocket, slipped free the sea-silk. "Samuel said you might know its origin."

The silk glimmered in the cottage's stony light as she lay it across Mother Aggie's table, a streak of otherworldliness on the scrubbed timber.

"Good grief," Mother Aggie whispered, tracing one finger against the silk. She looked up, searched Luce's face. "Where did you get this?"

Luce hesitated. She glanced at Samuel, unsure how much she could safely say.

"We will tell you, Aggie," Samuel said, meeting Luce's worried look with a slight nod. "But we would first need your promise of . . . discretion."

"You shall have it," Mother Aggie said, getting to her feet. "I know everything that happens in this village," she said, adding tea leaves and hot water to an ancient little pot. "When the fish are biting, and when the storms will come. I know where the revenue men roam, and who pays them to look away." She placed the pot on a tray and added three cups. "I know other things, too. Generations of secrets, the truth behind decades of carefully crafted lies—the fabric of any and every village." She set the tray on the table. "Your secret is safe with me."

Luce looked into Mother Aggie's sea-green eyes. Samuel believed the blood of the sea-folk ran in the old woman's veins. Looking at her now, she believed it.

"I am the adopted daughter of Jean-Baptiste Léon," she said. "His father, and his father before him, were shipowners. Corsairs. My father is a wealthy man, with many beautiful belongings."

"Of course," Mother Aggie said. She lifted the pot, poured them all tea.

"Thank you." Luce accepted her cup gratefully. "I found this silk within a sea chest in a secret chamber in my father's house."

Mother Aggie touched the silk with gentle fingers. "There are tales about women who look inside chambers and chests that are forbidden to them," Mother Aggie said. "They do not end well."

"Do you know what the silk is? Where it came from?" Samuel asked.

"Of course," Mother Aggie said. "It came from the sea-folk."

20

Half One and Half the Other

Luce's hands were shaking. She placed her cup carefully back on the table.

"Such silk cannot be woven here on our green shores," Mother Aggie was saying. "Its fibers are harvested from giant clams who exist far below the surface. Only the sea-folk can gather such fibers. And only the sea-folk are skillful enough to weave them into what you see before you."

She lifted the silk, ran it gently over her hands.

"It is not for mere decoration, though. Oh, no. The sea-women weave enchantments, wishes and hopes, along the strands. The magic gives the silk its color, its beauty."

"What kind of magic?" Luce whispered.

"The kind that comes when the moon is full and rising fast, painting a path of silver across the water," Mother Aggie replied. "The kind that comes when the night is close. When the tide is about to turn, or the ocean holds its breath before a storm. The in-between times. Not day, not night. Not high, not low. Half one, and half the other."

Half one, and half the other.

"By their very nature, the sea-folk are different to the other Fae. They are of the in between, creatures of both land and sea. They are light and dark, sun and moon, shallow water and deep. They love to swim, and yet they also love to walk upon the shore. Such duality would prove to be their undoing."

"Why?" Luce asked. Her tea lay cooling before her, forgotten.

Aggie sank back in her chair. "The tale of the sea-folk is not a happy one. They were ever the shyest of the Fae, preferring to dwell in the quietest coves, the most remote waters. For centuries they lived peacefully, taking only what they needed, using only what they had. Then humans learned to harness the wind, too. Ships became larger, fleets stronger, maps better. People began settling in those quiet coves, fishing those remote waters. They viewed the sea-folk with both reverence and dread, coveting their sweet voices, their beautiful forms, while at the same time fearing them. It has always been so. Sea-folk are as changeable as the moon. They can be dangerous. Vain, fickle, unpredictable. Yet they can be kind, too, when the mood takes them, calming a stormy sea or singing up a strong wind to fill a sagging sail. A seamaid can save a ship-wrecked sailor or show a drifting fisherman the way home, but she can just as easily drag him from his boat and drown him. A monster from the darkest of dreams."

Monster. Luce flinched at her casual use of the word. "Most were willing to risk it, for word spread across the seas that the kiss of a seamaid would bring good luck—calm seas, fair winds, good trade—to anyone lucky enough to receive it."

The image of Morgan the morning after the storm—the wonder on his face, the way he had pulled her to him . . .

There are two reasons, he had said when she had asked him why he had kissed her. *The first is that . . . I kissed you because I could not help it, Lucinde. I had nearly died. And you looked so wondrous. In truth? For a moment, I believed you were a seamaid.* And when she had asked him of the second reason, he had balked. *Does it matter?*

Had he heard the sailors' tales? Had he been thinking of his own success, his luck, even then?

She got to her feet unsteadily, pushed away from the table. Beyond Aggie's window the cove was calm in the morning sun, oblivious to her turmoil.

"But what of the silk, Aggie?" Samuel asked.

"Have you not listened to a word I've said, lad? The silk is the hinge. The door, the dusk. The key." Mother Aggie got to her feet and shuffled across the room. She fished about in a rickety drawer—the rattle of stone against shell—then drew out a piece of starlight.

"This," she said, bringing it back to the table and laying it beside Luce's, "was my great-grandmother's."

The two pieces of silk were identical in length and width. Both had the sheen of seashells, the softness of gossamer. Mother Aggie's, however, was darkly silver, glinting in every shade of the moon.

Luce looked anew at Mother Aggie; at her sea-soaked house, her long, wild hair. "Have you ever used it?"

"I tried, once. Many years ago. I hoped the stories were true, that I could do as my foremother did and turn my legs to a tail of shining silver. But alas—when I took this into the sea and held it against my skin, nothing happened." She shrugged. "Not enough salt in my blood, I daresay."

"You held it against your skin?" Samuel, it seemed, was well beyond being shocked by such a revelation. "Is that how it works, then? She—she simply has it on her when she's in the water?"

"Sea water, not fresh," Mother Aggie clarified. "But put simply, yes. At least, that's how my mother described it."

"And how would she breathe?" Samuel asked.

"The same way she would on land. A seamaid breathes air, like a porpoise. I have always imagined they can hold their breath for as long as a porpoise, too—and dive as deep, and swim almost as fast."

She imparted this astonishing information casually, as though she spoke of a seabird or a turtle.

"Jesus," Samuel muttered. He glanced uneasily at Luce, his face pale. "I never knew you knew so much about all this, Aggie."

"You never asked, Samuel. More tea?"

"God, yes."

He held out his cup while she poured, then drank it down fast, wincing at the heat. "I'm fairly certain I need something stronger than tea."

Mother Aggie was watching Luce.

"And what of you, Lucinde Léon? Do you need something stronger?"

"I am well enough," Luce said. It was a lie. Her blood was pounding in her ears. Nausea curled at the back of her throat, burning a trail along her neck. She returned to the table, sat heavily down. "Could your mother use the silk?"

"No." Her eyes glittered. "But *her* mother could."

Luce touched the silver silk. It felt completely different to the blue silk, which was alive, responsive; as though it wanted nothing more than to wind itself around Luce's wrist and remain with her always. The silver felt like nothing more than a piece of silk. Cool, ambivalent. Questions floated to the surface of her mind.

"How did she come to be here, in Lulworth?" Samuel asked Aggie. "Your great-grandmother, I mean."

"She fell in love with a fisherman after he caught her—by accident, mind—in his nets," she replied. "My great-grandfather. She was not the first seamaid to love a mortal. Nor will she be the last," she added, glancing at Luce. "She removed her silk and walked ashore with him, where she remained for the rest of her days. She made a choice."

Choice. The word hung heavy in the air.

"It was not easy for her," Mother Aggie said. "A sea-wife is caught always between two shores—one in the sun, one in the deep—and the desire for both is ever present." Luce looked around the little house, its treasures—shells and dried weed, scales and buttons and feathers—arranged almost reverently along dresser and shelf, table and windowsill. A shiver ran down her spine. It was not Aggie who had brought the sea into the house, who had sown it through the salty little garden. It was the seamaid.

"But she . . ." Luce gestured to the silk on the table, struggling to find words. "She could have returned to the sea if she wanted to?"

"Perhaps she did, from time to time. When the moon was new and the cove empty."

Luce wondered if the seamaid had longed for more than a solitary swim on a moonless night. Had she missed her family? Her home? Had she wanted to return to the sea?

"I like to think my great-grandfather loved her enough that he would have let her go, had she wished it," Mother Aggie said, as though she perceived Luce's thoughts. "But I cannot say. Not for certain. He was a man, and, like any man, he would have been loath to let something so precious go."

"Good fishing, then?" Samuel asked.

"Always. His nets were ever full, his boat safe in any weather, no matter how foul. Her very presence was a blessing."

Luce surged to her feet. "I think . . . I think I have heard enough." She smiled weakly. "Thank you, Aggie. For . . . trusting us with your tale."

"Yes," Samuel said, rising. "You've helped us more than we can say."

The old woman followed them to the door, which Luce had already flung open, eager to let the sea air calm the wild sorrow ravaging her heart.

"Trust your heart, Lucinde Léon." The older woman's eyes were soft with sympathy. She slid something between Luce's fingers. A dagger, its handle crafted of pale bone, its blade hidden inside a sheath made of countless overlapping shells. It was attached to a belt made of tightly woven sea-silk. Luce drew the blade free. It was bitterly beautiful, wrought of the same shimmering water-glass as her dancing slippers, catching the sunlight in every imaginable hue.

"Was this . . ."

"My foremother's. Yours, now."

"I cannot take it. It's too precious."

"I have no need of it," Mother Aggie said, staunching Luce's protestations with a press of her gnarled hand. "A woman knows her own truth. It's a gift she is born with that, like so much else, is quickly stolen by the world. By priests with their talk of sin and wickedness and shame, by men who learned long ago how best to use women for their own pleasure and advantage. Instead of speaking from their hearts, their souls, women are told to heed their father, their husband, their God. Instead of choosing their own path, they are told to obey. Even so, their souls always know the truth. Always. Do not be afraid to give yours voice." She squeezed Luce's fingers in farewell. "I will ask the wind to watch over you."

Luce bowed her head. "And I you."

"I don't suppose you're in the mood to meet *my* mother, after all that?" Samuel asked when they were on the rough road leading to the village. "I only ask because she'll be expecting me—she'll have seen Bones by now." He glanced at her worriedly. "We don't have to, though. If you'd rather I take you back to the—"

"No." Luce tore her gaze from the sea-knife and slipped it—rather reluctantly—into her coat before taking Samuel's hand. Her mind was churning like a swell after a storm, rolling over every word Mother Aggie had said, buffeting her this way and that. Samuel, his warm hand, his gentle voice, was like an island. She angled her steps closer to his. "No. I would love to meet her."

Samuel grinned. "She'll have food ready—I heard your belly grumble back at Aggie's."

"I didn't even finish my tea."

He wound his fingers tighter around hers. "You had other things to think about."

It was a relief to arrive in the heart of the village, its thatched roofed cottages and clever stone walls. They passed a tiny stone church and an inn. A group of men in blue uniforms were emerging from the latter's entrance as they passed.

"Curse it," Samuel muttered, walking faster.

"What is it?" Luce hurried to keep up with him, her feet whimpering in protest.

"It's nothing. Come on." He ducked into an alley between two houses, pulling her with him. Luce, looking back, saw three of the uniformed men peel themselves away from the group, and follow.

"Are they soldiers?" she asked.

Samuel hurried down the alley. A pair of chickens squawked and flapped, narrowly avoiding his boots. The stink of rotting fish was strong.

"Royal Navy."

Luce's heart panged with fear. She was far from home, in enemy country. "Do they know I'm a Malouin? Do they—"

"They're not after you, Luce." He gripped her tighter, swung her around another corner. "They're after me."

Down yet another alley, this one even tighter. Luce barely avoided being tangled in the folds of a petticoat hanging on a line strung between two windows. "Do they know about the smuggling?"

"You could say that."

He had told her of the risks. Of the near misses, the flights from revenue cutters and naval vessels. Smuggling was a crime and Samuel, a criminal. For the first time, Luce understood the risk he took every time he crossed the Manche.

They turned another corner, and swathes of forest appeared ahead, coating the steep slope of the hill overlooking the village. Samuel helped Luce around the last of the houses. She could see the woods now, hear the sound of running water.

"Damn it all to fucking Hell," Samuel hissed.

The remaining sailors waited at the edge of the woods, their dark blue uniforms and fresh white breeches bright in the gloom.

Samuel turned hard, dragging Luce with him, meaning to duck back into the maze of thatched houses. He drew up short as the first three officers emerged from the alley behind them.

"Welcome home, Thorner," said their leader politely. "We've been waiting for you."

"Not here," Samuel said, as two of the men clamped hands upon his shoulders. "I'll tell you what I know, I swear. But not here."

The leader flicked his chin lazily toward the tree line. "Into the woods, then." He glanced at Luce, paused. "Who's the quail?"

"My cousin," Samuel lied. "She has nothing to do with this."

The officer looked Luce up and down. "Bring the cousin, too."

"What?" Samuel demanded. "Wait . . ."

But there was no stopping or waiting. Samuel and Luce were seized by the officers and marched into the woods.

"Say nothing," Samuel whispered to Luce. "Pretend you cannot speak."

Luce gave a faint nod. She trudged through the undergrowth, awkward in her long skirts, her feet bleating in pain.

When the village was no longer in sight between the oaks and beeches, the sailors stopped. Luce was held between two of them some distance away while the rest arrayed themselves in threatening splendor around Samuel—a circle of wolves in sea-blue.

The leader began firing rapid questions in English. Luce strained to listen to what he said, but the man spoke so quickly and used so many unfamiliar words that, together with the distance between them, she struggled to make out half of his words. Saint-Malo was mentioned, again and again, as well as the word for *ships* and *fortress. The Manche* and *Saint-Servan* made appearances, as well as *City Guard, Fort Royale, garrison,* and the phrase *seventy-two guns.* Luce tensed at that—seventy-two was the exact number of guns that sat atop the ramparts of Saint-Malo. She knew them all, had counted them with her father many times as they'd walked the ramparts, watching for his ships. The officer was angry at Samuel, a cold fury glinting beneath his polished exterior, the golden braid on his uniform. It seemed the only way Samuel could defuse the man's wrath was to talk—to talk, and to talk, until at last the officer's bearing eased, and his steady stream of questions dried up, and he gestured to the men holding Samuel to release him.

"I trust you are telling the truth," the officer said. He glanced at Luce. "Of course, we shall know soon enough. And if I find you have lied, it will be not just *you* on the scaffold. It will be your mother, your sisters, your brothers . . . and your pretty cousin, too."

"Samuel?" Luce trailed Samuel through the woods, struggling to keep up with his furious strides. The officers were long gone, the gloomy canopy above hushed, clinging to her every word. "Samuel? What did those men want with you?"

The village came back into view beyond the trees, peaceful in the midday sun.

"Samuel?"

He stopped at the tree line and she caught him, reached for his arm. He pulled away from her.

"Please don't ask me, Luce." His voice was tight with anguish. "You won't want to hear the answer."

She stepped back, surprised. She had thought him angry. To find him shaken and defeated was infinitely worse.

"How do you know I won't?"

Samuel laughed bitterly. "Trust me."

"I do trust you, Samuel. You know my secrets. You heard even more of them at Aggie's. I have trusted you with everything. Why can you not do the same for me?"

He looked at her, torn.

Luce stepped closer, laid her hand on his arm. "What is happening? Why were you speaking of Saint-Malo to those men?"

He shook his head. "You will hate me for this. You will think me a monster. . . ."

He realized at once what he had said, winced. "I'm sorry. I shouldn't have said that."

Luce shrugged. "At least we will be monsters together."

"You could never be a monster." He touched her cheek. Sighed. "I will tell you, Luce. I promise. But first I want you to meet my family. Can you do that for me?"

Such hope, such despair, in those gray eyes. She nodded. "Of course."

Samuel's family lived in a house no larger or smaller than the others in the village. Its squat stone walls nestled welcomingly in the sun; its thatched roof was neat and well-kept, as was its rambling, walled garden and the flower-filled boxes beneath its windows.

Within, all was bright and warm: scrubbed floors, aged table freshly wiped, a posy of sea thrift sitting in a little pot at its center. It smelled delicious, of baking bread and something rich and fishy. Pie, perhaps. Samuel's mother, Martha, hugged him tight and beamed with pleasure when he introduced Luce.

"So *you're* Lucinde," she said, wiping her hands on her apron. "It's wonderful to meet you. Although . . ." She gave her son a reproving look. "Tell me you didn't load her onto that lug like a piece of contraband, Samuel."

"The *Dove* is not a *lug*!" Samuel said with feeling. "And why is everyone assuming I stole Luce and smuggled her into England?"

"Because that's precisely what you did," Luce said. She turned to Martha. "Although, I *did* ask him to bring me here, so I suppose we can't accuse him of the stealing part."

"That would be a first."

Samuel shook his head in mock dismay. "I deserve better than this."

"What do you deserve, you great moonraker?" A dark-haired

girl of perhaps sixteen sauntered into the room, her eyes a startling, and familiar, golden-gray.

"This is my sister Margaret, Luce," Samuel said, grinning. "Don't believe a word she says."

"Luce?" Margaret came to embrace her brother, all the while looking at Luce with interest. "Is this *the* Lucinde, then? You're prettier than Samuel described," she added, "which is impressive because he always says you are very, very pretty. No wonder he's a-took to you."

"Christ above," Samuel muttered.

"Has Samuel come home?" Two younger children scampered in, a boy of eleven or twelve and a girl of perhaps seven. They ran toward Samuel, the girl leaping into his arms, the boy catching hold of him around the waist.

"And these rapscallions," Samuel said, blowing the girl's chestnut-gold hair, so like his own, out of his mouth, "are Tobias and Flora." He wrinkled his nose, drew back and frowned at the little girl. "You smell like fish, Flora. What have you been doing?"

"Fishing."

"Makes sense."

She giggled, tweaking his nose between her fingers, then squealed as he swung her high and set her lightly on the ground.

"Mind the ceiling, Samuel," Martha scolded. It seemed they had interrupted her while she was preparing the midday meal. She returned to the kitchen, opened the oven, and drew out two loaves of bread.

"Are you from Saint-Malo?" The boy, Tobias, was looking up at Luce, his arms by some miracle still gripping Samuel's waist.

"I am," Luce said.

"Do you know any privateers?"

Luce smiled. "I do."

"*I'm* going to be a privateer when I grow up."

"I thought you were going to be a captain," Samuel said.

"I am," Tobias told him solemnly. "A *privateer* captain."

He followed Samuel to the door, watching while his older brother slipped out of his overcoat and tricorn and hung them on a pair of hooks, then, as Samuel moved away, promptly removed both and donned them himself. Samuel didn't say a word as Tobias, swimming in the folds of leather, his eyes all but disappearing beneath the hat, took his seat at the table. He only sat beside the boy and leaned his arm along the back of his chair.

"Come and sit, Luce," he said, gesturing to the seat on his other side. "We're just in time for nuncheon."

"Samuel always shows up when there's food about to be served," Martha said, leaning over as she slid a board bearing the bread into the center of the table. "And look; here's the other one. Right on time."

Bones entered the room, dropping to a crouch as little Flora ran to him.

"Bones!" she cried, hugging him tight.

"Hello, little Flora," he said tenderly. He waited until Flora broke their hug before rising and taking his seat at the table.

"Enemy in our midst, eh?" he said, winking at Luce.

"Mind your elbows, Bones," Margaret told him, returning to the table with an enormous pie in her hands.

"Where's Thomas?" Samuel asked as Flora scrambled onto her seat. She smiled shyly at Luce across the steaming food.

"He was helping William Anning with his nets this morning," Margaret said, easing the pie onto the table. She glanced up as something moved beyond the window. "Here he is, now."

Samuel's younger brother did not resemble him as strongly as Margaret and Flora did. His hair was darker, his eyes too. He was maybe eighteen years old, still growing, and yet to match his brother's height. Which, Luce realized as she watched Thomas hang up his coat and hat, would probably happen rather soon.

"Go gently on him, Samuel," Margaret murmured, before she took her own seat. "He's been crousty of late."

"Hmm," was all Samuel said.

Bones sighed wearily. Luce glanced at him, but he shook his head as though to say, *later,* then turned to watch Thomas approach the table.

"Thomas."

"Samuel." Thomas glanced at Bones. His face, which had been as stern as his elder brother's, broke into a grin. "Bones."

"Thomas. What's this we hear about you helping that fool Anning?"

"Someone needs to show him how to cast a net."

They grinned at each other, and then Thomas, moving around the table to take his seat, noticed Luce.

"This is Lucinde," Samuel said. "And before you ask, no, we did not smuggle her aboard the *Dove.*"

"Well," Luce said, tilting her head thoughtfully, "you *did* make me sit amongst all those packets of silk."

Everyone laughed. Thomas sat down, raising his cheek for Martha to kiss before she took her own seat and said a prayer of thanks for the food, for her children, and for the safe return of her eldest son and nephew. No sooner was it done than she was back on her feet, passing a bowl of butter to Luce before slicing up the pie. At the other end of the table, Margaret was cutting great slabs of bread for everyone.

"It is good to meet you, Lucinde," Thomas said, as his mother slid him an enormous helping of pie.

Samuel gave his brother an approving look, which quickly faded as Thomas added with a smirk, "*Now* we all know why you really spend so much time in Saint-Malo, Samuel."

"Spare me," Samuel murmured, raising his eyes to the ceiling.

Bones snorted.

"Here," Martha said, serving both him and Samuel. "Eat, the pair of you. Have you been taking care of yourselves? You look thin."

"They don't call him Bones for nothing," Thomas muttered. Bones threw a pea at him.

Samuel lifted his spoon. "Of course we have, Ma."

"Of course they haven't, Ma," Thomas said. "They risk themselves every day. And yet here we all are, benefitting from it. Sitting around doing *nothing* while Samuel and Bones risk everything to ensure that we have *butter.*"

"*I'm* not sitting around doing nothing," Margaret said into the silence. "Ma and I work hard—"

"Washing linens and baking bread doesn't count, Meg," Thomas told her.

"Watch your words, Tom," Samuel said quietly. "Be grateful for the clean shirt on your back, and the food on your plate."

"I'd sooner help pay for them."

Bones bent over his bowl, devouring his food with sudden vigor, while Samuel scrubbed a weary hand over his eyes. As though he knew the shape of the argument that was brewing, as well as how it would end. "I know what you want me to say."

"Then why not just say it?"

"You know why. You're too young, for a start—"

"I'm eighteen. Two years older than you were when you first went to sea."

"I've told you," Samuel said. "If you want to join a ship's crew, I'll pack your bag myself."

"I don't want to join a crew." Thomas's food lay forgotten before him. "I want to work with you two."

Bones glanced up from his pie, met Samuel's eye, and shrugged as though to say, *he's your brother; leave me out of it.*

Samuel glanced at Margaret, took a long-suffering breath. "I know. And I appreciate it, Thomas. I do. Bones, too. But we can't have you with us right now. It's dangerous—"

"I see," Thomas said bitterly. "So dangerous that you felt compelled to bring a *woman* across the Channel with you last night?" He banged an open palm on the table.

Luce flinched.

"That's enough, Tom," Martha said quietly. "Eat your dinner, now." The little house, which had bulged with good cheer and laughter only moments ago, now felt very different. Across the table from Luce, the youngest children watched their two older brothers with wide, worried eyes.

"I've told you half a hundred times, Tom," Samuel said tiredly, reaching for more bread. "You *will* come and work with us."

"And when will that be?" Thomas said bitterly. "Next niver'stide, I suppose?"

"Watch your mouth," Samuel said, his own tone hardening. "And it will be when I say it will be. Not a moment sooner."

Thomas pushed his food away and got to his feet. "Will it, then? And what if William Anning has offered me a place smuggling with *him*?"

Samuel, calmly eating, kept his eyes on his food. "Offering and taking up are two different things."

"What if I *did* take him up on it?"

The whole table stilled.

"Thomas . . . ," Martha whispered, horrified.

"You never did," Margaret said, staring at her brother in disbelief.

"I did," Thomas said, throwing out his chest. "Next time William makes a crossing, I'm to go with him." He placed his hands on the table, leaning toward his older brother. "Perhaps I'll see you and Bones in Saint-Malo."

Samuel got to his feet so fast his chair tipped back and crashed to the floor. "You will fucking *not* see us in Saint-Malo, Thomas, do you hear me? You'll see no one in Saint-Malo, because you won't be there. Not with Bones and me, and certainly not with William-fucking-Anning."

"You can't force me to stay here." The two brothers were toe to toe now, and Luce realized she had been wrong. Thomas *was* nearly as tall as Samuel, and as broad, and looked intent on finding out if he was as strong as his older brother, too.

"Easy now," Bones said, getting slowly to his feet. "Settle, the pair of you."

"I can," Samuel said, ignoring his cousin. "And I'll tell you why. You won't be smuggling in Saint-Malo because very soon there may not *be* a Saint-Malo. The king wants to divert the French armies from the fighting in Germany. He's had enough of Malouin corsairs dominating the Channel, interrupting trade, stealing English ships. He's planning a series of attacks up and down the French coast. A fleet is assembling in the Solent even now, under Admiral Howe's command. A hundred ships or more, by all accounts."

Luce felt a hot rush of fear. "They're going to attack Saint-Malo?"

"I'm sorry, Luce," Samuel said, throwing her a regretful glance. "But yes. They are." He turned back to Thomas, the rest of his family. "And I'll be damned if my dough-baked brother will be there to see it."

21

Those Bastards

The love Luce had witnessed in the Thorner house, the devotion Samuel clearly felt for his family, and they for him, was all that prevented her from stopping on the rough coastal path and shoving him backwards off one of his spectacular English cliffs.

That, and the growing conviction that he had betrayed Saint-Malo to keep his family, and Luce herself, safe.

If I find you have lied, it will be not just you on the scaffold. It will be your mother, your sisters, your brothers . . . and your pretty cousin, too.

"That was not the way I wanted to tell you about Howe's fleet," Samuel said. They were alone on the path; Bones had left them outside the Thorner house, ostensibly to bid farewell to his own family before sailing back, although Luce suspected he had been more concerned with giving Luce and Samuel a moment's privacy.

"Oh?" Luce stopped walking. "How were you planning to tell me?"

You will hate me for this, he had said when they had left the forest that morning. *You will think me a monster.*

They had reached the headland now. The grass on either side of the way was blanketed with sea thrift, the petals a softer, paler pink than those at the cove. Any other day, Luce would have gathered a sample. With Samuel glowering down at her, however, the sea wind catching at his overcoat, cold as the betrayal laying between them, there was no time for natural history.

"Since I only became certain of it *this morning,*" he said tersely, "I had planned to tell you here. Today. Right after you met my family."

True. He had asked her to meet his family before he explained what had occurred with the officer and his men. *And yet . . .*

"Why?"

"Because I knew that if you met them, you'd believe me when I said that I would do anything for them."

Damn my soul. How could she remain angry with him now?

"Tell me, then," she said, with a sigh.

He took a deep breath. "Those navy men we met—they caught Bones and me on a run. A stupid mistake on our part. We left late, arrived here at dawn. They spotted us, gave chase in their cutter. We could not outrun them, but nor could we risk them learning the location of the sea-cave. So, we let them catch us."

"When did this happen?"

"Around the time you went to the ball at Le Loup Blanc and met de Châtelaine," he said. *I leave you for a few days, and the wolf comes prowling.* "They were all for bringing us back to shore, throwing us into the nearest prison, and confiscating the *Dove.* I couldn't let that happen. My family relies on me to provide for them. So I did the only thing I could do."

"Which was?"

"Talk my way out of it. Before they questioned me, I overheard some of the officers speaking of an attack on Saint-Malo. I knew I could use my knowledge as leverage, and gain their trust. I told them I knew the Malouin coast as well as any local—that I had been sailing it for years. And that, if they released me, I could gather information that would help them prepare for the landing."

He leaned in, close, intent. "You need to know—I began spreading word about their plans as soon as I returned to the city. I have contacts in the garrison, and the City Guard, too. I made sure they each got wind of it, as well as many others. And I ensured that it would rise to the top of the chain, to the Marquis de la Châtre himself." Luce nodded. She had heard the men's talk around the supper table on the night of the Blessing. They had dismissed the threat, insisting the English would target Brest instead. "The news was not unexpected. The king of France knows the coasts of Bretagne and Normandy are vulnerable. The garrisons there have been preparing for months."

"So you courted them both."

"What choice did I have?"

"Were you not worried you'd be caught?"

He smiled darkly. "I live too near a wood to be frightened by an owl. Besides, I never really planned to betray Saint-Malo. It has been good to me, helped me feed my family. Bones and I have friends there. And you . . . Of course, when the officers never received word from me they became suspicious. I knew they were looking for me. I did not expect them to be sitting in the middle of the village this morning."

"But you told them the truth," Luce said accusingly. "I heard you. Seventy-two, you said. There are seventy-two cannon on the walls of Saint-Malo."

"There are," Samuel agreed. "And they will need every one of them when the Duke of Marlborough and his twelve thousand men arrive."

"Oh, my God." Luce covered her mouth with one hand.

"I take it you heard what else that officer said." Samuel stepped carefully toward her. "He swore that if he discovered I was lying—which he would have, quite easily, once the attack began—he would send not just *me* to the gallows, but my entire family. Which, after this morning, would also include my pretty cousin." He shook his head. "Better those seventy-two guns face English soldiers than my family. Than *you*. I can't be sorry for it, Luce. Were I faced with the same choice, I would make it again."

She rested her head on his chest, nodded wearily. "I understand."

His arms came up around her. "Besides, didn't you tell me that Saint-Malo has never fallen? That it never will?"

"I hope that's true." She turned her head against his shirt, looked southward over the wide, blue sweep of the Manche. "I really do."

They sailed through the afternoon and into the evening. With the *Dove* free of contraband, it mattered not who saw them, or where. Luce stayed beside Samuel throughout the voyage, her thoughts churning, her gaze returning again and again to the English coast, as though she might glimpse Admiral Howe's fleet sailing behind them, bearing down on Bretagne. She must have dozed. When she woke, her head was on Samuel's thigh, one of his hands moving gently against her hair, the other firm on the tiller.

The evening light was cooling by the time Samuel and Bones maneuvered the *Dove* between the rocks ringing the cove. Eight o'clock, Luce guessed. Perhaps a little later. Luce, dressed once more in her breeches, caraco, and overcoat, Mother Aggie's belt and sea-knife secured at her waist, leapt onto the shore, flinching as her boots splashed in the shallows. The sea-silk was tucked into her caraco, with a layer of wool and her chemise between it and her bare skin. Even so, she looked fearfully down, half expecting to see a tail.

"Careful there." Samuel was clearly thinking the same thing. "I'm still not sure how we'd explain it to Bones."

"Explain what?" Bones said, yawning.

"I'll tell you when I've figured out how to explain it."

Luce looked up at the cliffs, the forest, the path home. Her mother and Veronique had left for Nantes two days before, and would not arrive until tomorrow. After that would come the wedding breakfast, followed by a day or two devoted to shopping . . . Ordinarily, Luce would have hugged herself with happiness. Another five days, perhaps longer, before her family returned. Another five days of freedom. With the threat of the English fleet looming across the Manche, however, five more days without her father's reassuring presence seemed an eternity. Could she send St. Jean or one of the stableboys to Nantes with a message for him? No; that would take days. Could she ride to Saint-Malo herself, then, and beg to speak to the captain of the garrison? She scoffed at the mere thought of the soldiers' faces. Besides, Samuel had contacts enough in the city. She could always send a pigeon to one of her father's business partners. Or perhaps riding to the neighboring malouinières would be best? Monsieur Béliveau had always been courteous and kind. He would listen to her, she was certain of it, even if the precise details of the impending invasion would be, through sheer necessity, rather vague. If she rode out first thing in the morning. . . .

"Who's that, then?" Bones asked idly.

"Who?" Samuel turned.

"Those bastards right there."

Those bastards were five or six rough-looking men emerging from the forest above. They were armed to the teeth, flintlock pistols in hand and swords hanging at their waists. Luce swallowed. Several of those pistols were pointed directly at herself, Samuel, and Bones.

Samuel swore softly as more men appeared on either side of the cove, weapons drawn. They left the rocks, moving across the sand. Closing in.

"Samuel Thorner?" one of the men called, drawing steadily closer.

"Never heard of him," Samuel replied.

The man turned to one of his companions, half-hidden behind him. "That him?" he growled.

The second man nodded. "It is." Luce narrowed her eyes beneath her tricorn. She recognized this man. Had seen him at the Blessing, drinking with Bones and the rest of Samuel's friends.

Samuel saw him, too. "Morning, Debret," he said, so cold that

Luce could have sworn ice crusted along her spine. "Didn't expect to see *you* with de Châtelaine's dogs. Not happy with your cut, then?"

"Fucking traitor," Bones spat. "Couldn't resist blowing the gaff, eh?"

The ice spread, wending its way into Luce's chest, stealing her breath. She had been so caught up in worry for her family, for Saint-Malo, that she had not even considered the danger awaiting Samuel and Bones.

"How much was the reward again, Debret?" Samuel mused. "You should have come to me. Might be I could have matched it."

"I doubt that," the first man, clearly the leader, said. He spat in the sand and turned to his men. "Bring all three of them."

"All three?" Samuel stepped forward, palm raised. "You spoke of Samuel Thorner. Here I am. What need have you for my companions?"

"Me? None," the leader said. "You'll have to ask Monsieur de Châtelaine. He's the one said to bring you, and anyone you sailed with."

"I barely know these men," Samuel said. "I hired them to help me on the crossing, nothing more."

The leader turned to Debret. "That true?"

"That one there's his cousin," Debret said, pointing at Bones. "The two of them work together."

"And the boy?"

Luce kept her head down.

"I've not seen him before," Debret conceded. "But if he's sailing with Thorner, he's as like to be in his confidence."

"You're a rare piece of shit, Debret," Bones said conversationally.

"Leave the lad out of it," Samuel said. "He knows nothing of my business. He's less than useless to de Châtelaine."

"I'll guess de Châtelaine'll be the one to decide that."

"But—"

"Listen, you thieving bastard." The first man strode forward, squaring up to Samuel. Luce felt the rest of the men tense, heard the ominous clicks of pistols cocking. "We've been out here for two days waiting for you. Last night some fucking *gnomes* set fire to our camp and stole our supplies. We haven't eaten all day. So believe me when I tell you that I don't give two shits about your men, or how well you know them. You're all coming with us. *Now.*"

He turned for the path, not bothering to watch as his men closed in around Luce, Samuel, and Bones. Pistols surrounded them on all sides, black barrels staring with unmistakeable intent. *No choice.* Luce saw it in Samuel's eyes as he glanced at her, as Bones seized the *Dove*'s anchor and wedged it into the sand. No choice but to follow the men up the beach, to hunker low in her coat and draw her kerchief up around her chin.

A carriage drawn by two horses waited on the other side of the woods, its windows covered. Several saddled horses grazed nearby. Luce, Samuel, and Bones were bundled roughly into the carriage, then closed inside the dim space. The sound of a lock shooting home on the outside of the door, a creak and rock as someone climbed onto the driver's bench. Then they were moving.

"Fucking Debret," Bones muttered, as the sound of the wheels on the rough road and clop of hooves rose around them. "Always said he was a riotous prick."

"Debret is not my concern at this point." Samuel reached for Luce's hand in the darkness. "I'm so sorry," he said quietly. "If I'd known you'd be tangled up in all of this. . . ."

"No," she said. "This is all my fault. I should never have gone to Dorset with you. You and Bones should have gone alone, and stayed there."

"Where's the fun in that?" Bones asked. He swore as the carriage gave a sudden, rough jounce, clunking his head against the roof.

"I should have done a lot of things," Samuel said, "none of

which will help us now." His eyes glittered in the darkness as he turned to Bones. "What do you make of this?"

"Honestly? I have no fucking idea. But I will say I'd have been a deal happier if we'd found the City Guard waiting for us instead of these leery pricks."

"Agreed." Samuel was silent for a few moments. Then, "They didn't ask us where we've stored the stone." Luce could all but hear the whirring of his mind.

"No," Bones said darkly. "They did not."

Samuel turned to Luce. "Do you have the knife Mother Aggie gave you?"

She fumbled in her overcoat, drew it out. Shards of dark light gleamed on the blade.

"Best keep it within reach," he said grimly. "No telling when you might need it."

The carriage trundled along the rough road, its interior growing even dimmer and dimmer as evening spiraled toward night. At last, it drew to a stop. Luce heard low voices, the champing of horses, the squeak of harness and carriage springs as their captors moved about.

"Stay close to Bones, Luce," Samuel said quietly. "Don't let de Châtelaine see your face. The first chance you get, run. Both of you."

"We're not leaving you," Luce hissed. Bones grunted his agreement.

Before Samuel could argue further the door opened, revealing a rectangle of dusky sky and a familiar stretch of beach littered with hauled out boats for careening, slips, piles of timber, warehouses, and workshops.

They were at the dockyards in Saint-Servan.

The yards were empty now, the workers long gone. Luce stayed close to Bones and Samuel as they were pulled from the carriage and ushered through the gloaming, the bare bones of half-made ships rising like carcasses against the violet sky.

Two ship's boats waited on the shore. Beyond them, the water glimmered with the distant reflections of the candles and lanterns flickering to life in Saint-Malo, as well as on the many ships anchored in the harbor. Morgan's men did not stop to admire the view. They merely shoved their captives into the boats and pushed off, sculling for deeper water, where the shadowy shapes of new ships lay at anchor. One ship stood out to Luce from the rest. The *Lucinde* was even more beautiful now. Her three masts had been maneuvered into place, as well as her stays, yards, and much of her rigging. She would have her sails, and be ready for her first voyage, in a matter of days.

Her interest in the ship quickly turned to confusion when she realized that it was to the *Lucinde* that the ship's boats were bearing. As they neared, the subtle glow of lanterns glimmered from the deck, dancing over the water. A tangle of questions rose in Luce's mind. Had Morgan truly dared to board her father's ship without permission? What possible reason could he have for ordering his men to take them there? Samuel, craning his neck to take in the familiar features of the figurehead high above, swore softly.

"The *Lucinde*?" he whispered to Luce.

She nodded.

Another ship's boat had drawn up alongside the *Lucinde*, the men aboard it climbing a ladder rope to the deck high above.

"Up you go," the men at the oars ordered, guiding the boat beneath the ladder. Luce made to stand and climb, but Samuel caught her hand. Bones went instead, the little boat rocking as he stepped across Luce and took hold of the ladder. Hidden by the movement, Samuel gripped Luce's hand.

"*Go*," he mouthed, tilting his chin meaningfully at the water beside them. "*Now.*"

She shook her head, firm. *I won't leave you.*

He gave her a look that clearly meant he was about to throw her overboard himself, but was prevented from doing so by the nearest oarsman, who grabbed Luce's shoulder and shoved her toward the ladder. She stumbled on the boat's uneven bottom, the sea-knife, now secured at her waist, digging into her thigh. Righting herself, she gripped the rope ladder in both hands. Below her, the *Lucinde*'s hull curved into the darkness, the timber already roughening with a crust of pale barnacles. Above, Bones was about to reach the deck.

She took a breath, raised her boot, and began to climb.

Her feet bleated with every step on the narrow ladder, but even so Luce made it to the top. She struggled over the railing, almost staggering as her boots met solid deck, clutching at her tricorn as it threatened to slide off her head. Bones caught her, tugged her to his side with one firm hand, shoving her behind him.

"Good God," came an amused, velvety voice. "Is the boy drunk?"

Luce froze. The urge to look into Morgan's face, to demand why he had boarded her father's—*her*—ship as though he were entitled to, why he had ordered these men to snatch Samuel from the beach was overwhelming. Bones's broad hand, laid on her forearm in gentle warning, stopped her. She kept her eyes down, her chin tucked into her kerchief, hoping that the poor light, her tricorn, and Bones's wide shoulder would be enough to keep Morgan from recognizing her. She felt Bones tense as Morgan's shining black boots appeared on the deck before her. "*Is* he, though?"

At that moment Samuel boarded the *Lucinde*. Morgan, distracted by the arrival of his prize, turned away.

Luce, still shielded by Bones, risked raising her face slightly. No sooner had Samuel reached the deck and straightened than one of Morgan's men—there were half a dozen already on the deck, and more climbing from the boats below—seized his wrists, binding them behind his back.

"Samuel Thorner, I believe," Morgan said politely. He stepped closer, immaculate in a green silk frock coat and black breeches, his dark eyes narrowing as he took in Samuel's face. "Wait. I know you."

Samuel said nothing, his face perfectly neutral.

"You're the drunken scum who attacked me on the night of the Blessing!"

Attacked him? It took all of Luce's self-control not to shove Bones aside and run at Morgan herself.

Samuel, however, remained calm. "I believe it was *you* who kicked the shit out of *me*, monsieur."

"And glad I am for it, too," Morgan said. "For it would seem that you have stolen more than just the *Dauphin*'s storm-stone from me." Luce remembered the handful of ribbons shining in Samuel's hand. It was clear that Morgan knew exactly who had taken them from his pocket.

"It's not stealing if it never belonged to you," Samuel said quietly. "And, speaking of . . ." He gave the *Lucinde*'s decks an appraising look. "Is this pretty ship even yours?"

"It will be, soon enough."

Samuel raised his brows. "As you say."

"Enough with the pleasantries," Morgan snapped. "You know why you're here. Where is the stone?"

"The stone?"

"The stone."

"Which stone is that?" Samuel pretended to examine the bindings on his wrists. "There's a lot of it around, you know."

"The *storm-stone*."

"The storm-stone?"

Morgan clenched his jaw. "The storm-stone you salvaged—*stole*—from the *Dauphin*."

Samuel shrugged his shoulders, a movement that suggested he would have raised his palms had he been able. "I have no idea."

"Have it your way, then," Morgan said, gesturing to the yardarm above. It was near-dark now, but the men had hung lanterns from the masts, and set them around the deck. Gazing up, Luce could see that there was something unusual about the yard; extra ropes attached to the blocks at each end that should not have been there.

"Start with the boy," Morgan said. Luce flinched as she was grabbed from behind, as heavy hands clamped down on her arms. She fought to free herself, heard Samuel and Bones shouting at the men to let her—*him*—go. The men merely shoved her toward the section of decking where those strange ropes trailed down from the yardarms.

"Hurry up," one of the men snarled, nudging her forward. Luce, watching those ropes, wondering what on earth Morgan meant for the men to do with them, stumbled over her own boot, a wedge of pain driving up into her right heel. She went down, one knee smashing into the freshly polished deck.

"For fuck's sake." The man closest to her reached for her collar, wrenching her to her feet. Luce cried out as his hand caught the thick tail of her hair, hastily thrust down the back of her coat, ripping it free. In the instinct that comes with pain she shoved the man in the chest as hard as she could. He staggered back a step or two, shocked, then recovered himself and strode forward. The back of his hand crashed into Luce's jaw, sent her staggering.

"Insolent fucking whelp."

Luce felt herself falling, the deck sliding out from beneath her, Samuel's roar of rage dim in her ears. She hit something, shuddered to a halt. Smelled cologne and pomade. Almond and cloves, bergamot and musk. Someone knocked her hat from her head, dragged her to her feet.

"*Lucinde?*" Morgan was gripping her collar, staring down into her face.

Luce swallowed the fear that rose at the sight of the soulless rage in his black eyes. "What are you doing on my ship, Morgan?" she demanded. "How dare you do this?"

Morgan seemed not to hear her. He turned his head to Samuel, his entire body tight with rage. "What *else* have you stolen from me of late, Thorner?"

"As I said: it's not stealing if it was never yours." Samuel's eyes did not leave Luce.

Morgan showed his teeth. "And what of him?" he demanded, jerking his chin toward Bones. "What is *he* in all of this?"

Luce realized the man that had betrayed Samuel, Debret, was also there on deck. "That there's Bones," he stammered. "Thorner's cousin." He glanced nervously at the yardarm, the waiting ropes. "What do you mean to do with those sheets, sir? I gave you Thorner's name believing you'd take it to the Guard. I didn't know—" His gaze flicked worriedly to Luce. "I didn't know about any of *this*."

"Bones, did you say his name was?" Morgan asked. He smirked. "How apt." He pushed Luce toward two of his men. "Secure her on the quarterdeck." He turned to the rest of the men. "Run Cousin *Bones* up."

22

Wedding Present

Run Cousin Bones up.

The words echoed in Luce's mind as the two men bundled her along the deck and up the narrow stairs to the quarterdeck. They opened the first door they came to—a storeroom, Luce knew from the many hours she had spent studying the *Lucinde*'s plans—and shoved her through it, wedging it closed with a stray piece of lumber before returning to midships. Luce, trapped in the darkness, watched them leave through the small, rectangular grating in the door. They gave her no such attention; indeed, the men ducked back down the stairs eagerly, as though afraid they might miss whatever Morgan had planned.

Run Cousin Bones up. What could that mean? Sails and ensigns were run up, not people. She clung to the bars of the grate, heart pounding, straining to see what was happening on the deck below. It was fully dark now, but the lantern light gave her glimpses: the movement of those long ropes, the swing as they were hauled about. She heard the heavy clank of iron, and Samuel's voice, the words indistinct against the activity on the deck. Morgan replied, his voice tilting upward at the end as though he had asked a question. Samuel's answer came instantly. Words flowed out of him, fast and thorough—no riddles now—and Luce knew that he was telling Morgan where the storm-stone was. Her hands clenched on the grate. Whatever Morgan meant to do to

Bones was bad enough that Samuel was willingly, desperately, giving up the stone.

Silence. Luce strained her ears, waiting. For a moment she thought that it was over, that Morgan had released Bones, had stopped whatever game he intended to play. For it *was* a game to him; Luce had seen it in his eyes, in the relaxed, almost lazy way he'd waited for his men to bring Luce, Samuel, and Bones on board. He had known that the stone would be his, before he so much as uttered a word.

A deep and terrible wave of misgiving washed over her.

And then something—Bones, she realized, was hauled up on those ropes by his feet, dangling above the deck like a fish on a line. Luce stood on her toes, ignoring their protests, and peered through the grate. The men were doing something to his wrists—she heard the hiss of rope—and then he was swung out over the side of the ship.

One second became two, then three, then four. All the while Bones hung over the water, completely helpless, his hands and feet secured top and bottom by the ropes.

Samuel swore, loud, frantic. "You cannot do this! I *told* you where the stone is! I'll take you there myself!"

"Where's the fun in that?" Morgan drawled.

And suddenly Luce knew what Morgan had meant when he had said to "run Cousin Bones up."

One evening, when she was perhaps thirteen, she had crept from her chamber and sat at the door to the music room, where her father and his friends were gathered after supper. Her mother and the other ladies had retired to the salon, and Luce knew from experience that the best stories could be overheard when the shipowners were left alone with a good supply of tobacco and brandy. That night, however, she had heard more than she had bargained for. One of the men—Monsieur le Fer she suspected, though it was impossible to be sure—had spoken of a terrible punishment he had witnessed aboard a Dutch ship whose crew had attempted a mutiny. The captain, once he had restored order, had commanded that the mutineers be keelhauled—their hands and feet bound to ropes stretched from the yardarm while they were lowered into the sea and hauled along the bottom of the ship. Port to starboard. Luce, sickened by Monsieur le Fer's vivid description of the appalling injuries the sailors had suffered—as many had died from their wounds as by drowning, their clothing and skin torn against the thick layer of barnacles crusting the hull—had crept back to her bed. She had lain awake, trembling, for hours.

She was trembling now.

"Send him down," Morgan ordered. The sound of hissing rope cut through the silence, followed by a splash as Bones hit the black water below. Grunts of effort rose from midships—Luce imagined the men heaving on the rope, drawing it through the iron ring secured to the yardarm. And then the hideous sound of something dragging slowly against the *Lucinde*'s hull.

Heave, heave, heave.

Drag, drag, drag.

Each haul on the rope was followed by the sound of that appalling, distant dragging. *They can't be,* Luce thought. *They can't be doing this.* Horror swirled like ice in her blood. Her heartbeat thundered in her ears.

"*Morgan!*" She screamed his name. Gripped the bars of the grate, shook them as hard as she could. "Stop this! Please, let him go!"

She shoved her shoulder against the door, again and again. It held fast. She was trapped, with no means of getting out, of running down to Morgan and begging him to cease this madness. To dive into the sea and stop it herself. "*Morgan!*"

For one breathless moment Luce thought he had heeded her. The dragging stopped. There came the sound of something heavy being lifted from the water. She pressed her face to the bars and glimpsed Bones dangling limply from the yardarm.

Hands reached for him, drawing him back over the rail and out of sight. No matter; a glimpse had been enough. Bones's head lolled. Water and blood poured from his face, his hands. His feet hung limply down, bare, bleeding, and painfully fragile. Patches of bloody skin showed through his ripped clothes. No way to tell if he was breathing.

Luce flinched as the lines were loosened and he was dropped unceremoniously onto the deck with a sodden *thunk*.

"You fucking *bastard*!" Samuel roared, rending the silence. "I *told* you where the stone is!"

Morgan said nothing. Luce remembered his words to her weeks ago, right here on this ship. The coldness in his voice as he had spoken of his revenge.

You can be certain they will regret stealing from me.

"Do it again," Morgan told his men.

"*No!*"

Luce's heart broke at the anguish in Samuel's voice, even as her terror swirled and grew. She threw herself against the door, heedless of the pain flaring in her shoulder. She must stop Morgan. Must save Bones.

"Morgan!" she screamed. "Morgan, *please*!"

Perhaps the men hesitated. Morgan's voice, when it came again, was harder.

"I said, *again*."

"You don't have to listen to him!" Luce cried to the men. "You don't have to do this! My father is Jean-Baptiste Léon. I promise you that he will know of this and that there will be a reckoning! Stop now and I will ensure he knows that you were not to blame. That you are men of honor, who refused in good conscience to murder an innocent man!"

There was a long silence, ripe with uncertainty. Hope flared in Luce's heart.

Morgan laughed. "You forget, Lucinde," he called up to her. "Some men value money over honor."

Splash. Heave, drag. Luce could barely breathe as they did it all over again. This time it seemed to take longer for Bones to reach the other side of the ship. When they heaved him onto the deck, he was so badly mangled that Luce hardly recognized his face.

The sound of his broken, sodden body landing on the deck, of Samuel's agony when he realized his cousin was dead, would stay with her for the rest of her days.

"Cut him down," Morgan said indifferently. "And clean up this mess. I'd best check on our other guest before Monsieur Thorner enjoys *his* little swim."

"If you touch her . . . ," Samuel said brokenly.

"You'll what?" Morgan laughed cruelly. "I told you that night at the Blessing to keep those thieving hands of yours off your betters. You should have listened."

There was a sickening thud, followed by another, and another. Luce winced as she imagined Morgan's shining boot lashing into Samuel again and again.

"Get him ready," Morgan said, at last. For the first time since Luce had boarded the *Lucinde*, he sounded less than completely composed. "We'll dangle him when I get back."

Steps on the stairs, and Morgan prowled into view, a lantern in one hand. Luce, a caged bird, froze as he stopped in front of the grate, tilting his head consideringly.

"Not so talkative now, hmm?" He knocked aside the lumber securing the door and turned the handle.

"This was not what I had in mind for you," he said, taking in the storeroom with a disapproving *tsk*. He offered Luce his hand. It glistened with water and blood. "Come. Let's find somewhere more comfortable for you to wait while we entertain Monsieur Thorner. Somewhere less . . . drafty. I know just the place."

Like the rest of the *Lucinde*, the captain's quarters had been greatly improved since the launch. As well as the new table, bookshelves now lined the walls, a narrow ledge running along the front of each to stop their contents tipping onto the floor in rough seas. A long bench had been constructed beneath the windows, which were all firmly closed against the night.

"You needn't bother trying to keep what you're doing from me," Luce said.

"Come now, Lucinde," Morgan said blithely. "We both know that it is you, and not I, who has been keeping secrets." He set his lantern on the table at the cabin's centre, and gestured around the room with a flourish. "Cabin's coming along well, isn't it?"

"You want to discuss furnishings at a time like this?"

How could he be so calm, so courteous, after what he had just done? Luce was shaking so hard her teeth were chattering. The sound of Bones's body landing upon the deck played over and over again in her mind, melding with the memory of him flopping down beside her on the sand in the cove. That wide, warm grin of his, and the way his head tilted toward her whenever she spoke, as though he were listening carefully to what she had to say. The way he had pushed her behind him when they had first boarded the *Lucinde*, shielding her with his own body. His poor, ravaged body . . .

"Why not?" Morgan moved about the room, admiring the carved paneling, the furniture. "I'm not sure if you've heard, but I just discovered the location of my storm-stone. Which means that I can keep my end of our bargain."

"You just killed an innocent man—a man who was my friend—by *dragging him under a ship*," Luce spat. "If you think that I would even *consider* marrying you now . . ."

He raised a hand, lovingly stroking a gleaming bookshelf. "Keelhauling is a standard punishment in both the English and Dutch navies."

"This is *Bretagne*."

He dropped his hand, eyes narrowing. "So high and mighty. And yet look at you, Lucinde. Dressed as though you've come straight from the slop-chest. You would be fortunate to have *anyone* of worth consider marrying you now. Why, just being *seen* with those scum out there—and in such a state—could destroy your reputation. Fortunately, I am willing to look beyond it."

"How generous of you."

He shrugged. "My vision is grand, my plans far-reaching. They matter more to me than whether my wife has bedded a smuggler or two. To be perfectly honest, I enjoy slumming it myself, now and again. And again. You'll find me a forgiving husband, when all is said and done."

"Perhaps we can hire an extra valet to care for all your garter ribbons," Luce said icily.

He almost smiled. "You know about that, eh? I suppose that's why Thorner took them that night—he recognized yours. Can't blame him, really." The smile he gave Luce sent a chill creeping up her spine. "Do you remember when I took it from you? How wondrous you looked on those stairs."

"How could I forget?" Luce said, turning cold at the memory that had once set her aflame.

"I kept that ribbon with me every day, you know."

"That ribbon, and half a hundred others."

He chuckled. "It's true. I cannot help myself. I tell myself constantly that it's wrong to steal, that I should give the ribbons back. But I never do, Luce. I never do."

"You are despicable. You insult Samuel, and yet he is a thousand times the person you could ever be."

"Careful, now. You will make me jealous." Morgan moved, so fast Luce barely registered it. One hand slid to the nape of her neck, gripping her hair, tilting her face up to his. The table hit the back of her thighs. The lantern wobbled dangerously. "I brought you here to spare you from watching, and hearing, what I'm about to do to your gallant smuggler—a wedding present, of sorts. Don't make me change my mind."

"You have your stone," she rasped. His grip on her neck was

like iron. "Let me go, let Samuel go, and I will make you captain of the *Lucinde.* We can invest in any venture you want."

"That's not what we agreed." He had her pinned between him and the table, now, his two hands locked around her. "We made a deal, Lucinde. Your ship, my stone."

"If you kill Samuel now you may never find the stone." Luce shifted her weight against the table. Testing his strength, and hers. Morgan, perceiving it, edged closer, nudging his hip between her thighs. "He could have lied to you."

"He didn't." Morgan's lips were so close she could have kissed him, despite the hold he had on her neck.

"How do you know?"

"Because I promised I'd spare Cousin Bones if he told me the truth."

Luce went still. "And then you killed him anyway."

"Of course."

He was remorseless. Profoundly, coldly so. The thought gave Luce new strength. Her fingers tightened around the handle of the knife hanging at her waist. Morgan sensed what she was going to do, but too late—Luce slipped the blade free and lashed out. It was a clumsy movement, graceless, yet it did its duty: a harsh red line sprang up on Morgan's cheek, gleaming from his hairline to his nose.

"*Fuck!*"

He reared back, clutching at his face, and Luce scrabbled away, putting the width of the table between them, the knife held before her in one shaking hand.

For one endless moment Morgan went very still. Ignoring the blood running down his face and staining his snowy white cravat, he watched Luce with terrible intent.

"That's a pretty blade," he crooned.

Then he lunged. Missed, as Luce, panting, terrified, stumbled out of reach and threw herself for the door. He clawed at her hair, seized a handful, yanked her back. She slashed desperately at him with the knife, then, as he slid out of harm's way, lunged again for the door. He went with her, fast and light, blocking her escape easily. He seized the hem of her overcoat, gripped it tight; out of her blade's reach and triumphant.

"Give me that shiny knife, Lucinde."

She shrugged out of the coat, and he fell back with the sudden weightlessness, crashing into the table. Luce wasted no time: the cabin's large windows, and beyond them, the sea, were only a few steps away. She ran for the nearest of them, flicked aside the fastening, and shoved the thick panes open with one hand. Morgan was on his feet, careening across the cabin, bloody and rageful. He lunged at her, grasping with furious, bloody fingers.

And gripped nothing but air.

Luce had hoisted herself onto the window ledge and dived into the night.

"Find her!" Morgan's voice bounced across the surface of the water, thudding into the *Lucinde*'s hull. Luce, pressed against the bow, her long, webbed fingers clinging to the timbers, listened as booted feet thundered around the decks. As lanterns swung out over the water, and Morgan's men peered into the gloom.

"She's swum to shore, for certain," someone said.

"Then take a boat and find her!" Morgan ordered. "Don't stop until you've brought her back. She can't have gone far." A cruel little chuckle. "Not with those feet."

Movement to the ship's starboard side. Luce drifted around the bow, her tail silent and strong beneath her. Her breeches were gone, her boots and stockings too, sinking slowly to the bottom of the harbor. It didn't matter; she had what she needed. The sea-silk remained against her skin, safe within the confines of her chemise, stays, and caraco, while Mother Aggie's belt was cinched firmly around the place where her hips became tail, the sea-knife laying against the scales as though it belonged there.

Several of Morgan's men were clambering down to one of the ship's boats. Taking up the oars, they pushed away from the *Lucinde* and rowed swiftly for the shore. Two of their number stood at stern and prow, lanterns held high, searching the dark water.

"As for the rest of you," Morgan was saying from the deck high above. "You know what to do."

There came the sound of rope moving rapidly through iron blocks, the heave and grunt of working men. Edging down the ship's side, Luce strained to see which side of the yard Samuel was tied to.

It would happen fast. She must be ready.

At last she glimpsed the yardarm, Samuel's feet and legs dangling directly below it. Upside-down. She could not see past his waist—the ship's railing blocked it from sight—but it was enough.

"I told Lucinde that I would make you pay for stealing from me," Morgan said conversationally. "She didn't pass that on? A pity."

"She told me," Samuel grunted.

"And yet you did not heed her?"

"It was not the first time I'd heard such a threat."

The rope connecting Samuel to either end of the yard reared out of the darkness ahead, snaking alongside the ship before disappearing into the water. It began to wriggle as Samuel himself appeared, swinging as the men pushed him out over the water, his long limbs stretched tight between the ropes binding him at wrist and ankle. They had removed his overcoat and boots. Nothing but the thin linen of his shirt and wool of his breeches would protect him from the *Lucinde*'s hull.

"Of course it wasn't." Morgan leaned on the rail, a bloody kerchief pressed to his cheek. Luce shrank back against the ship. "But I'm sure we can all agree that it will be the last."

Luce braced herself against the timbers, every muscle alert to Morgan's next words. *Send him down.*

Samuel braced himself, too. "Your soul is forfeit," he told Morgan. "Know that. The sea should have taken it when the *Dauphin* wrecked. Luce saved you, and risked her own soul doing it. I'll never forgive you for that. Or for what you've done this night."

"The night is far from over," Morgan said breezily. "For some of us, at least."

"Your crew will never forgive you either," Samuel mused. "I've seen them walking the shore at dusk. Searching for you. You know what they say about a captain who abandons his own men—"

"Superstitions and stupidity," Morgan interrupted. "Nothing more."

"You don't believe a crew betrayed by its captain will rise from the deep?"

"I'm not some idiot deckhand to be spooked by tales!"

"What happened that night?" Samuel asked, softer. "You can tell me, surely?" He nodded at the dark waters below, as if to say, *I'll be dead in a few moments. What can it hurt?*

Morgan glanced at the men behind him, waiting, the ropes taut in their hands. "There is nothing to tell," he said. "The storm took us, there was nothing to be done—"

"Horseshit," Samuel said. "You were carrying enough stone to see out ten such storms."

"I suppose you'd know."

"I suppose I would. Your pilot was Malouin, no? Surely he knew the way through the islands and reefs to the harbor? Its ticklish for a ship that size, even in fair weather, but I heard he was experienced enough."

"He was a fool," Morgan hissed, stepping to the rail and leaning out so that no one but Samuel—and Luce—could hear. "Told me he knew the channels and would have us safely through."

"And he didn't?" Samuel sounded doubtful.

"There wasn't time," Morgan muttered. "The English were on our heels, the ship was damaged . . . I did what I had to do."

"You took the wheel yourself."

"Why not? It was my ship, my crew—"

"You'd lived in Cádiz for ten years or more. What made you think you had the skill to pilot a ship into Saint-Malo? Men more experienced than you have failed in kinder weather."

"I studied the charts—"

"Charts are not the same as water." Luce, clinging to the *Lucinde*'s side, all but nodded in agreement. "So, you hit the reef. What then?"

"What do you mean, what then?"

"What of your crew?"

"They tried to save the ship, the cargo, obviously. It was worth a fortune—"

"But instead of helping them, you lined your pockets with storm-stone and launched one of the boats," Samuel said. "Is that not so? And when the storm really worked itself into a lather and even *that* went down, you lashed yourself to the wreckage and tried not to think about the crew you'd left behind." Samuel's voice was grim. "In fact, you've tried not to think about your crew every day since. Tell me, how are you faring?"

Luce, pressed against the hull, waited for Morgan's answer.

It never came. One moment Samuel was high above her, the next he was falling, the hissing of the ropes loud as thunder. Luce dived as he hit the water.

Darkness. The looming shadow of the *Lucinde*'s hull. Ahead, a wash of bubbles, a pale figure plunging beneath the ship.

She surged toward it.

She reached Samuel as the rope at his wrists began to curve toward the keel. His eyes were closed, creased in fear, but he opened them wide when he felt her hands upon him. It hardly mattered; Luce knew he would not be able to see her in the dark. She gripped him tight as the ropes began their heaving rhythm, pulled him down, away from the wicked crust fouling the hull. Mother Aggie's knife glimmered in the dark water. Luce raised it to the rope at Samuel's wrists, began to cut.

Drag, drag, drag.

The blade was too small, the cutting too slow. Luce longed to reach up and seize the rope, hold it firm with both hands, but knew that to do so would leave Samuel exposed to the underside of the ship.

Drag, drag, drag.

They were halfway along the ship's width now, almost at the keel. The rhythm of the men above intensified, quickening Samuel's progress through the water. Luce held him harder, her tail working to draw him downward and away, against the ropes pulling him toward the hull. The faster the men hauled, the closer Samuel's body came to the barnacles. Morgan, Luce realized, knew this. This first run was intended not to drown, but to maim.

She stopped cutting. Slipped the knife back into the silvery belt at her waist and gripped Samuel tight about the shoulders, using all her strength to keep him away from the fouling. There was one of her against the strength of six men, however, and she felt him tense, felt the hideous catch and scrape of his back and shoulder against the hull. Blood bloomed in the water.

Drag, drag, drag.

Faster they hauled, and faster, as though Morgan were urging the men on. Barnacles hissed against Luce's forearms where they wrapped about Samuel's back, snarling at her skin. She did not let go. Not until the heavy shape of the ship disappeared above them, and the rope at Samuel's wrists began to tilt up. She watched him rise to the surface at the ship's opposite side, his shirt ripped half-off, blood dripping from his back, then swam for the bow and silently surfaced.

"Fools!" Morgan was saying to his men. "There's hardly a mark on him!"

"He should be more cut up than this," someone agreed nervously.

"The ropes were tight, I checked them myself!"

"Check them again," Morgan growled. "And send him back down."

They were going the opposite way now, and Samuel was dragged feet first, even faster than before. The ropes were tighter, this time, the pressure dragging Samuel toward the hull even fiercer. It took all Luce's strength to stay with him, dragging against the relentless upward pull of the ropes. Even so, when Samuel surfaced, once more on the side where this nightmare had begun, his shirt was gone, his back a bloody mess, one side of his breeches tattered against a lacerated thigh.

"Much better," Morgan said approvingly, as Samuel coughed and spluttered on the deck. "Again."

For this, Samuel's third run, he once again entered the water hands first. Luce seized the rope binding his feet and held it firm with one hand, slicing at it with the knife as they dragged him under the ship. They were slower on the ropes this time, perhaps hoping the water would finish the job they had started. The change in pace meant Samuel was further from the hull than before, and protected from the worst of its bite. Even better, it gave Luce precious time.

By the time they had reached the keel, she had breathed into Samuel's mouth twice and sawed through the rope binding his feet. Untethered, his legs and body drifted limply down as Luce worked on the rope dragging at his wrists. She sliced at it frantically, ignoring her own pain, willing whatever magic lingered within the blade to hasten her work. The edge of the ship was nearing, drawing closer and closer with every beat of Samuel's heart.

At last, just as they reached the open water, the rope tore free. Luce glimpsed its rough-hewn edge bouncing for the surface as she caught Samuel tight against her, dragging him away from the *Lucinde*.

She did not stop until she reached the nearest ship. With Samuel cradled in her arms, his head lolling on her shoulder, she caught her breath and watched the panic and confusion rising from the *Lucinde*'s decks. She pushed on, to the next ship, and the next, pausing in the shadows, clinging to the timbers as she rested and let Samuel breathe, doing her best not to hurt him further. Again, and again, ship to ship, the lights of Saint-Malo glittering like stars, guiding her to safety.

Please, please help us.

She did not stop, not when Samuel's breathing became shallow, not when he became cold and still in her arms.

Help me. Help us, please.

At last she reached a familiar beach beneath familiar ramparts. She slithered into the shallows, dragging Samuel with her, collapsing against him as the Manche ebbed and flowed over his hips, his back, licking at his wounds.

Only then did she let herself cry.

Please, please don't be gone.

Nothing, for several long, slow sea breaths. Nothing but the sea, and the moon, the ramparts behind her. Water lapped against Luce's tail, toyed with her long fins, melded with her tears. It was blessedly cold against her aching skin, her aching heart.

Then came the groac'h's voice. "What's this, then?"

PART 3

The waves rose high, great clouds gathered, and lightning flashed in the distance. Ah, they were in for a terrible storm.

—Hans Christian Andersen, "The Little Mermaid"

23

The Tide's Way

"I thought you'd gone," Luce said, watching the groac'h examine Samuel's back. "That you'd left Saint-Malo, like the rest of the Fae."

"Not yet." The shore-woman's skirts trailed in the water.

"Can you help him?"

She nodded. "The tide is still rising. And the water has cleaned his wounds." She hummed a little melody, brushed her fingers lightly over Samuel's wounds. "You have done well."

"I did nothing."

"Not true. It was you, and your kiss, that saved him."

"My kiss?"

A knowing glance. "You deny kissing him?"

"No, but . . ." Mother Aggie had said that the kiss of a seamaid would bring luck—calm seas, fair winds, good trade. "Is it true, then? What they say about a seamaid's kiss?"

"True enough."

The night bell, Noguette, tolled from the cathedral, marking the hour of ten and the beginning of the city curfew.

"I should have done more," Luce said brokenly. "I tried to keep him from the hull, tried to protect him." She wiped away fresh tears. "I wasn't strong enough."

The groac'h looked meaningfully at Luce's tail, its tendrils shining in the shallows. "You have much to learn. That is not your fault."

She laid a hand on Samuel's back, her low, soft humming growing stronger. Luce watched, transfixed, as the wounds marring Samuel's skin began to ease, *lessening* somehow.

"He will be scarred," the groac'h warned.

"He will be perfect." Luce swallowed, stroking Samuel's hair.

The tide-woman might have smiled beneath her tusks. "Here," she said, gesturing to Luce's wounds. "Your turn."

When Luce, too, had ceased bleeding, the groac'h got to her feet. "There is nothing more we can do for him here," she said. "He needs rest, and care. Come; he will be safe in your little cave."

Luce shook her head miserably. "We cannot go back to the cave. Morgan—Morgan knows the storm-stone is there." *And killed Bones anyway.* Fresh sorrow welled within her.

"There is more than one sea-cave near Le Bleu Sauvage," the fae said. She whistled, a beautiful quavering note that carried over the water. Luce made out the shape of her little witch-boat on the dark water, bearing toward the beach. She slid further into the shallows, pulling herself clumsily along, wondering how she might bring Samuel with her.

A bark tore across the sand, the sound of claws scrabbling on rock.

"It is the hounds." The groac'h clenched her jaw in irritation. "Cursed beasts."

"We must go," Luce hissed. The dogs, mastiffs imported from England generations before, were huge and terrifying. They had killed a soldier not three moons past, ripped him to pieces on the beach beneath the castle and eaten what remained. There had been blood on the driest, highest sand for months.

Several hair-raising growls carried up the beach. Long, four-legged shadows skimmed over the rocks and the sand, and through the shadows beneath the ramparts.

Closer, ever closer.

"They've caught our scent," Luce whispered.

"Into the water," the fae commanded. "Quickly." She slipped

her arms beneath Samuel's shoulders with surprising strength, dragging him toward the waiting boat. Luce plunged into the water, flicking her tail hard, arrowing along the sea-bed. She broke the surface at the boat's side and pulled herself aboard.

The dogs came into view, rending the sand with their huge paws, wet clumps of it scattering in their wake. They barked excitedly, plunged into the bloody shallows, growling and sniffing.

"Hurry," Luce called to the groac'h. "They will swim if the urge takes them."

She drew the sea-silk from within her chemise and slipped it carefully into the folds of her caraco. With the loss of its touch on her skin, her tail shimmered away into legs, bare beneath the thigh-length chemise and startingly cold in the night air. Shivering, she got to her feet, then leaned over the boat's side to take Samuel's weight from the groac'h while she hoisted herself lightly onboard. Samuel, for his part, remained resolutely unconscious. His eyes were closed, his skin frighteningly pale. Together, and with no small amount of help from the sea, which rose up, bearing Samuel over the witch-boat's side and depositing him gently in its belly, the two women got him settled. The groac'h whistled again and the boat turned smoothly, brisking toward the open water of the Manche.

Luce watched the beach disappear behind them. The hounds were moving, trotting toward the Holland Bastion. "They're leaving," she said.

"They will be back," the groac'h replied. "The shores of Saint-Malo are never safe at night." She settled herself by the tiller, though she made no move to take it. "There was a time, long ago, when the Fae Folk lived here, alongside the people of the city. These shores were shared, and rife with magic."

"What happened?" Luce asked. "Why did things change?"

"It is the nature of humans to seek, and to want," the tide-woman said, with a shrug. "First, they ripped our sacred stone from the earth and used it to build their walls and churches.

Then they razed our forests for their ships, butchering the oldest, most powerful trees for their masts. There is only so much conquest, so much thievery, the Folk can bear."

Luce leaned over Samuel. His eyes were still closed, but he was breathing, and the blanket covering him bore no trace of any bleeding.

"He's so cold," she murmured.

The groac'h produced another blanket, handed it to her. "If you wish to truly warm him, you need only summon the right breeze."

"The right breeze?"

The fae pursed her lips and blew gently through her tusks, catching her breath in her cupped hands. She leaned toward Samuel, opening her hands. A deliciously warm, drying breeze ruffled over him and Luce both.

"Could I—could I do that?" Luce asked, soft with wonder.

The groac'h chuckled. "Of course."

The witch-boat plowed steadfastly on, gliding around the Grand Bé before curling toward Clos-Poulet, faithful to the tide and the shore-woman's song. It rolled a little as it turned, and Luce wrapped her arms around Samuel, bracing him.

"Could I use my voice to control a boat like this?" she asked.

Another chuckle. "You, dear child, could control a *fleet*." The groac'h tilted her head, considering. "But yes, to begin with. A boat like this."

A fleet. Something stirred deep within Luce. The night, sparkling with promises of secrets and shadows, the stars and their reflections, seemed suddenly limitless. She gazed at the fae, sailing her little boat without sheet or tiller, capable, powerful. Free.

"You already knew, didn't you? About what I was." Luce motioned to her legs, tucked within a blanket. "About what I *am*."

A sideways glance. "I have lived in your cove for many, many years. I see everything. Remember everything."

"You did not think to tell me?"

"Would you have listened?"

Luce said nothing. Until very recently, she had avoided the tide-woman as much as the next person. All those who dwelled on the coast of Bretagne had been taught to mistrust the Fae. By the priests, by the tales. Had it been deliberate? Was it easier to steal from someone if you believed they were dangerous?

There is only so much conquest, so much thievery, the Folk can bear.

"What of the lutine? Did she know, too?"

"Probably."

"The jetins?"

"Most definitely. Why do you think they never throw stones at you?"

"Is that . . . is that why you helped me before the ball?"

A shrug.

Before Luce could ask further, Samuel moaned softly, stirring beneath his blankets. She took his hand, spoke soothing words until the witch-boat drew gently onto the sands of the cove.

The *Dove* was exactly where Bones had anchored it before Morgan's men had taken all three of them to Saint-Servan. It lay like a wounded whale, belly up and bleakly pale in the starlight. Luce did her best not to look at it as she and the groac'h helped Samuel ashore. Samuel, however, roused from his torpor.

"The Dove?" he rasped, straining to see the darkened beach.

"She's here," Luce murmured, holding him. "She's safe."

Inside the groac'h's cave, Luce's eyes widened in surprise. In place of the dim, rather chill chambers she had expected, she was standing in a cosy, comfortable home. Worn carpets furnished the sandy floors, and a fire crackled in a stone hearth. Ships' lanterns glowing with a magical softness hung everywhere—the stone walls, the sloping ceiling—filling the space with warmth.

The fae helped Luce bring Samuel to a smaller chamber behind a curtain made of salvaged sails. It contained a low bed with clean sheets and thick woolen blankets, as well as a shallow bowl of fresh water, clean linens, and a healing salve. A tray bearing two bowls of steaming hot soup, wooden spoons, and two small loaves of brown bread sat on a small sea-chest, and there were clean clothes for both Luce and Samuel, too, folded neatly on the blankets. Luce turned to the tide-woman, speechless with gratitude. "I don't know what I would have done without you."

"You'd have managed," the groac'h said gruffly, drawing the curtain. Beyond its folds the light dimmed, as though the cave itself was preparing for sleep.

Luce washed Samuel's back and covered it in the sweet-smelling salve, then helped him eat a few mouthfuls of soup.

"Luce?" he murmured, his brow creased with pain and weariness. "Where are we?"

"We're in the groac'h's cave, Samuel. We're safe." Luce stroked his hair, helped him settle on his belly on the clean sheets. She ate her own soup, and then, too tired and worried to contemplate returning to the malouinière, changed into the fresh chemise the groac'h had left her and curled up on the bed beside him. She did not let go of his hand all night, and woke to find him watching her, weary but alert.

"They killed Bones," he said, his voice cracking. Luce wrapped her arms—gently, so gently—around him.

"I know. I'm so sorry I couldn't save him," she whispered.

And then she held him while he cried.

Later, as the sun slanted westward and the air softened, Luce left the tide-woman's cave and went to greet the sea. The sand was cool against her bare soles, the Manche lapping peacefully at the shore.

She had stayed with Samuel throughout the day, cleansing his wounds, wrapping them in fresh bandages the groac'h had provided. The fae's cave was a wonder, neat and tidy, the furnishings, though clearly rescued from the sea, clean and comfortable, and her ability to sway the winds meant that it was always warm and dry. The little driftwood fire in its rough stone hearth was never without a flame.

All the warmth and comfort in the world, however, would not dispel the memory of Bones's limp, sodden body. It echoed in Luce's every thought, imprinting its shape on her mind. She knew Samuel was the same. With the help of the groac'h's magic, the wounds on his body were healing. His soul, she feared, would be slower to recover.

The water beckoned. Luce wore the sea-silk tucked into the fresh chemise the groac'h had given her; it would take a few steps, only, for the silk to do its work. For the saltwater to cast itself over her skin, changing it to scales. One push with her tail, and she would be heading for deeper water, its silence glossing over her, hiding her from the world, soothing her troubled heart.

Her fingers were working at the rusted pins holding her borrowed stomacher in place when movement on the water caught her eye. A ketch, its sails breezing across the tops of the rocks encircling the cove. She hastened back to the cave, one eye on the vessel as it struck sails.

The groac'h was waiting at the cave's entrance.

"Friends of yours?" she asked mildly, as Luce hurried inside.

"I very much doubt it."

Together, they watched the ketch drop anchor and launch a jolly-boat manned by several burly men. Luce narrowed her eyes, wondering if these could be Morgan's men, and, if they were, if they were the same ones who had . . . who had . . .

"Come for his precious stone then, has he?"

Never before had Luce heard such bitterness in Samuel's voice. She turned, found him leaning heavily against the stony wall, face wan and grim.

"You should be resting," she said gently.

"I've rested enough." There were deep shadows in his eyes.

All three of them watched, unseen, as the men reached the shore and dragged the jolly-boat onto the sand. It did not take them long to find the entrance to Luce and Samuel's erstwhile cave. Bearing large baskets, they disappeared inside, returning soon after loaded high with storm-stone. They repeated this process, moving back and forth between cave and jolly-boat, jolly-boat and cutter until the last of the stone was gone. Several of them helped themselves to the casks of whiskey and packages of lace and silk in the cave, as well. One or two even took some of Luce's meager treasures.

"Morgan isn't with them," she murmured, running her gaze over the ketch's decks for the third time.

"Why would he be?" Samuel replied. "When he can pay others to do such tasks for hin? A little heavy lifting, a little murder . . . Far better to avoid such unpleasantness." He shifted his weight against the wall, sucked a sharp, pained breath between his teeth.

"We should get you back to bed," Luce said, disliking the shadows in his eyes, the laboring of his breath.

"I am well enough." He glared after the ketch, which had weighed anchor and was moving slowly away from the beach. "Though perhaps a little rest might be beneficial . . ." He stumbled and Luce stepped beneath one shoulder, propping him upright. The groac'h caught his other side. Together, they helped him back down the corridor to the warmth of the cave.

"Stay down," the fae said firmly, when Samuel had eased himself, belly-down, on the bed. "Your wounds were severe. You must give them time to heal."

"We do not have time," Samuel said, wincing as he settled.

Luce frowned. "We don't?" It would be yet days before her family was due to return from Nantes. The freedom their absence afforded her had been Luce's only brightness in the depths of the night.

Samuel's face softened. "Have you forgotten what you learned in Lulworth, Luce?" The memory of a smile. "Can't say I blame you. A lot has happened since then."

It came back to her, then. Sudden and appalling. "The Duke of Marlborough."

Samuel nodded against the pillow. "And his twelve thousand men."

"Do you think they've left England?"

Samuel shrugged, then grimaced. "Impossible to say."

"Who is this duke you speak of?" The groac'h, who had listened to this exchange in silence, regarded them both with her strange, moon-colored eyes.

"An English fleet is preparing to cross the Manche," Luce told her. "It may be on its way even now. It carries an army set upon taking Saint-Malo."

The groac'h seemed unperturbed. "Such tidings are not surprising. Saint-Malo—indeed, the whole of Bretagne—is weak. How can it be otherwise, when so much of the land has been desecrated, and so many of the Fae have left?"

"Does it not concern you?" Luce asked. "Do you not fear for yourself, for your kind?"

"Most of my kind left these shores years ago."

"Why did you stay?" Samuel asked.

"Reasons," the groac'h told him, with a shrug. "Although perhaps I have lingered here too long. If what you tell me is true, it is time to make preparations of my own."

"Where will you go?"

The tide-woman shrugged. "Only the tide can say. There are still places of beauty and wonder left in the world. Places that men in their death-ships have not despoiled. A fair breeze and a path of stars is all that is required to find them."

"So you would simply go?" Luce asked, surprised. "You would leave your home, your lands, defenseless?"

"These are no longer my lands." The fae gestured to the cove, where Morgan's men were sailing with their cargo of storm-stone.

"The men of Saint-Malo have done nothing but take. Their very city was made with stolen stone. Perhaps the time has come for them to give something back."

Too much has been stolen. Something must be given back.

"It is the tide's way," Luce said softly.

"It is." The groac'h tilted her head, considering. "You could always come with me, seamaid."

A fair breeze. A path of stars. Luce's skin prickled, as though a faraway wind played over her hair, her dreams. What would it be, to feel such breezes? To sail upon starlight?

"My family is here," she said quickly. She felt Samuel's gaze upon her and was careful not to meet it. "What would happen to them if the city should fall? What would happen to *all* the people here?"

The darkness of a new moon glinted in the tide-woman's gaze. "Why should I care? Why should *you*?"

"Because they are my family."

The tide-woman's eyes narrowed almost imperceptibly. Then she nodded. "There is a way to know for certain if the fleet will reach these shores," she said, drawing aside the curtain and beckoning to Luce. "Come."

Seamaids, the stories said, were the loveliest, but also the vainest, of the Fae. Most longshoreman—old sailors who had given up the sea and settled on shore—had an encounter to share. Stories of seduction and mystery, of alluring songs and sudden, violent storms that arose mere moments after a seamaid was sighted. Some told of the maid's kindness, her ability to grant wishes to those who offered her aid. Others spoke of her cold-heartedness, her bitter, drowning fury. There was one detail, however, that all the tales shared: the seamaid's comb and mirror.

Luce had always thought the items a fancy, nothing more. What use would a seamaid have for a comb and mirror? Surely she had better things to do than sit by and idly comb her hair? Hair that would no doubt become salt-tangled and knotted as soon as she returned to the sea? So when the groac'h rummaged in a battered sea chest, withdrawing two items—a silver hand mirror and a matching comb—she knew a moment of doubt.

"You're jesting, surely?" She regarded the silver mirror, its ornate handle twisted and tarnished with time, and realised that it was the same one she had taken to the de Châtelaine ball. The comb was a perfect match, silver as spring rain.

"I never jest."

The tide-woman looked between the mirror and the comb, then returned the comb to the chest and left the cave, her bearing leaving no doubt that Luce's was expected to follow. The day had drowsed into evening, and the Manche lapped placidly upon the rocks.

"The tide is on the ebb," Luce said uncertainly. "Is this the right time for such things?" There was a reason that groac'hs were also known as tide-crones. Their magic depended entirely upon the rhythm of the sea. Luce had experienced this firsthand at the ball, when she had raced back to the cove in the magicked barge, the vessel and her gown crumbling as the tide ebbed away.

"For me? No. But for you . . . the magic of the sea-folk does not rely on the tide. It is one of the reasons they are considered so dangerous."

Luce struggled, and failed, to find an answer to that.

"Here," the groac'h said, when they had reached the water's edge. "Take the mirror. Hold it up, like this. Now, turn your back to the sea."

Mystified, Luce did as the she bid, turning to face the cliffs and raising the mirror until it was level with her eyes.

"What do you see?" the fae asked.

". . . myself?" Luce frowned at her reflection. She was unusually pale, and there were dark rings beneath her eyes. A broad bruise—no doubt where Morgan's man had cuffed her when she'd stumbled—glowered over one cheek, and cuts and grazes marred her brow. There were more on her shoulder and forearm, hidden beneath her dress. "More's the pity."

"Turn it," the groac'h said impatiently. "Like this." She tilted the edge of the mirror slightly, so that Luce was looking not at her own reflection, but at the Manche, mirror-flat over her shoulder.

"I see the Manche," Luce said.

"Yes, yes. Anything else?"

Luce peered into the silvery surface, spied a pair of gulls winging lightly over the water. "Birds?"

"The sea's face shines like glass," the tide-woman explained. "It reflects light, just as a mirror does. But underneath, its depths are filled with shadows. You must not fear the darkness. Indeed, it is there that you will see what you most require."

"I understand," Luce said, more confused than ever.

"You most certainly do not." The fae *tsk*ed softly and reached out one hand, trailing her long fingers over Luce's eyelids. "Close your eyes. Think of the fleet. Think of its danger, its power. Think of your family, of the people here, and what will befall them should it arrive."

Luce obeyed. Eyes closed, she pictured herself in Dorset once more, at the Thorner family's table. Little Flora and Tobias, clinging to Samuel with such devotion. His rage when his brother Thomas threatened to sail to Saint-Malo, and terror that his younger brother would be there when the city fell. *When the city fell.* She imagined the graceful spire of the cathedral, the steep rooftops, the castle, shattering apart. Flame devouring the streets and homes, the ships at anchor in the harbor. And the people, the people—she tried not to see her family running in terror through the streets, gripping each other as the city collapsed around them, flame and seawater alike threatening to tear them apart.

"Do you see it?" the groac'h asked. "Do you *feel* it?"

Luce nodded. Tears were gathering behind her eyelids, threatening to break free.

"Good. Open your eyes."

Luce did as the tide-woman asked. Tears rolled down her cheeks, but she hardly felt them. The calm, evening-soft reflection of the Manche was gone. Instead, the entire northern sky roiled with iron-gray cloud. Before it, riding on the wind, came the English fleet. A hundred ships or more surging atop the waves, soldiers lining the decks, as they sailed swiftly past the cove and westward, toward Saint-Malo.

Luce blinked and the fleet, the storm, disappeared. She lowered the mirror, turned. The same gulls, drifting peaceably. The same serene sky. The evening had taken its rightful place once more.

"What did you see?" the groac'h asked.

Luce brushed at her cheeks. "I saw the fleet. It is coming."

"When?"

"When the weather turns. A week, perhaps. Maybe longer."

The shore-woman nodded, then headed back to the cave. Luce, following, watched as she paused to scrape oysters and mussels from the damp rocks, stowing them in the folds of her net skirt.

"What now?" she asked.

"Supper, I think," the groac'h replied. "I'm hungry. And we should feed the storm diver now and then if he's to properly recover."

"And the fleet?"

A shrug. *Why should I care?*

"But . . . will you truly leave?"

"I will." The shore-woman, bent over a clustering of mussels, did not look up.

"When?"

"Only the tide can say."

It was clear the groac'h would say no more on the subject. Luce joined her at the rocks, tucking the mirror into her belt and gripping her sea-knife. She tried not to think of the last time she had used the blade; the way it had felt as it sliced into Morgan's face, or the ropes binding Samuel against the belly of the *Lucinde*. "The tales always say seamaids are vain and selfish. But they were never just looking at their reflections, were they?"

"The mirrors are used for all sorts of reasons." Mussels clattered into the groac'h's skirt. "To see the shape of the weather, to know if danger approaches. And other things, besides. When a seamaid looks backwards into her mirror, she sees therein that which she requires."

Luce prized an oyster free, added it to the growing pile. "Can you . . . will you teach me more of such things? What of the matching comb? What can it do?"

"It is too late in the day for raising storms," the groac'h said mildly.

"Raising *storms*?"

"Indeed." The fae straightened, eyeing Luce over her tusks. "Did the Lion never warn you not to comb your hair after nightfall?"

"Well, of course he did. Everyone knows not to do that." Luce looked sideways at the shore-woman. "Is it more than superstition, then? Can a comb—can someone's *hair*—truly control the weather?"

The groac'h, nodding in approval at their haul, started toward the cave. "Supper first. Then talk."

"Of course." Luce, following, realized she had taken the mirror from her belt and was holding it tightly, protectively, against her chest. She unfolded her arms at once. "I'm sorry. Here."

"Keep it," the tide-woman said, waving her away.

"It belongs to you," Luce protested.

"No," the groac'h said, as gruff as ever. "It belongs to *you*."

24

The Lion and the Wolf

The Léon family returned from Nantes five days later. Luce, who had spent their absence caring for Samuel, learning about sea-magic with the groac'h, and returning to Le Bleu Sauvage often enough to make her presence—and her recovery from her feigned illness—felt among the domestiques, was emerging from the chapel, smoothing the creases from her morning gown, when she heard the sound of the carriage. She hurried toward the gatehouse, quietly congratulating herself on her cleverness. She had spent spend more and more time at the malouinière over the last day or two, reverting to her former routine of rising early to visit with Samuel at the cave, and returning before the end of the forenoon watch in case her family returned.

Relief washed over her as the carriage rolled into sight. With her father home, she would finally be able to tell him of the impending invasion. Jean-Baptiste would listen carefully, as he always did. Would frown and lean in close. *Are you certain, mon trésor?* He would ride for the city at once, speak to the Marquis de la Châtre and the city's chief engineer, Monsieur Mazin, himself. He would ask them about strategy, ammunition, guns. And he would ensure that his family would be safe. The burden of Luce's knowledge would be hers to bear alone no longer. And then . . .

It had taken her days to pluck up the courage to return to the sea-cave after Morgan's men had raided it. Samuel, able to walk but slowly, had gone with her, watching in silence as she took down the canvas bag that had hung in the cave for so long, packed and ready for the moment of her long-imagined departure. Heaviness had filled her heart.

It was just a dream, nothing more.

"Is it wrong to think, and want and . . . and dream now, do you suppose?" Samuel had asked quietly. "Now that Bones is gone, I mean." *Now that it is all my fault.* She heard the words beneath the words, the aching guilt.

"I do not see how we can do otherwise," she said. "Thinking, wanting, dreaming . . . that is what we do. It is no different to sleeping or breathing."

"What do you think of now?" he asked. *Now that everything has changed.* He was watching the bag in her hands, the way she checked the clothes, the supplies, tucking them in with such care. Remembering, as she was, her plans to dress as a boy and slip away to sea.

"Too many things," Luce had said with a sigh. "So many that I can barely make sense of them all. It is like a . . . a constant crowd of people exists in my mind, speaking *my* words, my worries and fears. And my guilt." The sound of Bones falling to the deck, and Samuel's anguish. The hissing of rope through iron, the bloodied darkness beneath the *Lucinde.* Morgan's grip on her neck, the fury in his eyes when she escaped him.

Samuel nodded. "My mind is the same," he admitted. "But I find that I still want, sometimes. And dream. And it makes me feel so guilty, Luce, so ashamed. I can barely speak of it."

Luce had placed the bag gently on the sand at her feet. "What do you want, Samuel?"

"Honestly? I want to leave. I want to take the *Dove* and go." With the groac'h's help, Luce had beached the *Dove* in a rocky section of the cove the day after they returned. It had lain there hidden, as loyal as any hound, for almost a week.

"Where?"

"North?" He laughed brokenly. "West? I don't care."

Luce had stepped close, laid her hands on his chest. "And what do you dream of?"

He swallowed. "I dream that when I go, when I push out onto the water, you are with me."

She had nodded. Felt his arms come up around her, pressed herself into his warmth.

"I dream of you, too," she had whispered.

There it was. Five words, and a new course charted.

"Luce!" The carriage had barely rolled to a stop when the door flew open and Veronique spilled out in a rush of tangerine silk, bright as the sun. "Luce! You'll never guess what's happened!"

"We don't have to go to Dorset," Samuel had said, in the cave. "Whether I care to admit it or not, Thomas is a man now. Able—willing—to take on my responsibilities. You've met him. He will make a fine smuggler." He smiled, the first real smile she had seen from him since they had returned from the *Lucinde*. Hope unfurled its sails. "We can go anywhere you want. I don't care, as long as we're together."

Luce had nodded. "I must tell my father of the fleet first. I have to know that my family will be safe when the English arrive. But once he knows, Samuel—once I'm certain they'll be safe—we can go. Together. North, west . . ." She had leaned up, kissed him. "Perhaps we will find a fair wind and follow a path of stars."

Veronique was all but running across the gravel toward Luce. She was glowing like summertime, her cheeks rosy-bright. Behind her, Jean-Baptiste was handing Gratienne down from the carriage. To Luce's surprise, Charlotte had returned with them, along with her new husband. Her steps faltered. *Why is Charlotte here?* She had thought the newlyweds would be on their way to Paris. And whose horse was that? The handsome gray secured to the back of the carriage, its saddle and harness gleaming, seemed vaguely familiar.

Then someone else climbed down from the carriage.

Even with the bandage covering one cheek, Morgan looked as

refined and handsome as ever. He smiled as he straightened, his eyes gleaming as they looked straight into Luce's.

Her blood turned to ice.

"Isn't it wonderful, Luce?" Veronique said, her voice rippling with excitement. "Monsieur de Châtelaine and I are to be married!"

Morgan had traveled to Nantes, quickly discovering where the Léons had taken rooms, Luce heard over tea served with cheese tarts with lemon, blackberries, and sugar. He had been so lovelorn that he had gone on horseback, accompanied by his valet and a single laquais, making the trip in just two days. Luce, unable to take a single bite of the tart that someone, she could not say who, had placed on the low table before her, blanched as she counted back. Morgan must have left for Nantes the very morning after he had inflicted such violence on the decks of the *Lucinde*. Traces of Bones's blood, and Samuel's, might have lingered on his fingers as he took Veronique's hand in his. As he clasped Gabriel's arm as a brother, and admired the ring that Charlotte, newly married and glowing, proudly wore on her finger.

She could barely contain her shudder.

"Monsieur and Madame de Châtelaine have yet to give their approval," Veronique said. She perched beside Morgan in the grand salon, her hand resting on his sleeve. She turned to Luce. "They are on their way here now. They will stay for supper, and we shall make all the arrangements. Isn't that right, Papa?"

"Of course, ma chère," Jean-Baptiste said indulgently. "Though I have no doubt Castro and Camille will be as delighted as we are." He rocked back on his heels, brimming with pride. A man who just secured his empire by marrying his eldest daughter into the oldest and wealthiest ship-owning family in Saint-Malo. It was a wondrous match, his smile said, brimming with possibility.

Charlotte, across from Luce, rolled her eyes.

The day wore on, turning slowly into an evening rich with candlelight and the scent of roasting meats. Luce spent much of her time in her bedchamber and cabinet, the only places she could be guaranteed not to meet with Morgan. It was impossible to speak with her father about the English fleet; Morgan was always with him. Luce hated herself for her cowardice, for making herself small and meek, and allowing Morgan's presence to dominate her home. He knew about her relationship with Samuel, about her secret crossing of the Manche. Would he tell her father of her exploits? Surely not; to do so would be to leave himself vulnerable to a few retaliatory revelations of Luce's own. The events that had transpired aboard the *Lucinde*. The keelhauling, and Bones's death.

They had, it seemed, reached an impasse.

By the time supper began, Luce was wound tight as a fishing line at day's end. Nevertheless, she dressed carefully in a robe à la française of dark green silk and arranging herself dutifully in her seat between Charlotte and Gabriel. Morgan's elegant mother cooed over the fresh flowers, crystal and fine porcelain decorating the dining table, as well as Veronique's spectacular blue gown. Castro, for his part, barely waited for the wine to be poured before launching into the marriage negotiations. To no one's surprise, Jean-Baptiste was only too pleased to accommodate him, and a lively discussion dominated much of the first service. Luce, all too aware of Morgan's stealthy, and rather smug, glances, kept her eyes on her plate.

"And have you given any thought to your wedding gown, Veronique?" Camille de Châtelaine asked warmly.

Veronique looked up from her lobster gratin. She all but glittered in the candlelight, her cheeks flushed, her eyes sparkling. "I was thinking silk damask, madame."

"A lovely choice," Camille said approvingly. She took a delicate bite of pheasant, chewed thoughtfully. "Rose pink?"

"Yes. Or silver, perhaps."

"You will shine like a star."

Charlotte made a sound that might have been a snort. Gabriel glanced across Luce to his wife. Luce did not miss the twinkle in his eyes, and felt a surge of affection for her brother-in-law. It had become painfully obvious that, apart from herself, no one at the table was inclined to speak to him. It did not appear to bother Gabriel—he had eyes only for Charlotte—and yet the injustice of it, the fact that her parents and sisters were fawning over a bridegroom who was not only a liar but a murderer, too, while a good, kind, decent man was deemed unworthy . . . She steadied her breath, forced herself to eat.

The talk turned to chapels and flowers, guests and wedding feasts.

"We want to be married as soon as possible," Morgan said. "I intend to go to the bishop tomorrow and seek a dispensation. If it is approved, Veronique and I could be married within the week."

Veronique beamed at him. Her expression, so happy and trusting, shredded Luce's heart. She glanced at Charlotte and saw her own sentiments echoed there. Even Gabriel was watching Morgan warily.

"We will be married in Saint-Vincent's, of course," Veronique said. "And have the wedding breakfast on the ship. It will be intimate. Chic. Oh, but—" She glanced at Luce, bit her lip, and turned imploringly to Jean-Baptiste. "Papa?"

"Worry not, ma chère," he said soothingly. "Luce must find out sooner or later." He lowered his spoon. "Mon trésor, during our—negotiations—in Nantes, it was decided that the *Lucinde* would go to Veronique, as part of her dowry."

Across the table, Morgan sipped from his wineglass, barely concealing his triumphant smirk.

Ah. The truth came into focus for Luce, as clear and sharp as pieces of a broken mirror realigned. Morgan had ridden to Nantes, pursued Veronique, to secure the *Lucinde*. He had gained a ship, and revenge on Luce and Samuel for thwarting him, in one graceful maneuver.

Wolf, indeed.

Beside Luce, Charlotte gave a deep, disgusted sigh.

"There will be other ships, mon trésor," Jean-Baptiste promised Luce gently. "We have years and years ahead of us to build, to plan. . . ."

Luce said nothing. She should have been angry, hurt, yet found that she was neither. The *Lucinde* had lost its beauty—or, rather, Morgan had stolen it—on the night of Bones's death. The hope, the promise of freedom, it had once offered was gone; only sorrow and greed remained. *Besides*, some dim, new part of Luce whispered. *Such a betrayal will only make it easier for you to leave with Samuel.*

"Years and years, Papa?" Charlotte said, frowning. "What a thing to say. It is as if you fully expect Lucinde to never marry or find happiness of her own."

Silence of a profound and breathtaking nature settled over the table, so deep that the rumble of the storm-stone in the walls seemed like a distant storm. Even the laquais, who had been busily readying fresh bottles of wine and rinsing the family's used glasses, stilled.

Jean-Baptiste's expression was utterly cold. "If by 'find happiness of her own' you mean that Luce will leave this house in the dead of night with a man who is beneath her in every possible way, breaking her mother's heart and threatening our family's reputation, then, no, Charlotte, I do *not* expect it."

"Jean-Baptiste . . . ," Gratienne said, with a nervous glance at the de Châtelaines.

The silence, if such a thing were possible, grew even thicker. Luce stared at her father, shocked by the rage, the iciness in his eyes. What would he say if he knew of her plans to leave Saint-Malo with Samuel, a man who, in the eyes of everyone sitting at this table, was worthy of even less consideration than Gabriel? She felt a heavy gaze settle upon her, and looked up to see Morgan watching her, smirking ever so slightly as though he knew her thoughts. She straightened in her seat, chin raised.

"An English fleet is preparing to cross the Manche and attack the city," she announced into the void. "I have it on . . . on good authority that an English commander named Admiral Howe has assembled ships in the Solent and means to transport over twelve thousand men to our shores." She turned to Jean-Baptiste. "Papa, you must warn the commander. Howe could be here now, reconnoitering the coast for a landing point."

"*What?*" Veronique looked around the table, eyes wide. "The English? *Here?*"

"We are at war, Vee," Charlotte said. "Is it really so surprising?"

"But . . . what about the wedding?"

"I don't think your wedding is their main concern," Luce said.

"The English have been threatening to invade our shores for years," Monsieur de Châtelaine said airily. "Rumors such as these are a perfectly normal part of war. Do not fret, mademoiselle. The city cannot fall."

"Any city can fall," Luce told him, then flinched as her father flopped back in his seat, chuckling.

"*This* is why I adore you, Lucinde." He turned to Monsieur de Châtelaine with a grin. "Did you hear that, my friend? Have you ever heard such words from a young lady over supper?"

The tension in the room eased as Castro raised his glass to Luce, his eyes, so like his son's, twinkling. "Never!"

Luce looked between them, confused. "But—are you not concerned, Papa? Should you not send word to the commander and the chief engineer?"

"The Marquis knows," Jean-Baptiste said, nodding to Jean-Pierre and raising his glass so the laquais could re-fill it. "As does Mazin. Le Châtre has it on good authority that the English expedition will direct themselves against Brest, not Saint-Malo. Your fears are unfounded, mon trésor." He flicked his wrist at a silver platter brimming with fresh seafood. "Here—have some oysters."

"Are you certain, Papa?" Veronique asked worriedly.

"I would wager my life upon it, ma chère." Jean-Baptiste barely glanced up as St. Jean hurried forward, lifted the silver platter in gloved hands, and offered it to Luce. "Are we not Malouins? Kings of the sea? Our city shall suffer no enemy ships, nor armies to come against it. I promise."

Luce half-heartedly scooped an oyster from the platter with a pair of shell-shaped tongs. "But, Papa—"

Morgan cut her off. "Who gave you this information?" Polite. Curious.

"I heard it from the domestiques," Luce said coolly. "*They* heard it from the fishermen."

Morgan, still watching her, sipped thoughtfully at his wine.

"Let us make a toast," Gratienne said, getting to her feet. Due to the amount of jewels smothering her neck, wrists, and stomacher, the movement required considerable effort. "To my beautiful daughter Veronique and her handsome husband-to-be." She raised her glass, smiling around the table. "Just imagine how comely our grandchildren will be!"

Laughter tinkled upon the crystal and silverware. Behind her raised glass, Charlotte made a face.

"To the lion and the wolf, united at last," Jean-Baptiste added, lifting his own glass high.

"*To the lion and the wolf!*"

When supper was over Luce excused herself and stole down to the cove. A single slender silhouette stood at the water's edge, silver hair glittering in the moonlight. The groac'h glanced back as Luce made her slow way to the cave, but remained where she was.

"Samuel."

He had been sleeping, belly-down, his hair falling across his cheek. He roused at the sound of her voice, however, and opened his eyes. "Luce? Is everything well?"

"Not really, no." She swallowed, unsure where to begin, then plunged ahead. "My family has returned. Morgan—Morgan is with them. He followed them to Nantes, Samuel. The very day after . . . after the *Lucinde*."

He pushed his hair back sleepily, lifted himself up to sitting. Despite the turmoil of feelings, Luce noted that the usual grimace of pain he made when he moved had lessened. "Why would he do that?"

"For my sister. Or, rather, for the *Lucinde*." She told him of the engagement and her father's decision to give Morgan the ship as part of Veronique's dowry. Of Veronique's joy, and Morgan's calculated charm. "I have just sat through a family supper to discuss the wedding details with Morgan and his parents. Morgan is seeking a dispensation—he plans to marry Veronique within the week."

"Damn my soul." Samuel rubbed his face ruefully. "You have to admire the bastard's determination."

"It gets worse. I told my father and Monsieur de Châtelaine about the fleet."

"How did that go?"

"Badly. Monsieur de Châtelaine dismissed it as mere rumor. And Papa insisted that Saint-Malo is blessed. 'Are we not Malouins? Kings of the sea?' were his words. And Samuel—they said that the Marquis de la Châtre and Monsieur Mazin already know. They know, and have determined that Howe and Marlborough are set on attacking Brest, not Saint-Malo."

Samuel had gone very still. "Fools," he said softly, shaking his head. "I suppose it's not too late for me to do more. Speak again to my contacts in the city, the garrison. The right word to the right person could make all the difference."

"What? No!" Luce remembered Morgan's idle gaze at the betrothal supper, the dark rage lurking beneath his calm. "For all we know there is still a price on your head."

"I would be discreet." He leaned over, took her hand. "Until very recently, Saint-Malo has been good to me. I cannot simply sail away and leave it to its fate."

He had lost one of his swallow tattoos during his ordeal. Luce ran a thumb gently over the patchwork of half-healed scabbing. Did the remaining bird, alone at the base of Samuel's unmarred thumb, mourn its loss?

"I—we . . ." She took a breath, forced herself to speak. "I cannot go with you, Samuel. Not while Veronique means to chain herself to that . . . to that . . ." She shook her head. "And if my father won't believe me about the fleet, there is no telling what will become of my mother and sisters. I cannot leave them. Not until I know they will be safe."

He nodded. "I understand."

Tears threatened—disappointment, and something more. "I could follow you, afterwards. When I know they will be well. I could get passage to Dorset—"

"What?" He straightened against the pillows, reaching for her, then froze, wincing at the pain. "You don't really think I'd go without you, do you?"

"But—you must. Morgan will kill you if he can, I'm certain of it. The fleet is coming, the soldiers—"

"And you believe I'd leave you to face all that alone?"

Luce smiled. "I'd kiss you, you know, if I wasn't so worried about hurting your back."

"I'll have you know my back's perfectly fine."

"Liar." She leaned in regardless, pressing her mouth to his, breathing him in. Trying not to notice the painful hitch of his breath as his arms came around her, or the way his fingers brushed, ever so gently, against the faded bruise on her cheek. As though he were marking its shape, its size. Remembering every detail.

"Perhaps there's something I can do, too," Luce murmured against his mouth.

"Hmm? I was just thinking the same . . ."

She drew back with a grin, batted aside his roving hands. "Ambitious, aren't you? What a shame you're not the one I need."

"Ouch."

"Precisely." She leaned in, kissed him softly. "Go back to sleep."

The groac'h was still near the waterline, arms folded across her chest.

"I need you to show me how to raise a storm," Luce told her. It was a bold request. Over the last five days the fae had taught her many things—how to become one with the sea's movements, how to sense its moods. Luce was learning quickly, yet she had no doubt that she was a far cry from the lesson on storms and their summoning.

The tide-woman did not take her gaze from the water. "You think to save Saint-Malo from its enemies? You will be wasting your time."

"Perhaps not; I am a good student. You said so yourself."

The groac'h threw her a doubtful look. Then she gave a long-suffering sigh and reached into her tangle of skirts, drawing forth the silver comb. "You'll be needing this."

Luce took the comb. It was heavier than she expected, cool against her fingers. "Just this?"

"Your knife, too. Do you have it?"

Luce nodded. For reasons she could scarce explain—the still-too-near memory of the night of the *Lucinde* perhaps, or the strange, indescribable comfort the items gave her—she now kept Mother Aggie's knife, the groac'h's mirror, and the sea-silk with her constantly, the former tucked into the sea-silk belt beneath her skirts, the latter in its usual place between her breasts.

The fae eyed Luce's hair, pinned into elegant curls at the back of her head. "You'll need to take down your hair."

Luce was already drawing free the pins. "Thank you."

"As I said." The tide-woman turned back to the sea. "Waste of time."

~

If the preparations for the ball had seemed frantic, they were nothing compared to those for Veronique and Morgan's wedding. Having secured permission to marry at once, thus negating the need to wait the required three Sundays, when the banns would ordinarily be called, Veronique launched into the arrangements with remarkable zeal. A suitably opulent gown of silver silk damask was ordered, while the contents of her armoire—sheets, table linens, and nightgowns made of the finest silks in Paris—were removed, washed and pressed, then packed lovingly back inside. Gratienne resumed work on the precious baptismal gown, and a lavish wedding feast aboard the *Lucinde* was planned. The ship itself was receiving its final fittings, including its sails.

"I still cannot believe Papa gave Morgan your ship," Charlotte said to Luce the day after the betrothal dinner. She was sprawled on the small longue in Luce's cabinet. The small, comfortable chamber offered no small amount of privacy. "Although, if I'm honest, Luce, I must admit that I blame myself. In part, at least."

"You blame yourself?" Luce, perched on the little chair at her writing desk, turned to her sister. "Why?"

"Morgan made no pretensions about wanting that ship. And he used my marriage to Gabriel—the scandal of it, I mean—to leverage for a bigger dowry."

"A ship-sized dowry, you mean."

"Precisely." Charlotte glanced through the open door to Luce's bedchamber, ensuring it was empty. "I overheard the negotiations in Nantes," she said, conspiratorially. "Morgan made it clear that he knew the reason our family had rushed off—he said he was here that day, when Papa sent word that he'd found Gabriel and me."

"He was," Luce admitted, fiddling with the cracked vase on

It was brimming with bird feathers in every shape and ...ama tried to hide it. She said Papa had found a pair of ...ing side tables." The ploy had seemed amusing, then.

Morgan said he would only take Veronique if the ship was ...rt of the offer. I suspected then that he was more interested in the *Lucinde* than in our sister."

"And now?"

"And now, I suspect that I had every right to suspect him." Charlotte made a face. "I cannot help but feel that Morgan does not have our sister's best interests at heart, Luce."

"I must admit I feel the same." *If only you knew.*

"He hardly knows Vee, barely looked at her at the ball, and yet he rode all the way to Nantes to propose? *And* he arrived looking as though he had just come from a knife-fight at the docks. Speaking of . . . what happened to your face?"

"It is nothing." Luce waved Charlotte's concern away. "I tripped on the stairs. You know how my feet can be." She had said the same to both her mother, who had gasped in horror at the sight of Luce's face, and her father, who had ragefully demanded an explanation.

Charlotte sighed. "I know what that ship meant to you, Luce. It was more than a figurehead, more than a name. I'm so sorry. If not for me, Morgan would never have dared to make such demands of Papa."

Luce got to her feet. There was hardly room to pace in the cabinet, but even so, she tried her best. "The ship no longer matters," she said. "It is Veronique we must think of now. It is not too late, Charlotte. We could speak to her. Explain our misgivings."

"Are you mad?" Charlotte demanded. "*Speak* to Veronique? Have you seen our sister? She's besotted!"

"She will recover," Luce said firmly. "In time."

"Yes, but what of the rest of us? The lion and the wolf united, wasn't it? If you think Papa and Maman would even *consider* calling off this wedding . . . how many scandals do you think this family can endure?"

"Better another scandal than seeing our sister at the mercy of a man like that."

"When you say 'a man like that,' I'm assuming you mean young, handsome, and rich?" Charlotte said. "Because besides you, me, and Gabriel, that is all anyone sees when they look at Morgan. *Especially* our sister."

"She doesn't know Morgan," Luce said. On the bookshelf beside her, pooled in an iridescent shell the size of her palm, lay three black pearls. She lifted one absently, rolled it between her fingers. "Not truly. If she did, she would never have agreed to this."

Charlotte narrowed her eyes. "There's more to this story, isn't there?" She tilted her head appraisingly, taking in every detail of Luce—her face, her dark woolen dress, the pearl in her hand. Then, "Oh my God," she exclaimed, sitting up. "I cannot believe I didn't see it before. It was *you*, at the ball. *You* were the woman who danced with Morgan!"

"Don't be absurd!" Luce tipped the pearl back into its shell with too-hasty fingers. It fell, bounced once, and rolled across the wooden floor. She lunged for it, but Charlotte was too fast. She scooped the tiny orb up and held it before her, so that, from her angle, its inky shine was close to Luce's face.

"It most certainly was," she said decisively. "How did no one know?"

"Please, Cee." Luce held her hand out for the pearl.

"But where did you get that dress? Those magnificent *shoes*?"

"Cee." Luce curled her fingers, indicating that Charlotte should return the pearl and cease her questioning.

Charlotte's tone changed. "Surely you realize you can trust me, Luce? Unless . . . unless you still think it was *I* who stole your blue dress?"

"No," Luce said, slowly. "No, I don't think that."

In truth, she was sorely tempted to tell her sister everything. Yet if she told her of the ball, she would also have to tell her of the groac'h. Knowledge which could, in its turn, endanger Samuel. There were secrets within secrets, and none she could afford to have unravel.

"Perhaps one day I will tell you the tale," she said. "For now, know that I *do* trust you, Cee. And that I hope you will trust *me* when I say that we cannot sit back and simply allow Vee to marry Morgan. He is . . . he is not a good man."

"I will hold you to that." Charlotte, resigned, placed the pearl in Luce's palm. "And as for Morgan . . . Luce, we cannot mention our feelings about this wedding to anyone. Not Veronique, nor Maman and Papa. And even if we did, it would be too late. They've already signed the contract."

"They have?" Luce blinked. It was not uncommon for couples to sign the wedding contract a day or two before the ceremony.

Charlotte nodded. "They did it after supper, when the de Châtelaines were last here. You would have seen it yourself had you not retired so early."

I was at the cove, Luce wanted to say. *Learning to raise a storm so I might protect you all when the English fleet arrives.*

"Then there really is nothing we can do," she said wearily. With the contracts signed, Veronique and Morgan were as good as married.

No fleet, no storm, could protect her sister now.

25

Other Things, Besides

Veronique Léon and Morgan de Châtelaine were married in the cathedral on a sunny, Bretagne-blue morning. Luce, surrounded by her family in the Léon pew, was careful, for Veronique's sake, to appear joyful and serene as she watched her sister say her vows. Her searing regret—that she had been unable to save her from Morgan, just as she had been unable to save Bones—was a relentless ache in her heart.

By early afternoon the cream of Saint-Malo society, including the commander of the city and his wife, were strolling down to the quay, where boats waited to deliver them to the wedding feast aboard the *Lucinde*. Or rather, the *Veronique*. The newly renamed frigate had been moved from its mooring at Saint-Servan, and now graced the blue waters of the harbor, her rigging, yards, masts, and rails festooned with flowers and ribbons. A quartet of liveried musicians was already on deck, the sweet notes of Vivaldi drifting across the water as the guests climbed, or, in the case of the ladies, were winched upward in specially made seats that could accommodate their wide skirts. The dark-haired figurehead in her blue dress had been repainted: yellow hair and a rose-pink gown to capture the likeness of Veronique. Luce felt a strange sort of relief, at that. Perhaps Morgan meant to consider his new wife's feelings, after all.

As the boat bearing Luce and her family drew alongside the

ship, a terrible dread rose in her chest. Once, the sight of that sleek, dark hull had filled her with hope. The sight of it now, taken from her, gifted to another, should have, by rights, broken her heart. However, Luce found she could scarce look at the ship without seeing Samuel or Bones hanging beside it, their hands bound, their bodies mauled and dripping as they plunged beneath the surface.

"Come along, then," Charlotte said, taking Luce's hand. The ribbons on her hat fluttered as she tilted her head to gaze up at the ship, then back at Luce, eyes widening as though to say, *well, here we are. May as well enjoy it.*

The *Veronique*'s decks, freshly scrubbed, bore no trace of blood and violence. Garlanded chairs had been arranged in clusters beside long tables laden with delicacies: creamed scallops, fresh oysters and poached truffles, mille-feuille with marmalade and lavender cream, platters piled with lobsters and crabs, duck ballotine, quail stuffed with thyme, sparkling wine garnished with orange-blossoms, whole pineapples, and dainty meringues laden with crème Chantilly. The guests dined and chatted in their finery, as sleek and confident as kings as they admired the magnificent new addition to the Malouin fleet, supremely unconcerned about a potential English invasion. After all, why should they be? Hadn't the English commanders determined to target Brest? And besides, was Saint-Malo not invulnerable? Even now the harbor seethed with ships, three of Jean-Baptiste's most precious vessels—the *Lionne*, the *Thétis*, and the *Fleur de Mer*—among them. The sea had gifted the elite families of Saint-Malo with its bounty for generations: ships and cargoes, trade and riches. Surely it would not forsake them now?

Everyone clapped in delight when Morgan made a show of stealing one of Veronique's shoes, silk stockings, and garter ribbons, as was the custom. Luce tried, and failed, not to imagine *other* garters in Morgan's hands, in every shade of conquest. Veronique, glowing with joy, limped about on the deck until Morgan went to help her. He kissed his beautiful bride, while she, smiling, stroked his dark hair. Luce, unable to watch a moment longer, stole up to the stern. Found it, as she had hoped, to be blissfully deserted.

She crossed the deck, feet whimpering in the delicately-heeled wedding shoes Veronique had insisted she wear, and leaned on the taffrail, slipping the slippers free.

"Damn my soul." She sighed, reveling in the feel of cool timber against her stockinged soles. Absurd, that the wedding guests should be drinking orange-scented wine and eating pastries, when even now a fleet of English ships could be moving like sharks along the coast. She dragged her gaze along the horizon. The water, which had been calm and blue that morning, was now a steely gray, reflecting the clouds that were rolling thickly in from the north.

When the weather turns, the mirror had told her, and the groac'h had agreed. *A week, perhaps. Maybe longer.*

There was weather coming, no denying it. She could feel it in the air and on her skin, the same strange, faint prickling she felt when storm-stone was near. Luce threw her senses out into the Manche, tried to gauge its mood. She could have sworn it was holding its breath.

When the weather turns.

She glanced over her shoulder. She was utterly alone on the afterdeck, hidden from the other guests, still gathered at midships, by the height of the quarter deck below, the mizzen mast, and sheer distance.

To see the shape of the weather, to know if danger approaches. And other things, besides.

There was time enough, surely, to be certain. Besides, both the Marquis de la Châtre and Monsieur Mazin were aboard. If the fleet *was* approaching, both the commander of Saint-Malo and its chief engineer were only steps away.

Decided, Luce fished in her pockets—she had cut holes in the silk, allowing discreet access to the sea-silk belt at her waist—and slipped the mirror free. Turning her back to the sea, she held it up.

When a seamaid looks backwards into her mirror, she sees therein that which she requires.

"That which she requires," she whispered, focusing her thoughts on the fleet, the city, and her family. At once the reflection in the mirror changed. The glowering clouds behind her had made good on their threats, exploding into a storm both iron-gray and iridescent. Gulls wheeled, the last notes of sunlight harsh on their pale wings. And then—

Luce gasped. The sails, much closer to the city now, were as white as the gulls against the storm clouds. She turned the mirror slowly, the better to see the fleet in its entirety. Over a hundred sails, just as Samuel had said. At least twenty-five ships of the line, countless frigates, and three or four bomb ships, their telltale mortars gaping with infinite menace. There were many smaller ships, too. Fire ships, perhaps, destined to be set alight and sailed toward an enemy, or transport vessels. So intent was Luce on soaking in every detail of the fleet that she did not see the sliver of the *Lucinde*'s deck coming into view behind her. Or the figure that stood upon it.

When at last she *did* notice her father, she flinched guiltily and went to pull the mirror down. In that moment, however, his reflection wavered, until he was standing not on the afterdeck of the *Lucinde*, the flowers decorating its yards bright against the coming storm clouds, but on a rocky beach beneath a clear, blue sky. The sounds of the wedding rising from the *Lucinde*'s decks—laughter, chatter, the elegant strains of Bach—faded, along with Jean-Baptiste's embroidered frock coat, satin breeches, and white stockings. Instead, he wore a serviceable shirt and sailor's wide breeches, a heavy overcoat, and cracked leather boots. Gone was his fashionable, powdered wig. His hair was inky black, cropped far shorter than Luce had ever seen it. The weapons hanging at his belt, however, were familiar. She had seen them, many times, rusting and forgotten in the storerooms beneath the town house in Saint-Malo. A pistol, well-oiled; a short-handled axe; a fighting sword. He had a canvas bag slung over one shoulder, too; the kind sailors used for foraging on shore.

All this Luce noted in the time it takes to breathe in and then out again. Unable to look away, she watched as the strange, youthful version of her father moved along the unfamiliar beach, a tiny actor on a tiny stage meant just for her. The water behind him was a surreal turquoise blue, the sand clean and white. Luce frowned. Where was this place? And why did she feel as though she knew it?

Something small appeared on the sand ahead. As her father drew closer, Luce realized that it was a tiny child, perhaps one or two years old. It was naked, its softly-curling hair black. It looked up at her father's approach, and Luce saw that its eyes were a startling—and familiar—shade of blue.

The sound of her shocked breath was sharp in her ears.

"Lucinde?" Jean-Baptiste's voice carried across the deck, gentle and inquisitive, but Luce did not turn around. She could do nothing as her mirror-father approached the little girl and crouched beside her.

The child—*Luce*—was sitting at the water's edge. Water lapped at her bare feet and legs, which, Luce saw with a pang, were perfectly formed. Whole. A piece of sea-silk trailed in the water beside her, its blue-green folds barely visible in that outrageous water.

She looked trustingly up at Jean-Baptiste and smiled, offering him a shell. Jean-Baptiste smiled back, his face softening. "Where is your mother, little one?" At that moment the water pushed the silk against the child's bare legs. Jean-Baptiste, his hand outstretched to take the shell, froze, his gaze caught on the tiny, glimmering tail that had replaced her legs. Emotions played rapidly across his face—Luce noted wonder and shock—before something distracted him. He turned in time to see a woman—no, a seamaid, her hair as black as Luce's own, her face achingly similar—launch herself from the water as though the very ocean had risen at her command, her glorious golden-green tail splashing a wave of rage and seawater over the beach, her child, and the man who had dared to approach her. Luce's mother had a sea-knife in her hand, and a look of pure fury on her face. She coiled herself upon the sand, took Luce protectively in her arms, and hissed.

Jean-Baptiste's eyes widened in terror. For one endless moment it seemed that he might back away. Leave mother and child in peace, and return to his ship.

Then the sound of a gunshot pierced the air.

Luce flinched.

"Luce?" Her father had taken another step toward her. "You look lovely, I assure you. Put that away and come back to the party."

Luce ignored him, unable to look away from the motionless seamaid, the blood staining the sand.

A look of speculation crossed young Jean-Baptiste's face. Luce knew it well. *Here,* it said, *was an opportunity.*

He took his axe from his belt.

Luce did not look away as he cut her mother's hand off at the wrist, then used the axe to prize away some of her scales, storing them, bloody-tipped and oddly colorless now that they were separated from her, in the canvas bag.

A lion knows nothing of pity.

"Lucinde? Are you quite well?"

Luce watched, barely able to breathe as her mother's murderer prodded at the comb and mirror hanging from a belt at her waist, then peered closer, examining the belt itself. *Sea-silk.* She saw, rather than heard, his lips shape the sound. He pulled it free, indifferent to the tarnished mirror and comb that fell onto the bloody sand. Like so many men before him, he had deemed them nothing more than women's trinkets, and therefore, worthless.

When he had taken all of value, Jean-Baptiste went to leave.

He took three or four steps before he looked back at the child sitting beside her dead mother. A look of pity crossed his face. He hurried back, snatched the child up, and carried her along the beach.

A corsair lay at anchor beyond a rocky headland, its sails struck. Perhaps Luce knew that ship; perhaps she might have recognized the figurehead. As it was, she could not take her eyes off the blue-green sea-silk, still caught about the little girl's legs. She winced as Jean-Baptiste leaned down and ripped it roughly away. Startled, the child began to cry. She reached over his shoulder, her small, star-fish hands splaying for her mother, who grew smaller and smaller with every step Jean-Baptiste took. He held her tightly as she sobbed, tucking the piece of silk deep into his pocket.

"There, there, mon trésor," he said, stroking her hair. "You shall have a new family to love you, eh? A maman *and a* papa. And two sisters!"

"Mon trésor?"

He was right behind her now. Luce raised the mirror higher, so he might view what she herself beheld: the lifeless body of a golden-tailed seamaid, her blood staining the sand, the sea, in an ever-widening arc. When she was certain he had seen, Luce turned around, lowering the mirror.

Her father's face was bloodless.

"Mon trésor—" z

"I am not your treasure." And then, before he could utter another lie, she swung herself over the taffrail and dropped into the sea.

All through the afternoon, the weather worsened. The wind whipped the face of the Manche into a frenzy, while waves drenched the coast, plunging into caves and coves, carving into the stone.

Luce delighted in the sea's turmoil. She let it consume her, sinking gladly into its murky depths and then, just when she was certain she could not survive another moment without drawing breath, allowing it to push her back to the surface. Gasping in the spray, pale with the cold, she took a shuddering breath and plunged down once more, losing herself to the darkness.

Her dress and underthings were long gone, discarded beneath the *Lucinde.* Besides her scaled tail and Mother Aggie's belt, where those three precious items—knife, mirror, comb—were secured beside the knotted sea-silk, she was naked. Bare-breasted and wild, like the paintings of seamaids she had seen in her father's study.

Pain, sharp as a blade in her heart. She plunged once more beneath the churning waters, let them swallow her body and soul.

Somehow, she found herself back at the cove.

She hesitated before swimming to shore. Sculled in place upon the Manche's heaving surface—her massive tail working beneath her, keeping her clear of the rocks—torn between salty oblivion and the comfort of dry land. How would it feel to keep going? To dive again and again, not looking back until Saint-Malo, Bretagne itself, was far from sight.

Only the thought of Samuel, waiting for her, uncertain of where she was or when she would return, stopped her.

In the end, it was he who found her on the beach, exhausted and cold as stone, limbs trailing weed, frighteningly wild in the storm-light.

"Luce? What are you—holy fucking *Christ*!"

His hands were so warm, so warm. She lay very still on the sand, letting him gently untangle the sea-silk from her belt, lifting it away—like a fisherman freeing a seamaid from a line in an old tale.

"Shall I give you three wishes?" she croaked. "For your kindness?"

"I'd be satisfied with you not freezing to death," he grunted, pocketing the silk and slinging one of her arms around his neck.

The cold intensified with the return of her legs. Luce shivered uncontrollably as he hauled her against him, then pushed himself to his feet. She felt him tense, heard the sharp intake of breath as he strained his still-healing wounds.

"Y-you will hurt your b-back," she said through chattering teeth.

"Fuck my back."

Movement, then. Swift, rough. The cold silver of evening went dark, and was replaced by the dimness of stone, the warmth of sea-scarred lanterns and salted firelight. "Found her on the beach," Samuel was saying, his chest rumbling against Luce's ear. "She must have swum back." The groac'h's voice, stern and reproachful, replied—"not yet strong enough to swim such distances, and in such seas"—before Luce was laid somewhere soft—Samuel's bed?—and enfolded in warmth. She nestled into it gratefully, pressing her feet against the utter deliciousness of what could only be heated stones.

"Hand me her comb," the groac'h said.

"Her comb?" Luce heard the confusion in Samuel's voice.

"To dry her hair," the groach'h said. And then, lower, "And, perhaps, help with this weather."

Gentle hands smoothed Luce's brow, and then the comb was drifting through her hair. She exhaled deeply, as though she had stored all her shock and anger in her lungs, and the tide-woman's touch had allowed her to breathe again.

"Sleep, seamaid," the groac'h said, with surprising tenderness. Dimly, Luce heard the wind outside the cave ease, felt the Manche begin to settle. "When you wake, we shall speak of what has troubled you."

"You know." Luce, sinking into an oblivion of warmth and exhaustion and heartache, grasped at the words, muttered them before they slipped out of reach. "I think you've always known."

26

After That, the Stars

Impossible to say how long Luce slept. An hour? A week? The first thing she heard, as she drifted toward wakefulness, was Samuel.

"If this has something to do with that bastard de Châtelaine . . ."

"I have told you thrice, storm diver," the groac'h said patiently. "It has not."

Not a week, then, though it surely felt like it. Luce's body was anchor-heavy, her mind shrouded in weariness. Yet the sound of the sea, the color of the cave's walls behind her eyelids, revealed only an hour or two had passed since Samuel had found her on the shore.

"How can you be certain?" Luce sensed Samuel rise restlessly from where he had been sitting near the bed. She herself had sat in that same seat—a scratched and faded armchair that had washed up on the beach years before—when she was watching over him in those early days after the *Lucinde*.

"Reasons."

"Reasons? You'll need to do better than that, Margot."

Margot? Luce stirred, closer to full wakefulness now. She knew Samuel and the tide-woman—or, apparently Margot—had formed a friendship of their own. Often, when she arrived at the cave, she found them sharing a companionable meal or pot of tea, or, when Samuel first became strong enough to move about, resting in the sun at the cave's mouth. She opened her eyes and sat up, pulling the blankets against her bare chest and throwing the groac'h a wounded look. "You never told me your name was Margot."

"You never asked." It was clear the shore-woman would say no more upon it. She merely handed Luce a cup of water and waited, patient as ever, while she drank.

"How are you feeling?" Samuel took the empty cup, placed it on a small tea crate serving as a table, and sat carefully on the edge of the bed. "What in Christ's name happened, Luce? Did something go awry at the wedding?"

"You could say that." Luce turned to Margot. "Do you . . ." She hesitated, at once aching for the truth, and fearing its bite. "Do you know who destroyed my blue dress, the day of the ball?"

Margot nodded.

"You saw them do it?"

Another nod.

Luce swallowed. "Was it—was it Charlotte?"

Margot shook her head slowly.

Luce swallowed, her mouth suddenly dry. She had suspected for some time that Charlotte had not been the one to betray her. Which meant . . .

"Then who?" she rasped. Unwilling, even now, to admit the truth. Beyond the cave, the sea sighed sadly.

"You already know," Margot replied. "The sea told you its secrets, did it not? Why else would you come here as you did? Wounded and betrayed?"

"I want to hear it from you," Luce said. "I want to know what *you* know."

Wind rushed along the passageway, disturbing the threadbare hangings lining the stony walls, the curtains beside the bed, as though it, too, searched for answers.

"You already know who stole the blue gown," Margot said. "It was the same person who stole *you*. He knew what a blessing a sea-child would be. His ships would be safe through the grimmest of storms. His cargoes would remain intact. No weather, no enemy, no ill luck would threaten his trade. He—and all that was his—would pass safely across the face of the oceans as though the gods of the sea themselves commanded it. You know who hid your sea-silk, your mother's precious gift to you. And you know who made every step you take an agony. All this he has done for selfishness and greed. He kept you close, kept you from returning to the sea, knowing your presence, your magic, would fuel the storm-stone and his fortune. He took the dress to ensure that you would not leave him, nor lend your powers to any of his rivals. Everything he has, everything he owns, is his because of you. You are his greatest treasure."

Samuel's eyes widened.

"I saw my mother in the mirror," Luce said. "I saw *myself* with her. I-I watched her die."

Margot nodded. "We all of us mourned your mother. But no one as much as your father."

"My *father*?"

"Your true father. His grief, when he found your mother on the shore at Chausey, was boundless."

Your true father.

"Did you say Chausey?" Samuel asked. "You mean, the Storm Islands?"

"It was once a stronghold for the sea-folk," Margot told him. "Many lived there."

He nodded. "It is the reason storm-stone quarried at the Islands is best."

"It is the reason, too, why the sea-folk chose to leave. Luce's parents were among the few who remained." Margot turned to Luce with a weary sigh. "When your father returned and found your mother's body on the beach, her silver comb and mirror beside her, his grief was matched only by his rage. He discovered the name of the ship, and then the man, who had stolen you, and followed you to this very cove. Male sea-folk bear no silks—they cannot change their shape as the women do. He could not walk upon the land and take you back, and he knew that you were behind high stone walls, out of reach. Out of *everyone's* reach. For years your father waited, hoping for a chance to take you back, even as more and more of the sea-folk left these shores. Until, one day, he was the only one who remained. Overcome with sorrow and loneliness, he finally left Bretagne. He trusted me with your mother's comb and mirror, and bid me give them to you, should you and I ever chance to meet. I promised him I would do so—and that I would watch over you in his stead."

"You should have told me all of this long ago," Luce said. *Your true father.*

"Would you have believed me? Taken my word over that of a man who, until very recently, you loved above all others? No; far better for you to learn the truth about Jean-Baptiste Léon yourself."

Luce thought of the hand in the cabinet of curiosities at Le Loup Blanc. She had no doubt that it belonged to her mother, and that the friend who gifted it to Monsieur de Châtelaine was none other than Jean-Baptiste. She thought, too, of the sea-silk—her only means of returning to the sea—hidden away between walls of stone. The lutine and the jetins, always so kind to her, had doubtless known the truth. *Thievery,* the water sprites had cried, again and again. Luce had thought they feared that she might steal from them, but now she realized they were simply trying to tell her what her father—the man who claimed to treasure her—had done.

Everyone wants to take a bite.

She curled her hands around her belly, wondered if she might be ill.

"The mermaid's kiss," Samuel said slowly. "Every time Luce kissed her father goodnight, or thanked him for some gift or kindness, she was gifting him with good fortune."

Give your papa a kiss.

Margot, watching Luce, nodded. "You yourself have benefitted from the seamaid's kiss, storm-diver. She did much more than dive beneath a ship when she saved you from the wolf."

Luce, pressing her mouth to Samuel's in the bloody shadows beneath the *Lucinde*.

Morgan, opening his eyes as he lay on the sand. The way he had looked at her, with such wonder and greed.

In truth? For a moment, I believed you were a seamaid.

"And then there's the matter of storm-stone," Margot was saying. "Jean-Baptiste Léon is known for having the very best, no matter the scarcity, no matter the cost."

"He let you help him with his ships," Samuel said, his voice soft with dismay. "Invited you to join him at the dockyards, to look over the construction. Took you into the holds where the storm-stone was stored . . ."

Luce stared at him. Her horror was a live thing, cold and slimy in her gut.

"He was using you to keep his storm-stone strong," Margot said. "Why, just by living in his house you were protecting him."

The betrayal was worse than anything Luce had imagined. Every conversation about navigation and trade, every map and book gifted to her, every new ship her father had proudly taken her to inspect, had been for his own benefit. He had never had any intention of letting her sail on the *Lucinde*. Had never intended her go *anywhere*. Every promise he had made, every word he had said, had been a lie.

Have you had any adventures today, mon trésor?

And she, a mere child, had trusted him. Loved him.

Give your papa a kiss.

She opened her mouth to speak, but the sound of cannon fire stopped her: three distant *booms*.

"The guns at Ile Harbor," Samuel said softly.

"Men and their g—" Margot got no further in her grumbling, for three more shots cracked the air, followed by three more.

"La Conchée and La Varde," Luce said, imagining the men at

the forts hurrying to load the guns, bracing themselves for the fire, smoke rising over the battlements. She waited, and heard still another repeat, and another—the forts dotting the coast to Cancale repeating the signal.

"They've spotted enemy sails," Samuel said.

"Yes." Jean-Baptiste had explained the warning system to her when she was a child. "As soon as one fort along the coast spies an unknown sail, they signal by firing a cannon three times. They continue to fire three shots every hour, until the two nearest forts to the east and west repeat it. And on, and on."

"And when does it stop?" Luce had asked him uneasily, flinching as another cannon roared.

Boom, boom, boom.

"It stops when the threat has passed, or the ships have landed," Jean-Baptiste had said. Seeing the fear in Luce's eyes, he had leaned down and put his arm around her. "Have no fear, mon trésor. No harm shall come to us."

"Why, Papa?"

"Because we are Malouins, ma chère. Blessed by the sea. It will protect us always."

Boom, boom, boom.

A new cannon awoke, quieter than the others, and further away. By the time the last of its pounding had faded, the entire coast between Saint-Malo and Cancale would have woken to the danger.

"Luce?" Samuel touched her arm. "Tell me what you want to do."

The mood in Margot's dwelling had changed. The sense of peace and comfort—the slow ebb and flow of a simple, hidden life—was gone. Beyond the curtains, Margot was moving about, mumbling to herself, hastily gathering items and stowing them in a pair of canvas sacks.

"What are you doing?" Luce asked the shore-woman.

"Leaving," she replied simply. "Like the rest of our kind. The time for dwelling in Bretagne is over."

Boom. Boom. Boom.

"You're going? Just like that?"

"If I stay, I will die," Margot said simply. "The land is weak, its magic fading. I have kept my word to your father. Told you the truth, given you your mother's things. My promise was all that tied me to this place." She looked from Samuel to Luce. "Come with me," she said. "The world is large, the oceans endless. There is magic left in it, still. Let us find it."

She blinked, her tusks pearlescent in the lantern light. And then she moved away, distracted with her preparations.

"What do you want to do, Luce?" Samuel asked. "Say the word, and I'll ready the *Dove*. We can sail west, to Saint-Malo; check on your family, do what we can to help. Or we can bear north, for Dorset. I'll need to speak to my brother, make arrangements. . . . But after that? We can sail anywhere. Go with Margot; find a fair breeze and a path of stars. Whatever you want."

Luce looked at him. At the still-healing wounds on his shoulder, visible beneath the collar of his shirt. At his beautiful eyes, gold and gray.

There are still places of beauty and wonder left in the world. Places that men in their death-ships have not despoiled. A fair breeze and a path of stars is all that is required to find them.

Boom. Boom. Boom.

What do you want to do, Luce?

She thought about that as she pushed aside the blankets and reached for the salvaged clothes Margot had left on the chair. As she accompanied Samuel out into the gloaming and fetched her sailor's bag and treasures—the sextant she had found in the cove that long-ago day, her earnings from storm-diving with Samuel, her charts and maps—from her sea-cave, stowing them in the *Dove*. As she gathered up a badly beaten tricorn and overcoat, rolling them tight and laying them on top. As she checked the belt at her waist, where the sea-knife, comb, and mirror hung.

What do you want to do?

The question was overwhelming in its simplicity. It was what she had wanted to be asked so many times, over the years. And of course, she knew the answer. She had had enough of walls, of the fanciful, yet stifling, society that bound her and her sisters—stays and panniers, tiny shoes—within its narrow confines. She had had enough, too, of Jean-Baptiste Léon's lies. (Never again would she call him "father.") She was ready to chart her own course; to chase the horizon she had craved for so long.

She had every right to go.

Even so, as she helped Samuel rig the lugger, the Manche and its veil of early stars glittering with promise, doubt shadowed her steps. She pushed it aside. She owed Saint-Malo nothing. She owed *Jean-Baptiste* nothing. The sooner she removed her presence from his life—and the fortune she had brought him all these years began to dissipate—the happier she would be.

And yet.

And yet.

Jean-Baptiste was not the only one who would be affected by her leaving Saint-Malo. Her mother and her sisters were in the city, too. The city which, due to the negligence and arrogance of its leaders, including the man who had stolen her, was unprepared for an invasion. True, the walls were high, the stone strong—Luce tried not to think of all the times Jean-Baptiste had asked her to walk around the ramparts with him, pretending to admire the ships coming in and out of the harbor, or the gulls, or the light on the island forts—and the garrison well-manned. Reinforcements would come. Her family would stay within the walls. And the walls, when the English began their bombardment from both land and sea, when they hoisted their ladders and climbed to the top of the ramparts with sword and pistol, would hold.

Wouldn't they?

"Ready?" Samuel pushed the vessel into the shallows. He lifted Luce onboard, catching at her knotted skirts before they could drag in the water. An old habit; it no longer mattered if Luce's clothes got wet, if anyone knew she had been on the water with him.

She was free.

She settled herself in her usual place near the bow, took up the jib sheet in readiness for departure. Margot's little black witch-boat was already drifting in the darkness beyond the cove's rocky embrace. When the *Dove* remained motionless, Luce looked astern and saw Samuel standing in the shallows.

"Before you decide on our bearing," he said quietly, "you need to know that the invasion may not go well for the people of Saint-Malo. The women, especially."

The sheet slipped from between Luce's fingers. What would happen to Gratienne, to Veronique and Charlotte, if the city fell? Would Jean-Baptiste protect them? Once, Luce would have trusted him with her own life, and each of theirs as well, but now . . .

Samuel shoved the lugger onto the water, hauling himself aboard.

"It's still your choice, Luce," he said, settling at the tiller. "Say west, and we'll bear west. Say north, and we'll bear north."

The dusking horizon was hers. The last of the light, the scent of salt on the wind. The *Dove* shivered and creaked, impatient.

"I want to be sure my mother and sisters are safe," Luce said, at last. "And then, I want to see the endless oceans. Find the magic left in the world. With you."

"West, then." He smiled. That new, careful smile that broke her heart. "Then north."

"Then north." Luce whistled, low and sweet, and wind filled the sails. "And after that, a path of stars."

27

Sharp Teeth

Saint-Malo hunkered in the dusk, preparing to defend itself.

The Sillon, the single roadway joining the city to the mainland, was all but cut off, with only a narrow, straggling line of people fleeing the countryside still able to make it across. Soldiers were working by torchlight to establish fouglasses, improvised mortars, on the quays. The ramparts were bright with flickering torches, moving hither and thither as soldiers and volunteers scurried to and fro, readying the cannon. Even the tide was on the rise, covering the sands as if it, too, knew that an enemy approached.

Luce and Samuel secured the *Dove* on the beach at Rocabey, then joined the line of terrified people filing into the city. Luce scanned the waters beyond Fort Royale as they went; Margot and her witch-boat were waiting for them there. The shore-woman had refused to sail anywhere near the city. "Saint-Malo *will* burn," she had said quietly to Luce, before they left her. "The sea, the sky, the stone . . . all will be flame and ruin. I have seen it." She had leaned in, lowering her voice, so that Luce, sitting alongside the witch-boat in the *Dove*, was forced to pull the little vessel closer. "Have a care with the storm diver. There is a new, and very old, darkness within him."

At Saint-Vincent Gate, the last to remain open, they were forced to wait while a company of mounted volunteers—some of whom Luce recognized from receptions and suppers at Le Bleu Sauvage—rode out to defend the Sillon. Armed with double-barreled rifles, pommel pistols, and swords, the men urged the fleeing villagers to *hurry, hurry.* When they reached the end of the Sillon, they would cut it off completely.

Inside the walls, the streets were barricaded with furniture, wagons and barrels. Fear hung, thick and soupy, in the air. Luce and Samuel hurried along the torch-lit cobbles, passing the empty fish market and Our Lady's Gate. A crowd had gathered there, praying to the marble statue of the Lady herself, nestled in her niche above the gate. Luce did not need to go near the cathedral, or any of the city's smaller chapels and churches, to know that it, too, would be filled with Malouins seeking such comfort.

"They think they are doing what is best," Samuel murmured, steadying Luce as she stumbled on the slick cobbles.

"Margot spoke the truth," she said bitterly. "They do not deserve the protection of the Fae."

They pushed on. Away from the flurry of movement near the fortress and the Sillon, the city was eerily quiet.

The Rue Saint-Philippe was in turmoil, the elegant street buried beneath hastily-constructed barricades. Luce rushed through the open gates to the Léon town house, through the little garden and up the curling stairs to the grand salon. The beautiful room was silent and dim, the candles unlit, the fireplaces gray and cold. She checked the rest of the rooms and found them all empty. The paintings, the candlesticks, and the best furniture had been removed, no doubt locked away in the cellars.

"Maman?" she called, in the vestibule. "Veronique?"

There was no answer.

Panicked, she ran out to the street, Samuel close behind. A group of soldiers barreled past, torches flickering in the damp. They reached the steep stairs leading to the ramparts above. A handful of armed Malouins trailed behind; Luce, pushing through a broken dining table and three of its erstwhile chairs, recognized one of them.

"Gabriel!"

He turned on the stairs, peered into the gloom. "Lucinde? Thank God. Charlotte was so worried when you disappeared at the wedding. We *all* were. . . ."

"Where are my sisters, Gabriel?"

"They're safe. They're up above, on the walls. Your father thought it best to stay out of the house in case of a barrage."

"The house is made of the best storm-stone in Saint-Malo," Samuel said, flicking Luce a sideways glance. "Surely he has faith in its protection?"

Gabriel frowned at him. Had they met under different circumstances, Luce was certain he would have demanded to know exactly who Samuel was. "Perhaps he thought it best not to test the stone's strength with his family—and my wife—inside."

Or perhaps he fears the sea and the storm protect him no longer. "Is my father with them, Gabriel?"

"No. He was at the castle helping with the artillery when last I saw—"

A chorus of shouts erupted from the battlements above. All three of them hurried up the stairs, where the walkways were crowded with people—soldiers and Malouin volunteers, but also women and children. Jean-Baptiste, it seemed, was not the only one who feared the an English bombardment. To the east, a line of torches had appeared on the slope above the harbor. Snatches of shouted commands and war drums drifted on the breeze.

"They're here," Luce said.

Samuel took her hand. "They're here."

"*Luce!*"

Charlotte pushed her way through the crowded walkway and seized Luce in a viselike embrace. "I've been so worried—you disappeared from the wedding! Simply *disappeared*! It was as though you'd fallen overboard!" She released Luce and stepped back, her keen gaze roving over Samuel.

"I don't believe we've met," she said, with a significant glance at Luce. "Monsieur . . . ?"

"Samuel Thorner, madame." He cleared his throat. "At your service."

Luce's heart clenched protectively. Despite everything, he was nervous. She tried to see Samuel as her sister might—hair unbound, battered greatcoat salvaged from Luce's sea-cave. Beneath its dim folds he wore a pistol, knife, and sword.

If Charlotte was shocked, she hid it well. "Thank you for taking care of my sister this night, Monsieur Thorner," she said politely.

"In truth, madame, it is she who has taken care of me."

A company of soldiers hurried past, and forcing them all to cluster together and make way.

"One day, sister, you will tell me *everything*," Charlotte hissed to Luce during the confusion.

"One day," Luce agreed.

"Maman and Vee are not far away," Charlotte said, louder. "It seems we're all to spend the night up here. Can you imagine?"

She led them to a sheltered section of the ramparts, where Gratienne and Veronique were settled together in a nest of blankets and cushions, their maidservants and laquais around them. Both women leapt to their feet when they saw Luce, and Gratienne pulled her into a fierce embrace. "Thank God. We were so worried."

"I am fine, Maman."

"Where have you been? And what are you *wearing*?"

Samuel, who had remained a discreet distance away, stifled a chuckle.

"The wedding was spoiled, Luce." Veronique sounded close to tears. "And it was so perfect, too. . . ."

"I know, Vee." Luce held her sister tight. "I'm so sorry."

Veronique sniffled. "Thank you. Morgan and I were supposed

to be leaving for Paris in the morning. And now *he* is at the castle defending the city, and *I* am sleeping on top of a wall! I am astonished, truly."

Luce, glancing at Samuel, saw him tense. He never mentioned Morgan by name—had not, since the night of the *Lucinde*—but she saw his gaze slide to the northeast, where the fortress lay. Something in his face, hard and intent, unsettled her deeply.

"Although," Gabriel said cautiously, "that's not *precisely* what Morgan is doing."

Veronique frowned.

"There are more than a hundred ships anchored at Saint-Servan, Trichet, and Val, including several of your father's," Gabriel explained. "The very ships that have been hounding the English Navy. To leave them defenseless would doom them to certain destruction. Morgan, his brothers, and several other captains have gone to Trichet. They plan to move the ships while the tide is high."

"The English could be there already," Luce said.

"It's a chance they're willing to take," Gabriel said. "To lose so many would be devastating. Besides, the *Lucinde*—I mean, the *Veronique*, is there. Morgan refused to abandon her."

"Of course he did," Charlotte said tartly.

"He knows the waters well enough to get safely out of the harbor," Veronique said, misreading her sister's tone. "Have no fear."

Luce, unwilling to discuss Morgan's navigational abilities, remained silent.

"You doubt him?" Veronique demanded, glaring at them all. "You think him foolish to risk himself for a ship?"

"No one suggested that," Gabriel soothed.

"And what of you?" Veronique rounded on him. "Why have *you* not gone to help him?" She was frightened, for herself and her new husband. Gabriel seemed to understand this, for his patience did not falter.

"I am afraid I would be of little use in such an endeavor."

"Gabriel is a scholar, Vee. Not a sailor," Charlotte snapped.

"Besides," Gabriel said to Veronique, raising a placating hand. "Morgan asked me to stay behind and protect you."

A lie. Luce saw it in his eyes, along with his pity. Veronique, however, softened. "He did?"

It was Charlotte's turn to frown. "Surely it will not come to that? Surely the English commander—"

"Lord Marlborough," Luce offered.

"Surely Lord Marlborough will try to negotiate?"

"He did," Gabriel said. "He sent a summons to the Marquis de la Châtre asking him to surrender the city or capitulate."

"And?"

"The Marquis replied that capitulation was in the mouth of his cannon."

There was a silence, punctuated by echoed shouts and footsteps on the ramparts, the beat of distant drums, and the nervous sigh of the sea below. The light from the nearest torches wavered eerily. Veronique had complained about sleeping on top of the walls, but Luce could not help but think there would be no resting this night, not while the threat of the English cannon lay so close.

She went to her mother's side. "I have something for you, Maman."

"Oh?" Gratienne's seemed small and frail in the half-dark.

Luce slipped something soft into her mother's hands. "It's your baptismal gown, Maman."

Gratienne frowned, looking from the gown to Luce's face and back again. "How did you get this?"

"It doesn't matter now." The domestiques had been in an uproar when Luce had returned to the malouinière for her mother's treasured gown. Word had arrived that the English had landed at Cancale and were marching across Clos-Poulet, burning and looting everything in their path. Taking the gown from her mother's armoire and telling the remaining domestiques to lock the gates and get themselves to safety were the last things Luce would ever do at Le Bleu Sauvage.

"I suppose it doesn't." Gratienne pulled her into a long embrace. "Thank you."

"It is I who should thank you, Maman."

"Indeed? For what?"

For taking a stranger's child into your home without question, even when the rumors swirled that your husband had been unfaithful to you. For caring for her, keeping her warm, fed, and clothed. For doing everything you could to ensure she might have a chance of a safe, strong marriage—the best and only gift you could have given her, in such a world as this. For loving her like your own.

"For everything."

"Is that Maman's baptismal gown?" Veronique asked, drawing near. She reached out, touched the fine fabric. "You saved it for her, Luce?"

Charlotte, too, was there. "She saved it for *us*," she said, slipping her arms around Luce and Gratienne. Veronique did the same, and the four women held each other closely, heads bowed.

The gut-wrenching boom of a cannon ripped through the night. Screams, panic fluttered over the city. A wave of movement on the walls as people surged to see what was happening.

Boom, went the cannon. *Boom, boom.*

"That's Fort Royale," Luce said. From where they stood, on the northern side of the city, it was impossible to see the fort, which had been designed to cover both the Sillon and the city's southern face. If the gunners there were firing, there was every chance the English had reached the Sillon and were attempting to enter the city.

"They must be at the Sillon." Gratienne had reached the same conclusion. Her voice quavered with fear.

"They will not get across the causeway, Maman," Luce assured her. "Fort Royale is well able to cover the Sillon and Saint-Vincent's Gate."

Another bone-jarring *boom*, then another. Luce gave Gratienne's shoulders a comforting squeeze, looking around for Samuel.

He was gone.

She moved through the crowds, searching for him, hope battling the dreadful certainty that he would not be found. The weapons he wore, the way he had not tried to convince Luce not to return to the city, despite the danger, the risk for them both. The way he had looked when Veronique and Gabriel had spoken of Morgan's whereabouts.

Have a care with the storm diver, Margot had warned. *There is a new, and very old, darkness within him.*

Luce knew that darkness well. It was within *her*, too, ever-present in her waking thoughts, her dreams. An ancient temptress calling her with a sweet siren-song. Her name?

Revenge.

Luce swam between the ships moored at Trichet, her petticoat clinging to her tail. Samuel was close by; she was certain of it. The temptation of finding Morgan, of making him pay for what he had done to Bones, to Samuel himself, even to Luce, had proven too much.

There were men aboard some of the ships. Malouin, by their voices. She could hear them, could feel the vibration of their boots upon the decks. They worked in stealthy darkness, readying the vessels for sail, a handful of ship's boats bobbing in the shadows.

The *Veronique* stood out against the rest, her rigging still thick with wedding flowers and ribbons, the ladders from the wedding celebrations still in place. Luce's heart skittered as she spied a lone ship's boat affixed to its side.

Was Samuel already aboard?

Muttering came to her over the water, punctuated by the

rhythmic slap of oars. She swam to the shadows at the *Veronique*'s stern as Morgan and a handful of men approached. They made the boat fast and began to climb, disappearing in the darkness above.

Luce removed the sea-silk from her chemise and tucked it into her belt, away from her bare skin. Her legs thus returned to her, she followed Morgan up the ladder, cutting the journey short—and avoiding meeting him directly—by hauling herself into an open gun-port. Once inside, she slithered gracelessly onto the gun deck, then lay gasping in her wet underthings, blood pounding. Had the men above heard her? She lay very still, listening to the low voices of the men as they readied the ship.

She was safe.

Luce blew a warm breeze into her cupped hands, quickly drying her chemise, stays, and petticoat. She tucked the now-dry silk between her breasts once more and got to her feet, ensuring her knife was within easy reach. Then, as quietly as she was able, she climbed the stairs to midships.

There were men nearby. She could hear them, their urgent whispers, the creak of rope and sail as they worked. *Was Samuel among them?*

The thud of a fist into flesh sounded near the mainmast, followed by a grunt of pain. Something heavy—an unconscious man, perhaps—hit the deck.

Yes. Yes, he was.

Luce crept to the mainmast, expecting to find Samuel there. The deck, however, was empty. The sound of further scuffling came to her from the direction of the quarterdeck, along with a whimper or two. She hurried toward it, flinched as a shout, quickly silenced, shattered the quiet.

The quarterdeck, too, was deserted. She opened the passageway to the officers' quarters, a shiver of foreboding rippling through her. She had no interest in being locked belowdecks again. She closed the door, edged back toward the relative safety of midships, and froze.

Samuel stood beside the mainmast. He held a pistol, its iron grip gleaming in the half-dark.

The barrel rested on Morgan de Châtelaine's chest.

"We don't have time for this, Thorner," Morgan said. As though to prove his point, an explosion thundered in the east. Luce ran to the rail, and saw that flames smeared the water between the Talards and the ship. The English soldiers had reached the island, which contained a rope works, dockyards, and a powder magazine. The latter, now on fire, was the undoubted source of the blast. "Those redcoat bastards are coming."

Samuel, apparently unmoved by this observation, merely shoved a length of rope at Morgan's chest. "Tie that to your feet."

Luce heard a muffled groan from the forecastle. Had Samuel truly disarmed every one of the men helping Morgan move the ship?

"Samuel," she said uneasily. "What are you doing?"

He ignored her. Lost completely to the siren song of revenge. Morgan, however, gaped. "*Lucinde?* What the hell are you—"

"Tie it to your feet," Samuel repeated. There was a sharp click as he cocked the pistol. "Now."

"Are you mad?" Morgan was trying, and failing, to contain his irritation. "They'll burn the ship beneath us!" He turned to Luce. "For God's sake, Luce. *Tell* him."

"Tie the fucking rope to your feet," Samuel said. Gone was the warmth, the light, the smile. *There is a new, and very old, darkness within him.*

Luce's gaze traced the length of the rope.

It was fixed to the block at the end of the yardarm.

"Oh, Samuel, no," she said, in dismay.

"Listen to her, Samuel." Morgan had come to the same realization as Luce. Concern had replaced annoyance; his face, in the fireglow from the Talards, was grave.

"You don't really want to do this," Luce said gently to Samuel.

"Oh, but I do, Luce. My only regret is that I don't have the men to help me run him over that lovely keel once or twice first." He jerked the pistol toward the rope. "*Tie it to your feet.*"

Morgan seemed to realize there was no way out. He lowered himself slowly to the deck, then tied the rope around his ankles.

"Tighter," Samuel ordered. He crouched and checked the rope, the pistol never leaving Morgan's chest, then hauled his captive, hissing in protest, to his feet.

"Time to dangle," he announced, and punched Morgan hard in the jaw. Morgan's head rocked back. One, two, three steps, and Samuel had dragged him, limp and whimpering, to the rail. He heaved Morgan over without hesitation.

Luce, watching it all happen as slowly as a dream, heard not the splash of Morgan's body hitting the water, his strangled cry, but the sound of Veronique's sobs. Felt not Samuel's rage, but his regret when he woke from the fever of grief and rage that consumed him, and realized what he had done.

A step or two of her own, a moment of freefall, and she was in the sea.

She felt Morgan before she saw him, his panicked struggles prickling against her skin. She swam toward the sensation, and Morgan appeared in the darkness, growing sharper as her sea-eyes adjusted. Stunned by Samuel's blow, he was barely struggling, his bound feet twitching uselessly as he sank.

Luce caught the rope. Drew her blade, its wicked beauty reflecting fragments of her face, her drifting hair. Perhaps . . . perhaps Samuel had been right. Perhaps this *was* what Morgan deserved. Better than he deserved, really, after all that he had done.

A new, and very old, darkness was waking within Luce. An instinct born of hunger and desire that had nothing to do with her tail. A song as old as the sea, promising rapture and ruin. She wound her long, webbed fingers into Morgan's overcoat, bunching it against his chest. He opened his eyes, beheld her, recognition, and then terror, bubbling out of him. Luce smiled.

Sharp teeth.

She had saved him once, when the sea would have sucked the flesh from his very bones. Had plunged into the Manche and dragged him free of its clutches, pulling him toward the light. All that she had been, all that she was, had upended, as though she glimpsed herself through a mirror, darkly.

Luce dived. Tail arching, fins flowing, thoughts of death filling her heart, she plunged Morgan into shadow and bore him down.

Down, down.

Down.

28

A Light in the Storm

"*Luce!*"

Her name was light across storm-dark water. Breaking the surface, Luce swam toward the sound. Samuel had abandoned the *Veronique* and stood in one of the ship's boats, a lantern held high in one hand.

"Are you all right?"

"Yes." She angled her body slightly, the better to drag Morgan, limp and heavy, along with her.

"Is he—"

"He's alive."

Barely. The sea had yearned for him, had begged and wept. It must, after all, have its number. And for a long, terrible moment, Luce had been more than happy to indulge it. Had it not been for Veronique, she might have.

Hoofbeats and voices sounded on the beach. Torches, their flames leaping across the sand, revealing, through the ribs of the half-finished ships, the crimson coats of English soldiers.

A hiss of startled breath in Luce's ear. She turned, saw Morgan's eyes fixed on her—on the impossible, glittering length of her—in wonder.

"I knew it," he muttered. "I knew it when your slipper turned to water in my hands."

He wound his fingers through her hair as though he would steal one last, treacherous kiss.

In the dark water below, something brushed against the flukes of Luce's tail. She peered down. There were faces in the water, bloated and unseeing, rotting hands grasping. She yelped in panic as more and more men appeared in the darkness, reaching up from the deep.

"Luce!" Samuel had seen them, too. "Luce, get away from him!"

"Don't leave me!" Morgan was choking with terror. He clawed at Luce like a drowning man. Shoved her under, into those hideous, bloated faces, and used her to launch himself toward the *Veronique, clutching desperately at her side.*

The drowned men barely glanced at Luce. As one, they drifted after Morgan.

On the beach, flames flickered and danced, growing and spreading. The soldiers were torching the ships in their stocks, the ropeworks and timber mill. Others were upending a row of beached fishing boats and carrying them to the water.

Something flared against the *Veronique*'s sails. Flame kissed canvas.

Morgan, still struggling to save himself, gazed up in horror as fire danced across the ship, licking along the yards, teasing at the rigging.

Fire above, and darkness below.

The *Dauphin*'s crew reached Morgan, closing their rotting hands around his ankles, his waist, oblivious to his cries, to the flames spreading across the *Veronique*'s decks. He kicked and punched at them, screamed and splashed and fought, but it was no use. The strength of the dead was with them.

"Stay back, Luce," Samuel warned. "The debt must be paid; you cannot stop it now." She felt the truth of his words. Understood that, even had she wanted to, there would be no interfering with the sea's ancient reckoning.

Down they pulled him, down and down, until Morgan's terrified eyes and white face disappeared beneath the surface; until he stilled beneath their hands, graceful in his drowning, and the darkness swallowed him whole.

Impossible not to be shaken after witnessing such a loss, even when the person being lost was Morgan de Châtelaine. Luce wanted nothing more than to be out of that dark water, and as quickly as possible. With one powerful push of her tail she swooped beneath the surface, angling rapidly toward the ship's boat. She emerged at its side with a gasp, reached up. And there, reaching down for her, as he always did, as he always would, was Samuel. He hauled Luce out of the water and into the belly of the boat. Drew her against him, heedless of water and cold and fins, and held her close.

"I'm sorry," he whispered. "So sorry."

A wind blew across the harbor, snatching at the flames from the *Veronique* and tossing them playfully into the rigging of the next ship. The English soldiers, too, were busy—rowing merrily between the ships, hurling flaming bundles onto the open decks and severing the moorings. There were cries of dismay from the Malouin volunteers aboard the *Veronique* and her sisters, splashes as they leapt overboard to escape the growing flames. The pride of Saint-Malo, its beautiful corsairs—with seven or eight of Jean-Baptiste's finest among them—was in danger of becoming a fleet of fire ships. Nothing, not even the storm-stone ballast many of them would carry in their dim, damp bellies, could stop it.

Except . . .

Samuel brushed the comb at Luce's belt with his fingertips. "Will you do it?"

She knew what he was asking. With a whisper, a word or two, she could stop the wind, saving every one of those ships, including the *Fleur de Mer,* the *Lionne,* and the *Thétis.* She could save, too, any valuable cargo that remained unloaded in their holds, ready to spill more wealth and power into the pockets of the gentlemen of Saint-Malo. And, even more precious, their storm-stone ballast.

Every piece of it taken from the Fae, from the land itself, without permission or payment.

Every piece of it stolen.

"No," Luce said.

Too much has been taken.

She whistled a few notes, soft and enticing, and the breeze picked up the little boat, pushing it smoothly back toward the city. Together, they watched the flames spread through the ships. On the shore, the houses, the stores, and the dockyards were ablaze.

Luce flinched as the cannons of Saint-Malo roared.

"They're trying for the city again," Samuel said, getting to his feet. Luce, removing the sea-silk from her chemise, did the same. The Sillon was crawling with soldiers, their crimson coats blistering bright amid hundreds of torches. Shouts and commands rolled over the water. The soldiers were working hard, digging into the earth, unhitching cannon from stamping horses and maneuvering them into position. More cannon fire, a dull boom as the guns at Fort Royale made their displeasure at this turn of events known. There was an explosion of dirt and bodies, smoke and stone. The high-pitched screams of a wounded man. The remaining soldiers, however, continued staunchly in their task, angling their own guns toward the city walls between strike after strike from the fort. Held between them in the seething, smoky mist, Luce glimpsed several enormous siege ladders.

Samuel was looking between the Sillon and the burning ships in horror. "They're not going to stop, Luce."

"Yes," she replied calmly. "They are."

It is a matter of breath, the raising of a storm. Breath and water, intention and will.

It begins slowly. A knife swirled in the shallows. A whisper.

Awaken.

What is this? the sea, jolted from its rhythm, replies. It had plans. Purpose. It is loyal only to the moon, its true and ancient mistress. *You are not my mistress.*

You must persist.

Yes, I am.

Next comes air. A gentle breath, a whisper, to alter its course. To summon.

It likes its freedom, the wind. Always has. It will cling to its wide skies. It wants no mistress, needs no mistress.

Yes, you say. *You do.*

Whistled notes, a sweet-worded song; your choice. The music brings forth a hush, a calm. The stars cease their glimmering to listen.

The weavings of the world tangle with your breath.

Waves are rising now, summoned by the turning, turning of a sea-knife through still waters.

Like this? The sea, finding its new rhythm, asks. It is eager to please, now, shuddering and rolling.

Yes.

The wind is singing, too, bellowing the notes you feed it, whipping up the waves. Spray and salt, roar and heave.

Heed me now.

Unbound hair and a silver comb. Ripples and snarls, weavings and tangles.

The sea's might lies in a clenched fist.

Awaken.

That is what you hold to, as the skies blacken and the clouds roil. As day becomes night and the ocean shows its teeth.

Breath and water. Intention and will.

Light. Dark. Beauty. Violence.

And then the rain will come.

When the sea was good and riled, the rain sheeting across the rooftops and the lonely spire of the cathedral, Luce summoned a wave. It bore her obediently upward, pushing her over the city wall before waiting, as polite as any dance partner, for her to step smoothly onto the ramparts. Only then did it shatter and plunge back into the churning maelstrom below. Luce had selected a particularly lonely section of the wall to attempt this feat, one that faced neither the Sillon nor the harbor, and—hidden by the wind, the rain, and the dubious pair of breeches, shirt, and overcoat she had stolen from the ship's boat—managed to remain unseen.

Dimly disappointed by this fact—Margot and Samuel would surely never believe her—she hurried along the walls to join the crowds of sodden townsfolk gathered on the eastern walls. It seemed the entire population of Saint-Malo was there, hunched against the rain, dripping with apprehension as they watched the roiling sea, the burning ships, and the horror unfolding on the Sillon.

It took but a moment for Luce to understand why. Why they were choosing to remain on the walls—exposing their elderly folk and children to the weather—while the streets beneath them were empty, the houses shuttered and dim.

The English soldiers would soon be close enough to bombard the city and scale the walls.

The wind and rain Luce had summoned—which had just moments ago seemed so powerful, so relentless—had not been enough to deter Lord Marlborough. As the smoke cleared between rounds of deafening cannon fire from the fort and Saint-Malo both, Luce could see the redcoats plainly. Struggling in the mud, slipping in the rain, roaring at each other as they dug in? Yes. Bleeding and screaming, falling as a ball cut through their midst? Undoubtedly. But stopping? Retreating?

No.

Saint-Malo will burn, Margot had said. *The sea, the sky, the stone . . . all will be flame and ruin. I have seen it.*

Luce longed for the groac'h's presence now. She was, Luce hoped, still waiting on the seaward side of Fort Royale. Samuel, for his part, had stowed the stolen boat and gone to join the Malouin volunteers preparing to defend the gates. "You cannot expect me to hide away like a shell-less crab while you do all the work," he had told her, before leaving her on the beach.

He was right. She knew it. Even so, Luce's chest tightened at the thought of him standing alongside Saint-Malo's people—*her* people—as they fought to defend the city. She touched the wall before her, taking comfort in its low, familiar hum, the gentle prickling in her skin. Thanks to her presence, the city's supply of storm-stone was strong.

But was it strong enough?

As though in answer, the squall sweeping the battlements began to ease. *No, no.* Luce willed the last of her dwindling strength, her faeness, into the sky, the water. It was no use. The storm was fading. All her strength, all her need, had not been enough.

"O God," someone muttered, into the stillness. "You have willed that Our Lady should shine forth as the Star of the Sea and protectress for us who are tossed about on the stormy waves. . . ."

A second voice, further along the wall. "Our Lady, Star of the Sea, you have provided a light in the storm. . . ."

Then a third: "Grant that we may set a course through these times to reach our safe haven with you. . . ."

Another prayer, and still another. The boom of the cannon, the roar of the flames on the vessels on the harbor, could not drown them out.

". . . through her help and direction, we may be safe from dangers of soul and body . . ."

". . . protectress for us who are tossed about on the stormy waves . . ."

Down on the Sillon, red-coated soldiers were moving tentatively onto the causeway. Stretched between them were several ladders.

More voices rose, a soft litany of prayer beneath the misting rain.

". . . we turn to you for protection."

"... shine forth as the Star of the Sea ..."

"... save us from every danger ..."

Luce glimpsed her mother and sisters among the many faces. They were pale and bedraggled, clinging together. And then, beside them, she saw Jean-Baptiste. He was watching her, not the Sillon. As though it were only the two of them on the crowded battlements, and Luce, not the encroaching soldiers, was his greatest threat. Luce was taken with the sudden urge to leave the city. To step into the sea's embrace and give of herself no more. It was only the presence of her sisters and her mother, the other innocent people around her, that stopped her.

"... a light in the storm ..."

"... Star of the Sea ..."

"Save us, or we perish. ..."

Raising the weather had taken everything Luce had; all of her skill, all of her power, and it still wasn't enough. Margot had once said that she could control a fleet, but it would take time and practice to master such magic. Luce looked helplessly again at the vessels blazing on the harbor, the thick smoke lathering the Sillon, and the men creeping, ever so surely, toward the city gates, and wished fervently for more of both. As though it felt her presence, the storm-stone prickled softly against her fingertips. Distant thunder; threat and promise.

"... protectress ..."

"... light in the storm ..."

"... shine forth ..."

And there on the crowded ramparts, the rain-soaked stone gleaming like the fiery night around her, she knew what to do.

29

A Path of Stars

Luce had never before climbed to the top of the cathedral's tower. The stairs had taunted her so often, over the years. Now, they were all that stood between saving the city, and watching it fall.

She had run from the ramparts to Saint-Vincent's, and pain was already her loyal companion as she slid inside the darkened church, silent but for a handful of pious souls. Despite the oily blackness of the night, the scent of gun smoke and terror on the air, they were deep in prayer, heads bowed as the windows above rippled with hell-light from the burning fleet. No one looked up as Luce limped across the nave and into the tower. No one stopped her as she began to climb.

Every step was a new devastation. An exquisite, bone-slicing pain that caused her to bite her lip and cling to the rounded wall. Every stone beneath her fingertips mocked her cruelly. Every turn urged her to go back, go back. Worry for Samuel at the gates, for her family on the walls, drove her on. Yes, the storm-stone and the guns at Fort Royale and along the city walls would deter the English soldiers, but for how long? And how many redcoats would it take to scale the walls and open the gates for their countrymen to stream inside? A dozen?

Less?

At last, *at last*, she reached the top of the tower and the rain-slicked coldness of the night. All around her, Saint-Malo's rooftops glinted with silver and gold, storm and fire.

Was she too late? Had the soldiers broken through? She tottered along the landing, leaning heavily on the stone railing surrounding the bell tower, and peered out to the east. The Sillon looked just as it had when she left the walls, a chaos of smoke and cannon fire, masses of crimson-clad soldiers working frantically. To the south, an armada of hell-ships dominated the harbor, reddish waves reflecting the flames. She flinched as a burning ship imploded, its mast crashing into its own blazing hull, groaning like a wounded leviathan. All the while, countless ships' guns were firing, expelling their ammunition into the inferno.

"Christ," she whispered, forcing herself to look away. To focus on the storm clouds ruminating over the city, the rain silvering gently on her face.

Her prickle was overwhelming now; never before had she beheld so much storm-stone. It was above her, in the spire; around her, in the tower; below her, in the church itself and the surrounding houses. The fortress and its walls, the ramparts, bastions and towers. All ripe with stolen power.

Too much has been taken. Something must be given back.

"Shine forth," Luce whispered. Setting her palms on the stone railing before her, she drew a breath from the depths of her very soul. Power crackled through her in an eager rush, as though it *wanted* to be freed from the stone. It soaked into her hands, her arms, her body. She leaned into the wind, urging it to rise once more.

Heed me now.

There was no hesitation, no question, this time. The wind responded to her song at once, whipping itself against the tower, the sea, her hair. The water far below heaved and gasped.

Breath and water. Intention and will.

Sing to us.

Luce caught up her hair. Pressed and crumpled the tangled lengths in her fist. Below, the water mirrored each knot and snarl, seething against the quays and walls.

And still the magic surged into her from the stone, until there was no telling where the storm-stone ended and Luce began—

"Lucinde."

She turned her head, distracted, and saw Jean-Baptiste framed by the murky sky. He looked exhausted, his clothes wet and dirty, his fingernails, clutching a musket, black with powder.

"Don't do this," he said softly. "Please, mon trésor."

Rage of a different kind settled over Luce. She drew her hands from the stone, from her hair. Around her, the rising storm skipped a beat, waiting for her to resume her song. *Be patient,* she told it silently. *There are things to be said.*

"When I was a child," she began, turning to face him fully, "and you were finished with your work, I would go to your study. The sun would be sinking over the western fields, the light like honey. It was always my favorite time of day."

The memory stood in harsh contrast to the glowering sky, the malignant clouds.

"'Mon trésor,' you would say," she continued. "'Come, come! Tell me of your day. Any adventures?' I would clamber onto your lap and I would tell you all that I had done, and seen: the house and the kitchens, the orchards and the attics, the stables and the gardens; all that made up my small world."

"It was always my favorite time of day, too." Jean-Baptiste glanced worriedly at the burning harbor, the roiling sea, the churning sky, as though he wondered how, and when, Luce's world had grown so very large and powerful.

"As I grew," Luce said, "I dared to go further. One day, I walked out the open gates and through the woods to the cove. The next, I went even further. And again, and again, until I glimpsed the abbey of Mont Saint-Michel in the dim blue distance, and realized that the coast, and the sea, was much larger than I had believed them to be."

"Everything I did, I did to protect you," Jean-Baptiste insisted. "You cannot blame me for trying to keep you safe!"

"You frowned when I told you what I had done," Luce said, ignoring him. "'But that is too far, mon petit oiseau,' you said. 'What if something had happened to you? What would I do without my treasure?'"

She laughed brokenly. A cold wind, wracked with bitterness, swirled about the bell tower.

"The gates were always locked, after that. Not that it mattered; I did not dare to leave the malouinière's walls for a long time. The look on your face—the fear and worry—squeezed my heart. I loved you above all others." Her voice cracked at the betrayal, at the memory of love and safety, lost.

Jean-Baptiste raised a hand as though he would interrupt her, explain himself. Luce lifted a hand of her own, and the storm clouds rumbled, silencing him.

"But love did not stop me regretting my promise to you." Luce forced herself to go on, to push through the shattering of her heart. "The taller I grew, the smaller the house and kitchen, the orchards and attics became, until I had no choice but to break it. By then, of course, you had learned how to distract me. Books and tutors. Music and maps. Dreams of horizons you would never allow me to reach."

He moved toward her. "Perhaps, one day, we might have sailed together, mon trésor—"

"*Don't call me that!*"

The wind kicked up, whipping his peppery hair, shoving him roughly against the stone railing. He caught himself, turned to her, white with fear.

"How many lies would you have told me? What reasons, what excuses would you have found to keep me within your walls? Would you have blamed Maman? Would you have blamed my *feet*?"

He sighed heavily. "I am so sorry, mon trésor."

"For what? For locking me away? For destroying my feet? For

pretending you wanted me to go to the ball? You gave me that blue gown, and then you threw it into the sea!"

The wind was rising of its own accord now. Below, in the harbor, the Manche sucked threateningly at the city walls.

"Or perhaps you are sorry for giving the *Luci*—the fucking *Veronique*—to Morgan de Châtelaine. How convenient that must have been for you. 'There will be other ships, mon trésor,'" she mimicked. "'We have years and years ahead of us to build, to plan . . .' You never had any intention of letting me go. You needed me, needed my faeness to maintain your storm-stone."

The wind howled greedily around the cathedral spire, eager to have its way. Jean-Baptiste looked at the roiling clouds fearfully.

"No, Lucinde." He made to step closer, caught himself. "I loved you."

"You loved what I brought you," Luce said. "Good weather. Good fortune. The sea's blessing. '*Give your papa a kiss, mon trésor.*'" The words snarled out of her, dark with malice. Above, the storm murmured its approval. Rain splattered.

"Of course I loved those things," he said. "But I loved you more!"

"Love, is it? Is that why you killed my mother and gave parts of her to your friends?"

A webbed hand floating in a tiny sea of fear and fascination.

Jean-Baptiste's face was the color of ice. "I—I have always regretted that," he said. "I was young, and foolish."

"You took *everything* from me. Every promise you made, every word you said was a lie. The sea-silk would have stayed hidden forever if I had not found it. You would have kept me with you, trapped, for the rest of my life."

"No!"

"*Yes!*"

Boom.

Down in the harbor, another burning mast fell, the ship beneath it erupting into flames.

"That looked like the *Fleur de Mer,*" Luce said coldly. "I rather hope it was."

Jean-Baptiste approached her again, palms raised. "What you are saying is true, Lucinde. I *did* do all those things. But I have suffered every day for it. Every time I *look* at you. Do you think I don't know what I took from you? Do you think I don't know that I'm a monster?" He shrugged, helpless. "But . . . I do love you, mon—Lucinde. More than anything. I swear it on my blood. My bones. My very soul."

Despite everything, Luce hesitated. The man before her *was* a monster. He had murdered her mother. Kept Luce from the sea. Benefited from her presence, year after year. Told her a thousand little lies. But she knew—bones, blood, soul—that he had spoken a thousand little truths, too. He believed, truly believed, that he loved her.

She thought of what Mother Aggie had said of her great-grandmother, the seamaid who had given up the sea for a fisherman. Like Luce, her very presence in his life had been a blessing. *I like to think my great-grandfather loved her enough that he would have let her go, had she wished it. But I cannot say. Not for certain. He was a man, and, like any man, he would have been loath to let something so precious go.*

"That's where you're wrong," Luce told Jean-Baptiste. "You never loved me. Not truly."

He stared at her, aghast. "How can you say that?"

"Because if you had, you would have set me free."

There were tears on his face. Sorrow and regret, mingling with the remnants of the rain. The storm howled its pleasure.

"In any case, it no longer matters," Luce said. "I loved you once, Jean-Baptiste Léon. Above all others. But no more."

He brushed at his cheeks, as old and broken as Luce had ever seen him. Then anger glimmered, mutinous as the clouds swirling over the cathedral.

"Hate me, then," he said. "I deserve it. But whatever you are doing here, to the weather, and the stone—don't. You will doom the city. It will—*we* will—never recover. Our protection, our strength, will be gone."

Luce smiled bitterly. *Of course.* It did not matter to him that the Duke of Marlborough's men were at this very moment crossing the Sillon with ladders to scale the walls. That there was only so long Saint-Malo and Fort Royale's guns could keep them from breaking through. That the lives of his wife and daughters, of everyone in the city, were in danger. Why would it? Wasn't the entire family, the entire household, all of Bretagne—indeed, the entire *world*—arranged for his arrogance and pleasure?

"It was never *your* strength," she said. "You stole it, as you steal everything."

"But—surely you don't mean to help the English? To leave the city vulnerable?"

"Everything I do, I do to save Saint-Malo and its people," Luce told him. "The enemy shall not take the city this night; I will see to it. But you should know that Saint-Malo will burn. Not tonight. Maybe not in a hundred years. But it *will* burn. Fire will rain upon it from the sea and the sky. And there will be no stormstone, no Fae, left to protect it. Everything you have done, everything you have built, will be ashes."

Jean-Baptiste's eyes widened as he looked upon the truth of her—the wildness of the creature he had tried so hard to keep contained. Beauty and violence. Terror and rage. And something else, too. A glimmer of light on dark water.

"Too much has been taken," Luce said above the monstrous cry of the wind. The sea-knife shone in her hand. "Something must be given back." Before Jean-Baptiste could stop her, she plunged the blade into the stone of the bell tower.

A peal of thunder cracked over Saint-Malo, louder than any cannon, any burning ship.

Magic rippled over the surface of the world.

Lightning razed the sky.

Weather more terrible had never been seen in Saint-Malo. The rain fell with such force, and the storm was so violent—the noise of the thunder and the sea, the burning vessels in the harbor, the waves ablaze with immense red flames—that the English soldiers were forced to return to their ships, their siege ladders washed away, their hopes of conquest with them. When the cathedral bells heaved into life, pealing the city's victory, Luce released her hold on the weather and limped down the tower steps, barely glancing at the old lion slumped, alone and mourning, before the altar. She stepped out of the church into the dawn, and Samuel's arms.

The groac'h, as promised, had waited for them at Fort Royale. The storm was in its death-throes, the last of the waves lashing against the fort on its rocky little island, whipping across the Manche, but the witch-boat, like the *Dove*, remained unmolested. They sailed north together, watching the coast of Bretagne growing ever more distant, and Luce's mother and sisters with it. Luce thought of Charlotte, and whether her sister had found the letter Luce had slipped into her pocket during the confusion on the ramparts.

One day, you will tell me everything.

Luce had written it in haste, on paper stained with salt: the tale of a child brutally stolen from her parents. Of a seamaid raised among earthly sisters. Of a shipwreck, and tears in the sea, and a pair of sea-glass slippers. Of a lion, a wolf, and a smuggler. And Charlotte, who was never the favourite, would be first to read the letter. First to know the truth. That Luce loved her, as she loved Gratienne and Veronique. And that perhaps, one day, she would see them all again.

The tattered clouds soon cleared. The Manche, a great mirror, shone every shade of gold and mauve. Luce leaned over the *Dove*'s side, traced her fingers through the spray.

"North," Samuel said, at the tiller.

She smiled at him over her shoulder. "And after that, the stars."

He was bone-pale, his eyed smudged with sleeplessness, but he managed a grin.

"It's been quite the night." Luce straightened wearily, grasping the mast for balance. "You—we—should rest."

"Rest?" He smiled faintly. "We're sailing to England, in case you hadn't noticed."

"Believe me, I noticed." She drew the *Dove*'s store of blankets out from beneath a bench, arranged them on the boards.

"Luce?" Samuel was somewhere between confusion and concern. "You cannot lie down in the middle of the Manche. I may need you."

"I can," she told him, yawning. "And so can you."

"But—"

"She's a seamaid," Margot called, between the boats. "And you are in safe hands. Sleep, storm diver."

Luce was cocooned in the blankets, drifting on the edge of wakefulness when she felt Samuel lay himself reluctantly beside her.

"If anything happens to my boat . . ."

"Sleep, storm diver," she murmured, with a smile. He scooped her against him, his grumbles subsiding as he, too, drifted into slumber.

Moments later, it seemed, the *Dove*'s keel was scraping rhythmically against a smooth, pebbly shore. Luce lurched into wakefulness, pushed the blankets away. Samuel was gone, the *Dove*'s anchor line stretched tight. High above, a gentle evening sky.

"Samuel?" She peered over the side and beheld a familiar cove. Ringed by gentle white cliffs, the grey-pebbled beach was a perfect circle, the water a clear blue-green even in the fading light. Nearby, drawn up on the beach like the *Dove*, was Margot's witch-boat.

Dorset, then. They had sailed, without incident, throughout the day. Grinning, Luce clambered from the boat. Samuel and the groac'h were further along the shore, and she crunched toward them, the pebbles small and deliciously smooth against her bare feet. She paused to pick up a handful: gray and caramel-brown, white and burnt-cream. So different to the sands of Saint-Malo. At the sight of those pebbles in her palm, the beautiful cove and the golden air, her chest tightened.

She had done it.

She was free.

There was no containing the delight; it was pure, wild, joyous. She tossed the stones into the evening-colored water, careless as a child, and watched them ripple and sink.

Samuel and Margot's heads snapped toward her.

They had been talking, Luce realized, taking them in properly for the first time. Samuel was sitting on the beach, head low, knees bent, bent arms resting wearily upon them. Margot was standing over him, hands open at her sides. As though she were trying her very best to explain something to him, and he was trying *his* very best not to listen.

"Is everything well?" Luce hurried toward them. Perhaps there was a problem with the boat? Or Samuel's family? "Samuel? Is everything—"

"Everything's fine, Luce." Samuel glanced up at her, then quickly away.

Luce froze. Were there tears in his eyes?

Margot, too, seemed troubled. She was watching Samuel worriedly. When it was clear he would not meet her eye, however, she gave a heavy sigh and walked back to the boats, patting Luce's arm as she passed. There was something strange about the gesture, something almost . . . apologetic. Luce watched her go, unease anchoring itself deep in her belly.

"What is it, Samuel? What's wrong?"

He got to his feet as though the effort cost him dearly.

"I have just been speaking with Margot," he said.

A scraping in the shallows. Luce turned to see the witch-boat leaving the shore, its sails slowly filling with an enchanted breeze. Even at this distance, Luce could see that the tide-woman was watching them closely.

She swallowed, nervous. "Samuel?"

"I cannot go with you, Luce."

The shock of it was the winter sea in her face, the heavy surge of a sudden wave before she'd taken breath.

"What?" Luce stared up at him, at the sorrow in his eyes, and felt the weight of oceans. "What are you saying?" Flailing, floundering, desperate for air. "Do you—do you not *want* to come with me?"

"Of *course* I do." He reached for her hands. That lone swallow, sorrowful in the dying light.

"Then why—"

"Because Margot just told me it is impossible."

He was so calm. Anger clawed at sorrow, taking its place. "But why would she do that? Why would she ask us to go with her, only to change her mind?"

"She never asked me," Samuel said. "I was there that night, it was true. But she was speaking to *you*, Luce. Not me. Never to me."

"No." Luce shook her head, unwilling to believe it. "No." Margot liked Samuel. Had healed him after the *Lucinde*. She trusted him.

"You remember what she said to you, don't you? 'There are still places of beauty and wonder left in the world. Places that men in their death-ships have not despoiled. A fair breeze and a path of stars is all that is required to find them.'"

"Men in their death-ships," Luce echoed, stricken.

"Men in their death-ships."

Beyond the pale, curving arms of the cove, the sun was hastening into the west, staining the water.

"But—the *Dove* is a fishing boat," Luce said. "Not a ship. And you don't mean anyone harm."

"That's what I said to Margot. She agreed, and yet it makes no difference. I'm not like you, Luce. I'm not Fae."

Sorrow took Luce unto itself, binding her tight. She sank onto the pebbles, legs useless, limbs heavy, heart broken.

"Then I cannot go either," she said. "I cannot go without you."

"Yes, you can." He was on his knees beside her, gathering her close. "You can. And you will."

"No—"

"Yes."

"No!" A hundred memories flooded Luce's mind. Samuel hauling her on board the *Dove*; passing her a blanket for her aching feet; waiting for her so often in the dawn. Teaching her to read the wind and water. Listening to her every word, nursing her through her hurts, making her laugh. A light in the darkness, endlessly patient. She thought of how his brothers had teased him for spending so much time in Saint-Malo. He had forsaken his home, his family, to be close to Luce. When she had turned into a seamaid right in front of him, he had not turned from her, he had not reviled or feared her. He had wrapped her in his overcoat, held her, promised her that they would find answers. Together.

"It's all right," he said, rocking her. "It's all right."

She thought of the smuggler's cave, the way her body had clung to his, curving itself about him. How he had caught her hard against him when it was over, held her so tight she was sure he would never let her go.

"I can't leave you," she whispered through her tears.

"Yes, you can. You *must*, Luce." He grasped her chin, tilted her face up to his. "Your father—your real father—is out there somewhere. Perhaps other family, too. You need to find them. And that . . ." He gestured to the witch-boat, the shining water beyond. "*That* is everything you wanted. You must take it, Luce. You must. If you stay here with me, we might be happy for a time.

But part of you would always wonder what might have been. And one day, perhaps sooner than you think, you'd resent me for making you give it up."

"No, I wouldn't—"

"Yes, you would. You remember what Mother Aggie told us about the sea-wife, don't you?"

A sea-wife is caught always between two shores—one in the sun, one in the deep—and the desire for both is ever present.

"Aggie said she liked to think her great-grandfather loved his wife enough to let her return to the sea, had she wished it." Tears spilled down Samuel's cheeks. "I love you enough, Luce."

Delight it is. And perhaps my doom, as well.

The Manche was whispering of sorrow and sea-wives. It slid along the shore, lapped at Luce's bare toes. Knowing, as Luce knew, what must be done.

Be brave.

Be free.

"I'll wait for you." Samuel kissed her, soft. Wiped away his tears. "Go, Luce."

She listened to his fading footsteps. Told herself, again and again, that she would rise and follow him. And yet, when she *did* at last rise, it was to shrug out of her stolen coat and shirt, her breeches. The water was calm, flecked with the first of the stars.

One, two, three steps and she was shin deep. Four, five, six and the cold glimmer of scales dragged at her thighs. Water surged around her, melding with her tears. She opened her arms and scooped them back, gliding toward the horizon, where a little black boat was cutting a path to the stars.

Behind her, on the empty sand, a trail of footprints ending at the water's edge. A puddle of clothing, dark with salt and time. And sea foam, as delicate as lace on a blue, blue gown.

But perhaps it would always wonder what might have been. And [illegible] perhaps sweeter than you think, you'd [illegible] to the [illegible] that life you have [illegible].

"I don't want to—"

"Yes you would. You remember what Mother Aggie told us about the sea [illegible]."

[illegible] one in the deep [illegible].

Aggie had she liked to think [illegible] rather loved the sea [illegible] though [illegible] return to the sea [illegible] had she [illegible] smiled down [illegible]. *I love you enough* [illegible].

Delighted [illegible].

The [illegible] along the shore [illegible] knowing [illegible] knew what must be done.

Be brave.

Be free.

"I'll wait for you, Samuel," [illegible] "Go on, Pearl."

She listened to his fading footsteps, told herself again and again she wouldn't [illegible] follow him. And yet when she did at last rise it was to slip out of [illegible] coat and [illegible] the water was [illegible] with the first of the [illegible].

One, two, three steps and the [illegible]. Four, five, six [illegible] glimmer of scales [illegible] under [illegible]. Water [illegible] around her [illegible] she opened her arms and [illegible] toward the horizon [illegible] the black [illegible].

Behind her, on the empty sand [illegible] with [illegible].

At [illegible] as dark as [illegible].

Epilogue

Time can never truly be contained. We try, of course. With ships' watches and glasses filled with sand; with clocks and church bells. We name the holy days, the months, the seasons; mark the turning of the year. We believe that, by naming time, we have captured it, forcing it to bow to us.

In truth, it is *we* that bow to *it*.

Even the tide will conspire, to a degree; offering an illusion of order, of timeliness. Ebb tide. Flow tide. Dead tide. And yet it, too, will inevitably forsake us, unwilling to be checked. Time weaves through the tides, and beyond them. Past the turnings of the moon, its silvery, changeable face. Light to dark, and back again. Past the falling leaves, the misty frosts, the warming sun.

An endless net, is time. Catching nothing.

He marked its passage the only way he could. Day, by day, by day. Each morning he slid his boat into the sea, and he fished. In the afternoon he dried and mended his nets. Sometimes, he passed a word or two with the other fishermen. Other times, he went to the village and partook in celebrations there. Weddings and baptisms. Funerals and holidays. But every sunset without fail he went down to the shore, to the place where she had last stood. He gathered driftwood, built a fire. Watched violet flames dance against the evening sky.

His own tiny seasons.

His own light in the dark.

At first, he wept. Or, worse, sat in broken stillness, the ocean of his tears run dry. Tides came and went, and the moon turned its back to him again, and again. The tales were always of men taking to the sea, and women being left behind to long and worry, to take comfort in their children and in the certainty that a husband or a sweetheart cannot stay away forever. That one day, he *will* come home again. They would abide by the old ways, those women, the customs known to keep sailors safe: praying in the village church by day, and refraining from brushing their hair at night. Lighting a candle on a storm-wild eve, when the sea roiled and the wind raged so hard the windows shook. A light for lost souls.

There were no such comforts for him. No children of his own, no songs or prayers to hurry his beloved's return. His hair grew wild, his beard thick, despite the certainty that no brush, nor blade, could threaten her. She needed no light, was not lost, and yet on stormy nights he lit a candle in the window of his small cottage. Slept alone in his narrow bed, assuring himself that the tiny golden flicker would show her he waited still.

Years passed. Day, by day, by day.

And then, one summer's end.

Something.

The night was cool, autumn's breath riding on its back. He had been working on the fire, coaxing it to life, when the smallest movement in the dusk—a disturbance in the warp and weft of his world—caused him to look up.

A wild thing looked back at him. Half in the water, half without, her tail coiled in the shallows, her hair a veil of night. She was moonlight and sunlight together. Pearl and storm. Dream and nightmare. So Fae, so *other,* that he knew a moment of fear. Six years had passed since she was here. Did she even remember him? Or had some instinct, dark and hungry, drawn her to this shore?

Was she a predator, and he merely her prey?

He found he did not care. She was all that he had dreamed of for so long. Bare shoulders and smooth arms; long torso, shapely hips. Skin glimmering with seawater and magic. There were ropes of pearls in her hair, and shells at her wrists. The curve of her breasts, almost visible beneath the layers of sea-silk binding them, near undid him. She was magnificent in her beauty and her terror.

Delight and doom.

"Luce?" Her name, a light in the never-ending dark.

He rose slowly, achingly so, one palm raised. *No harm.* He had blankets with him. Warm clothes and food; a basket of just-in-case. He took the corner of a blanket, drew it free.

"Luce?"

She frightened him: there was no denying it. Time, and the sea, had changed her. Her eyes were large and dark, her wildness, her faeness, a warning. He thought of the drowning tales: seamaids who lure and take. Their kisses a curse, their beauty a trap.

Delight and doom.

Then let it be so.

One, two, three steps and he was halfway down the shore. Heart thudding like a boy's, legs shaking. Blanket trailing in the sand.

Four, five, six and the cold glimmer of her scales, of her eyes, were dragging at his soul. She wore her sea-knife at her waist, her mirror, and her comb. He braced himself. Did seamaids kill with knives? Teeth? Or would a simple drowning do?

And then—

"You grew a beard."

Her voice was low, rough with disuse. But it was *her* voice. *Her* smile.

He fell to his knees in the shallows. "Christ, Luce," he muttered, reaching for her, barely stopping himself.

Long, cool fingers on his jaw. "I like it, Samuel."

His name on her lips undid time. He crushed her to his chest, cold and Fae and wild. Ran his hands down her hips, the first, smooth meeting of skin and scale.

"I missed you," he muttered into her hair. Tears and seawater, mingling. "Did you—did you find the horizon? The path of stars?"

She nodded against him.

"Your father?"

Another nod. "And more, besides."

She drew back, her smile, her joy, star-bright. "I found it all, Samuel. Everything I wanted."

Everything I wanted. His heart, so close to broken, did a little death dance. *Fool,* it leered. *What did you expect? A seamaid for a wife? Trapped and miserable?* Look *at her, for Christ's sake.*

"Everything I wanted, Samuel," she said. "Except you."

Except you.

His heart stilled. Listening.

"There are places," she whispered against his ear, "where the Fae and humans live closely together, yet. Where you and I—where we could—"

It was all he needed, and more. Tomorrow morning, when one of his family came to check on him as always, they would find the cottage empty, the *Dove* gone. And they would know that Luce had come back from the sea, and that Samuel had gone with her to follow the stars.

He took her face in his hands and kissed her tenderly. It was answer and promise. Longing and joy. She smiled against his lips, weeping too, as the Manche washed happily around them. Tears and salt. Sorrow and sea.

There is magic in such meetings.

ACKNOWLEDGMENTS

I've often described *Upon a Starlit Tide* as a mash up of the "Cinderella" and "The Little Mermaid" fairy tales. While this is true, it also includes elements of two more tales: Bluebeard, which has roots in Brittany, and a lesser-known Breton folktale about a merchant or a shoemaker who finds a mermaid on the beach and takes her home to be part of his family. The girl possesses the power of the fairies, but she is wild and unruly, and forever escaping the house and wandering the shore. She begs to be set free, eventually granting the family their hearts' desires when they let her return to the sea.

Saint-Malo seemed to be the perfect setting for a story using a combination of these tales, a lush, beautiful and compelling canvas with a fascinating history from which to draw upon. Known as the Corsair City, it flourished in the late sixteenth and early seventeenth centuries, and became notorious for its corsairs, or privateers, who dominated the English Channel and amassed incredible wealth. The Raid on Saint-Malo really *did* take place in June 1758—an English fleet landed at Cancale, soldiers burned over a hundred Malouin ships, and a terrible storm rose up and ended their attempts to take the city. (Of course, the walls were not made of storm-stone, and a mermaid was not responsible for protecting them, although it must be noted that the city did succumb to heavy Allied bombing after it was occupied by German forces in 1944—just as a certain tide-crone foresaw.)

I travelled to Saint-Malo and surrounds in May 2023, my husband accompanying me as research assistant, tour manager, driver, photographer, porter, and navigator. He suffered through too many visits to historic houses and museums (the hair exhibition at the Musée des Arts Décoratifs in Paris was a low point) and hiked miles of Clos-Poulet and Dorset coast with me (much more enjoyable), patiently waiting as I examined the color of the water, wildflowers, and sea-caves. Thank you, honey—I can't wait to do it all again.

Saint-Malo is a tourist town these days, its population booming when swarms of visitors, many of them British, arrive during the summer. There are, however, around two hundred permanent residents who live there year-round. One of them, Stephane, was born in Saint-Malo and rented us his apartment (overlooking the site of the old vegetable market) while we were in town. Over a drink or two in the historic Hôtel France et Chateaubriand, Stephane pored over old maps of Saint-Malo with me and answered as many questions as I could throw at him in in his excellent (though, according to him, terrible) English. Thank you, Stephane!

Thank you, too, to Olivier de La Rivière, descendant of Malouin shipowners and owner/guide of the Magon de la Lande mansion (the Corsair's House Museum) in Saint-Malo. Built in 1725 for François Auguste Magon de la Lande, Corsair of Louis XV and ship-owner, the mansion has almost sixty rooms including salons, cellars, old servants' quarters, and a hidden staircase leading to a secret chamber (!). Olivier is also an author, and his books *Album Secret de Saint-Malo* and *Sur La Route des Malouinières* were invaluable to me, too.

While I'm thinking about books . . . I used many, but I'd like to acknowledge the following titles and their authors: *Les Malouinières Ille-et-Vilaine* by L'inventaire général des monuments et richesses artistiques de la France; *Les élites malouines: Histoire et dictionnaire* by Luc Boisnard; *Seafaring Women* by David Cordingly; *Saint-Malo et l'Angleterre* by René Henry; *The Corsairs of Saint-Malo* by Henning Hillman (thank you for publishing one in English, Mr Hillmann!) and *Building the Wooden Fighting Ship* by James Dodds and James Moore.

There are one hundred and twelve malouinières in the Saint-Malo hinterland, but only a few are open to the public. We visited two of them, Malouinière de la Ville Bague, a magnificent 1715 malouinière which I leaned on heavily when imagining Le Bleu Sauvage (it even has a private chapel set half within and half without the wall) and Château de Montmarin, built in 1760 by shipowner Aaron Magon. Located on the left bank of the Rance, with views over the estuary, Montmarin played the part (in my imagination) of Le Loup Blanc, location of the de Chatelaine ball.

I must mention Lieu dit Bienlivien B&B in Saint-Coulomb, too. We stayed here because the historic farmhouse and buildings were once part of the neighboring, privately owned malouinière. Owner Jeanne-Marie (and her family) was incredibly warm and welcoming, made us home-made croissants and other French treats, and patiently suffered the barrage of questions I fired at her through Google Translate, generously sharing her local knowledge.

Closer to home—thank you to Richard Miller and Stan Brown for talking sailing, boats, smuggling and Dorset with me, Dr Nigel Helyer for helping me with the finer points of luggers, and James Kesteven for taking me sailing.

To Sarah Taylor—thank you for answering all my questions about French words and their meanings, and for helping me with research. Merci beaucoup!

Thank you (forevermore and always) to my agent, Julie Crisp, without whom [this is a placeholder line].

To the team at Tor Books—Emily Honer, Emily Mlynek, Libby Collins, Greg Collins Rafal Gibek, Jeff LaSala, Jacqueline Huber-Rodriguez, Debbie Friedman, Jessica Warren—every day you magical people go to work and make my dreams come true. Thank you! [Placeholder for sensitivity reader acknowledgment. This will probably be another sentence or two.]

Lindsey Carr—thank you for creating the most exquisite mermaid (and endpaper art) ever, and Katie Klimowicz for designing the most exquisite cover to go with her. And to my wonderful editor, Aislyn Fredsall—thank you for helping me dive deep and draw the shiniest parts of the story up to the light.

Enfin, merci à ma famille.

ABOUT THE AUTHOR

KELL WOODS is an Australian historical fantasy author. She lives near the sea with her husband, two sons, and the most beautiful black cat in the realm. Woods studied English literature, creative writing, and librarianship, so she could always be surrounded by stories. She has worked in libraries for the past twelve years, all the while writing about made-up (and not so made-up) places, people, and things you might remember from the fairy tales you read as a child.